NEUTRINOMAN AND LIGHTNINGIRL: A LOVE STORY

NEUTRINOMAN AND LIGHTNINGIRL: A LOVE STORY

SEASON 2 (EPISODES 4 - 6)

ROBERT J. MCCARTER

LITTLE HUMMINGBIRD PUBLISHING

Neutrinoman & Lightningirl: A Love Story

Season 2 (Episodes 4 - 6)

Copyright 2020 by Robert J. McCarter

Cover images: 123rf.com/profile_kitleong, 123rf.com/profile_stokkete, 123rf.com/profile_kesu87

Version 1.0, August 2020

ISBN: 978-1-941153-44-4

Find out more about this book at: Neutrinoman.com

Visit Robert's website at: RobertJMcCarter.com

Published by:

Little Hummingbird Publishing

P.O. Box 23518

Flagstaff, AZ 86002

www.LittleHummingbird.com

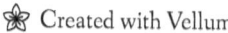 Created with Vellum

NEUTRINOMAN & LIGHTNINGIRL: A LOVE STORY

- Meteor Attack!
- Toxic Asset
- Protocol X
- Season 1 (Omnibus edition of Episodes 1 - 3)
- Off Book
- Hard Times
- Elemental Factors
- Season 2 (Omnibus edition of Episodes 4-6)

Find out the latest at Neutrinoman.com

These are for my love, Aleia... Always!

Inside you will find the complete text of *Off Book*, *Hard Times*, and *Elemental Factors*. These three books take us another step forward in the adventures of Neutrinoman and Lightningirl and a big step forward in the relationship between Nik and Licia.

The tag line for the first episode, *Meteor Attack*, and Season 1 is: *Falling in love and saving the world.*

But what happens after you fall in love and save the world? You have to stay in love and, if you are our heroes, keep saving the world. And, given that I'm quite the romantic and lucky enough to be with the same wonderful woman for nearly three decades, you get to keep falling in love and that has always been the thing that has saved my world.

But, since these books are fast-paced action/adventure stories with a strong dash of romance, I can further sum up the season with the tag lines for the three books:

Off Book: An impossible mission

Hard Times: Everything will change

Elemental Factors: A team arises

This season delighted me with all its changes and surprises—everything really does change. And if you like these stories (and I sure hope you do) there is a ways to go for our heroes. A lot more world saving and a lot more falling in love with a Season 3 and maybe even a Season 4.

So I hope you enjoy these adventures and I hope they give you some moments of escape and a few smiles during this crazy year of 2020.

Robert J. McCarter
August, 2020
Flagstaff, Arizona

OFF BOOK

NEUTRINOMAN AND LIGHTNINGIRL: A LOVE STORY, EPISODE 4

1 / A QUIET MOMENT

WHAT HAPPENED AFTER BOY MET GIRL, AFTER THEY FOUND out they both had powers, after they saved the world together and shared a kiss? After they began defending the world against an alien aggressor and things got hard for both of them? After the girl pushed the boy away because of what was expected of them. After the girl broke up with the boy. After the girl saved the boy from those aliens and lost someone she cared about in the attack. After the boy bared his soul and told her that she was the personification of what he was fighting for, that she was what made the world worth defending, how she made him stronger not weaker. After she agreed to be his girlfriend and they agreed to be a mess together?

What happened after a hopefully happily ever after?

Have you ever wondered? After the initial romance, how does the couple stay together through tumultuous times? How do you save the world and stay in love, grow deeper in love?

If you were Nik Nichols aka Neutrinoman (that would be me) and Licia Lopez aka Lightningirl, that "being a mess together" meant holing up in a little A-frame cabin in Flagstaff, Arizona, that was nestled up against the ponderosa pine forest and playing Scrabble while a fire crackled in an old iron woodstove.

It was late, past midnight, and she was dressed in a fuzzy black bathrobe and I was in sweats, a blanket spread in front of the woodstove and a game of Scrabble sitting between us, the tiles crawling all over the board in a game that was clearly near completion. It was dark outside and quiet, the red wine in our glasses from the local winery where we had our first date, a homemade ceramic platter with cheese and crackers on the blanket next to the Scrabble board, the taste of Munster and dry red wine lingering in my mouth. Her face was intent on the board as she chewed on her lower lip.

She was petite and alluringly feminine with dark, silky hair that was disheveled and cascading down past her shoulders, deep brown eyes, and a round face. She was beautiful and intelligent and powerful and I loved her, but I didn't really understand her. I wanted her, I needed her, but I didn't get her yet.

Yes, some of it was the whole differences between men and women, but we weren't just a man and a woman anymore. We were quantum-metamorphs, our powers bestowed upon us eighteen months ago when the cosmic rays struck and our accidents happened.

Me at the Palo Verde Nuclear Generating Station, she while working as a line woman for the local electric utility.

The woodstove had a glass front and the undulating yellow light was caressing her light brown skin, making her already beautiful face even more lovely. I couldn't get enough of that face, of those eyes, those lips. I wanted to caress her with the tenderness and intimacy of the firelight, but we had had our fill of that for the moment.

We'd been here for almost two weeks, after what happened at the Battle of Palo Verde where she saved my life but had to kill to do it. For the first time. After she quit the military's q-morph program. After she decided to stop being Lightningirl. After she agreed to be my girlfriend.

We used to be regular people with regular problems, but we were no longer quite human. We each can transform at a quantum level, her into a controlled electrical reaction in the form of a beautiful woman and me a controlled nuclear reaction in the form of a man.

We used to have simple lives and simple problems, and they were anything but now.

Powers changed things. Working for the military changed things. Taking lives changed things. Having our identities revealed changed things. Saving the world changed things.

I didn't understand her because of all of these things. And, if truth be told, I didn't understand myself. I liked to think that I was the same old Nik, the same guy who had cruised rather aimlessly through his twenties, who had gotten the job as a janitor at Palo Verde just so he could see the inside of a nuclear power plant, who did what he did during that accident, exposing himself to a lethal dose of radiation during the day the cosmic rays hit, because lives were at stake and it was the right thing to do.

But the powers and the saving the world and the falling in love all made it so much more complicated.

"Okay," Licia said, her eyes meeting mine, a grin on her face as she nodded down at her tiles. After all that saving the world, we both need a whole lot of mundane, and this late Scrabble game was just about perfect for that.

I shifted away from the crackling fire a bit, my left side quite baked from its lovely radiant heat, the distant scent of smoke in the air.

Licia picked up four tiles, her smile growing wider. "Double letter on the 'O,' triple word, that's thirty-three points!"

She added "OXIC" to the "T" in "TOAST," forming "TOXIC." She looked at me, but now her smile was rather shy. Was this an opening? A conversation she wanted to have? Tom Tyree aka Toxicwasteman was something of a frenemy. He was a villain, there was no doubt about that, but he wanted to defeat the aliens too and had taken an interest in me.

One that wasn't always comfortable for me and was never comfortable for Licia.

"Nice one," I said with a nod. "You've been holding onto that X for a long time."

She nodded, her lips pursed. "I was waiting for the right word."

"I don't trust him, you know," I said, easing into the opening.

"Completely," she said, taking a sip of wine.

"What?" I asked.

"You don't trust him... completely," she said, her eyebrow arched and gaze appraising.

And there it was. Since I had met Tom, my trust for the military had decreased as I interacted with him. It didn't feel good, but she had a point.

"I don't trust him," I said, "except when it comes to defeating the aliens."

She took a deep breath. "Even though he will lie, he will cheat, he will do whatever it takes to—"

"Defeat the aliens," I finished, interrupting her.

She pursed her lips and nodded. "He is not like you, Nik. Just because you both have the same goal, don't fool yourself. He is using you, and when he's done with you..." she ended in a shrug, her robe opening just a bit, but I kept my eyes locked with hers—this was not the time to get distracted.

I sighed. "I know. It's..." I leaned forward across the board, close enough so that I could smell the wine and cheese on her breath, my voice a whisper. "I think I trust the military less. What would they have done with Sarah, the alien I saved? Interrogated her? And how? What kinds of measures would they have resorted to? She is so much like us I think there has to be a way to stop all this. And what hasn't the military told us? You know that there is a lot. Colonel Williams is a great guy, I'd follow him just about anywhere, but he has to follow orders. I don't trust General Markus any farther than I can throw him. I..."

I stopped when I realized that my face was flushed and my tone had gotten loud. Too loud. I leaned back and nodded. "I don't trust him and I don't trust the military." I gave her my best smile and added, "But I do trust you."

She smiled back, it was sweet, but brief, a small reward, but not what she was after. "And..." she prompted, giving me no direction on which way she was thinking the conversation should go.

I took a sip of wine to give myself time to think, letting the rich, velvety flavor linger.

My shoulders fell. "And... it's too much. It's too damn much. Just because I can fly, because I can shoot neutrino bolts, because I can explode, they both want... they all want..."

I was breathing too fast and felt tears stinging my eyes. I wanted Licia to know all of me but thought it might be too soon for this, but she had agreed to be a mess with me.

"There is an alien threat," I continued, "one strong enough to point an asteroid at us, one clever enough to almost maneuver me into setting off the super volcano below Yellowstone. I'm just a regular guy and barely know how to use these powers, how the hell am I supposed to save the world? Why does everyone want me to save the world?"

I trailed off and looked back at Licia. There was compassion written on her beautiful face. She licked her lips and nodded. "Nik," she said slowly. "Why do *you* think *you* should save the world?"

I was too hot. I wanted to run out into the freezing cold mountain night. It was so quiet, just the crackling of the fire while Licia stared at me. This here, this was intimacy, true intimacy, way beyond the physical. I still worried that if she really knew me that she wouldn't want me. But I couldn't hide this from everyone, and she was one of the only people on the planet that could understand.

"Because..." I began, taking a deep breath. "I do have this power. I have to try."

She nodded and reached out and I let her take my hand. She kissed it gently. "You are a good man, Nik. This, more than anything, gives me hope."

I blinked, the tears so close to escaping. Hope for our world? Hope for our relationship? What did that give her hope for?

I opened my mouth to speak when my phone chimed, and at the same time, Licia's landline rang. Her brow furrowed, but she held my gaze for a breath before getting up.

"Hello," she said. "Yes, Colonel Williams. What's going on?"

I flipped my phone open and read the text. It was from Williams:

Report to Palo Verde at 0800. Urgent meeting. Bring Ms. Lopez.

Licia came back, her arms wrapped around her chest as if she was cold in that big fluffy robe. "We have to get up early. Let's get some sleep. We'll have more time."

I nodded and smiled. I got up and pulled her into a hug.

I didn't know it, but everything was about to change, and it would be a long time before we'd have a chance to talk like this again.

2 / SARAH SPEAKS

THE VIDEO WAS GRAINY, BUT CLEAR ENOUGH. IT SHOWED A picture of the alien Sarah dressed in a silver jumpsuit, like when I had rescued her from her crashed spaceship. The classic *The Day the Earth Stood Still* look. She looked good, the cut on her forehead was healing well, her long blond hair was pulled back, her blue eyes intense, her youthful Nordic looks making it hard to believe that she was not from this planet. The audio was crisp and clear.

This video had been received by mail, sent to Diane Madison at WNN on a thumb drive. The world hadn't seen it yet, but Diane was going to air it this evening.

Licia, Colonel Williams, General Markus, Jennifer Johnson, and I were in a hushed little conference room at the Palo Verde Nuclear Generating Station, the lights off, the glow of the large screen making everyone look a little bit ghostly.

I was tired. After our late-night Scrabble session and our conversation, I hadn't slept much. We'd gotten up early and hit the road before 6:00 a.m. neither of us talking much on the way down from Flagstaff. I think we both had too much on our minds. We didn't know what we were being called in for and Licia was only here as a favor to Williams. She didn't want to be anywhere near the military's q-morph program.

"I am known as Sarah," the tall alien began on the video. She looked nervous. Behind her was a flat white wall, no clues whatsoever to her location. "I represent the Arcturian Alliance. I am no one, but I will speak for you and all will listen. This is our way."

The room was dead quiet, all eyes fixed on the screen. Sarah's smooth forehead was furrowed and she spoke slowly as if the words were hard to say, her accent strange and unidentifiable.

"Your planet has been classified as threat. We have been listening and watching you for sixty Earth years. We have been studying you. You are an immature and violent species. The Arcturian Alliance has determined that extermination is required. Several attempts have been made and have failed."

The meteor attack that started all this madness and the "Incident at Yellowstone" came leaping to mind. I wondered if there were others.

"None then spoke on your behalf," she continued. "I speak now."

General Markus caught my eye and gave me a small nod, his round face relaxing a bit and his green eyes sharp. Releasing her had been my idea, and it had caused a major fight between me and the general. This video was starting to sound like Sarah was keeping her end of the bargain. That we did the right thing.

"I have been to your planet. I have witnessed the kindness and compassion of the yellow one. When we fought, he saved me. I am no one but he saved me, he saved others, he fought for my release from your military. So now I speak on your behalf and hostilities will stop.

"While I speak, while the council listens and debates, there will be no more attacks by the Arcturian Alliance. This is our way."

She stopped, her head falling and her blue eyes hidden. I could see her chest rise and then fall in a shuddering exhale. When she finally looked back at the camera, the wrinkles on her forehead were gone and her blue eyes were hard. It looked to me like she was about to go off script.

"Look in your hearts, people of Earth. Find compassion for one another. Stop your wars and fighting. Stop putting the needs of the individual over the whole. Stop killing each other. This is your chance to change, your one chance. Once I speak, once they listen, the decision will be final. We will either leave you be or we will destroy you for the sake of all."

I sat there blinking, my chest tight. I couldn't breathe and it didn't sound like anyone else was breathing.

"Look to the yellow one," she said. "Be more like him. I am called Sarah. I am no one, but because of the yellow one, I speak for you."

The video ended and Jennifer turned on the lights. The room was silent, the air thick and heavy, all eyes on me. Colonel Williams rubbed his salt-and-pepper hair and shook his head. General Markus had this faraway look on his round face. Jennifer just stood there in her ever-present white lab coat, her arms wrapped around herself just like she was cold.

I am Neutrinoman, the "yellow one," and what Sarah just said made my heart pound hard in my chest and sweat trickle down my back. She was asking the world to be more like me. She was holding me up as an example. It's what Licia and I just talked about. It was too much. I wanted to bolt, to run away. To leave all this behind and just have a normal life with Licia. I didn't want to be the hero.

Under the table, Licia grabbed my hand and squeezed it hard. Her soft brown eyes in her beautiful face were compassionate as she looked at me.

She didn't speak, her lips pressed into a thin line. She knew what this fight with the Arcturian Alliance had cost her, had cost me. She knew how things were getting more complicated. She had been with me when I had been served last week. Some people of

Las Vegas suing me because of the damage the alien's meteor attack had done there, citing my incompetence in not completely destroying the threat.

Peace had come, but for how long? And if Diane Madison outing me as Neutrinoman wasn't enough, if this new lawsuit wasn't enough, I now had an alien telling the entire world to stop fighting and to look to me as an example.

It was just too damn much.

3 / WHAT HAPPENS IN VEGAS...

I HAVE COME TO KNOW AND UNDERSTAND THE BEAUTY OF THE desert. It's not a flashy beauty like the tropics, it's a quiet beauty, deep and abiding, entirely mysterious.

Quinn Rask, my new dark-haired and muscular q-morph partner, drove my 1990 Ford Focus down US-93 in the northwestern corner of Arizona between Kingman and Las Vegas. It's a long, lonely stretch of desert with plentiful cactus and craggy hills in the distance.

Spring had come and with it hope. After Sarah's video, the full truth of the alien attacks on our planet had come to light. The governments of the world had even started releasing details they had about previous alien visits: Roswell, New Mexico in 1947 (it wasn't a weather balloon); the Rendlesham Forest incident in 1980 (alien ships did land in England); Japan Air Lines flight 1628 in 1986 (alien ships seen over Alaska); the Phoenix Lights in 1997 (not airplanes); and more.

I had done more interviews and had become a celebrity. I was dealing with paparazzi when I was out in the world and then with endless training when I was with the military.

Some lawyers had taken up defending me against the Las Vegas lawsuit pro bono, wanting to grab a piece of the limelight, which I was happy to share. Still, it took too much of my time.

This "speaking" Sarah was doing was of an unknown length with a decision-making process we couldn't fathom. Everyone was worried the attacks would resume. Just because Sarah implored us to "stop killing each other" and had promised that "we will destroy you for the sake of all" if they perceived the need, didn't mean we could change.

The US was still at war in Iraq and Afghanistan, the Middle East was a disaster, and fighting terrorism was a major pastime here since 9/11. School shootings. Gun violence. Murder a daily occurrence in all big cities. There was no shortage of humans killing humans.

The threat of annihilation often made us less logical, not more.

And the worst part was that I hadn't had much time with Licia. Not the kind of time we needed, not the kind of conversation we were about to have over that Scrabble game in front of the crackling woodstove.

I stared out of the car at the dirt and sage brush whipping by me. The signs of spring were not overt in the desert, but they were there. Growing green grasses, instead of the usual brown, the lighter green of new growth on the sage brush.

"Are you going to be this pensive the whole trip?" Quinn asked, his blue eyes boring into me as we roared down the two-lane road at ninety miles per hour, the fastest my little Ford could manage.

I looked at him and smiled, but it didn't work very well. I only managed a grimace. As much as I liked Quinn, I finally had some R&R and was spending it with him instead of Licia on our crazy "off book" mission. The military thought we were going to Las Vegas to blow off some steam. In truth we were going there in search of Chaosboy. Since our "little heist" on the train I couldn't stop thinking about him, about how he could bend probabilities with his will, about how he left a wake of chaos and bad luck for others, about how blasé he was about collateral damage.

An alien threat. Overwhelming celebrity. A lawsuit. Not enough time with Licia. Chaosboy and the damage he could cause. I had reason to be pensive.

"Because if you going to be big wet blanket, then I think we should turn around now," he said. Quinn had this odd accent that is impossible to place. He said it's because of his Army brat upbringing, spending the first sixteen years of his life in five different countries in Europe, and his French mother.

I took a deep breath and tried to shake it off. Quinn was still staring at me as we roared down the road. It made me nervous, but I understood that it wasn't dangerous for him. Quinn is a q-morph—quantum metamorph—like Licia and I. But unlike us, his powers are always present, just like Chaosboy and Byte. And that makes him sound like a quantum biomorph, but he earns the "meta" with what he can do.

During the day the cosmic rays hit, he was working in the Relativistic Heavy Ion Collider in Upton, New York. He was inside the collider inspecting some of the sensors when the collider was accidentally triggered. The collider is a 3.8-kilometer track where ions traveling at relativistic speed (a significant portion of the speed of light) collide so physicists can study the primordial form of matter that existed shortly after the Big Bang. Those particles went through Quinn's body and mixed with those cosmic rays turning him into the q-morph he is today.

He doesn't have a single superhero name like most of us do. Actually, he has a lot of superhero names, but no one knows that they all belong to him: The Hammer, Stretchman, Jumper, and others. Actually, he's the reason that most counts of the q-morphs created that day in 2003 are too high. He can control his body at a molecular level and, in reality, is each of those q-morphs.

And this is why I didn't need to be worried about him looking at me while he was driving down a two-lane highway like a maniac. In his normal form, a handsome and muscular 6'4", he has the best reflexes on the planet and amazing peripheral vision. He could look at me and still drive safely.

But this isn't his natural form. I think it's the body he wanted to have when he was young. He was in his late fifties when the accident happened, but he looks like he's about thirty now.

"Come on, Nik," he said. "We need to have some fun. We've been cooped up for weeks."

"We're going to Vegas for a reason," I said.

"Yes! To gamble and drink and chase women—"

"To find Chaosboy," I said, interrupting. "To stop him."

Quinn was silent, his eyes turning to the road, the smile melting off his face. He ran his right hand through his jet-black hair in a gesture I have come to understand signals nervousness for him. His hair was slicked back and perfect as always. The gesture was completely unnecessary.

"How do you know he is there?" Quinn asked quietly.

I sighed. We had been over this. "Chaosboy has a fan club, a private group on Yahoo. I'm a member."

"And how did you get into the group?"

"Byte got me in last month." Byte was Tom Tyree's (aka Toxicwasteman's) tech guru. She was a q-morph that could control the Internet with her mind and is part of LoVE (League of Villains Extraordinaire).

"Chaosboy and Byte are both part of LoVE," he said slowly. "Why would she do this thing?"

I shrugged, but I suspected why. There was something Tom and his gang wanted me to do. I knew that Byte had probably run one of her computer simulations, known that evidence of Chaosboy being close might draw me out. I knew that they were probably manipulating me, but that didn't change the fact that I wanted to have a serious conversation with him. That I wanted to bring him in.

The time I spent with LoVE changed me. I no longer doubted that we both had the same goal (eliminate the alien threat, save the world) but it was their methods that disturbed me. I had also come to believe that LoVE was approaching the problem in ways far more innovative than the military.

So maybe this was some convoluted way to get me to do something, but it was in alignment with something I wanted to do. So be it.

"And what will we do with this Chaosboy if we catch him?" Quinn asked.

I stared back out at the desert again, trying to catch more signs of spring, the light green of new growth, the color of a blooming cactus.

In truth, I didn't know. I wanted Chaosboy stopped, but how far would I be willing to go to do that?

———

LICIA DIDN'T KNOW WHAT WE WERE UP TO. SHE THOUGHT WE were just out for some fun, some male bonding, cutting loose time. And oddly, she wasn't hurt that I was spending time off without her. Well, that wasn't odd for her, but odd for other women I have known.

She had been rather withdrawn since she left the program ten weeks ago. At first, she tried to go back to her job at Arizona Public Service (APS), but since the world knew who she was and what she looked like, crowds would gather when she was doing dangerous work on high-tension power lines.

She had a fan club, and members of it would roam Northern Arizona and tell others of her location if they found her.

Lately, Licia had been holed up in her cabin backing the forest south of Flagstaff. Taking long walks, wearing a blonde wig and dark glasses so her neighbors didn't recognize her, trying to have something of a normal life. But there was no "normal" for us anymore.

"You thinking of her?" Quinn asked. He was still driving my old Focus and we were past the Hoover Dam and Lake Mead and were headed down towards Boulder City and then Vegas. From here we could see the sprawl of Las Vegas laid out over the flat desert below.

"Yeah," I said.

"I could help if you like, I could—" he said, and I knew what was coming.

"No... please, Quinn. That would just make it..." I trailed off because it was too late. Quinn was morphing, the strange sound of it emanating from his side of the car. It's a disturbingly organic sound: kind of like a cross between flowing water and crickets chirping. His jet-black hair suddenly started growing long, his features changing, his limbs thinning and his body growing shorter. From the bulky 6'4" frame of Quinn Rask to the lithe body of Licia Lopez. Or at least a close enough reproduction to be completely unnerving.

He got the body proportions right, his new body dressed in shorts and black tank top, but the face wasn't quite there. The cheekbones were too high, the eyes a bit too big, the lips puffy. And his blue eyes were still there instead of Licia's brown. When Quinn changed, for some reason his eyes didn't.

"Hey, big boy," Quinn-Licia said. "Don't be sad little puppy dog. I am right here." The voice was feminine but definitely not Licia. It takes Quinn a long time to get good at another form. It takes a lot of practice. He wasn't that good at Licia.

"Stop it."

"But hey," she-he said as she-he looked down at her-his chest, "I've always thought these were a bit inadequate."

The clicky/squishy sound resumed and Quinn-Licia went from a B-cup to a D-cup, her breasts swelling under the black tank top. "That better? You like?"

I looked away. That weird face, that strange voice, it was just too much. I stared at this abandoned western-themed casino, built to look like an old fort, as we passed it. I didn't want that nightmare version of Licia to stick with me. And for the record, I have never found anything about her physicality to be inadequate.

Quinn's transformation sound started up again for a minute or so. "It's okay now," he said in his normal, deep voice. "Sorry, thought you might find that funny."

"Don't *ever* do that again," I said, glad to see him back.

He smiled at me, this perfect white-toothed grin. "Of course not."

We drove in silence the rest of the way to the Golden Nugget Casino on Freemont Street in old Las Vegas. We knew Chaosboy was there. We had a plan.

"Quinn Rask," Licia said, her jaw set, her arms folded across her chest, her normally soft brown eyes hard and dangerous. It was midday and we were working on the new greenhouse at Casita de Soledad, our isolated home in central Arizona where Homeland Security basically kept us under house arrest.

After the madness was all over and we signed the Quantum Metamorph Accord in 2020, this is where we ended up. My love and I in the high desert of Arizona building our own home to keep ourselves busy and me busily doing a lot of navel gazing writing these memoirs.

Licia's electrical powers made her very good with plants and this was the second greenhouse we had taken on. The foundation and flagstone floor were laid and we were now getting ready to put up some posts to support the roof.

I had just shorts and work boots on, my skin pasty white as always—it dealt with the UV light in a different way. Licia had a black tank top on, her already brown skin slightly darker from all the time we had been spending outside. Her silky black hair was pulled back into a ponytail.

It has been over twenty years since all of this began, since the cosmic rays hit and we got our powers, but Licia still looks to be in her thirties and so do I. Our frequent transformations into our quantum metamorph selves seem to be keeping us young, slowing the aging process, which means we might be stuck out here alone in the desert for another fifty years or more. So the building was partially about keeping us busy, but also about making our time out here more enjoyable because it seemed we were going to have a lot of it.

I spent about a month away from writing as I dug the foundation, mixed cement, and laid in the floor. But it was eating at me. This story has kind of taken on a life of its own now, the story has to be told. I've started a new schedule. I get up early and write for an hour or two before we start on the greenhouse.

Licia knows I need it and has been supportive. When I came out today, she was already here and working and asked me what I was writing about. I told her Quinn had just been introduced.

"So you're finally to it," she said, shaking her head.

I shrugged. Back when I was first starting this project, she asked me if I was writing it because of "him." And in truth that was one part of it, and Quinn is that "him." We'll get to it all, but for now let me say that our relationship was more than a little complicated.

"I hope this helps you," she said. What she didn't add, and I think she meant was, "because this isn't going to help me."

Quinn's relationship with Licia, and really all of us, was... I wish I had a different word, one that better described the breadth and depth of it all, but "complicated" is all I can come up with. It wasn't at first, but boy did it get complicated. There is a residue left there that I would love to shed myself of. I don't know if writing about him will make it better or worse. I guess there is only one way to find out.

In the car sitting in the parking garage of the Golden Nugget, Quinn started transforming again. That sound always sent a chill down my spine. What he did just wasn't natural. I looked away. I didn't want to witness it.

"It's a little hurtful, you know," he said, his voice feminine and sultry.

"What?" I asked, looking at him. He was now a statuesque blond dressed in heels and a tight red cocktail dress. This was one of his go-to forms he had practiced and was good at. He called her Sadie, so I'll refer to Quinn as this when he is her. (His transformations can certainly challenge the use of pronouns.)

"You are disgusted by who I am," Sadie said, a pouty frown on her face.

I took a deep breath. I couldn't believe he was bringing this up now. Here.

"We are partners now," she said. "We need to embrace each other's unique capabilities." She then pulled up the front of her strapless dress, in a move that is entirely distracting to the hetero-sexual male. Sadie was well endowed so it was quite the show.

As I tried to come up with something to say I realized that when Quinn turned into Licia earlier and then into Sadie, he didn't leave any clothing behind. His clothing as Quinn had been part of his form. Part of him.

"You've been naked this whole time?" I asked. "Seriously, dude? That is not cool."

Sadie shrugged, her blue eyes looking me up and down. The eyes were the one part of Quinn that was still part of Sadie and the lecherous look she gave me freaked me out. "Clothing just gets in the way, don't you think?"

I got out of the car and slammed the door. "Oh, hell, Quinn. What is wrong with you?"

Sadie got out of the car, her movements slow and sensuous. "Do you know how much fun I can have with this body in a town like this?" Her feminine hands raked up and down her hourglass figure, the dress leaving little (or just enough) to the imagination.

I sighed. "Just stick to the plan, okay?"

She shrugged and tugged her dress up again. "Chaosboy won't be able to resist me."

Of that, there could be no doubt.

<hr>

MY INTEL PUT CHAOSBOY PLAYING CRAPS IN THE GOLDEN Nugget right now. He was having what he called one of his "Chaos Meets" with a few of his fans. It was basically him showing off to a crowd and raking in lots of money from the casino. His groupies bet with him and made money too.

There were reports of previous versions of this on his Yahoo group. Since they're such a public thing he really had to bend prob-ability hard for the casino to not catch on too soon. Inevitably someone got hurt. A stumble leading to a broken arm in Reno, a fatal heart attack outside of Phoenix, and lots of dropped electronics.

The weird thing was, his groupies didn't seem to mind. They seemed to get off on the danger of being near him. This world has no shortage of weirdos.

Our plan was simple. Quinn—or rather Sadie—would go in playing the role of a groupie and lure him away up to her room. Not that we had a room, he was to get Chaosboy to the elevators where I would be waiting.

I had a Bluetooth headset on and was listening through Sadie's phone. She had dialed me once she had spotted him and then stashed the phone (I didn't know where and didn't want to know). The Golden Nugget is a bit of a labyrinth, just like all casinos, and I was hanging out in the south tower lobby at the end of a long hallway with garish orangish and brown carpet that I tried not to look too much at. The hall went past the outdoor swimming pool, large windows showing the oval pool and waterfall (this is before the shark tank with a slide through it went in).

"Hey, Red," Sadie said through the phone line. And I do have to admit that she has a wicked sultry voice, a bit Demi Moore, a bit Scarlett Johansson.

"Well, hello there, beautiful," Chaosboy said with his Irish accent. "You're just in time to blow on my dice for luck."

"On this peach of a day," Sadie said. "I'd love to." The phrase "peach of a day" was the code phrase from the Yahoo group. It identified Sadie as one of his core groupies. There was then a very exaggerated blowing sound and a boyish giggle from Chaosboy. I can imagine how Sadie bent over giving him a fine view of her epic cleavage.

No. I don't want to imagine that.

There was a lot of background noise, his cheering groupies, overlapping conversation, the jangle of slot machines, but I could hear pretty well. I went over to the small Starbucks near the elevators and got a coffee. I was nervous, and knew the caffeine probably wouldn't help, but I needed something to divert my attention from Sadie seducing Chaosboy.

Not that it was much of a seduction. I suspect Chaosboy was pretty sure he'd get "lucky" at all of these. He probably didn't even need to bend probability to do it.

I pulled the Red Sox baseball cap low on my head and adjusted my mirror shades. This amounted to my disguise. It wasn't much, but enough. No one recognized me.

There were a few small tables in front of the Starbucks and I took a seat and waited. I listened over the phone to the cheering as Chaosboy had an improbable run at the craps table, as Sadie gushed at his brilliance as Chaosboy did his occasional boyish giggle.

The coffee was bitter and I drank it slowly. By the time I was down to the cold dregs, the "Chaos Meet" was breaking up and Sadie had convinced Chaosboy to go to her room.

He was twenty-one, short, with flaming red hair and green eyes. He was wearing white pants and shirt and a straw hat, the kind of outfit some Florida mobster might wear. Sadie towered over him in her heels. Chaosboy had the biggest damn grin on his face as they walked past the Starbucks to the bank of elevators.

I relaxed a little. It didn't look like he suspected, and he didn't even glance my way when they passed. He was telling her a dirty joke about an Irish priest and a donkey, one I will do you the favor of not repeating.

After they passed, I tossed my coffee cup in the trash and ambled towards the elevator. Sadie made a show of bending over to press the up button and Chaosboy took the opening and stared at her ass. I shook my head, the two of them were just a pair. Sadie really looked like the right kind of dumb blond that would go for Chaosboy.

The elevator door dinged, some tourists spilled out before some more got in. Chaosboy made a step towards it but Sadie held him back. "Maybe we can get lucky, Red," she said. "Maybe we can get an elevator to ourselves."

Chaosboy looked her up and down (his head came up to her bosom, so it's more looking up than down) and grinned. It wasn't long until an empty elevator opened up and they walked in.

I walked in right behind them. Well, I almost didn't. I was positioned properly, only a few steps away, but somehow a guest with a huge trolley of luggage got in between me and the elevator at the last moment. Very unlucky.

Quite ungracefully, I plow right through the middle, spilling their luggage on the floor, and stumbled into the elevator just as it closed.

"Hey, lad," Chaosboy said. "This here is a private party."

"Yes, it is," I said, grabbing him by the lapels of his fancy white suit and slamming him against the back of the elevator.

He hit with an "oomph" and then the elevator suddenly stopped as Sadie hit the red emergency stop button. Sadie didn't turn back into Quinn. It was part of the plan, if we could confuse Chaosboy in any way during this it was worth a shot.

I kept him pinned to the back of the elevator with one hand and took off my sunglasses.

"Neutrino!" Chaosboy said. "What is this?"

"It's time for us to have a long talk. A very long talk."

━━━

WITH A LITTLE HELP FROM CHAOSBOY, THAT REQUIRED A little coercion from me, we managed to make it to the roof of the Golden Nugget's Carson Tower without interruption. It's a flat expanse of dull white with a waist-high wall all around. We were twenty-two stories up in the air and I didn't think it would be easy for Chaosboy to escape us.

Except once we got up there, once the door slammed behind us, once I let go of his neck, his demeanor changed. Radically.

"Well, Neutrino, I'm mighty glad you got my meetin' invite," he said as he strolled across the roof like he was taking a walk on the beach. There was a swagger to his step and a lilt in his voice that made me want to punch him.

"And Quinn," he said, turning to Sadie. "As much as I enjoy ya like this, ya can drop the disguise. We know all about ya, lad."

Sadie looked at me and I nodded. The click-squish sound emanated from him again and soon he was back to Quinn.

It was hot up here, over a hundred degrees, and I was starting to sweat. "What is this?" Quinn asked, looking at me.

"Chaosboy, here," I said, gesturing to the still strutting redhead, "and his gang set this all up. He was expecting us."

"You knew?" Quinn asked.

"I suspected, but it doesn't matter. We can still do what we came here to do."

"Okay, gents," Chaosboy said. "If we're done with pleasantries, let's get down to it." He trotted over to the north edge of the roof that bordered the outdoor ground-level pool and courtyard below and hopped up on the low wall, a big grin on his face.

Quinn rushed over and said, "Don't jump."

I took my time. I wasn't worried about Chaosboy hurting himself. Quinn didn't have much firsthand experience with him yet. Chaosboy was in no danger. I was beginning to doubt that we would be able to contain him, though. I was casting about for a plan when he started talking.

"Your mission, gentlemen," he began in a comical attempt at a deep voice, "should ya decide to accept it, is to stop the q-morph known as Gaia from causing major loss of life in the Las Vegas area and to, if you're able, bring said q-morph onto our side in the battle against the Arcturian Alliance."

He stopped, his hands spread wide, a huge grin on his face. Quinn and I were about five feet away.

Chaosboy pulled a keycard out of his pocket and tossed it to me. "That is for the penthouse suite. Ya have it for the night. A dossier on Gaia is in there—it won't self-destruct or anythin', so don't ya worry. The odds are long on this one, lads," he said, looking at me. "So ya will need your little firefly if you have any chance of capturing Gaia alive." By "little firefly" he was referring to Lightningirl. As I stood there, I hoped to be around when he called her that in person. "There is a plane waitin' for her in Flagstaff. Details in the suite."

Quinn and I stood there with our mouths open. In truth I had suspected this as a setup, but not to this degree. A mission? And from the *Mission Impossible* speech it sounded like a hard one. And who the hell was Gaia?

His smile broadened and he looked to Quinn. "If Sadie ever really wants a good time... Well, I'm game."

He took a step back on the wall and looked down before meeting our gazes again and continued in his not-so-deep voice. "As always, should anyone get caught or killed in this mission, LoVE, the League of Villains Extraordinaire, will disavow any knowledge of your actions."

He got this blank look on his face and then stepped off the wall, falling out of sight.

5 / MISSION IMPROBABLE

CHAOSBOY SURVIVED. OF COURSE HE DID. BUT YOU WOULDN'T believe me if I told you how. Or maybe you would. You've heard the stories of him, and these things for most q-morphs are really exaggerated. For him, not so much.

In some ways I suspected this was easy for him because of where we were. Chaosboy was created by the accident on Freemont Street. The Golden Nugget is on Freemont Street.

We were atop the south tower and that didn't face Freemont Street, but let's just say we were in the epicenter of his "luck."

The towers of the Golden Nugget surround the pool area. After he jumped, Quinn and I rushed over and saw what happened.

The little guy was falling with a grin on his face looking at us and waving enthusiastically with one hand while holding onto his hat with the other. He was headed for the roof over the conference center that fans out below the tower and borders the pool area. Then, out of nowhere a huge breeze rushed through the courtyard, shoving Chaosboy over the roof, over the sunbathing tourists and into the pool. It was a freak wind out of nowhere, a million—no more like a billion—to one. A big splash and then moments later he was out of the pool and walking calmly away.

Seconds later, I heard the crunch of steel and honking horns over on Casino Center Boulevard. The chaos left behind in the wake of his lucky fall.

"We should—" Quinn began.

"Don't bother," I said. "We lost him as soon as I let go of his scrawny neck."

Quinn gave me a look but didn't question further. We went down to the suite to find out about this "Mission Impossible."

THE SUITE WAS MAGNIFICENT. TWO LARGE BEDROOMS, A common area with a bar adjoining the two, and floor-to-ceiling windows overlooking old Las Vegas. More awful orange and brown carpet, but up here, with this view, I could live with it.

Next to the brown couch was a thick manila folder and a laptop sitting open, the screen said, "Press Enter."

We sat down on the couch and I tapped the enter key. A video came up of Tom Tyree. He's got his usual wolfish grin on his face. The background was of a nice room done in shades of brown. Looking around I can tell that he was filmed right here in this suite.

"Don't bother, Neutrino," he said. "We did film this here, but we are long gone."

It's frankly eerie how close Byte, the q-morph that is one with the internet, and her simulations are. And scary.

"And welcome, Quinn," he continued. "I look forward to us meeting in person one of these days. You are a fine addition to our mutual battle against the Arcturian Alliance. I believe you will soon come to know, as our friend Neutrino here has, that it will take all of us working together to defeat them."

Quinn looked at me, his brow furrowed. I just shrugged my shoulders and nodded.

"But for today, we've got a crisis brewing. Gaia is a powerful q-morph that has recently surfaced." The laptop showed a picture of a dark-skinned African woman dressed in a kaftan that flowed loosely around her body. Her brown eyes were intense, as was the grim frown was on her face. She was standing outside in front of a devastated area. It looked like it was recently a forest, but there was not much left but ragged stumps and browning foliage.

"Her name is Jena Grange. She was born in England but spent much of her life as an ecological activist in Africa. Here she is standing in front of a recently destroyed rainforest in the Democratic Republic of the Congo that was cut down to make room for cattle grazing."

The picture changed to show a large hole in the ground, edged with crumbling asphalt, a house slumping into it. "She became Gaia when this sinkhole swallowed her on that day in 2003 when the Earth was bathed in the cosmic rays that changed us all. Jena was presumed dead, but recent events have made us believe that she survived. That she is bent on the destruction of the human race. That she is in the United States now and her target is Las Vegas."

On the screen Tom blinked and rubbed at his long chin, his face becoming grim. "This is a distraction we cannot afford. We don't know her target yet, but we expect to know in the next twelve hours."

Tom paused, looking slightly to the left and then to the right like he was looking Quinn and me over. "I know you have some question, so I will answer them. But believe me when I tell you that time is of the essence."

He then looked to the right, at me. "Neutrino, you must get Lightningirl here and you must not contact the military. You need Lightningirl to have a chance in hell of catching Gaia, and if the military gets involved the loss of life goes up. Way up.

"I know this puts you in an awkward spot with your masters. But please trust me here. This is the only way."

He then turned to the left, looking right at Quinn. "Don't try to take Gaia on directly. She is too powerful. Follow Neutrino's lead."

Tom took a deep breath, clasping his hands in front of him.

"The rest that we know," Tom continued on the screen, "including details of Byte's simulations, are in the folder. Good luck." The wolfish grin returned to Tom's face. "This message, will in fact, self-destruct in five seconds."

LICIA CAN BE TOUGH TO TALK TO ON THE PHONE. HER emotional cues are not always verbal... often they are not. They are mostly visual and mostly subtle. A raising of one eyebrow, a brief frown, a quick roll of the eyes.

I knew that when I dialed her from one of the suite's bedrooms looking out over Las Vegas. It is a mud-brown expanse of desert with craggy hills in the distance that has improbably filled up with mankind and its stuff. As the phone rang it didn't surprise me that Gaia would want to attack Vegas. It's all about excess. About man's domination of nature.

"You boys having fun?" she said as greeting.

"You might say that," I replied.

"What's going on, Nik?"

"I wasn't quite forthcoming with you on why we came up here," I said.

"Oh," she said flatly. I wished that I could see her, it would help me gauge the level of surprise and/or disappointment.

But I couldn't see her so I just told her everything. In detail. And then I apologized for the deception and tried to explain. "It's Chaosboy. I... he... The kid is dangerous in ways that are hard to explain. I thought maybe we could..." I trailed off with a heavy sigh and waited for her reply. It took a while for her to speak and in that time my stomach felt like it was falling out of my body.

"Why are you telling me this now?" she asked. Again no clues as to her emotional state, just straight to the practicalities.

I took a deep breath and sighed. "We need you. We need Lightningirl. There is—"

"No," she said cutting me off, her tone so flat that I knew it wasn't good. Our relationship had truly started when she had stopped being Lightningirl, had given up on it after the trauma of the Battle of Palo Verde. What had developed between us had been strictly q-morph free.

"They say it will go bad, really bad, without you," I said.

"Who is 'they'?" she asked.

I bit my lip before replying, sitting down on the big bed with a sigh. "Tom told me, but there are simulations that Byte did. I am sure—"

"Oh, so you and Toxicwasteman are on a first name basis now?"

"Licia, it's not like that. They know things we don't. Byte's simulations are eerily prescient. If they say we need you, I believe them."

There was silence on the other end of the phone. I could hear the sound of her pacing on her hardwood floors in her cabin that backs to the pine forest of Flagstaff.

"I need you, Licia," I said. The pacing stopped, but she didn't speak. "I am a better man with you, and a better Neutrinoman with Lightningirl. This is now about preserving innocent life. Please."

More silence and then she sighed. "I'll do this for you, Nik. Just this once."

"Thank you."

"I'll pack up and get headed towards you as quickly as I can," she said.

Now was the tough part. She wasn't going to like what was coming next. "There is a plane waiting for you at the Flagstaff airport."

"Oh?"

"And a car should be arriving at your house right about now."

I heard her walking on the floor again and then her sucking in a breath in surprise. "But I'll need some clothes... some..."

"There is a change of clothing in the car and toiletries too," I said.

"Nik, what the hell? This... I..."

"I know, honey. It's weird how good they are at this. Please just grab your purse, lock up the house, and get in the car. I'll see you in a few hours."

WHILE WE WAITED FOR LICIA, QUINN AND I POURED OVER the information on Gaia. It was a bit sketchy. We did know her powers revolved around the manipulation of earth. She could trigger an earthquake, cause a sinkhole, travel unseen underground.

There were a few blurry pictures of her too. A naked black woman looking over the destruction caused by La Conchita landslide in California. Or a blurry picture of the back of her in Sterling Heights, Michigan, after a sinkhole opened up in 2004. There were five of these in total. Images that might be her near recent natural disasters. The implication was that these disasters weren't exactly natural.

There was also a thick wad of paper outlining the simulations Byte had run—seeming endless data about actions, participants, and the odds of what would happen.

We were just digging into these when the door opened and Licia walked in. She had a keycard in her hand (I presume that was part of what was waiting for her in the car) and a confused look on her face.

I walked over and took in her in my arms. She let me, but didn't really hug me back. "Thank you for coming," I said.

She nodded and took her bag into the room I was using. I heard the door to the bathroom shut and the sound of water running.

Quinn gathered up the packet of simulation information and got up. "I think I'll go find another place to review these."

"No," I said. "I should look at them too."

Quinn smiled and looked towards the bedroom Licia had disappeared into. "Look, this is going take time. You and Licia have not seen much of each other of late. I am sure you need to catch up."

I was about to protest again when there was a knock on the door and someone said, "Room service."

Quinn and I looked at each other. We were both surprised. I walked over, opened the door, and a young man dressed in black and white rolled the cart it. On it was champagne on ice and meals for two.

I lifted the metal covers on the two plates. One had a grilled portabella, brown rice, and steamed vegetables. The other had some salmon but was mostly cheese.

It was clear this meal was for Licia and I and neither of us had ordered it. More prescient action by LoVE.

Quinn chuckled and dashed out the door. "Call me if you need me. Otherwise I'll see you in the morning."

I was about to protest, but the waiter was leaving.

"What do I owe?" I asked him.

"It's already been taken care of, sir," he said with a smile.

Of course it was. This entire event had been carefully arranged. I had to wonder what was coming next.

6 / IN THE DOG HOUSE

A RELATIONSHIP IS NEVER CONSTANT, ALWAYS CHANGING. Sometimes you are closer than you can imagine, thinking each other's thoughts. Sometimes things are awkward and it seems you hardly know the person.

Licia and I ate, mostly silently, at the suite's small round table overlooking Main Street and a slice of old Las Vegas. The sun was gone, leaving only a dirty orange glow to the west. The champagne sat in its ice unopened.

You have to remember, we were early in our relationship, one that only began after Licia told me no repeatedly. I was scared. I didn't want to lose her, but I knew what I knew. That this Gaia was a real threat. That we needed her.

And that's just the big picture. Zoom in and what I knew was that I needed her, too. So at war in me was the desire to do what I knew was right (try to stop Gaia) with the desperation to do anything at all to keep her in my life. Our relationship was untested, of unknown strength.

These things are delicate.

Licia was dressed in jeans and a khaki-colored short-sleeved shirt with her silky black hair pulled back. She's petite with moderate curves, and looking at her was a balm for that caricature of her that Quinn became on the drive up.

Sometimes it's honestly hard to look at her. Because she is beautiful, yes. Because I love her more than I can express, yes. But today because I was afraid of losing her to this need.

"Can we talk about this?" I asked.

She speared a piece of asparagus, popped it in her mouth, and nodded towards me. Meaning, *if you want to talk, you start it up, buddy.*

"I know you want out of the q-morph game. I know you are still recovering from what happened at Palo Verde, about what happened to Ben." Her eyes darkened and she looked down at her food. Ben was a guard she was friends with that died during that battle. And she had killed for the first time during it—to save me. I had a similar trauma from the Incident at Yellowstone. These kinds of things aren't dealt with easily.

I took a deep breath and sighed, pushing around the cheese left on my plate. "How can we stand by while innocent lives are on the line?"

Her brown eyes met mine and they were hard. "Nik, you are always going to have to try to save the world. I know that about you. I accept it. And I already agreed to help. Why are you going over this again? Besides, it's not really the point, is it?"

And there it was. I didn't really understand what was bothering her. Except it's clear that my lack of understanding was an additional layer of the irritation.

It's one of those moments in a relationship. Do you understand your love well enough to empathize with them? Can you put yourself in their shoes and get a glimpse of their world?

This is a very valuable skill in any relationship. Empathy matters. But we were still early on in our time together. Was I supposed to know her that well already?

She smiled at me, a weak little smile full of irony. She wiped her mouth with the white cloth napkin, slid her chair back on the beige carpet, got up, walked into one of the bedrooms, and closed the door.

IT WAS NOT THE ROMANTIC EVENING I HAD BEEN HOPING FOR. I slept on the big brown couch just in case Quinn came back. He did, at 4:00 a.m., reeking of alcohol and stumbling.

"Ohh... Poor Nik," he said in an exaggerated whisper. "No lovey-lovey for poor, poor Nik." He added an uncharacteristic giggle to the end.

I was irritated. You have to understand, I was sleeping on the couch and Quinn was very drunk and making a nuisance of himself. And for Quinn to be drunk he has to want to be drunk—he can easily adjust his biology and drink all day long and not feel a thing. So instead of studying the simulations he went out on the town and purposely got drunk—and God knows what else.

"Go to bed, Quinn," I said.

He slapped the papers with the simulations down on the dark wood coffee table. "Screwed, Nik-o. We are screwed."

I pushed myself into a sitting position and looked at Quinn. His handsome face showed clear signs of worry (and inebriation). Maybe the simulations were why he got drunk.

And then I was really mad. Not at Quinn, but at myself. I can have empathy in two seconds for my partner, but not for my lover? What the hell?

"Sit down," I said, indicating the overstuffed chair near the couch. "Explain it to me."

"Well..." he said, pointing at me in a very exaggerated fashion. "If this simulation stuff is good—and I know you believe it is—there is only one way to stop her and avoid disaster. Only one way, my nuclear friend, to avoid big disaster."

I was puzzled. "That doesn't sound so bad."

He laughed loudly, the sound of it bouncing around the suite. His laughter was too high pitched, too manic. I had never seen Quinn this out of sorts. I didn't like it. "The problem is," he said, leaning towards me, his eyes wide. "You will never do it. Not in million years."

"What, Quinn? What won't I do?"

"Kill her. The only way to stop her and big disaster is for you to kill her the moment you see her."

———

Licia made Quinn coffee. He didn't need it—he could sober up in an instant if he wanted to. But I let it be. If Quinn "needed" coffee to get sober, then so be it.

She was dressed in a fluffy white robe with the Golden Nugget logo on it. Quinn's ranting woke her up. She found out what was going on and got all practical (she's very good at practical). She started the coffee and started digging through the printouts of the simulation data.

"He'll never do it," Quinn said with a slur. "And even if he did, it just makes it worse."

It was silent in the room for a while as Licia flipped through the papers scanning them rapidly. "Here it is," she said. "'Scenario 20a: Eliminate with extreme prejudice. Action: Neutrino must attack at first sight with a barrage of neutrino bolts. Result: 85% chance of Gaia's death, destruction averted. Long-Term Ramification: Chances of winning war are halved; we need Gaia's power long term.'"

Licia got up, poured three black coffees, gave one to Quinn, one to me, and sat down with the other. It was nearly 5:00 a.m. and I could see the sky starting to lighten just a touch outside.

"What do we do?" she asked. "Presuming these simulations are right, there must be something we can—"

Licia was cut off as all three of our phones chirped, signaling that text messages were received. The laptop, still sitting on the coffee table, then came to life. On it was Tom Tyree. For once he didn't have a grin on his face, but a deep frown.

"I'm glad you're awake," he said. "We know what Gaia's target is. You need to leave now if you have any chance of stopping her."

7 / TARGET: HOOVER DAM

SPRING 2005, HOOVER DAM, NEVADA/ARIZONA BORDER

I DROVE. QUINN WAS STILL TAKING HIS TIME SOBERING UP AND we didn't have a moment to spare.

"You two are adorable couple," he said from the backseat, his voice a bit slurred. "Make up, okay. What is old saying..." He trailed off, and I thought he might have dozed off or something, but about a minute later he finished. "A couple should never go into battle angry at each other. That's it."

The saying was about going to bed angry, of course, but Quinn's point was well taken.

"Is it Tom?" I asked, glancing at Licia sitting in the passenger's seat. "That I let him go? That I trust him on this?" We were out past the edge of Vegas and making the climb towards Boulder City. She was staring out the window as the desert whipped by in the yellow light of dawn. Just like I had been doing when Quinn had driven us to Vegas.

She sighed and glanced at me before staring back out at the desert. She was silent for a long time and I was about to open my mouth again when she said, "That is irritating and disturbing. The man is a psychopath. The man is using you—and now us. But no, that is not it."

I tried to engage her more, but it wasn't happening so I gave up and drove us to Hoover Dam as fast as I could.

⊏⊐

THE HOOVER DAM. SEVEN HUNDRED TWENTY-SIX FEET TALL, 3,250,000 cubic yards of concrete. Holding back the Colorado River and sixteen million acre-feet of water. Providing electricity to Nevada, Arizona, and California. The Hoover Dam is an epic piece of human engineering, and I love epic pieces of human engineering.

Things like the Hoover Dam give me hope. Hope that we as a race can find ways to work with nature in ways that aren't so invasive and terrible for the planet. And, yeah, I get that the river isn't free and all, but it's better than choking the air with coal smoke.

The dam sits in a narrow river gorge carved by the Colorado River. And the Colorado is no slouch—it also made the Grand Canyon. It holds back Lake Mead, the largest reservoir in the country, when it's full.

This was Gaia's target. She wanted to destroy the dam and free the waters trapped in Lake Mead.

In 2005, when this happened, the bypass bridge over the river gorge was still under construction and traffic on US 93 went over the dam itself. Because of the early hour, there wasn't much traffic. We wound our way down through tight switchbacks carved into the reddish-brown rock of the canyon and onto the west edge of the dam. I stopped the car and got out.

"The Hammer?" Quinn asked from the backseat of the Focus. He had finally sobered up.

"Yes," I said.

Licia was out and looking around. We didn't know all that

much. Just that this was the target and Gaia was expected this morning.

The click-squish sound came from the car as Quinn transformed into The Hammer.

A couple cars stopped behind us and were honking. Several security guards were yelling at us and running our way.

The Hammer got out of the car and said, "Need steel." Quinn's already deep voice was an octave lower.

I guess I should take a moment and talk about q-morphs and the conservation of mass. Quinn weighed about 250 pounds, so when he transformed, he still weighed 250 pounds. So Sadie weighed 250 pounds, and even that petite, nightmare rendition of Licia he did weighed 250 pounds. He can't suddenly weigh something different unless he acquires or releases mass.

So when The Hammer got out of the car, he weighed 250 pounds.

You know what The Hammer looks like, right? All dark grey skin, flat features, huge chest, fists as big as your head. In most images of him he's covered in steel armor plates and weighs more like 350 or 400 pounds. That's why he asked about steel, he needed it to complete the transformation.

"Car?" he asked looking at my Ford Focus with its faded blue paint.

The Hammer also has a different personality than Quinn. His endocrine system and metabolism are significantly altered. He is constantly adrenalized and has epic amounts of energy (and needs epic amounts of food).

"No," I said and pointed him towards the steel guardrail along the road as I moved to intercept the guards. Licia was at the edge of the dam, tendrils of electricity starting to flow from the power lines above us to her outstretched left hand.

"Sir, you will have to..." the lead guard said. He was a grey-haired man with brown eyes. He trailed off when he noticed The Hammer and what he was doing with the guardrail.

It's that whole molecular manipulation thing. The Hammer had his hands on the guardrail, and the steel was flowing onto his body. By touching it, he was able to manipulate it at a molecular level, the molecules relocating to his chest, his arms, his forehead, his fists. It looked like the metal was liquid as it crawled all over his body. The metal was making a high-pitched groan as it flowed onto him.

"Do you know who I am?" I asked. I didn't have my hat or sunglasses on. I wanted to be recognized.

He and the sandy-haired guard next to him looked at me and the older one nodded.

"Good. I'm here because of a credible terrorist threat against the dam. I need you to initiate an evacuation and start any kind of disaster protocols you might have."

"Excuse me?" the sandy-haired one asked.

"There is a threat to the dam that could destroy it. We need to move fast. Evacuate. Warn everyone downstream."

"Sir, you'll have to move your car, or I'll have it towed," the older man said. Maybe it was just too much, but they didn't seem to be getting it.

"What now?" The Hammer asked as he came up next to me. He's about my height, six feet, but so much wider. He's strong as an ox and relatively quick on his feet. In a hand-to-hand battle between anything biological and The Hammer, well, The Hammer will win. And I mean anything—he could take on a rhinoceros, I'm sure of it.

"Block the traffic on the other end of the dam," I said to The Hammer. The guards were still talking, but I wasn't listening to them anymore.

The Hammer ran off, I could feel the vibration of his pounding feet through the asphalt. "And don't hurt anyone," I yelled.

"There she is," Licia yelled. Licia was standing on the low concrete wall that edges the sidewalk that goes across the dam. To her right was the visitors center with several floors of glass looking over the canyon and the damn. Right above her were high-tension power lines and she was starting to draw a thick bolt of electricity from it.

I ran over next to her. She put her right hand on my shoulder and began to pump electricity into me. It felt good to have her by my side again.

I didn't have time to appreciate the dam, the massive concave form of it holding back hundreds of feet of water, the generating station a U far below that hugged the bottom of the dam and the sides of the canyon. All off-white against the rough rocks. Clean, renewable energy and a stark emblem of mankind's manipulation of their environment.

I looked and could see a figure across the gorge standing on a rocky protrusion above the other side of the dam. I couldn't see her as well as Licia, but I could tell it was a woman with brown skin. She was naked and standing proud. Jena Grange. Gaia.

And suddenly I knew why Licia was upset with me. "I'm sorry I didn't tell you the truth about why we came up here."

She looked at me and smiled. I finally figured it out. It wasn't that I asked for her help or that I had this weird relationship with Tom Tyree. It was the most basic of things. I hadn't been honest with her.

"That's it. Right?" I asked.

The ground rumbled beneath us, rocks falling from the cliff Gaia was standing on. This wasn't the pounding of The Hammer's feet. This felt like an earthquake.

"Not now, dear," Licia said as she transformed into Lightningirl, her clothing burning off of her as her flesh transformed into blue-white swirls of her q-morph form. "We've got a mission."

INTERLUDE 2: WHAT A WOMAN WANTS

Not surprisingly, Licia and I worked well together as we built the greenhouse. I am physically stronger, but she has a better eye for detail and more patience with the small stuff.

We've got the steel frame in place and are getting ready to start installing the windows. It's a much bigger greenhouse than our old one. It will be nice and will let us grow more of our own food.

The hot sun was beating down from a clear blue sky. It was a lovely summer day in the high desert. We're both standing off a few paces, eyeing our work, taking a break.

The rolling high desert hills framed the greenhouse and we were far enough away from I-17 to the west that it was dead quiet.

"So..." I began, my brain still full of the past and the story I had been writing that morning. "Honesty. Is that what a woman wants most?"

She gave me an appraising look. "We're about to fight Gaia, right?" she asked.

I nodded.

"Hell of a time for a realization," she said, a smile on her face.

"Quinn said we shouldn't go into battle angry." I said it like a joke, but her smile disappeared and her face darkened.

"Well... is it?" I asked, trying to change the subject. "Is honesty the most important thing?"

A slight breeze came up and was licking at the sweat on my skin. It felt good. I had nothing but shorts and shoes on, as usual, so I could absorb as much UV radiation as possible.

"It's not that simple," Licia said.

"Well, explain it to me."

She smiled and shrugged. "Think of it like baking bread."

I wasn't much of a baker, but I nodded for her to continue.

"Honesty is like the yeast. If you don't have any yeast, your bread will turn into a dense, inedible block of wheat. Yeast makes the bread rise. Yeast makes bread, bread."

I pursed my lips and nodded, thinking about it. "So yeast is the most important ingredient in bread as honesty is the most important ingredient in a relationship."

She shook her head and sighed. "No. You need all the ingredients. Leave out water and you still don't have bread. Leave out the passion in a relationship and there is no relationship."

I love my wife. How much I can't even convey to you. We have managed to stick together through so much. Our lives have changed radically many times. She even puts up with my dredging up the past and my philosophical meanderings.

"So it's kind of like alchemy?" I asked.

She smiled and nodded. "Exactly. Don't get me wrong, honesty is a basic requirement, but it takes passion and commitment and trust and patience and so much more to make it work."

"So you like honesty," I said, a silly grin creeping onto my face.

Her brow furrowed as her eyes searched mine, but she said, "Yes, I do."

"Great, then let me be honest with you about something very serious."

"Okay..."

"I'm horny," I said with a big grin. "How about we take a break and—"

She sighed and rolled her eyes, stopping me.

"Too much honesty?" I asked.

She laughed and nodded. "We've got work to do." She walked back to our construction site. I gladly followed.

SPRING 2005, HOOVER DAM, NEVADA/ARIZONA BORDER

Standing there on the edge of the Hoover Dam, the ground rumbling beneath us, we didn't speak. We just acted. Licia transformed into Lightningirl. I transformed into Neutrinoman. Our clothes burning away and dropping to the ground.

She hopped on my back and I flew us across the river gorge toward the salmon colored outcrop of stone above the east end of the dam.

Despite our time apart, despite Licia's fear of flying, we knew what to do. I missed her acutely in that moment despite her proximity—it had been too long since we had been Neutrinoman and Lightningirl together.

I was a contained nuclear reaction, swirling motes of yellow with neutrino jets shooting out of my palms and feet to power our flight.

Lightningirl was a contained electrical reaction, blue-white, her left hand outstretched while she continued to pull electricity from the Hoover Dam in the form of a coruscating lightning bolt. Her hair was a halo of sparking electricity around her, and with her feminine curves she looked the part of a goddess.

Where our bodies met, they did their dancing exchange of energy, my yellow to her blue-white, the two of us together making a whole that was more than the sum of its parts.

As I flew, I noticed a few things.

The Hammer bodily moving a car on the far end of the dam below the rock. He punched the tire, blowing it out and made sure the car couldn't move. The road down to the dam had been carved into the rock so the outcropping Gaia stood on rose as a cliff about fifty feet above him.

It was early, but a few cars and trucks were backed up trying to get across the dam. There were guards on that side too, wisely keeping their distance from The Hammer. In fact, there were people running away from The Hammer (and the dam), which was a good thing.

I heard and saw out of the corner of my eye a helicopter flying high above us. It seemed too early for a tour, but I didn't think anything of it.

And then there was Gaia. She stood there calmly, her head turning to watch The Hammer below and then Lightningirl and me flying towards her.

We arrived and landed on the stone near her. She was still calm, which was beginning to worry me. Lightningirl hopped off my back and the three of us stood there staring at each other.

It was a spectacular spot. The off-white expanse of the Hoover Dam squatting in the deep canyon, its concave surface holding back the vast blue of Lake Mead. Seven hundred feet below us, the Colorado River. Dark blue skies above us, slowly lightening as the sun rose.

Gaia was about 5'5" with brown skin and long, curly black hair that fell across her shoulders and down her back. She had full lips and a wide nose showing her African heritage. She was completely nude. Like most of us transforming q-morphs, there is no costume that can survive what she can do. She had wide hips and large breasts. She wasn't fat, but she wasn't skinny either. She looked like an ancient carving of a fertility goddess. She had the kind of body suited to childbirth.

"Hi," I said, filling the silence. "I'm Neutrinoman, this is Light-ningirl. You must be Gaia."

Her brown eyes, deep and intense, turned on me.

"You are the one that stopped the meteor," she said. She had a British accent, not cockney, more upper crust, like she came from a wealthy family.

"Yes," I said with a nod and a smile.

"I hate you," she said, her tone flat.

Lightningirl had stopped drawing power from the high-tension power lines and had tamped down her electrical reaction. She was still a swirl of blue-white electricity, but not as intimidating as when she is fully powered. I banked down my nuclear reaction too. We were just having a conversation. I had, obviously, rejected the strategy of killing her on sight.

"I'm sorry," I said. "Have I done something to harm you?"

"You stopped that meteor," she said, her lips twisted in a bitter frown.

I just stood there, my mouth moving. I had no clue as to why that would upset her.

"You mean you wanted the meteor to strike the earth?" Licia asked.

"Yes," she said. "Mankind is a disease. Mankind must be stopped. I must stop it."

———

BACK THEN, IF YOU WERE TALKING ABOUT GAIA AND IF YOU were being generous, you would use words like "passionate," "dedi-cated," and "uncompromising." If you weren't being generous you would use words like "crazy" and "radical."

Her tone as we talked was calm. Way too calm, really. Her arguments were unfailingly logical. Her conclusions were... well, they were scary as hell.

"Disease?" I asked. "How is mankind a disease?"

"It spreads across the planet unchecked," Gaia said, sweeping her hand to encompass the dam and all its support structures. "It uses resources for individual gain without thought to the whole or to the planet. Mankind is selfish and gluttonous, taking much more from the Earth than it needs. This is the behavior of a disease. The behavior of a virus or a cancer so virulent it will foolishly kill its host in the name of its own greed."

"Oh," I said. How the hell could I counter that? She wasn't exactly wrong. I just happened to value human life too much to go there.

"Mankind is a mess," Licia said. "I will give you that. But things are getting better."

"Better?" Gaia asked, turning her gaze on Licia.

"Yes, better. Look at this country a hundred years ago. African Americans were much worse off, not treated as equals. The plight of women has also improved radically—we're not expected to just raise a family anymore. We can go out into the world and make our own way, although it is maddening we don't have a ratified Equal Rights Amendment. The Clean Air Act of 1970 did much to curtail pollution and the Endangered Species Act of 1973 helped with extinction of our animals."

"And yet there is an island of garbage in the Pacific," Gaia said. "Species are still becoming extinct all the time. Poverty is rampant in the third world, and first-world countries like this one do so little to help. Global warming is denied by the western powers despite mounting evidence."

"But it is getting better," I said. I was amazed at how well educated Licia was on this topic. I had no idea. "The Gates Foundation is putting billions towards dealing with problems like malaria and trying to pull the poorest nations out of poverty." And I only knew that because Bill Gates was the richest person in the world and even I hear news about him.

"Though we fight, our world is getting more civilized," Licia said. "You don't have to do this."

"We need you," I added.

Her brow furrowed as her deep brown eyes searched mine. "You need me?" she asked.

As we talked, I noticed a few things. First, she was completely unashamed of her nudity. I really envied that. Maybe she grew up someplace less uptight about such things than Arizona. Second, her feet were buried in solid rock up to her ankles. No sign of the rock being disturbed whatsoever. It was like she was part of the rock. In fact, the lower half of her calves appeared to be sandstone.

"Yes," I said. "We need you. Humans aren't perfect, but we are getting better. We are trying to improve. We need you to help us..." I trailed off. We needed her to help save the human race, but she didn't seem to be very much interested in that.

"To save the planet," Licia interjected, phrasing it in a way she might actually be able to hear. "Neutrinoman is famous now. He can help get you a forum to speak on these issues. He can get you in with the Gates Foundation to see if they can help address your concerns."

My mouth dropped open. She was committing me to a lot, but something clicked then. I *was* famous. I *had* a forum. Shouldn't I be doing something about it? Wasn't poverty, human rights, and climate change worthy of more attention? "Yes," I said. "I will do anything I can to help address these issues. You can join us, Gaia. You can help us and we can help you."

"But..." Gaia began, her eyes looking towards the northwest, towards Las Vegas. "That place is such a blight. Such an affront to Mother Earth. I must strike against it. I must..."

Lightningirl and I were getting through. I knew it. I could see it in her eyes. But then along came The Hammer.

IF YOU THINK OF THE HAMMER AS A ROIDED UP FOOTBALL player with way too much testosterone flowing through his veins, you are pointed in the right direction, but you are under the mark by quite a bit. He's all that and much more.

While we had been talking, he had been acting. Blocking the east end of the dam and then running to the west end and chasing people off. The Hammer is not dumb, he's just filled with so much fight that he often misses the obvious. When he was on the west side of the dam he looked across and spotted us up on the cliff. He saw Gaia. He knew she was dangerous. He acted.

"Please," I said to Gaia. "Let's leave this place. Let's talk. I promise I will help you address these concerns. I..."

I heard him grunt as The Hammer finally found a way up the cliff. He had to go up the road to the east a ways, find a slope not too steep to climb, and come up the back side of the rock.

When I saw him, his head was down and he was running hard with a branch of some sort of bush sticking out of his mouth. That's the other thing about The Hammer, to keep that energy going he eats anything organic he finds in his path.

"No!" I shouted, holding my hands up and running towards him. But it was too late to reason with him. There was not enough time for my intent to get through his brain. I ran towards him intending to push him out of the way, but he threw me aside.

Licia threw her left hand back and a lightning bolt leapt from the high-tension power line to her left hand, and from her right hand it spiked out to The Hammer. It wasn't a lot of electricity, she was just trying to get his attention.

But that wasn't enough either, his momentum shot him towards the wide-eyed Gaia. But when he should have connected with her, she was gone and The Hammer went flying over the cliff towards the Colorado River seven hundred feet below.

⊏⊐

I WASN'T HAPPY WITH THE HAMMER, BUT I WENT AFTER HIM anyway. I wasn't thinking, just reacting. After taking a single step, I was flying after him, yellow neutrino jets firing out of my feet and palms.

Once I got over the outcrop we had been on, I could see that he had cleared the service road and was falling down the gorge. I spotted him when he bounced off the side of the canyon.

This was a fool's errand, really. It takes all of five seconds to fall seven hundred feet, and I was about a second behind. That bounce, though, helped. It slowed him down just a touch.

I flew hard and fast, and by the time he was halfway down, I had a hold of his hand. He had this wide-eyed look on his flat face. He was afraid. The Hammer can take a lot of damage, but slamming into the ground at 140 miles per hour would probably cause him some issues, maybe even do enough damage fast enough so he wouldn't be able to heal himself.

Not that I could stop him from slamming into the ground, not at the pace we were going. What I could do was slow him down. So as I clung to his arm, I pointed my feet and my free hand down and put out as much thrust as I could with the neutrino jets. The Hammer screamed.

There was a reason Quinn was my partner. His ability to control his body at a molecular level made him able to heal quickly. To heal from radiation. He wasn't immune, it was just that he could take a good amount of it without any lasting damage.

When I grabbed him, my reaction was hot. I was slowing him down, but I was burning his hand at the same time, at a rate his body couldn't quite keep up with. It hurt, thus the deep-throated scream of The Hammer as we fell.

At the bottom of the dam was a U-shaped, white-roofed building that hugged the downstream end of the dam and ran along both sides of the river. This was the roof of the hydroelectric generation station. Water from Lake Mead was funneled through turbines here to generate electricity. Water flows out the bottom of it into the river gorge.

I had slowed us down. Not completely, but enough to make the landing survivable. We slammed into that white roof hard and kept going.

The generator room was huge. About ten stories tall with a long row of massive round turbines. We crashed through the roof, which was reinforced with steel girders, and slammed to the floor below, debris from the roof raining down upon us.

The floor was concrete and I landed first, cratering it out a bit. The Hammer landed on top of me.

Not a pleasant landing, but I've had much worse.

There were large walkways to either side and a few hard-hat-wearing workers were staring at us. I didn't blame them. It's not that often you see two superheroes crashing through your roof.

We got lucky in that on the far end of the station there were no generators for us to land on. Only hard floor.

"Thanks," The Hammer grunted as he got up and brushed

himself off. I could see his hand and forearm repairing the damage from the radiation.

"Sure," I said, standing and looking up through the hole in the roof.

We were grinning at each other. In truth these kinds of things are exciting. A near brush with death, a daring save you can walk away from. I was starting to feel better about the day. And I had always wanted to take a tour of the dam, not that this was the way I imagined it. I loved these kinds of big engineering projects. It's what led me to become a janitor at Palo Verde—I really just wanted an inside look. I wanted to learn how it worked. And that simple curiosity led to the accident at Palo Verde on the day the cosmic rays hit that turned me into Neutrinoman.

That's when the floor started to shake underneath us and I could hear rocks striking the roof above. A few came through the hole we had made and fell on us.

"Oh no," The Hammer said.

"I don't think this is over," I said.

I looked through the hole above us. I could see clear blue sky, still slowly lightening as the sun rose, and then I saw... Well, I didn't believe what I saw, but it looked like a flash of rock framed in the blue sky. The rock looked like a clenched fist, and then it was gone, and then the whole building shook hard.

I looked around and at one end of the room there was an observation deck and a group of tourists there gawking at us.

I looked at The Hammer. "Get this place evacuated and get out of here. I'm going to go see what this is."

The Hammer nodded and started running to a set of stairs that went up to the observation deck.

"And be gentle," I yelled after him.

I looked up and saw that huge fist-shaped rock pass over and the whole room shook again. People were screaming and a high-pitched alarm went off.

INTERLUDE 3: AN INTERVIEW REQUEST

Licia had a puzzled look on her face as she walked out of our little adobe casita and towards the greenhouse we were building. She had two glasses of iced tea in one hand and a plate of cheese in the other. I could smell the cheese from fifty yards away and it made my stomach grumble.

I was obsessed with cheese and had an extraordinary sense of smell because of the rat that bit me the day of the accident, the day I became what I am.

There are always three elements for those of us that transformed into q-morphs. For me it was a rat, endowing me with an excellent sense of smell and an everlasting need for cheese. For Licia it was a raven and giving her excellent eyesight and an unerring sense of direction.

I was glad to see her. It was just past noon and hot as hell. Construction is hungry work, but the puzzled look on her lovely face gave me pause.

"What's up?" I asked when she got close.

She handed me the plate and one of the glasses of tea and sat down on the flagstone floor, but she didn't speak.

I sat next to her, taking a long drink and then popping a piece of Munster in my mouth.

"That was Diane Madison on the phone," she said quietly.

I was in mid-swallow and choked on the cheese, coughing hard.

"She wants to interview you," she said when I had cleared my throat. "Actually, she wants to interview both of us."

Diane Madison. The woman who had outed our identities. The woman that had inserted herself in our business every chance she got. The woman who had... Well, we're not to that part of the story yet, but suffice it to say we had reason to be wary of Diane Madison.

"You told her no, right?" I asked. "Preferably loudly and then hung up on her."

Licia slowly shook her head. "I told her yes."

"What!" I stood and began pacing the floor of the greenhouse. We had the main posts in and had started on the glass roof. "Why? Why would you do that?"

Licia took a deep breath and slowly sighed. "For you, hon." She added a small smile, her eyes tracking me as I paced. "You said it was time that we have more of a life, aren't cooped up here all the time. Isn't that what you want?"

I stopped in front of her. Her expression was still an odd one. Part shock, part determination. Her brow was furrowed as she stared up at me, her lips forming the barest of smiles, her eyes wide.

"Diane is doing a segment in her 'Where Are They Now?' series about the war. She's got two presidents booked and General Markus. She's calling all of us q-morphs that survived."

I sat back down on the cool stone next to my wife. "Why would she be doing that?"

"She tied herself to you early on," Licia said. "Her star was hitched to your wagon when it all went to hell in the end. When we had to sign the Q-Morph Accord of 2020 and were all gotten out of the way, she went down too."

I took another bite of cheese and ate it slowly. Diane was in it for herself, and knowing that made me feel better.

"America loves their heroes," Licia said.

"But they love to see them fall even more," I added. We had said this to each other many times when things had gone to hell.

"I reminded Diane of that," Licia said. "And you know what she said?"

I shook my head.

"That what America loves even more is to see their heroes redeemed. She thinks it's time, Nik. She thinks it's all because of these little books you are writing."

I bristled at the adjective "little" being associated with my writing. It didn't feel "little" at all, although they were fairly short, so maybe that is what she meant. But I let it pass. "But what if she doesn't behave? What if she screws us over again?"

A wicked smile played on Licia's lips. "She'll be good," she said.

"How do you know?"

"I told her if she wasn't, she would have me to deal with. That I would wait until it was a dark and stormy night in LA when lightning rained down on the city. And a stray bolt of lightning would stab out from her TV or a wall socket. That that lightning would kill her, and that lightning would be me."

It was suddenly quiet around us. The heat of the high desert day had driven all the animals underground. The air was still, and the sun hung in a clear blue sky.

"Seriously?" I asked.

She laughed. "Seriously, although my tone was much more menacing when I told her."

I wanted to ask her if she would really do something like that, but then stopped myself. I really didn't want to know the answer.

She grabbed my hand. "You want more of a life, we need the public to remember us, to remember all that we did. We need her and she needs us."

I nodded, feeling my stomach tighten at the thought.

"Besides, if she screws us in the edit you have your own forum now. You can write about the interview, tell the truth about it. It'll be okay."

I nodded, but I wasn't sure.

"So," Licia continued. "I guess we need to get Agent Peters out here."

Agent Peters is with Homeland Security. He's what I affectionately think of as our "landlord." He's really more like our "guard" or "warden," keeping us happy so we stay on our reservation and don't bother the people now that the war is over.

And yes, I used the word "reservation." I'm from Arizona, I've been to the Navajo and Hopi reservations numerous times. I don't use that word lightly. With the Quantum Metamorph Accord of 2020, all of us surviving q-morphs were basically restricted to our own plot of land.

We are not living in the third-world conditions of the real reservations, but we are isolated and restricted here. We are treated differently because of who we are. Our plight is not anywhere near as extreme, but there are parallels.

"Well," I said with a smile, pointing up. "I know how to get his attention."

Licia smiled and nodded. We wrapped up our work and headed towards our launch pad, an area of flagstones near the high-tension power lines that run near our home. We had been seeing Agent Peters a lot more. I would fly us up into orbit every week or two where I could soak up some nice radiation from the sun. And every time Agent Peters would be here when we got down, questioning our unauthorized use of powers, making us fill out a ton of paperwork.

After we had transformed into our q-morph selves, Licia standing on my feet, her arms around my neck, I said, "Thank you." I would never have agreed to an interview with Diane Madison myself. I needed the push. "I think this could help."

She smiled and held me tightly as we soared into the air.

SPRING 2005, HOOVER DAM, NEVADA/ARIZONA BORDER

WHEN I FLEW UP OUT OF THE GENERATING STATION, I couldn't believe my eyes. And, frankly, I wouldn't expect you to believe what I write here, but you've all seen the videos and pictures shot that day. It was early, but a few tourists did capture some images, and someone in that helicopter had a camera recording the whole thing.

What I saw was a seven-hundred-foot-tall rock giant. A colossus. Gaia, fully transformed and mad as hell.

That rock outcropping we had talked to the humanoid Gaia on was the head, its features roughly that of a woman, her rough features that of Jena Grange. The fist I had seen from below was the left fist of the rock giant, and as I flew up, that fist flew past me and slammed into the dam again, taking out a chunk of the top of the dam and throwing debris into Lake Mead.

The colossus Gaia appeared to be pinned by the dam. Her left side was in the open on the downstream side of the dam while her right side was on the upstream side of the dam.

It was unbelievable.

I flew up to the height of the dam and out of reach of the giant, my mouth hanging open. I mean, this was not something I had ever imagined seeing. And as I watched, the colossus began to look more like her human self as rock fell away. The chest pinned by the dam, one breast visible. The hips forming down the rock gorge. A long leg and foot now stomping on the transformer station at the bottom of the river gorge just downstream from the generating station. Rocks fell. Sparks flew. And a deep shout of rage escaped Gaia's rock lips. The sound was like rock against rock and I could literally feel it when the sound hit me.

Mother Nature was angry. She didn't like this dam. She was going to destroy it.

As I gawked, as I tried to get my mind in gear, tried to figure out how to stop Gaia, Lightningirl acted.

Lightning stabbed out from behind me and struck the rock giant. I looked back and saw Lightningirl in full goddess mode standing on top of the visitor's center, the ornate patinaed copper roof behind her, a hundred feet of windows below her, the main tower of it rising out of the rocky canyon all glass and copper accents.

She was drawing a large bolt of electricity from the high-tension power lines to her left hand and lightning was arcing from her right hand and striking the giant. She was fully powered, tiny bolts of electricity sparking off her swirling blue/white form, her electric hair haloed around her head, her hair snapping and sparking all around her face.

It was like the Goddess of the Earth was fighting the Goddess of Electricity.

I flew over to the roof and landed next to Lightningirl.

"I'm going to kill Quinn," she shouted over the crackling noise of the lightning bolts. "How do we stop her?"

She shot a bolt of electricity into my back. It's intense, it hurts, but it also feels good. There is something about our powers that are complementary. She can strengthen me with her electricity and I can strengthen her with my radiation. It's why we work so well together.

I started firing neutrino bolts at Gaia, yellow balls of coruscating neutrino energy leaping from my palms. About the size of a baseball, they fly straight and true and explode on impact.

I felt bad about doing it. I honestly didn't want to hurt her, but I didn't want her to destroy the dam, to send all that water rushing down the Colorado River towards Lake Mohave, which it would probably overrun, sending another wave of water farther down the river.

The area is sparsely populated. Below Lake Mohave is Laughlin on the Nevada side and Bullhead City on the Arizona side. Laughlin is kind of like a mini Las Vegas, with casinos lining the Colorado River. They would be decimated.

Farther down the river is Lake Havasu and then Yuma.

The desert southwest uses so much of the Colorado River that it is barely a trickle by the time it reaches Yuma and crosses into Mexico. It doesn't even make it all the way to the Gulf of Mexico anymore.

And maybe this was just the first dam on the Colorado River that Gaia was going to target. Maybe she would take out Lake Mead and Lake Havasu and then go upstream and take out Glen Canyon Dam and drain Lake Powel, which would send a torrent of water through the Grand Canyon.

So I shot neutrino bolts at the rock giant pinned by the dam. She kept pounding at it with her left fist and then her right. Breaking through the top of the dam, the remnants of the road falling into the lake. Starting at the top, each blow knocked away a part of the dam. Left right, left right, her rhythmic beating quickly destroying the dam where she pounded, throwing debris down the canyon or back into the river.

The lake's water levels were low, the top of the dam a hundred feet or so above the water, so she could fully use both fists in aid in the destruction. Her position pinned by the dam gave her perfect leverage. Concrete flying out with each blow, cracks radiating, the sound of it like small explosions each time the colossus's fist struck. We could feel the vibration of it under our feet.

She didn't waste any energy on the intake tower rising up out of the lake even though it was within reach. She was focused on the dam, beating a chunk of it away with every blow.

The loud sirens continued to scream and I saw that they were finally evacuating, people spilling out of the visitor's center below us and running up the road away from the dam.

My bolts had an effect. Where they hit Gaia, rock would explode, but soon it would be replaced by other rock. On my second attempt, a few bolts hit her hand taking out the top third of it. But it wasn't effective, soon rock flowed down her arm and the thumb and index finger were recreated.

I landed some bolts on her left elbow, same effect. She would just draw more rock from the cliff and repair the damage. This caused the cliff to erode back behind her.

My bolts seemed to cause her pain. Each time one landed, that grinding rock-on-rock scream would escape her, drowning out the drone of the siren.

I stopped firing at her. It wasn't working.

Lightningirl, though, was getting somewhere. At first her lightning didn't seem to have any effect at all. She struck Gaia's fist and arm and chest and hip and leg to no effect. The giant just seemed to absorb the electricity.

But then she landed a bolt on the giant's head right between the eyes and that got its attention.

The pounding of the fists stopped and Gaia turned her gaze to us. Her rock face now looked very much like her human face and she looked mad.

"Uh oh," I said.

Gaia cocked her left arm back—and I must remind you it was over two hundred feet long, so it was quite the display. She cocked her arm back, and instead of slamming her fist into the dam, she swung it towards us with it ending up pointed directly at us, fingers splayed. A boulder flew from her hand right at us. I grabbed Lightningirl and started flying us up just as the boulder hit where we had been standing.

The roof of the visitor's center exploded around us, debris flying everywhere.

As I flew us, Lightningirl didn't stop. She kept targeting the giant's head with her lightning bolts. I had grabbed her from behind and had both of my arms around her. My flight was wobbly using just my feet and I quickly landed her on the now abandoned dam not far from the visitor's center.

"I'm fine," Lightningirl shouted. "Target her head, right between the eyes. There's something there."

The Hoover Dam is forty-five feet wide at the top and over six hundred feet wide at the bottom. Gaia had done a tremendous amount of damage the short time she had been beating on the structure. She had opened up a gap on the Arizona side almost down to the water line, the break in it making it clear how the dam widens the lower you go.

Even with all that concrete it was clear that given even a little more time, she would work her way down to the water level if not completely destroying the structure.

The man-made dam was strong, but it appeared that the earth goddess was stronger.

Gaia was cocking her arm back again to launch another boulder at us as I took flight. I didn't love the idea of leaving Lightningirl, but I knew her capabilities. She was in full-on Goddess of Electricity mode—she could take care of herself.

I flew hard and fast just downstream of Gaia away from her swinging arm. I didn't fire, I looked. I wanted to see what Lightningirl had been referring too.

Right in the middle of the rock giant's forehead, right between the eyes, was a darker-colored spot. The head of this thing was over one hundred feet tall, and this brown spot was only about a foot tall. At first it looked like some random aberration of the stone, but as I flew closer, I saw what it was. I saw a face.

———

Jena Grange can manipulate the earth. That is her power. So this rock giant, this colossus that had formed, that was pinned by the Hoover Dam, was controlled by Jena, really was Jena. That face I saw was the human in the giant. She was still physically there, still physically part of it, still flesh and blood.

This is why the giant reacted when the lightning struck her there. By the time I had the realization, I was almost upon her. Gaia had just hurled another boulder at Lightningirl, but I wasn't aware of that at the time. I was focused on this tiny face buried in the rock of this huge giant. I was trying to decide what to do.

I didn't want to kill Jena but her actions were not acceptable. I ended up taking precious moments to ponder this as I flew towards her. It wasn't long, a second or so, but it was long enough so that I didn't have any maneuvering room. I was going to run right into that huge rock head.

So I used my final moments to adjust my trajectory and slammed right into the middle of the giant's forehead, right where Jena's head was embedded in the rock.

I didn't explode, like I had done with the meteor, I just slammed into the rock hard and then I was falling with rock, dirt, and boulders all around me, having no idea what was going on.

11 / GOODBYE FRYING PAN, HELLO FRYER

Tumbling... disoriented... bouncing between rocks like I was the ball in a pinball machine. As I tumbled, I tried to see light, but my vision was obscured, everything a gray haze around me. It took me a moment to realize water was falling on me and turning to steam, which is why I couldn't see.

And I could hardly think. The blows from the rocks didn't really damage me in my neutrino form, but the painful jolts kept me from thinking clearly.

It was only seconds, but then, through the mist, I saw lightning, a small tendril of it stabbing through the fog. I flew hard towards it and was soon out of the jumble of rocks and water as they tumbled down the side of the canyon and fell on top of the generator station.

When I had struck the colossus's head, it had fallen apart, like a puppet with its strings cut. All the rock that had moved, that had formed the legs, chest, arms, and head of Gaia, fell. It left a gap around the eastern edge of the dam, like a very badly receding gumline. Water was spilling over the gap, a huge torrent from the lake suddenly draining into the river below.

It was a massive waterfall, strangely beautiful.

I landed on the dam next to Lightningirl. "Thanks," I said.

"Anytime," she replied with a smile. The bolt arcing from the power lines to her hand had stopped. "Generator's out," she said.

It wasn't a surprise. Much of what had been Gaia had fallen on the generating station.

I looked back to the dam, the gap went about five feet below the water line. That meant the lake was about to go down by five feet and that all that water was going to hit Lake Mohave. I was hopeful that word had gotten out, that they had opened their flood gates. That the lake was being evacuated and that they could handle all that water.

I felt a thump, thump through the cement below my feet and had a bad moment. I was worried that Gaia was back, but I turned and saw The Hammer running from the visitor's center towards us.

The visitor's center was in shambles, the roof ripped off by the boulder Gaia had thrown at us. A few people were running out of it and away from the dam.

"What did I miss?" The Hammer asked.

"A seven-hundred-foot-tall rock giant," I said.

The expression on The Hammer's flat face was hard to read. It was a strange combination of disappointment and awe, with maybe a touch of fear.

"I think we're going to be okay," Lightningirl said. "Not great, but okay."

The waterfall was still going, a brief Niagara Falls in the Arizona desert. It was going to take quite some time for all that water to drain, but the dam was intact, Gaia was gone, and we had *kinda* saved the day. Well, let's put it this way: it could have been much worse.

"Yeah," I said with a smile. "I think we are. The dam gets thicker as you go down, there is no way that—"

A sharp bang both heard and felt through my feet stopped me short. I looked over at the dam and saw that more of the generating station's roof had collapsed and black smoke was roiling out.

"Oh no," The Hammer said. "You spoke too quick."

I smelled burning diesel and melted plastic. That first bang was followed by a much larger one, the dam moving below our feet, a blossom of yellow flame escaping the generating station six hundred feet below as more of the roof collapsed.

"This is not good," I said.

Lightningirl turned to The Hammer and said, "Unless you can fly, you best get off this dam right now."

You didn't have to tell him twice. The Hammer headed west, the thumping of his feet rapidly retreating.

I leaned over and looked at the dam, at the ragged V-shaped gap where Gaia had been beating on it, where water was spilling out. The line wasn't sharp, all crumbly edges with small cracks radiating out from it in all directions.

Gaia had been banging on the dam from both sides and had weakened it significantly, and the exploding power station had just made it worse.

As I looked, I heard a different kind of cracking sound. This one not as loud and much sharper. As I watched, the edges of the gap crumbled and it got bigger, especially at the bottom, the pressure of the lake and the water flowing rapidly, increasing the damage, the water flowing faster and getting stronger.

"Oh, shit!" I said.

"You've got to do something," Lightningirl said as the sharp cracking sound continued.

"What the hell can I do?"

"You have to do something," she said again.

"What!?"

We were a little freaked... Okay, a *lot* freaked out. This whole trip was supposed to be about having a conversation with Chaosboy, maybe bringing him in. But instead we were overseeing what was looking like the destruction of the Hoover Dam.

Not really how I saw this little "off book" adventure going.

Lightningirl looked at the lake spread out behind us. A blue expanse of water as far as the eye could see. She then looked down the deep and narrow river gorge. She then looked at me.

She was opening her mouth to say something when we were rocked by a third explosion from the generating station. The loud bang of the explosions was accompanied by even louder cracking from the dam.

It was starting to sound like thin ice when you walk on it. A sharp crack like gunfire that makes your heart race.

"Find a narrow area in the canyon," she shouted, pointing downstream. "Blow it to hell. Do something to slow this water down."

As if on cue, the cracking became loud and continuous and the dam shook beneath us. The small waterfall was getting bigger faster, the water pushing its way through the damaged dam.

With a flash of light, Lightningirl was gone and I was left there alone on the dam as it started to give way.

INTERLUDE 4: THE FUTURE

SUMMER 2025, CASITA DE SOLEDAD, CENTRAL ARIZONA

When we came down from orbit, Agent Peters and several other agents from Homeland Security were there. They stood stiffly in the desert sun dressed in their dark suits and sunglasses with a black SUV on our barely passable road. They looked like they stepped out of a *Men in Black* movie.

"This is becoming excessive," Peters said in lieu of a greeting. Peters is not a tall man, with short sandy hair and a rapidly receding hairline.

Licia and I had gone into our tin shed, transformed back to our biological bodies and put our clothing on. He had been out here regularly lately and each time he became grumpier.

"You are in clear violation of the agreement you signed," he added, mopping at his forehead with a handkerchief.

"What are you going to do?" I asked. "Throw us in a deep, dark hole and throw away the key?"

I didn't like Peters and he didn't like me. It was the nature of the relationship.

"Now, boys," Licia said with a disarming smile, "let's talk about this civilly, over iced tea."

She took Agent Peters's arm and escorted him and the other agents into the house. She sat with him at our small table in our sun-drenched kitchen with fresh wildflowers in a vase and windows all around. She served iced tea and cookies. She smiled and was charming. She cheerfully filled out the paperwork and made our jaunts into orbit sound like the most reasonable thing.

Agent Peters softened under the onslaught, but it wasn't like the first few times. This was obviously becoming a bigger issue.

And then she told him we had accepted an interview with Diane Madison in a month.

"No," he said flatly.

"Come again?" I said.

"No interviews," he said, his pale grey eyes connecting with mine. "It is against policy at this time."

"I don't care," I said.

Peters pursed his lips and folded his arms across his chest. This place is in some ways like a reservation or a prison, but in other ways it is not. We are superheroes. If we are dead set on something, they will have to go to extraordinary measures to stop us. I didn't think they were willing, seeing how we were insurance policies just in case our powers were ever needed again.

"Gentlemen," Licia said, her light tone slicing through the tension. "There must be a way. Contact Diane Madison and her producers, Agent Peters. This piece will be good PR for all of us."

The discussion went several more rounds with Peters saying "no" in several different ways, and me saying "try to stop me," and Licia trying to keep it reasonable.

When the agents left, we still hadn't come to an agreement. As soon as they walked out of the house, her smile was gone. "I hope this is worth it," she said.

"You set up this interview."

"You know what I mean, Nik. You want things to change, you

want a future where we can move around with some freedom. That is why I agreed to the interview. For you."

I sighed and rubbed at my face. Peters always wore me out. "I hope it is worth it too," I said.

I wanted change, that much was true. But I've been around long enough to know that the change you get is not often the change you envisioned.

12 / TOXIC ASSISTANCE

I FLEW HARD AND FAST—AND YES, THAT MEANS I WAS USING the infamous butt-thruster. After I stumbled into the ungraceful method of flight when battling the missile the aliens fired at Palo Verde, the military had me practice it. A lot. But the practice didn't make it look any less silly. With my legs drawn up against my abdomen and a huge yellow jet coming out of my ass, it was anything but dignified. But it was fast.

When I was about half a mile away from the Hoover Dam, I heard it. Barely. The white-noise roar of a wall of water headed towards me. The dam had eroded further. The water was coming. There wasn't much time.

I flew up a few hundred feet above the canyon, so I could get a good view. The canyon below the dam was not all good for what Licia had suggested. Some of it was deep and narrow, but in other spots the desert sloped steeply down, but not sheerly. I was trying to get ahead of what was coming to buy some time.

Out of the corner of my eye, I noticed that tour helicopter

again. It seemed to be following me. This didn't surprise me, but the green flash I saw jump out of it did.

Toxicwasteman.

Like Lightningirl and I, Toxicwasteman is a contained reaction, a chemical reaction. While my q-morph form is swirling motes of yellow, his is similar but a sickly green, iridescent green.

He was soon flying next to me, jets of green flame coming out of his feet, hands, and posterior, a trail of thick black smoke following him. He had developed his own chemical-based butt-thruster.

Now we both looked silly.

"This is going to be fun, Neutrino," he shouted at me. He sounded like some little kid about to get on a roller coaster and had a smile on his pulsing green face. "Let's do this!"

———

You may be puzzled as to why I was surprised to see Toxicwasteman jumping out of the helicopter and coming to help me. You may have figured out who was in that helicopter the first time I mentioned it.

But I was surprised.

This surprise was part of what was going on for me. I tended to take people and situations at face value. Although it was an obvious thing, it didn't occur to me that LoVE would be monitoring this encounter or that Toxicwasteman himself would be on site just in case.

So I was surprised and mad. Mostly mad at myself for not seeing the obvious. For being so naïve.

"Next bend," I shouted, pushing down my anger and surprise, pointing to a narrow spot in the canyon. We were right in the middle of an emergency, this was not the time to get all introspective. "You take the right side, I'll take the left. Blast down low, let's see if we can bring down enough rock to slow the water down."

Toxicwasteman gave me his green-toothed wolfish grin in

answer. This was going to be fun for him, it was obvious. This was way too serious to be fun for me.

We dove down into the canyon, Toxicwasteman to my right and slightly behind me. We flew above the dark blue waters of the Colorado, tranquil and as yet unaffected by the coming torrent. And when we rounded the bend, we blew the hell out of the canyon.

I fired a rapid barrage of neutrino bolts low, just where the canyon rose sharply up. Toxicwasteman fired balls of green that exploded on contact on his side.

We were a mile or so down from the dam. We both circled around to survey the damage. Rock from both sides had fallen into the river forming a low dam that reached barely above the water level. It wasn't enough. Not nearly enough.

We hovered there staring.

"You are going to have to go elemental," Toxicwasteman said.

"No shit," I shot back. Yes, I was a bit grumpy. I don't like going elemental, and I certainly didn't like him pointing it out, but I didn't see a choice.

13 / ELEMENTAL

I HAD DONE IT WHEN I HAD TAKEN ON THE METEOR THE aliens had sent towards the Earth. Just like Licia has an elemental electrical form, when she travels on high-tension power lines and when she fought at the Battle of Palo Verde, I have one too. Except mine is kind of like turning into a nuclear bomb. I explode.

In that brief time that we paused above the Colorado River downstream from the badly damaged Hoover Dam, a wall of water fifty feet high came roaring down the canyon. I heard it first, like a massive wall of white noise, and still I was not prepared for the sight of it. The water was surging and sloshing down the canyon, a wall of it five stories high, a hungry torrent splashing up the sides of the canyon. It was epic.

I surged forward, flying low over the river as fast as I could. I flew so fast, I left Toxicwasteman behind, which gave me some sliver of satisfaction.

I wanted a spot where the canyon narrowed, before Lake Mohave started. There were only a few miles to go until the upper end of the lake and I feared I wouldn't find it.

And then I did. It was on a straight portion, but the canyon was narrow and the right side had already been undercut a bit by the river. I increased my reaction to the max, carefully containing most of my energy, and slammed into the cliff. I let my reaction bleed hot and I could tell the rock around me was melting as I burrowed farther into the canyon.

I explained this "exploding" before. I let my nuclear reaction build and build, but I contain it. And then, just like a balloon, it becomes too much and explodes forth. I explode.

And that is what I did.

I went elemental and for a few moments there was no Neutrinoman anymore.

———

I HONESTLY HATE GOING ELEMENTAL. IT'S KIND OF LIKE WHEN Quinn becomes The Hammer, he loses a lot of himself to become a more primal being. Going elemental, exploding, is like that times one hundred. The essential me is gone and I never know what's going to happen or where I'm going to end up.

And this time where I "ended up" was in total darkness unsure of where I was or what had happened. I felt a suffocating pressure all around. Where was I?

I was still Neutrinoman—which was fortunate or I wouldn't have survived. I instinctively ramped up my reaction and the earth started to glow and melt around me. I couldn't see much but the orange-yellow glow of molten rock, but at least I could see something.

So rock... I must be underground. It started to come back to me. Hoover Dam breached. Flood waters heading downstream. I could tell which way was up by how the rock flowed around me. I started thrusting upwards with my hands and feet making my way towards the surface.

It was taking a long time and I started to freak out a bit. One part "buried alive" and another part "did it work?" I started going faster and faster, tunneling my way up, melting through the rock and earth. I could feel my energy depleting. I hoped I had enough left in me to get out. And just as my mind was telling me I would die here alone burned to death by the rock I was melting, I burst forth through a massive pile of loose rock into a bright and beautiful desert morning.

The cliff that I had burrowed under was now slumped into the canyon forming a barrier four hundred feet tall. It had worked. Water was building behind it, some of it seeping through the bottom of the impromptu dam, but not much.

It worked.

I flew over, inspecting it, seeing if it looked like it would hold. It wasn't a tall, tapering dam like Hoover had been. It was a thick jumble of rock and dirt clogging the canyon. Not elegant, but serviceable.

I looked back and saw that the explosion had been directed. Earth didn't go everywhere, most of it went directly into the canyon. And that's the thing about being elemental. I'm gone, but not completely. My intent, to block the canyon, came through.

That's when I noticed Toxicwasteman standing on the opposite cliff. He was smiling and waving for me to come over, like we were both eight years old and his mother had just baked cookies. No, that's not right. He was waving like a twelve-year-old that had just found his older brother's secret stash of Playboy Magazines and wanted to show it off.

SPRING 2005, COLORADO RIVER, NEVADA/ARIZONA BORDER

"Well done, Neutrino," Toxicwasteman said as I landed beside him. We had a good view of the river and the new dam. The water was sloshing behind it, a thick brown, the color of chocolate milk.

He extended his green hand for me to shake but I ignored him.

"Right," he said. "We don't have much time."

I didn't know what he was talking about, so I ignored that comment too. "Do you think it will hold?" I asked.

He nodded. "Over ninety percent chance," he said. "It will hold long enough for the dams downstream to prepare."

I looked away from the churning water and back at him. How the hell did he know that?

He saw the question on my face and turned his head and pointed at his left ear. In it I could see a little metal earbud—he was in communication with someone. I also noticed that the green swirls of his Toxicwasteman form were less pronounced around his ear. They had figured out a way to get comm equipment on him. I was jealous.

"We've been simulating everything live," he said. "Byte sends on her congratulations." He gave me an exaggerated wink, making me remember Byte's offer to me in her crystal cave in the LoVE base.

"So you know they're pissed, right?" Toxicwasteman said.

"What?"

"The military. They are *so* pissed. You let Chaosboy go. You oversaw the destruction of the Hoover Dam. And you didn't tell them a thing, not one tiny little thing about it." He held his green index finger and thumb close together. "It's that last bit that really has their panties in a bunch."

Well... when he put it that way. "Yeah, I guess they are. But I was—"

Toxicwasteman held his hand up, cutting me off, and tilted his head. Byte must have been talking to him. His expression fell as he slowly nodded his head, suddenly looking very serious.

"Okay, listen up," he said, turning back to me. "There's not much time at all now. I know you have some questions, so I'm going to just answer them." He didn't give me a chance to say anything and plowed right on. "One, there is a good chance that Gaia survived. Byte has reviewed the footage we shot and done her simulation thing and we believe she withdrew down into the Earth fast enough to not get injured."

I nodded, glad to hear that. I hadn't wanted to hurt her.

"We will do our best to send her back your way," he said.

"Send her my way?" I asked.

"You and Lightning were getting through to her," he said. "Surprising, really. But true."

His insistence on calling me Neutrino and Lightningirl Lightning was really starting to annoy me. The suffix of "man" or "girl" reinforced our humanity, which I have found important with the power we wield.

"Next, we believe that the military has been observing you this entire time. Is observing you right now, you apishly dense Boy

Scout! We've got to do some damage control!" He was yelling at me now, gesticulating wildly with his hands, which made absolutely no sense.

"What are you—" I began.

"No time!" he yelled. "Just listen. You aren't going to like what comes next. I am going to fly away and you are going to have to make a good show of trying to stop me. But, please, just make it a show."

"What?" I was still confused. I didn't know what he was talking about and why he kept yelling.

"Just fly after me and fire a few neutrino bolts, then turn back, look concerned about your little dam here, and then come back. They'll be here soon, you yellow excessively moral buffoon! And when they come, your best bet is to go in easy!"

Now I was just getting angry. A sickly green super villain yelling at you will do that. Not having the full picture—ever—will do that. Realizing that during your secret "off book" adventure everyone was watching your every step, will certainly do that.

Toxicwasteman turned, as if he was going to go, and then swung around fast, his green fist connecting with my yellow chin. Hard. I went down.

We established this in Yellowstone, Toxicwasteman and I don't mix. Where his green toxic touch connected with my chin, I felt a sharp, deep pain and knew that I had been infected with his greenness.

He laughed, a high-pitched manic kind of thing, flexing his fist which had a patch of yellow on it from our contact. It looked like it hurt him too. He then turned and flew away, trailing thick, black smoke.

He didn't have to remind me to fly after him. I wanted to. He didn't have to remind me to shoot neutrino bolts at him. I gladly did.

He flew low above the river and I followed. One bolt grazed his back and he glanced back at me, then. The look on his face is an image I'll treasure. He was scared. He thought I was really going to take him down.

I wanted to. But I didn't.

I fired a few more bolts, came to a halt, and gazed back at the dam I had created with a worried look on my face. I looked back at the retreating Toxicwasteman once more and then went back to monitor the dam.

Just as I had been instructed to do.

The truth was I didn't know enough to do anything else. Toxicwasteman hadn't given me enough information. No one ever gave me enough information.

As I landed back on the cliff and watched the muddy water build behind the thick rock dam, I heard the thump-thump of helicopters approaching. They were coming.

15 / STANDOFF

ONE HELICOPTER BUZZED AROUND ME BRIEFLY BEFORE leaving. I ignored it. I was firing neutrino bolts at the cliff just in front of me trying to force more rock into the canyon. I really was worried about the dam holding long enough.

In my training with the military, I have found that not all neutrino bolts are created equal. I can fire some that will go a long way and remain hot. I can fire others that are short range and will explode. I was working with the latter here, trying to modulate them so they didn't have much range, just enough to get a few feet into the rock, but had a great big bang.

It was working pretty well. I was slowly carving off more of the cliff, the side I hadn't exploded earlier. This is where Toxicwasteman and I had had our conversation.

I wanted to go check on Licia. I wanted to—and this is a surprise—have a long conversation with Toxicwasteman. I was doing my best, but I didn't have enough information. Licia might have some wise words on how to get more information out of him. And I knew Toxicwasteman knew a lot more than he had told me.

And then it occurred to me. In some ways both the military and Toxicwasteman treated me the same. They gave me just enough information to get me to do what they wanted me to do.

And that produced anger. And that next neutrino bolt I fired was a whopper. The sound of the explosion rumbled through my feet and the rock underneath me fell. I used my neutrino jets to hover while a full ten feet of the cliff slumped off and tumbled into the canyon, splashing into the frothing brown water, making the dam bigger.

It was then that I noticed the three dull-green UH-1 choppers. They were hovering around me, the open side door of each facing me. In each chopper was a soldier holding one of the alien energy weapons, the ones that could drain my power and return me to flesh and blood. They were all aimed at me.

And there is no mistaking these alien energy weapons with their bright metallic barrels and black tube snaking around to a big backpack. I hate them. I really do, and even though I was Neutrinoman, the sight of them made my stomach turn over.

"Stand down, Neutrinoman," a voice said over a loudspeaker on a fourth helicopter that was a ways off. "Find a place to land and return to your human form."

Now the military was threatening me. Great. Just great.

———

TOXICWASTEMAN HAD TOLD ME TO "GO IN EASY." I REALLY didn't want to but saw no other acceptable choice. I flew over on top of the cliff, landed, and let go of my neutrino form.

Those three helicopters kept hovering, soldiers pointing the alien energy weapons at me.

And I knew those weapons well. I had first encountered them at Yellowstone when aliens wielded them against me, and then a larger version at the Battle of Palo Verde. And I had encountered them repeatedly over the last few months in training with the military.

Soldiers shooting them at me had become part of my training. They wanted to find out if I could build up a tolerance, so they had shot me repeatedly with those purple balls of energy. It hurt like hell each and every time, and while I had begun to find ways to resist them, I wasn't very good at it. The threat was real.

The fourth helicopter landed twenty yards away. I just stood there naked, covering myself as best I could, and watching the brown water build up against the dam. The morning air was cool and dry, the heat of the day not yet here.

I've talked about my lack of a costume, that no material can survive my transformation to Neutrinoman. How it causes me constant embarrassment. It's my upbringing. Maybe if I was born in France or was psychotic like Toxicwasteman, I wouldn't care about letting it all hang loose. But I do.

When the two soldiers jogged over with their rifles pointed at me, I had my hands over my genitals and red blossoming on my face. I think part of it is the transition: going from being a contained nuclear reaction to being mere flesh and blood is kind of a letdown. And by "kind of" I mean, "oh my God, is it a massive letdown."

Being Neutrinoman can be addictive. And in that moment of vulnerability, naked, the desert morning light of Nevada reflecting on the disaster I was just a part of, with soldiers pointing guns at me... Well, it can be a long way to fall.

"Hands up," one of the soldiers said. He was young, maybe nineteen, and he looked scared.

"No," I said quietly. "Bring me something to wear and I'll be happy to put my hands up."

It was a line for me in that moment. Being naked in that situation was one thing, but at least I was able to cover myself. I just wasn't willing to let go of what little dignity I had left.

"Hands up now," the other soldier said. He was in his twenties and had a hard look on his face, like he'd seen battle, like he would fire upon me.

I smiled, as best I could, and shook my head. "Get me a jacket and I'll go in quietly." I left the "or else" unsaid. I figured these boys could think that through.

We had a bit of a standoff there. Three helicopters hovering around me with their now useless energy weapons pointed at me (they work against Neutrinoman, not flesh and blood). One helicopter on the ground twenty yards off, two more soldiers coming forth. Two nervous young men with automatic weapons pointed at me.

I don't know. Maybe it seems like a silly time and place to make a stand, especially such a small one. But it was an important moment. It may have been a small thing, but I wasn't willing to budge.

Give me dignity or give me...

Give me what? Young soldiers firing on me? A direct conflict with the military? Becoming a fugitive? Death?

I wasn't worried about death right then. I had enough juice left to turn into Neutrinoman and fast. The odds of them delivering a killing shot before that were not that great. The military had been training me. Constantly. For months. I had plenty of tricks up my sleeve.

And while I couldn't withstand those purple energy balls, I was pretty sure I could evade them and I knew I could outrun the helicopters.

And then I thought of Licia. What kind of position would that put her in? Had they arrested her too? The weight of what had just happened crashed down upon me. I had dragged her into this, my stand here could cost her even more. And what about my parents? What would happen to them if I didn't "go in easy."

With a sigh, I raised my hands in the air.

Before I knew it, the older soldier had me on the ground face-down and zip-tied my hands together. He wasn't gentle in the least. He pulled me up and marched me to the waiting helicopter.

I laughed. I was Neutrinoman, what the hell good did zip-ties do? I heard the sound of my own laughter as it bounced off the bare rock, rose above the sound of the roaring river. I sounded a bit manic. It sounded a bit like Toxicwasteman.

SPRING 2005, ARIZONA, NEAR THE HOOVER DAM

THE EASTERN PORTION OF THE HOOVER DAM WAS BADLY damaged. Where Gaia had been, where she had beat on the dam with her giant fists, there was a large gash about two hundred feet tall and one hundred feet wide at the top, narrowing as it went down, forming a ragged V.

A huge torrent of water was flowing through the gap down into the river gorge. The generating station wasn't even visible anymore under the onslaught of mud-colored water. The darker color was caused by all the silt at the bottom of the lake mixing in with the clean water at the top.

Dams are not forever. They collect silt from the day they go into operation. The silt will eventually render the dam useless, although Hoover was far from that point.

The image of the crippled dam made my chest hurt. This was something that I had been a part of, something I hadn't prevented. There would be blackouts as they found ways to compensate for the loss of this clean energy. It would be massively expensive to rebuild the dam—if they even did.

This was my fault.

I got a good view as the helicopter flew by and then headed to the east over into Arizona. We didn't go far. There were a few green tents setup on the desert not far from the road. The helicopter landed and I was escorted, still nude, into the largest tent.

Licia was there pacing, her arms wrapped around her chest, dressed in fatigues way too big for her. Quinn was there too, back to his normal dark-haired self, standing quietly in a corner. There were several other soldiers, some communications equipment, a table with maps spread out on it, and Colonel Williams.

When Licia looked up and saw me, my heart almost broke. Her cheeks were stained with tears and she looked so small, not like a goddess anymore, but like a normal girl. She ran to me, ignoring the protestations of my two guards, and hugged me tight. I was glad that she wasn't handcuffed.

"It's bad," she whispered in my ear.

"I love you," I whispered back. Maybe not the most useful thing to say, but at that moment, for me, it was the most important thing to say.

"I love you too," she whispered back.

Another soldier roughly pulled her off of me. Licia gave him a look that could melt solid steel and shook him off.

Colonel Williams had ignored us thus far, but finally turned around. He's not a tall man but has this coiled energy to him. He looked fit in his army fatigues with short salt-and-pepper hair and a sharp chin.

He looked angry when he turned, but his expression changed when he saw me there nude and filthy from being thrown to the ground, my hands behind my back.

"For Christ's sake," he said loudly. "Will someone get the man a blanket, at least!"

Before long I had a scratchy wool blanket hastily thrown over my shoulders. The three of us, Licia, Quinn, and I, were alone in the tent with Colonel Williams. He had dismissed the other soldiers. I was still handcuffed.

Williams looked tired, he kept rubbing at his face as if trying to wake himself up. He was pacing the small space in front of the three of us. We were standing together by the edge of the tent.

"Perhaps I should explain," I began. "I—"

Williams held up his hand, cutting me off, and resumed his pacing. "Don't bother explaining, Nichols. We're past that at this point."

Past that? What the hell were we past? Things had gone badly, but we had tried our best. We had managed to mitigate the level of the disaster. We were past explanations?

"We know what happened," he said, walking to the table with the maps and pulling out a folder of pictures underneath. He walked over and showed them to us. Several were Quinn as Sadie, Chaosboy, and the three of us on the top of the Golden Nugget. The pictures were taken from several angles. They had had a lot of people watching us. There were also some grainy pictures of Toxicwasteman and I talking on the cliff above the river.

He took that folder back and brought out another folder. It contained the research about Gaia that Tom Tyree and LoVE had left for us in the suite at the Golden Nugget. I had stashed it in the trunk of my car, which is where they must have gotten it from.

I felt my cheeks flush again. Not so much from embarrassment, but from anger. Toxicwasteman had often told me about the "short leash" the military had me on, but I had no idea just how short it was. If they had followed us to Vegas, had they been observing everything we had been doing whether on duty or off?

I think Licia was having the same thought as I was. She was blinking rapidly and wouldn't meet my eyes. Had they been spying on Licia and me during our private time?

"This is serious," Williams resumed. "We have you consorting with, and letting go, two members of a known terrorist organization. You received intel from them. You took instructions from them.

You didn't inform us of your actions." He sighed, rubbing his face again. "God, Nik. What were you thinking?"

I opened my mouth up to answer, but he held up his hand again. "Don't tell me," he said. "This is beyond me and I have done what I can."

My stomach twisted sharply. Williams was the man that made our time with the military bearable. If he was out, what did that mean for us?

"I have a deal to offer you," he continued, his green eyes softening somewhat. "It is all I could do." He resumed his pacing briefly and then returned and stood erect in front of us, his hands behind his back.

"The deal is this. Nichols, you are going to be 'detained' and you will be the only one being detained providing that Lopez and Rask cooperate."

I didn't like the word "detained." I would prefer being arrested, that implies lawyers and publicity. "Detained" sounded much more nefarious and a lot more quiet.

"Cooperate?" Quinn asked.

Williams gave him a sharp nod. "Have you mastered impersonating him?"

Quinn nodded.

"Let's see," Williams said.

The click-squish sound started and I watched as Quinn turned into me. He was soon standing there, four inches shorter, with my messy brown hair, pale white skin, and a kind of goofy grin on his face. He still had his own blue eyes instead of my brown, but otherwise he looked just like me.

Licia stiffened next to me. I had told her about this, but she hadn't seen it.

Williams looked closely at both of us, slowly nodding. "You'll need contacts, of course, but that will do. And the voice?"

Quinn-Nik shook his head and said, "Not yet. Voices are much harder." His voice wasn't as deep as Quinn's, but it certainly wasn't mine.

I think it has to do with all the complexities that go into making a voice sound like it does. The physiology of the vocal cords and the tongue, the shape of the throat, mouth, and sinus cavity. The speech patterns and idioms of the speaker.

With the body, he had a visual reference he could use to match another's appearance. With the voice, he didn't have any of that. It was much more trial and error.

Williams bit his lip. "We'll manage. So the deal is this. Nichols, you go in quietly. Lopez, you reenter the program and are seen from time to time with Rask as Nik. Rask, you will make it so the world thinks Nichols and Neutrinoman are still on the job, still protecting us from the alien threat."

Back when Tom Tyree had first told me about Quinn, he said the military wanted to see if he could emulate my abilities. It was an utter failure, and near disaster. Quinn almost killed himself. I am a contained nuclear reaction, after all, and while Quinn can handle a lot of radiation, his forms are all flesh and blood. But what he can do is "appear" to be Neutrinoman. No flying or anything, but he can do a reasonable facsimile of the yellow motes and swirls of my neutrino form.

The air in the tent was thick and still. It was midmorning and hot now. I could smell sweat and fear. Not just mine and Licia's and Quinn's, but Colonel Williams's too.

"No," Licia said. She didn't say it loudly or quietly. She just said it like she was saying no to desert at a restaurant.

"What?" Williams asked, surprised.

"I will not cooperate," she said, her arms crossed. "If you think we did something wrong here, then accuse us of a crime. Arrest us. Give us a trial. You will not hide Nik away and have me pretend you didn't."

Williams pursed his lips and nodded. "This is not my choice. This came from General Markus directly. He wanted to 'detain' all of you. I convinced him leaving you and Rask free would be better for everyone." Williams sighed, his normally erect posture falling. "I can tell you that there are contingencies in place. There will be no arrests today."

"It'll be okay," I said to Licia. I could imagine what those "contingencies" were. There were more soldiers with alien energy weapons tuned to take Lightningirl and me out. There were armed soldiers surrounding our tent. I could hear the soldiers walking outside, vehicles and helicopters approaching. The only way out would be to fight our way out. I knew I didn't have the stomach for that and Licia didn't either.

"But..." she began, a worried look on her face.

"I promise you that if they take this too far, I will take action." I said it to Licia, but I was saying it to Williams (and whomever else was listing) too. "Put on their little show for them. Can you do that?"

Licia nodded and I turned to Quinn who nodded too.

"I will go in quietly," I said to Williams. "But I do have one condition."

SPRING 2005, ARIZONA, NEAR THE HOOVER DAM

My one condition was not a lawyer or to plead my case and explain myself. It wasn't clothing to wear—I still only had the itchy wool blanket. It wasn't certain concessions during "detention" or anything like that. It was ten minutes alone with Licia and no handcuffs.

And at this point, I had no doubt that we were being listened to, but at least we were physically alone. I held her and she held me. We silently did our best to reassure each other.

"I don't like Quinn," she whispered after a time. "What he can do..." I was holding her and a shiver ran through her body.

"Quinn is a bit strange, but he's all right," I whispered back.

"But how will I know if it's really you?" she asked. "I mean, he looked *exactly* like you."

"His eyes are always the same blue when he changes. He sucks at voices and always has that weird accent of his."

"And if he puts on contacts and figures your voice out? I just..." She trailed off. We were standing in the middle of the tent, her body against mine, that blanket wrapped around both of us.

"This really bothers you, doesn't it?" I asked.

She nodded and looked up at me, her brown eyes wide with worry. Not just about Quinn convincing her he was me. But about the whole thing. Me going away. Her back in the program. An alien threat that could come back at any moment. At the time, I thought she was focused on Quinn as a way to avoid thinking about those other things, but she always had better instincts than I did.

"Okay," I said, leaning down so I could be eye to eye with her. "Then we have a word that I will say so you know it's me."

She nodded and smiled.

I thought for a moment and then leaned close and whispered in her ear. The smell of her and her closeness was rather distracting. When I leaned back up, she had a quizzical look on her face and then recognition dawned.

I had whispered "pot roast" to her. It was the meal my mother had served when her family had dinner with mine. The day we had met. That dinner was my mother's attempt to set me up with a "nice girl." And it had worked, a fact she would never stop bringing up. I had also noticed that Licia, being a vegetarian, didn't eat her pot roast, just pushed it around the plate. Noticing that, I believe, had done a lot to get her attention.

It was such a mundane word, but for us "pot roast" has meaning.

"We're going to be fine," I said, pulling her into my arms again.

"Promise?"

"I promise."

We had too much to say so we just didn't talk. I held her tight. I held her past the ten-minute mark and didn't let go until Williams and several soldiers with those bulky alien energy weapons came in and took me away.

I was escorted across the hot desert to a waiting Huey helicopter, its rotors spinning fast. As soon as we boarded, it took off and headed to the east.

Licia was out of the tent staring at the helicopter as it rose in the air. Her hand was above her eyes, shielding them from the sun. She blew me a kiss and I blew her one back. The door to the Huey was still open and I had a good view of her.

I watched her stand there in the desert, surrounded by soldiers, Quinn, back to his normal look, coming to stand next to her. I watched her until we passed over a plateau and she was gone.

Even before she was out of sight, I was missing her. But, for now, this was best. But how long would this last? Where were they taking me? When would I be with her again?

Colonel Williams was staring at me. I sank down into a seat next to him and shouted into his ear so he could hear me. "I'm holding you personally responsible for her safety."

His eyes widened briefly and then he nodded.

I didn't know what the future would bring, but I was dedicated to being back with Licia as soon as possible.

My thoughts weren't for alien threats or for civilization-ending disasters. Nor were they for the Goddess of Electricity, Lightningirl. My thoughts were for the flesh and blood Licia, the woman I loved.

I had to find a way back to her.

EPILOGUE

"THAT'S IT?" LICIA ASKED, HER EYEBROWS HIGH. SHE PUT down the stack of papers she had been reading on the glass table of our flagstone patio at Casita de Soledad. "Seriously, Nik. You're stopping there?" She took a sip of iced tea, the ice cubes clinking together musically.

The hot sun was edging towards the horizon, the blue of the sky washed out from the heat of the day. My pale, radiation-loving skin was sucking in the UV as my muscles relaxed from building our new greenhouse.

This had become our ritual of late. I would write early, then join Licia at the greenhouse, and when the shadows started to get long, we would come out here and she would read and we would relax.

I smiled. While her tone was unexpected, I took it as a sign she was fully engaged in the story.

"You've got your brown puppy dog eyes on," she continued, her eyes stabbing down at the manuscript. "You're on the helicopter watching me fade into the distance being taken to God knows where, and you stop?"

"Puppy eyes?" I asked.

She nodded. As the greenhouse neared completion, I had taken to writing more, feeling drawn back into the past, feeling the need to get to and then get through the dark times right around the corner. "Let me rephrase," she began with a laugh. "'Adorable, cute, but *manly,* brown puppy dog eyes.'"

We had been over "cute" before, and while it still made me a bit uncomfortable, I let it be. "We're at the end of this story. Two important q-morphs have been introduced. Things are transitioning and this episode sets it up."

"But... But..." she said. "They're dragging you away. The Hoover Dam is destroyed, Gaia is believed to be on the loose... We have no idea how long it will take Sarah to 'speak' and what the outcome will be. I mean, things are getting crazy."

"The next episode will be along soon," I said with a shrug.

"But, don't you think you should treat your readers with more respect?" she asked. "Not play silly games with them."

I opened my mouth to speak, but then closed it. This ending was a cliffhanger, much more than what I had done before. I liked to think I was getting better at storytelling. And then I remembered something. "Do you remember that night we went out to that fancy restaurant in Flagstaff? This was shortly after you left the program."

She nodded, a quizzical smile on her face.

"We had been taking it slow, being a mess together, when you said you wanted to do this. You knew the owners, close family friends. They snuck us into their private room in that historic house that had been converted into a restaurant."

"Yeah," she said. "Not sure what this has to do with your ending here."

I smiled, looking her up and down. She was dressed in her usual shorts and tank top, but I was imagining what she was wearing that night. "Remember that little black dress you wore that night?"

She nodded.

"When I saw you in it, I could barely breathe. How it hugged your curves, how it amplified your considerable beauty. You also had your hair up, with makeup and earrings. You were stunning, absolutely stunning."

She was smiling now. "I remember."

"That dress, it was a promise that there was something wonderful coming." I paused, feeling my cheeks flush from the memory of that promise fulfilled. "You knew exactly what you were doing, I knew what you were doing too, and we both loved it."

Her brow furrowed. "Are you comparing the ending of this story to that evening, to... to..."

"No. No." I held my hands up. "Of course not. All I am saying is that dress was a promise, one we both knew we were making to each other. The ending of this story is a promise too. One that the readers know about and are used to. I am promising if they come back there is much more to come. I am promising the story of how our hero and heroine overcome challenge after challenge and reunite."

She slowly nodded. "But they'll want more right away."

"Yes. And just like the promise that black dress made, sometimes waiting, sometimes anticipation makes it that much better."

She reached across the glass patio table and grabbed my hand, a devious smile on her face. "You know, I still have that little black dress."

"Really?" I said. That dress is a legend in my mind, marking a turning point in our relationship.

"If you make us a nice dinner tonight," she said with a smile, "maybe I'll put it on."

We switch off on cooking duties and it was her turn. Also the word "nice" signaled that she wanted something more than baked potatoes, steamed veggies, and a bunch of cheese.

"What do you mean?" I asked. "It would take all of two minutes to put the dress on. Why do I have to make dinner?"

She smiled broadly and got up. She moved slowly and sensuously—quite on purpose, I am sure. "You can't just put on a dress like that," she said. "I need a bath first and time to primp. It's not just a dress, you know. It's the mood and attitude. That takes time."

I was nodding, watching her walk to the sliding glass doors that lead into our casita. "Besides, didn't you just say that sometimes anticipation makes these things better?"

I nodded and watched her go into the house and close the door behind her, full of anticipation of what was to come.

I sat there happy as could be, unaware of the change that was about to descend on our current lives. The seeds had been sown, but I didn't have a clue what was coming.

HARD TIMES

NEUTRINOMAN AND LIGHTNINGIRL: A LOVE STORY, EPISODE 5

PROLOGUE: A SMALL CELL

I paced my cell counting the steps. One, two, three, four. Turned, paced the next wall. One, two, three, four. Turned, paced. Turned, paced.

I'm not Neutrinoman, I'm decidedly biological now, just Nik Nicholas, and have been since they brought me here. They made sure I didn't have enough power to transform.

I let my fingers slide over the smooth white walls where I can walk next to them. Past the narrow bunk, the metal toilet and sink, the tiny shower with a white plastic curtain, the shelf that has some toiletry items and the two books I have, and finally the workout wall. It's studded with a couple pull-up bars, a weight bench that folds up into the wall, and some free weights.

Twelve feet on a side, I knew these four walls much better than I should. I knew this cell so well that I hated every square inch of it. I took a deep breath, smelling the stale air and my own despair.

I stopped at the five-foot-wide section of my cell that was not two-foot-thick walls, but bars, a door. They were smooth and silvery, duller than steel, and much stronger, made out of some kind of exotic alloy. I could see thirty feet down the plain, unadorned hallway where it made an abrupt turn to the right. On the wall at the end of the hallway was a mirror and I saw myself reflected there. Short brown hair, fairly rumpled, medium height, medium build, dressed in bland grey coveralls.

I was just a man and I had been for over six months. I wasn't Neutrinoman flying out to save the Earth from an asteroid aimed at us by the Arcturian Alliance. I wasn't battling aliens to keep them from setting off the super volcano underneath Yellowstone National Park, and I wasn't trying and failing to stop Gaia in the form of a seven-hundred-foot-tall rock giant destroying the Hoover Dam.

I didn't have Lightningirl/Licia by my side. I wasn't alone, but I was so very lonely.

Behind that one-way mirror was a guard with one of the alien's energy weapons. It was always powered up. It was always pointed down the hall at me. Just in case I figured out how to transform into Neutrinoman. Just in case I tried to escape, they could easily stop me, the alien's weapon built just for me to sap my powers.

That turn in the hallway, that guard station, was only one of four getting to this cell.

I looked up at the ceiling twenty feet above me. It glowed evenly, light transferred here fiber-optically. There was not one joule of electricity anywhere I could reach to help power my transformation. Not one switch, one battery, nothing.

There was a TV hanging about fifteen feet down the hallway, but I have to ask a guard to turn it on or change the channel, so I didn't bother anymore.

I'm far underground in this prison built just for quantum metamorphs, q-morphs, like me. This cell built specifically for me. This had taken a lot of time to plan and build. The government must have started the process as soon as they found out about us and understood our powers and our weaknesses. The thought was a bitter taste in my mouth, like sucking on an aspirin.

I sighed, letting go of the cool bars of my cell door and kept on pacing. Kept on breathing. Kept on living.

What else could I do?

As prisons go, this was probably the best it could be. They fed me well, a kind man named Ronald brought me books, they had given me space and tools for exercise, but it was still a prison. It was still confinement. It was still punishment.

My fingers slid over my books as I paced past them, the noise loud in the silence, but comforting. Skin against paper. A rough splash of white noise. It sounded like freedom to me. And I don't mean freedom as in escaping into another world. I mean freedom as in getting out of these four walls. Real escape.

The books make me think of Licia, and the memory was so strong that I caught a whiff of her ozoney scent and saw a glimpse of her smile in my mind's eye. She would be happy that I've been reading so much. Before the military imprisoned me for "consorting with known terrorist, willful destruction of public property, blah, blah, blah," I had been more of a TV guy. But one of these books, it holds the key.

I'd been in here one hundred ninety days. I had a lot of time to read, to learn, to contemplate, to grow. I was almost there. I was close, I could taste it.

I was starving for freedom, for the wide-open sky, for Licia. I knew I'd be getting out one day, I knew I'd see her again. They'd either let me out or I would blast my way out. It was only a matter of time.

Escape was a simple, inevitable thing in my mind that day, but that's not the way it turned out. It wasn't a simple thing at all. I knew there would be a price to be paid, but I had no idea how hard it would be to bear.

1 / APPROACHING CHANGE

TIME PLAYS WITH ME AS I WRITE THESE MEMOIRS. AS I DANCE between past and present, reliving the past as I write and then coming back to the present, twenty years later after the war is long over and all the madness we all went though.

When I'm in the present, the past still lingers and Licia has been tolerant of the process, letting me ruminate and relive it all.

When I started these stories, I thought it would all be about the past with just a splash of the present, of Licia and I now to put things in context, to make us more real.

But one summer night in the hills near Casita de Soledad, our exiled home, it all changed.

We like to walk after dinner up a hill near our adobe home that we built with our own hands up onto a hill that gives a fine view of the rolling high desert so we can watch the sunset.

Our life was like that. Long walks. Time to talk. Plenty of time to sleep. We kept busy, continuing building here and my writing, but there was a gentle leisure to our days.

We were standing there holding hands watching the sun kiss the top of some craggy hills as it made its nightly journey.

"Someone's coming," I said. The third element of me acquiring my powers, after the cosmic rays that bathed the planet and the lethal dose of radiation I received, was the bite of a rat. It left me with very good hearing and an insatiable desire for cheese.

"Who is it?" Licia asked, her face close to mine, her breath smelling of curry, the low sun kissing her beautiful features.

I shook my head. "No idea. It's not time for a delivery, is it?"

"No," she said, shaking her head, her silky black hair sliding across her shoulders.

She hooked her arm in mine and leaned her head on my shoulder. She hadn't transformed into Lightningirl for a while, so I could smell soap and shampoo, not her usual ozone-laced scent.

It wasn't long until we saw two black SUVs slowly bouncing over the barely-there road that leads to our exile home. The view up here is vast, the dry land rolling away and diving into canyons, the dry dirt decorated with scrub brush, dried grass, and prickly pear cactus.

"It's got to be Homeland Security," I said. They are our current masters.

"But it can't be urgent," Licia said, "or they would have flown out."

"I doubt that it's anything good," I said. "It never is with them."

Several decades had passed since my imprisonment and countless challenges, but those days locked up had left me with a distrust of governmental authority. Those SUVs, as benign as their mission probably was, made me tense up. Made me remember that small cell and all that happened there.

I felt Licia nod, her silky hair rubbing against my arm.

We could leave. Licia could draw power from the high-tension power lines close by, transform into Lightningirl and then shoot lightning into me until I could transform into Neutrinoman. I could take her in my arms and fly her away from here.

But where would we go? And besides, I had gotten fed up with hiding. It was one of the reasons for the memoirs. It felt like it was time to be seen, time for our side of the story to be known. And it was time to meet whatever challenges those two SUVs were bringing and deal with it.

I laughed. It came out strained and too high pitched.

"What?" Licia asked.

"I'm worried about a couple of suits in SUVs. In the old days it would be Toxicwasteman, Gaia, or the Arcturian Alliance. Now I'm worried about agents."

She separated from me, her brown eyes searching mine in the rapidly dimming light. The sun had sunk below the horizon and was a fading glow on this cloudless night "Is that a good thing?" she asked.

I swallowed and studied her lovely face. It's round, her skin the color of creamed coffee and the most beautiful thing in the world to me. But she was serious, and I couldn't tell what kind of answer she wanted from me, so I stuck with the truth. "It's not a bad thing. I don't mind not having to save the world every other day. I just..." I shrugged weakly. "I don't trust them, Licia. "

She nodded, but I could tell she wasn't quite sure about my answer. "You're writing about your imprisonment now, aren't you?" she asked. I have never been able to hide anything from her.

I bit my lip and nodded. "I've been putting it off for a few weeks now, but I just started."

She pulled me into a fierce hug and held me tight while the SUVs slowly bounced closer. Our banishment here to Casita de Soledad, "The Lonely Little House," was implicit instead of a cell like they had locked me in.

"I'm here," she whispered.

"I know," I whispered back.

I held her and watched those SUVs as the sky darkened and the breeze brought the dry, dusty scent of the desert. The rumble of their engines was an intrusion to our quiet home, one that was more annoying than usual.

"We better go find out what they want," she said after a time.

"No more prison cells for me," I said, my voice surprisingly steady. "Never again."

She let go of me and took my hand. "No cells. Not with me here," she said quietly and led me towards what was sure to be change.

AFTER THE DISASTER AT HOOVER DAM WITH GAIA AND before they threw me in that cell, Colonel Williams put me in handcuffs and hauled me away. He did give me some fatigues to put on first, so at least I wasn't naked anymore.

Terrorism. Destruction of public property. Consorting with a known terrorist. I wasn't arrested. I was to be "detained." Which meant they were going to toss me in a deep hole and throw away the key.

Things had gone badly, very badly. Chaosboy and Toxicwasteman had warned us about Gaia and her plan to destroy the Hoover Dam. My new partner Quinn, Licia, and I had gotten there in time, but we hadn't been able to talk her out of it. She had transformed into a seven-hundred-foot-tall rock giant. We had fought. Gaia had been defeated, but the dam broke.

Toxicwasteman and I stopped the downstream flooding by blowing up enough rock to create a makeshift dam, but it wasn't enough for the military. The orders had come down, and Colonel

Williams had followed them. He put me in handcuffs and led me away.

The deal was that Quinn and Licia would stay free as long as Quinn used his q-morph powers to appear to be me and Licia played along.

That image of Licia is etched into my brain. She was dressed in oversized fatigues and standing on the reddish rock in front of the bland green military tent. As the UH-1 helicopter lifted off, I could see the Hoover Dam behind her, water still spilling out the huge gash, a temporary Niagara Falls in the dry desert. Quinn was standing a few paces behind her, and despite his bulk compared to her petiteness, I could only see her. The wind of the rotors tossing her silky black hair about, her hand was to her forehead shielding her eyes from the rising sun. A look of grim determination and fear alternately playing on her face.

I had fought for her, for us, and we had finally been together, finally a couple. And now this.

"Can you hear me? We don't have much time," Williams said in his gravelly baritone as we flew away. The noise in the helicopter was overwhelming. The thump of the rotors, the howling of the wind. Neither of us had headsets on and I could only hear him because of the enhanced hearing. Williams knew all about my abilities.

I looked at him, but he wasn't looking at me, instead staring in the other direction. His face turned away from the two soldiers in the back of the helicopter with us. I gave a slight nod and kept staring at Licia. I could barely see her, but I wasn't about to look away, not until her tiny form disappeared completely.

"Don't fight this, Nik," he said, his hand brushing at his short salt-and-pepper hair. "There are some, plenty actually, that are scared of you. No, terrified. That are hoping you do fight this. They are looking for any excuse."

I gave another nod, just so he was sure I was listening.

"You are powerful," he continued, "and if they can't control you, they would rather destroy you, the alien threat be damned."

I bit my lip. I couldn't see Licia anymore, but I kept staring at the rough reddish-brown land where she had been.

"I won't be with you much longer," Williams continued. "Remember what I've said when it gets bad. And it will get bad. I will do everything I can for you from the outside."

I wanted so badly to turn, to look him in the eyes, to express some sliver of gratitude. But I didn't. I sat there staring at the desert, terrified of what was coming next.

⸺

FROM HOOVER DAM, THE HELICOPTER FLEW US OVER LAKE Mead. I didn't enjoy the stark, eroded landscape or marvel at the beauty of that much water in the middle of the dry desert. The handcuffs were tight and felt heavier than they should. Williams wasn't talking, his jaw set, his eyes never meeting mine. He didn't like this, but he was a soldier, he followed orders.

But I wasn't a soldier. I thought of jumping out of the Huey. Transforming into Neutrinoman, melting those damn handcuffs off, flying back to Licia. Maybe finding Toxicwasteman and letting him hide us.

It was a distasteful vision, but not as distasteful as "detainment." It was the colonel's warning that stopped me.

A few miles north of the lake in a desolate stretch of flat desert, the helicopter touched down. There was another UH-1 waiting for me there full of soldiers not dressed in uniforms, but dressed in black. Black sunglasses, black cotton pants, black long-sleeved shirts, black ballistic vests with fat pockets, thick belts with a gun and pouches hanging on them, all of them looking alike but for the different shades of their hair and slightly different heights.

Williams guided me out of the helicopter, one strong hand around my right bicep.

Two men got out of the other helicopter. They were beefy and square jawed, looking kind of like marines to me (or at least how I imagined marines looked if you dressed them all in black).

"You boys treat him well," Williams said to the soldiers in black, "or you'll be answering to me on down the line."

With that he left me standing there and got back into the UH-1. I turned and gave him an awkward salute—handcuffs, you know—as the helicopter lifted off. He saluted me back. I watched until the helicopter was out of sight.

When I turned back all four of the soldiers were out of the helicopter. Two of them held the alien energy weapons, the ones that drain my power. Without a word they began firing.

The bolts didn't exactly hurt, I wasn't in my neutrino form, but I did feel my reserves quickly fade. I couldn't have transformed into Neutrinoman if I had tried.

The big one, the one who seemed to be the leader, came forward and threw a black bag over my head and I was roughly loaded into the helicopter and we took off. No one said a word.

The bag stunk of oil, and in that darkness with only the roar of the helicopter to keep my company, I felt despair. This "detainment" was looking to be worse than I imagined.

———

THE HELICOPTER RIDE WASN'T LONG. I WAS THEN transferred to the back end of a C-5 transport and the bag removed from my head. We had to be at Nellis Air Force Base, which sits on the northeast corner of Las Vegas.

My four square-jawed, beefy companions were still there. They didn't talk to me, they just watched me, one of them always had an alien energy weapon trained on me, and another always had a pistol pointed at me.

We took off. There were no windows and I felt the plane shift course multiple times. This, I suspected, they were doing for me. Making sure I didn't know where we were going. And I didn't.

We were in the air for five hours, and believe me, this was a long five hours. I felt like a teenager sitting outside the principal's office, waiting for my punishment. I kept going over what had happened with Chaosboy and Gaia and Toxicwasteman. Could I have prevented the destruction of the dam? Should I have attacked Gaia right away, as Tom had suggested in the video he had left me at the Golden Nugget? What would have happened if Quinn, in his Hammer form, hadn't charged Gaia? It had seemed like we were getting through to her.

But the more I thought about it, the more I began to realize it wasn't the Hoover Dam that had pissed them off. It was that Chaosboy had gotten away. That Toxicwasteman had gotten away. That I really didn't even try to bring Toxicwasteman in. That I wasn't playing by their rules anymore.

I believed that Tom Tyree (aka Toxicwasteman) was a sociopath, I also believed that he was hell-bent on destroying the aliens and that we needed him if we were going to have any chance of winning this fight.

I didn't feel sorry for letting him go. And I knew that was not the right mental state when waiting for punishment. They would want me recalcitrant, sorry for what I had done, that I had strayed from the path.

But I wasn't sorry.

This was no high school principal I was waiting for, though. This was serious.

3 / AN OLD FRIEND

IT WAS DARK AND LICIA AND I WERE WAITING OUTSIDE OUR little adobe home when the two SUVs pulled up. Agent Peters got out of the backseat of the lead SUV. He was dressed in his usual black suit with a dour frown on his face.

He was generally the lead agent when we had visits. Licia's managed to develop a good rapport with him, but we don't talk. I hate the look of his bald head and thin lips. I hate what he represents.

But this time, something was different. His shoulders were slumped as he walked around the SUV and opened the other passenger-side door. An old man dressed in jeans and a cowboy shirt got out.

"Thanks, son," the old man said to Peters who nodded and pointed to the rear SUV and then to our house.

The old man's voice was rough, like sandpaper on metal, but still strong and he stood erect. Two agents, a man and a woman, both young, leapt out of the rear SUV and started carrying things towards our house. An olive-green duffle sack and a few cardboard boxes.

I was still putting it together, steeped in worry about an agent visit. But not Licia. She squealed with delight and ran to the old man, embracing him.

Colonel Williams. It had been twenty years since I met him and, unlike Licia and I, time had extracted its usual price. He was now in his mid-seventies with snow-white hair and a deeply wrinkled and leathery face. But he still had his usual brush cut and his piercing green eyes, and aside from a mild widening around the middle he looked as fit as usual.

"Colonel," I said after I walked over, a wide smile cracking my face. You don't go through what all of us did and survive and not have feelings for each other. I couldn't have been happier to see him.

Licia had him by the hand and was talking rapidly. "Are you hungry? We've got some leftover curry I can heat up. No meat, of course, but it's good. You always liked my cooking. God, I'm glad to see you. What are you doing here?"

When she stopped to take a breath, Williams laughed. It was a happy thing and I felt the tension in my shoulders melt away. "I'm here," he said, "because Sunni kicked me out."

"What?" Licia said, her brow crinkling in worry. "Is there anything wrong?"

"No. No. We're fine. Retirement is... well... I'm not so good at it. I was starting to get on her nerves, so she told me to go find something to do for a few days."

"Well, you're welcome here," Licia said. She was still bubbly, a smile lighting up her face. "Any time. As long as you like." Clearly Licia needed some company. We were just so isolated out here.

"Yes, Colonel," I added. "As long as you like. Or should I say General." I was truly glad to see him. Because I too needed the company, I genuinely liked and respected the man, and I could ask him some questions to help my storytelling along.

"For Christ's sake, Nik," he said, clapping me on the shoulder. "Call me Walter, will you. I'm neither a colonel nor a general now, and we've been through far too much for such formality."

Our eyes met when he said it. We were still standing under the starlight, agents moving about us, hauling what Williams had brought into our house. He sounded happy, he looked happy, but his eyes were telling a different story. There was something else going on here. Something else behind his visit.

I shook it off, chalking the paranoia up to old habits from the old days, from revisiting my time in that twelve-by-twelve cell.

"It's good to see you, Walter," I said, embracing him.

His still-strong arms held me tightly and longer than I expected. There was a slight tremor, maybe a shiver, as he held me. Maybe he was just old, but it convinced me there was something else. Something worthy of the worry.

4 / PRISON

I TOLD MY INTERROGATOR THE TRUTH—WELL, ALMOST ALL OF the truth. I told him that Quinn and I had headed to Vegas specifically to capture Chaosboy. That I feared what he could do and how casually he did it. I told him that he had warned us about Gaia, that Tom Tyree / Toxicwasteman had left us a briefing in the suite of the Golden Nugget. That I had enlisted Licia to help us and kept the military out of it.

We were underground, how far I couldn't say, but it was a long ways. The elevator ride had taken a few minutes. I was alone in the room, a plain square box with white walls and one metal chair.

This was before I saw my cell and my first interrogation. There was a camera pointed at me and the voice of my interrogator came out of some speakers mounted on the wall. He wasn't in the room with me. I couldn't see his face, which was starting to bug me.

"You don't trust us?" he asked, his voice smooth and calm. He sounded like he should be narrating audio books or something.

"I trust some of you," I answered.

"What does that mean?" he asked.

"It means I've worked with people in the government I would trust with my life," I said, taking a breath of the stale air. "But the organization as a whole? Not really, no."

"Then why didn't you leave the program like Miss Lopez?" he asked.

"Is that an option now?" I said, flashing a sarcastic grin at the camera.

"No."

I was dressed in grey coveralls and had thick handcuffs made of that dark grey metal on both my wrists and my ankles. My square-jawed friends had stripped me down, executed a rather intimate search, and had put me in the jumpsuit and matching accessories. I didn't resist. It wouldn't have done any good.

"Was it an option then?" I asked.

The voice was silent. I imagined him, my interrogator, switching off the microphone and conferring with the other men in a little room next to this one. My interrogator, as I saw him in my mind's eye, was short and bald, with pale brown eyes and a weak chin. I had no idea what he looked like, it just helped me to imagine him that way.

"Let's go back to when Chaosboy got away," he finally said, ignoring my question. "He just jumped off the roof?"

I knew he knew the answer. We had been closely observed in Las Vegas. "I'm sorry I didn't try to leave the program," I said, ignoring his question as he had ignored mine. "Licia is smarter than me. Much smarter. But I guess the reason I stayed is I believe in what we are fighting for."

"And what is that?" the voice asked.

The smile I gave the camera took effort. It was like swallowing a bitter pill without any water. "Freedom. Freedom from the aliens. Freedom to determine our own fate."

Silence again. They must be conferring. "Do you still believe in that? The fight for freedom?"

I smiled, this time easier. "I will always believe in that."

IT SEEMED TO BE A KIND OF GENTLEMAN'S PRISON. No violence. No torture. And almost no human contact except for Ronald, the man who brought me books.

The interrogations happened daily for the first two weeks. Each morning three of those square-jawed, beefy boys would escort me to the little room. They all had mirror shades on and they never said a word.

One would point an alien energy weapon at me with its metal tube and bulky backpack. They still had a jerry-rigged look to them. Another one would have a handgun pointed at me, and the third would have a pair of handcuffs on a long pole. They weren't fooling around. After the cuffs were on, they'd escort me a ways down that winding hallway to the little room.

There I would sit and talk to that smooth, disembodied voice. He asked me the same questions over and over. It was boring, and I think that was the point. That big-bellied, little bald guy—as I imagined him—was trying to break me through sheer boredom. Like if he just asked the question enough times, I might answer it differently.

After about a week I just stopped answering. We had been over it. I told them almost everything. I left out the conversation that Toxicwasteman and I had had after stopping the flood waters from the broken Hoover Dam, and I left out the location of the real LoVE base I had been at.

The rest of it, including my belief that we needed Tom and his crew, I was totally upfront about. But that smooth voice kept digging, so I stopped talking.

After a week of me not talking, things changed. Right after one of the beefy boys delivered my dinner, I met Ronald, an older, elegant-looking black man.

He wasn't dressed that elegantly in tan slacks and a black T-shirt, but it was more the way he moved. There was a grace to his walk, an elegance in his long fingers and thin limbs. He looked to be around seventy with his hairline having receded back to a strip of short white hair. I was surprised to see him.

"Who are you?" I asked, slumped on my bunk. I was so bored, I had nothing to do but workout, sleep, and refuse to talk to the smooth-voiced man. No books, and I was sick of TV and the endless commercials. In truth, I had slipped way past boredom into a deep depression.

"My name is Ronald," he said, extending his hand through the bars.

I was shocked. No one had talked to me since I got to this place, not face to face. "Um... yeah..." I got up and shook his hand. His grip was firm and his hands were rough, as if he did a lot of manual labor. "I'm Nik."

"Is there anything you need?" he asked.

It took me a moment. After two weeks of silence—except for the damn interrogations—I found it hard to speak. "Umm... I don't know... a book would be nice."

Ronald smiled and nodded and walked slowly down the hall. I found myself smiling as I ate my food, remembering how Ronald's hand had felt, his white-toothed smile, his deep, reassuring voice.

The next day in interrogation instead of being silent, I asked, "Who's Ronald?"

The room was intentionally bland. White walls. Metal chair. The only thing of interest to look at was the white camera facing in in one of the corners. The air was stale and warm. There was nothing of interest in this room but the conversation.

There was silence on the other end, like he was conferring with someone. "Who do you think he is?" the smooth-voiced man asked.

Another surprise. I had tried to steer the conversation in a different direction many times, but it had never worked. "I... I think he's a spy." I was kind of surprised to hear the words tumble out. I hadn't been consciously thinking it, but it made sense. "He's ex-CIA or something. You are hoping I open up to him."

Another bit of silence. "Let's go back to when Tom Tyree tried to recruit you. What exactly did he say to you while you were in their base at the Grand Canyon? Try to remember every word."

I had come to hate that voice. It was too calm, too smooth, too in control. "He said the military would eventually do something stupid and that I couldn't let it take me out of the game."

"But you are out of the game now," the voice said.

"Am I?" I asked.

Silence again. This conversation wasn't a fair one. They had a camera on me, they were, undoubtedly, studying my face, gleaning more information than I was giving them verbally. I couldn't see the person (or rather, I suspected, persons) on the other end.

"You look like you are out of the game to me," he said.

"Maybe the game has changed. Maybe I want to be here." And yes, I should have known better. I should have learned my lesson about picking a fight on someone else's turf from my interview with Diane Madison. But I was sick of this. I felt trapped and powerless. I wanted out. If all that was left to me was a verbal game, I was going to try something.

"Why would you want to be here?"

"The food," I said, "and the companionship. It's excellent." This verbal game wasn't me, and that was a problem. Tom, now he could do this kind of thing all day and love it, but me, I only had a bit of sarcasm as defense.

"Let's go back to when Tom Tyree tried to recruit you. What exactly did he say to you while you were in their base? Try to remember every word." He said it exactly the same way he had the time before. The same words, the same intonation. It was maddening.

I just shook my head and didn't say another word.

Their plan wasn't clear. What did they intend to do to me in this "gentle" prison? Just feed me and interrogate me and then expect me to go fight for the planet if the aliens returned?

I could see no way out and my only hope was that Ronald would talk to me again, would bring me a book, would help break the monotony before it broke me.

THE FIRE CRACKLED, THE STARS SPARKLED, AND WALTER Williams and I drank.

After we had gotten him settled in our guest room at Casita de Soledad and he had eaten—and thoroughly praised—some of Licia's curry, he had grabbed a mason jar out of one of the cardboard boxes and said, "Come on, Nik, get drunk with an old friend, will you?"

"What is that?" I asked.

"Whiskey. Homemade. Sunni, she said to me after I retired, 'You better get a hobby, Walt, or we'll be getting a divorce.'" He paused, a wide grin on his angular face. "Not that she entirely approves of *this* hobby."

He invited Licia too, but she declined, saying she had to clean up. I think we all knew she was going to call Sunni and make sure things were okay between them.

I took Williams out to our flagstone patio. It juts out from the front of our house, has a built-in firepit, and a hell of a view of our high-desert home during the day and a stunning view of the stars at night.

There are no cities near Casita de Soledad. Most nights, and this was one, you can see the milky way above, a dense swath of stars strewn against the dark velvet void.

I lit the fire and Williams poured us drinks.

"To the fallen," he said, raising his glass to the stars. "May the sonofabitch aliens never come back, and may you be here if they do to kick their grey asses once again."

"To the fallen," I echoed, our glasses clinking as I shot the tea-colored liquid down. It burned my throat and I coughed like some kid taking his first shot of hard liquor.

Williams slapped me on the back and chuckled. "It's not the smoothest drink you'll ever have."

"You ain't kidding," I said when I could talk again.

"I have not mastered the art," he said while he refilled our little shot glasses. "But it's a hell of a lot better than my first attempt, and it gets the job done."

The warmth was spreading into my stomach and I felt my shoulders further relaxing. I took measured sips while Williams knocked the whiskey back.

He was sitting hunched over a bit, his right hand against his chest moving in an odd pattern. It took me a moment to realize that he was signing. American Sign Language had been part of our training with the military. It provided useful numerous times, like when we were out of the atmosphere and couldn't speak, or around enemies and needed to talk privately.

He was only using a single hand and was spelling out a single word. *Danger.*

When my eyes widened in recognition, my mouth opening to speak, he said, "Think about it, son." He then took a breath before adding, "I haven't been doing this long, so I'm not going to be that good at it. On Sunni's insistence, I did pull some strings and get a license to do this, so at least I'm not..." He trailed off, for just a second, like he had drunk a bit too much, but I knew he hadn't. He finally finished, a serious look on his grizzled face "...breaking the law.

He was asking me to think about why he was signing to me and was he telling me he was breaking the law? I closed my mouth, feeling the tension crawl back into my shoulders, and took another sip of the rot-gut whiskey.

He was signing again, this time with two hands, his back to the desert, hunched over a bit. *You must get drunk. It's important.*

I nodded and shot back the rest of the whiskey. Colonel Williams was here passing secret messages, breaking the law, why the hell not get drunk?

6 / EATING EGGS AND DRINKING COFFEE

I THINK I WOULD HAVE LOST IT DOWN THERE WITHOUT Ronald. Every time I saw him ambling down the long hallway, I smiled. He had this presence to him that reminded me of the seventy-ish Morgan Freeman. Not that he looked like Freeman; Ronald was bald with only a strip of white hair remaining, and rather homely looking. It was more the vibe he put off. Like he was a man that you could trust.

"Special delivery," he said that next morning after I had met him. My breakfast had just arrived, runny eggs, underdone toast, and cold coffee. The lock rattled on the pass-through I got my meals from. It was a beat-up hardback book. *Killing Floor* by Lee Child.

"It's the first Jack Reacher novel," Ronald offered. "I think you'll like it. Reacher is a man of action, kind of like you."

"Thanks, Ronald. But... How... Why are they letting me have books now?"

He just smiled and shrugged his shoulders. "Enjoy," he said as he ambled back down the hallway.

I sat there on my bunk holding the scarred book while my food got cold. The spine was broken, the cover ragged, and the pages a bit yellow. The book had been well used. I cracked it open, flipped to the first page and started reading:

I was arrested in Eno's diner. At twelve o'clock. I was eating eggs and drinking coffee.

I looked over to my eggs and coffee and felt a chill go down my spine. The coincidence seemed bizarre. Did Ronald know I had just received the food the book opened up with?

When I was young, I had read a lot. Mostly fantasy, things like *The Lord of the Rings* and it's progeny. But when I hit college, that had stopped in favor of studying. And after college and Ashley when I entered my coasting phase, I never took it back up.

With its short sentences and quick pace, the book was clearly a thriller of some sort. I started reading, my breakfast forgotten. It was such a relief to escape that cell—even if only in my mind—for a while.

A few hours later, at the top of chapter 13, was a note scrawled in bright red ink:

"Hold on. We're making a plan. Will come if they don't let you out. Look to my boy, Ron."

It was signed with two looping Ts. Tom Tyree. It had to be him.

I slammed the book shut and put it down on my bunk. My eyes darted around the cell. Where exactly were the cameras? Was there any chance that they had seen that? Should I tear the page out and flush it? No, no. That would just bring more attention to it.

So Ronald wasn't CIA or even working for the government. Ronald was sent here by Tom.

I knew the emotions I was feeling were all over my face so I got on my rowing machine and started working out. The rowing machine, like everything in this cell had no electricity, no power. It had a handle that you pulled back that moved a fan. Nothing special, but at least I could get an aerobic workout.

My mind was reeling. What would it mean if LoVE came and

got me? How many would die for my freedom? Could I live with that?

The walls of the cell were a boring white. No color. No pictures. Nothing. Before Ronald all I had to keep me sane was exercising, and it was clear that wasn't going to be enough. But if Ronald was Tom's "boy," how did he get in here? How were they letting him talk to me and bring me a book?

After the workout I pulled the little plastic curtain around the tiny shower area and let the hot water run over me for a long time. Tom Tyree and his boy Ron were my lifeline down here. Tom Tyree was saving me... again.

Once I was clean and dressed, I went back to the book. I had decided to do nothing about the note written in chapter 13. I kept my face calm and opened the book back up and when I got to chapter 13, I gasped.

That red ink was gone. I flipped back, looking through each chapter page until I got to the beginning, but didn't find it. I then flipped forward, but it wasn't there either.

I did my best to calm myself. I hadn't imagined the note, had I?

━━

AFTER *KILLING FLOOR*, RONALD BROUGHT ME *DIE TRYING* AND then *Tripwire*. All Jack Reacher novels. I would gobble them up in a day or two, going back and rereading my favorite parts.

I did my best to keep track of days, but without a pen or even something sharp to scrape on the walls, I lost track of time, but I had a feeling that spring had slipped into summer.

My daily interrogation sessions with the smooth-voiced man continued, but I had strength again. I started asking more questions and refused to answer his. We had strange little conversations.

"When are you letting me go?" I asked one day.

"When you answer all my questions," he replied.

"But I have."

"No you haven't," he said.

"Okay, what question haven't I answered?" I asked.

"This woman that worked for Tom Tyree, this 'Byte.' What is her real name?"

"I can't answer that question because I don't know the answer," I said.

"No one ever used another name for her? A nickname?" he asked.

"No."

"And you don't know anything else about her? Where she's from, where she worked, how she got her powers?" he asked.

"No," I lied. That was one other area I had been less than truthful about. No one knew who Byte was—my gut told me it needed to stay that way. "I didn't interact with her all that much."

"But you robbed a train together," he said.

"That we did," I replied. "It was fun."

"And you never had a private conversation with her?" he asked.

"A few, but not about anything private," I said.

"I don't believe you," he said.

"I don't care," I said.

Those books were making me stronger. Jack Reacher was one tough son of a bitch. He wouldn't take this faceless man's crap, and neither would I. The books and the sliver of human contact with Ronald had changed things for me.

I suspected they had enough equipment trained on me to tell when I was lying and when I wasn't. But I didn't care about that either.

There was one thing that didn't make sense. Ronald and his books had given me this strength. Even if Ronald was working for Tom, why are they letting him talk to me? It didn't make sense.

"Who is Ronald?" I asked after a minute of silence.

He didn't reply right away, once again. "Who do you think he is?"

"I don't know," I said.

Another long silence. "What have you been reading?" the voice asked.

"Jack Reacher novels. Ronald brought them to me." At first, I felt guilty telling him, like I'm ratting Ronald out or something. But they have to know what he's doing. They're watching, always watching. "Is he some sort of librarian?" I asked.

"Is that what you think he is?" the voice asked.

I shrugged my shoulders. "Maybe now, but I don't think he was always one."

"What do you think he was before he was a librarian?" he asked.

"A spy... no, maybe a diplomat," I said. "He's a very trustworthy kind of a guy. But it doesn't really matter, I've told you everything, so sending him in to try to get more out of me is just a waste of time."

This game was dangerous and I needed that. Part of me believed that the note written on chapter 13 of *Killing Floor* was real, that somehow Tom had turned someone down here. And another part of me thought that I had just imagined it, that maybe I wasn't doing as well as I thought, that I was slowly losing myself.

Silence, I again imagined my pudgy and bald interrogator conferring with people. "Maybe we should stop his visits," he finally said.

My heart started thumping in my chest, like it was trying to escape the prison of my body. I didn't know if I could take it if Ronald didn't come by, didn't bring me books. I swallow hard. "Your choice," I said, trying to sound casual and failing utterly.

"We'll take it under advisement," the voice said.

BY THE TIME LICIA JOINED US OUTSIDE, THE FIRE WAS burning nicely and Williams and I were drunk. He hadn't signed much more to me, but kept me drinking just enough to be drunk, but not enough to get too stupid.

It was a beautiful night, the fire chasing away the chill and the stars resplendent and bright in our isolated location. Earlier the yips of coyotes had bounced across the rolling desert land.

"Licia!" I cried when she came out. She had a grey sweater pulled tight around her and looked serious. "Come have some of Walter's wonderful whiskey." I giggled at the rhyme. I had drunk enough that I was actually liking it now.

"I don't think so," she said to me and then looked to Williams. "Sunni says to take it easy on the whiskey."

"Well Sunni's not here, is she?" Williams said, his eyes narrowing and looking around at the shadows around us. He then looked very serious. "She's not here, is she?"

"She's worried about you," Licia said, her arms crossed. "You've been preoccupied, restless. And at this point, I'm worried about both of you."

"We're just having a little fun," I said, my words slurring more than I wanted them to. "We don't have enough fun around here."

Licia's eyes met mine briefly, her lips a thin line.

I made an exaggerated nod of my head, indicating that I wanted her to look at my hands. I was hunched over, just like Williams had been and I signed, *Something is going on. We are in danger.*

Licia's eyes widened, and her mouth opened to speak, but Williams lurched up and put his arm around her. "You won't refuse to have a drink with your old friend, will you? I made this whiskey with my own two hands and you can't refuse me."

Licia looked back to me, confused. If there was danger, why were we getting drunk? Williams was sitting back down and signed, *I must tell you both something important, you must drink first.*

Licia sighed and sat down, pulling one of our patio chairs up next to Williams. "Okay, one drink. But only one." And then she signed, *Why drink?*

So they don't hear the stress in your voices when I say what I need to say, Williams signed.

Licia took the proffered whiskey and shot it back. She gasped but didn't cough like I had.

Who? I signed. *There is no one out here.*

Williams gave me a grim smile as he refilled all three of our glasses. The air was thick with the smell of smoke and the tang of alcohol. "To the fallen," he said, raising his glass, repeating the toast he had done with me earlier. "For those that died so that we might live."

"Hear, hear!" Licia cried.

After we drank, Williams signed, *Homeland Security. They listen to every word you two say.*

"I think I'll take another," Licia said, the flickering yellow of the fire making her look fierce.

Licia quickly joined us in our drunkenness and then Williams told us what he had come here to tell us.

FOUR WALLS. FOOD TO EAT. MEANS TO EXERCISE. FACELESS sessions with the voice.

I don't think I ever imagined a prison to be like this, and if I had, I wouldn't have understood the difficulties of it. I see one of those beefy square-jawed guards twice a day when they bring my meals, and three times a day when they escort me to my interrogation, but they never speak to me, and they have on dark sunglasses so there is never the possibility of eye contact.

They were depriving me of human contact, of real interaction. Isolating me. Giving me one, and only one, avenue of expression, my interrogations.

A week of that seemed easy. I worked out, caught up on sleep, enjoyed the verbal banter of the interrogations, ate my food.

At four weeks it was starting to get hard. I felt myself wanting to treat my faceless interrogator as my friend. To talk to him like a friend. To tell him things. But I resisted.

Eight weeks in and I woke up one morning and couldn't remember what Licia looked like. I had been having a dream where

I wandered through an empty Phoenix, cars parked on the freeway, houses vacant with the doors open and the TVs on, no one home, not even a cat or a dog. Just emptiness under a blazing hot summer sun.

I found myself, after walking for what seemed like days, at my parents' house. The place where I had grown up and the place my parents had had to abandon when Diane Madison revealed my identity. The front door was open and I walked in calling for my mother and my father. I could smell my mother's cheap perfume and the house was clean, everything put away, like someone was living there.

I rushed through, opening doors, checking in the garage and finding my Dad's 1972 Dodge Charger, but not my parents.

I went into my bedroom and flopped onto my little twin bed. This was my room when I was a kid and is still very much like it had once been. The shelf of Star Wars models I had built as a kid. A few trophies from my time running cross country in high school. A picture of me and Robby Holmes, my best friend in high school and college, with our cap and gown on at our high school graduation. And a picture of me and a dark-haired woman.

I'm puzzled by the picture. It's just a normal picture, but for some reason I can't see the woman's face. It's not like it's blurred out or anything, it's just that my mind doesn't register it.

I can see that she's got long black hair, she's wearing a red tank top with a yellow lightning bolt emblazoned on it. I'm sitting close to her, a big goofy smile on my face. You can see part of my forearm, it's a selfie. We're sitting on a picnic table and you can see a hill rising in the distance behind us with noticeable horizontal lines running across the hill.

That's a vineyard on that hill. I know that place. It's a winery in the Verde Valley that sits right on Oak Creek. I've been there... with...

It was a dream and my mind was sluggish, trying to grapple with the feelings of isolation. I know that woman, her name is...

Lisa? No, that's not it. Alice? No, it doesn't start with "A." I sit down on my bed holding the picture, still not able to see the face. She's beautiful, I know that. And petite. Powerful, she's somehow very powerful.

I feel tears running down my face. For this lost world I am trapped in, for this woman that I know I love but can't remember, for this ache in my heart.

When I woke up, my heart was pounding and real tears were running down my real cheeks. I rolled over on my bed, facing the smooth wall, pulling the thin blanket over my head. I didn't want them to see me cry.

And as my mind went over the strange dream, I knew that girl's name. It was Licia. It was Lightningirl. My love. My reason for holding on. My reason for going to this prison without a fight. My reason for getting up in the morning.

Licia Lopez. Beautiful black hair and thick eyebrows, coffee and cream-colored skin, deep brown eyes.

But I couldn't put those features together. I closed my eyes shut and I couldn't "see" her. I bolted upright, too freaked out to care about my watchers. I began pacing my cell trying to force my mind to see her. It'd been eight weeks—how could her image have faded so fast? What was wrong with me?

Silky black hair. A slightly turned-up nose. A round face.

But these were just words, the image wouldn't come to me. I knew I was losing it, that my isolation had worn me down. But knowing it didn't help me stop my tumble.

The next time the voice asked me what I hadn't told him, I was going to spill it. I was going to tell him everything I know about Byte. About the real location of the LoVE base where Tom Tyree left me a supply of uranium ore. About the conversation we had after Gaia breached the Hoover Dam.

All of it would come spilling out of me. I would trade it for a picture of Licia. She felt like she's slipping away and I couldn't stand that.

9 / PROJECT VULCAN

UNDER THE STARS, WE THREE WERE DRUNK, COLONEL Williams, Licia, and me. Our drinking slowed but we all stayed at that balance point. Definitely drunk, but some control remaining.

The fire popped and sparked, a cool breeze kicked up from the west, and the stars continued to dazzle.

Williams signed to us as we drank and talked about silly things. He told us about project "Vulcan." When we had moved out here in 2021, the land had been prepared for us. The rudimentary road built. The foundation for our casita laid. A well drilled. And one more thing.

They had buried a bomb below us. It was called Project Vulcan. It was a failsafe. If we became a threat or too much trouble, they would trigger the bomb and we would be gone.

This was why Williams had insisted we be drunk. We were chatting, having the conversation old war buddies might have, but below all of this was the serious talk of impending doom. The slurred speech of the intoxicated was—Williams was hoping— enough to mask the stress of what he was telling us.

I threw another log on the fire, crackling sparks rising briefly into the night, throwing too much light on our grim faces.

"I can see why Sunni frowns on this little hobby of yours," Licia said while signing, *Why would they do this?*

We all signed carefully, our bodies leaning towards the fire, our backs facing the desert, our hands in front of our abdomens. We knew they were watching.

"That she does," Williams said. "But she told me to find something to occupy my time. This does it two ways. While I make it and while I drink it." *Humans fear what they can't control, what is more powerful than they are. You two are both.*

"Well I think it's the best damn whiskey I've ever had," I said. *What do we do now?*

"That's the booze talking, son," Williams said. "It's terrible whiskey, but not as bad as my first batch." *I have a plan.*

What is it? Licia signed.

"Ahh hell," Williams said as he poured the last drop from the mason jar into his glass. "This one is empty." *Time to dig that root cellar. Time for Nick to remember some old skills.*

"I'll get us another one," I said, rising to my feet, my body swaying like I was a sailor on choppy seas. *Root cellar? Skills?*

"No," Williams said. "This old man is tired. It's a hell of a bumpy trip out here." *In the morning tell me about where you plan to dig your root cellar. I know you've been planning it. Dig where I tell you not to.*

With a groan he got up, putting his hand on Licia's shoulder to steady himself. "It may not be the smoothest whiskey," he said with a laugh, "but it sure as hell gets the job done."

With that he walked, his steps slow and careful, to the house.

"To the fallen!" I cried as he got to the door.

He raised his fist into the air and stumbled into the house.

With Colonel Williams gone, it suddenly seemed cold and the vast sky above us seemed dangerous. Like we were mice that had been enjoying an open plain in daylight before we remembered the eagles. Licia shivered, and I looked up. They were watching us. They were listening to us. They were plotting against us.

I looked at Licia and her face looked stricken. "I'm glad he came," I said. "It's been too long."

Licia nodded, yawned, and grabbed my hand. "Let's go in. I'm cold."

Licia and I didn't sleep much that night. We didn't speak either. We held each other, my mind racing. A new threat, this one from within.

10 / RESISTANCE

THAT DAY IN THE INTERROGATION ROOM I TRIED NOT TO SAY anything. I was feeling so vulnerable from my dream, about not being able to close my eyes and see Licia's face. I knew if I said anything, I'd say everything.

"Did you not sleep well?" the voice asked. It was as smooth as ever, calm and even, entirely in control.

I didn't answer. I didn't want to be here anymore. I needed to get out.

I was starting to hate that smooth voice and I was truly hating the little walks down to this room. I used to like it, any reason to get out of my cell, but they treated me like I was radioactive, and that was wearing on me too.

Yes, I know that I can be literally radioactive, but maybe a better way of saying this is that they were treating me like a leper, like the mere touch of my skin could taint them.

When it was time, three of them came. One with an alien energy weapon, one with a handgun, and one with a long grey metal pole with my handcuffs attached. It's the pole that got to me. They made me go to the back of the cell while they unlocked the cell door. The man with the pole then extended it to me and I had to put my wrists in it. He triggered something on his end and the cuffs snicked into place and I was led that way to interrogation.

Yes, they were afraid of me, I get that. But there was no talking at all. The first time they held up signs for me so I knew what to do. They all looked the same, blank expressions on their faces with dark sunglasses over their eyes. There was no human connection here.

They marched me down to the room, the man holding the pole in front of me walking backwards, the two with the guns behind me.

"We can end this right now. Today," the voice said, interrupting my thoughts. "Tell me the truth, all of it, and we will let you go."

I squeezed my eyes shut tight trying, again, to remember what Licia looked like. I could smell her in my mind, that ozone tang she emits after she's been Lightningirl, I could feel her hand in mine, I could even hear her laughter, but I couldn't see her face.

"You can go back to her," he said. "We don't want to keep you apart, but we need to know everything."

I clenched my fists tight and squeezed my eyes closed tighter.

Why was I resisting? Was it for Tom Tyree the psychopath and his gang of villains? Was it shame for the choices I've made, letting Tom go twice, not going after Chaosboy after he jumped off the roof of the Golden Nugget, failing to stop Gaia at the Hoover Dam?

For a moment I didn't know why I didn't tell them. I didn't understand my resistance. I lifted my head up and looked around the empty room. There was the camera, its big black eye staring at me, but nothing else. Smooth white walls, a single door, nothing else.

"No," I said, the first word I had uttered this time. They had kept me in the dark, they had treated me as a tool, not a person, they threw me in this cell and treated me like a pariah. This wasn't a conversation. This wasn't a partnership.

"Please be reasonable, Nik."

His use of my first name made me madder. We weren't friends —hell, we weren't even acquaintances. I didn't know his name, or what he really looked like. I didn't know how old he was or if he liked baseball or football better. I didn't know if he had kids or if he liked to ride motorcycles.

I slowly stood, my fists clenched, my jaw tight. "Don't call me that."

There was a pause. "What should I call you?"

"I'm done. Take me back to my cell." I could feel my heart pounding and my face flushing red. I was angry and that was enough to keep me from giving away my secrets. But I feared it wouldn't last, that I would grow weak again.

"We are not done here," the smooth voice said.

I walked to the door and tried the shiny silver nob. It was locked.

"Don't do that," he said.

If I just had a knife maybe I could jimmy the lock. I looked around the room, knowing it was silly, but still needing to do something, but there was nothing. The chair in the middle of the room bolted to the floor. The camera mounted on the wall.

"Please sit down."

The chair was metal, the back of it made up of square hollow pieces of metal. Maybe I could break it and jimmy the lock with that.

I walked over to the chair and started kicking the back of it from the side. It was strong and the blows were painful to my foot. The metal on the left side of the seatback bent a little, but it wasn't much.

"You must sit down." The voice was still as calm and even as ever.

I ignored it and kept kicking, switching to my other foot.

"This is your last warning."

I was working up a sweat and it felt good. With each blow I gave a growling grunt of effort, giving voice in a small way to my anger. It was going to give way, eventually. I could see that.

Then there was a strange smell in the air, it had the sweetness of almonds, but was sour too. What is that?

I paused to catch my breath. I was dizzy.

The smell was getting stronger. I didn't like it. My legs gave way and I knew nothing.

"Do you feel better now?" the voice asked as if from very far away. My mouth tasted like greasy metal shavings and my head hurt. I was sitting in the bland interrogation room, sitting in that metal chair, I could feel the damage I did to it, the bent side pressed against my back.

I tried to rub my face, to wake myself up, but I couldn't, my hands were down by my side. They had me handcuffed to the chair, a chain passing under the chair keeping my hands low.

I spit on the clean floor trying to clear that awful taste from my mouth.

"Let's resume where we left off," the smooth voice said. "This Byte woman. You haven't described her to me yet."

That weakness I felt when I woke up from that dream, not being able to see Licia's face, it was gone. I still couldn't see her face, but it wasn't making me weak anymore. It was making me angry. They took me away from her. They locked me up down here. Except for the brief visits from Ronald, they deprived me of the simple comfort of human interaction.

I groaned and strained against my handcuffs feeling them cut into my skin.

"Please don't do that," he said evenly.

I slowed my breathing, taking deep and measured breaths. I knew how to transform into Neutrinoman, it's all about finding that spark and igniting that change. Like a match to kindling.

"What are you doing?" he asked.

I had no charge, no fuel if you will, but I was determined.

"Stop that," he said.

I knew that this is what they feared, and I wanted to give it to them. I had no fuel but my anger and my body. Let it be the fuel. I will change to Neutrinoman. I will fly out of here. I will not listen to that voice one more minute.

"I am afraid that I must insist," he said, his voice still even. "Open your eyes now or I will be forced to take measures."

It's will that does it. Just like I can will my hand into a fist, I can will myself to turn into Neutrinoman. I felt hot and sweat trickled down my back. The voice was still speaking but I didn't hear it. That trigger was there, I knew it was there. My anger was the fuel. I was the fuel. I flipped the switch and...

Nothing.

I slumped in the chair exhausted, defeated, vulnerable.

⸻

THERE WAS NOTHING LEFT OF ME AFTER MY FAILURE TO TURN neutrino, handcuffed to that chair. Powerless.

The voice asked more questions, but I wasn't listening. I was falling into a deep, dark pit of despair. It was just me down here. The guards weren't really people. The voice, my interrogator, wasn't either. He was too calm and collected. That voice could be a computer for all the empathy and humanity it contained.

I know the isolation was meant to break me. They had my psych profile. They probably knew my mind better than I did.

They had chosen this isolation purposefully to break me. But they broke me too well.

I chuckled, a brief bitter bark.

"What are you laughing at?" the voice asked.

Tom Tyree and his gang had used my psych profile to manipulate me. First at Yellowstone, tapping into my sense of duty. Then at the LoVE base, presenting me with an open exchange of ideas which I had been longing for.

And what had the military used to manipulate me? My most basic of human needs. My need for human interaction and dignity. They had done something much more villainous than Tom had to me.

Tom had tried to build me into something that could defeat the Aliens. These people had just torn me down. If not for Ronald's brief visits it would have happened much sooner.

And that there, that anomaly, tickled at my brain, but I had no time for it, it was just a whisper against the scream of my despair.

I laughed then. I laughed hard, the sound coming deep from within my belly with a high-pitched manic tang to it.

"Can you please share?" the voice asked.

I laughed until my belly hurt.

"What is so funny?"

"This is working," I began. "This scheme of yours. You are breaking me. You will get what you want this way. Congratulations."

"Why is that funny?" he asked.

"Because of you," I said, "I won't be there to fight if aliens come back. The Earth will fall."

"Let's go back to this Byte woman," he said as if nothing had happened.

I laughed again until my body was too tired to laugh. I knew I sounded crazy, but I didn't care. They eventually uncuffed me from the chair and led me back to my cell.

"MAYBE WHAT YOU NEED IS SOMETHING MORE REAL," RONALD offered.

"What?" I asked. I had heard him arrive, but hadn't stirred, slumped on my bunk, the scratchy wool blanket underneath me. It wasn't mealtime, it wasn't time for him to be here. Despite the fiction, I had slipped back into that dark place. The place where I didn't believe I'd ever get out. Where I believed I was powerless to change my situation.

"As good as it is, a man can only take so much Jack Reacher." Ronald had a compassionate smile on his face. It was a kind face. A trustworthy face. I didn't trust it.

Keys jangled and I heard the snick of the pass-through door opening and closing.

"Give that a shot," he said.

I levered myself up from my bunk and stumbled over to the pass-through, which was in the wall right next to the door. It had a lockable opening on the outside and it was just big enough for a food tray, wide, but not very high, making it a good size for books. In it was a slim, beat-up book. *A Gradual Awakening* by Stephen Levine. The cover was in sepia tones with a tall spindly tree leaning towards the right and a mountaintop just visible through a misty barrier.

It looked like new-age nonsense to me.

"Why?" I asked him, my face close to the metal bars of my cell.

He licked his lips and looked me up and down. I hadn't show-ered or shaved in days and I stunk. He looked over his shoulder, as if checking for observers. Which was strange. They were watching, we both knew it.

"Look," he whispered. "I'm not supposed to be giving you any books at all, but this one... you need this one. Just read it."

"They're not going to let me out, are they?" I asked.

Ronald's face darkened and he licked his lips again and sighed.

"In or out, prisoner or free, you need to read that book. You need to get your head in the game."

I snorted and shook my head, "Why?"

His old brown eyes locked with mine. "I believe in you, even if you don't believe in yourself."

With that he turned and walked away.

⸻

"Who were you talking to yesterday?" the voice asked. I'm back in the interrogation room, the bent metal of the chair pressed against my back.

"Please no games today," I said, my voice low, my head down. "You know who I was talking to."

A pause. In my mind my interrogator was no longer short and bald. He was tall and handsome with thick black hair. I could see his symmetrical face clearly in my mind, but I still couldn't see Licia's.

"Let's go back to after the breach of the Hoover Dam," the smooth voice said, "when you were talking to Toxicwasteman. What did he tell you?"

"He told me what he always tells me," I said. "That the military, you guys, would screw this up if you were given enough time."

"Can you try to remember the exact words, please?" he said.

"What does it matter?" I asked. "He was right, you know."

"Right about what?" he asked.

"About you screwing this up," I said.

"What have we screwed up?"

I shook my head and got up, started pacing around the room. It was much smaller than my cell, but I felt better moving than I did sitting. I stayed close to the walls. Two and half paces to a side. It seemed to be perfectly square.

"What have we screwed up?" the voice repeated.

I stopped right below the camera. I wasn't sure if it was the only camera in the room, but if it was, this made the conversation more even. I couldn't see him and maybe he couldn't see me.

"The military and I are done," I whispered. I didn't feel strong enough to say it out loud.

"We are not part of the military," the voice said. He said it in his always-even tone, but it made my blood run cold.

"Who are you?" I asked.

"Let's go back to after the breach of the Hoover Dam," he began, but I wasn't listening anymore. If they weren't the military, who were they? CIA? FBI? Homeland Security? It was some sort of governmental organization, wasn't it? It had to be, didn't it?

THE NEXT MORNING—WELL, IT WAS CLOSER TO NOON, WE were all nursing hangovers—we took Colonel Williams for a tour of our little home. He had been here before, but it had been over a year, and we didn't get many visitors, so we probably gave him the kind of in-depth tour that would make most people run for the hills.

We showed him my workshop—really just an oversized shed stuffed with tools—the small greenhouse, and the large greenhouse that we had just completed. The plants were just sprouting and Licia was very proud. She went in depth on each plant, how long they take to mature, how we were going to be able to grow all our own produce.

It was overkill, on both of our parts, but we had gotten so isolated that we needed someone else to talk to. Williams took it in stride, nodding at the right places, asking questions that showed he had been listening. Asking Licia what it would take if he started a small garden, telling her that maybe he needed a hobby other than the brewing of whiskey.

"So what's next?" he asked. "Do you have plans to build something else?"

"A root cellar," I said.

"Really? Why?" he asked.

"The same reason anyone has ever had a root cellar," Licia said, "to keep canned goods cool. With this greenhouse we're going to produce enough food that preserving makes sense."

The truth of the matter was that we could grow produce year-round in the greenhouses. We didn't need a root cellar, what we needed was something to do with our time. But this was a pleasant and civilized conversation, so I kept those thoughts to myself.

"We're currently scouting for a location," I said. "The ground here is full of rocks, so it's not going to be easy."

Williams gave me a raised-eyebrow look. "No powers then?"

I shook my head. "Just us. Just shovels and picks."

He looked like he was pondering the situation. This conversation we were having was a little play for our listeners. Our voices were a bit rough, our words a bit awkward, but that could easily be blamed on the hangovers.

"Well, let's take a look," he said.

We walked the property, showing him the spots we had discussed. Just in back of the house, over by my little workshop, and next to the new greenhouse.

At the last stop he kicked at the ground and then stooped, pulling a beige rock out of the soil. "I wouldn't do it here," he said looking at us, his eyes squinting against the bright sunlight. "Looks like there's more rocks than average."

"I don't know," Licia said. "It's all rocky, and I like the things in orderly lines."

Williams shrugged. "Suit yourself. It's your backs, not mine."

So we had our spot. That night as we sat around the fire under the stars, we had another one of those weird conversations. We spoke of things unimportant and signed of the things most important. We drank wine, Licia insisted, and didn't get nearly as intoxicated, but did drink enough to make our spoken conversation full of laughter.

Next step, Williams signed, *Nik needs to revive his EMV.*

EMV: Electromagnetic Vision. It was a skill I developed while I was being "detained." It requires a half-meditative state and allows me to "see" electromagnetic radiation.

I groaned in response. I never found the skill an easy one to maintain. The mental state can be very frustrating to achieve.

"Oh," Licia said, "looks like you need more wine." She was covering for the groan.

"Yeah, Nichols, it's early. Don't stop now." *It's the only way you'll find the bomb,* he signed.

"If Sunni could see you now," I said.

Williams grinned. "Oh, after fifty years together, I can assure you she knows exactly what I'm up to." *And you must find the bomb. Soon.*

"You should bring her along next time," Licia said.

Williams nodded. *The writing, the interview you agreed to with Diane Madison, some people are getting very nervous. So dig and quick.*

13 / THE PRISON INSIDE

THE BOOK RONALD LEFT ME WAS BORING AND HARD TO READ. A book on vipassana meditation. The reasons, whys, and techniques. I longed for a better escape, one with heroes and heroines. One with action and adventure.

And that was sad. I wasn't longing to physically escape from these four walls but to mentally escape, what I wanted right then was some good fiction with some action and adventure. I could no longer imagine physical escape.

I don't know that I really identify with being a "hero." I find the word to be troublesome. I mean, in fiction I know what it is, but not in the real world. The real world is a lot messier and a lot more complicated. Someone looking at my actions and not living through them with all the doubts and second-guessing might use that word, but I wouldn't.

Lee Child's Jack Reacher was very much on my mind. Highly skilled and capable, Reacher only got involved when he had to, when things got too close to him personally. When there was no other choice.

He seemed more of an anti-hero to me, and that was appealing. He just wanted everyone to leave him alone. He just wanted to wander. And right about then, that sounded perfect to me, provided Licia was along for the wandering.

But I didn't have a Jack Reacher novel and boredom did its job and I would pick up the meditation book and read a little, it's words mostly bouncing off me, mostly making no sense. And then I would pace until I couldn't stand it anymore and then flop down into my bunk and read a little more.

In fits and starts, I read that book about the nature of the human mind written by an American Buddhist. How the real prison we all face is inside our own minds, not in our circumstances. A treatise, if you will, on the care and tending of the human mind.

I didn't buy it at first. I was a hot dog and football kind of a guy, an "I'll believe it when I see it" person. Just a nobody drifting through my life until the accident at the Palo Verde Nuclear Generating Station. But that book was the only one I had. Ronald had taken the Jack Reacher novels back when I was done with them. What else was I going to do?

The foreword and introduction threw me off. They seemed too full of words that didn't make sense to me and written decades ago from a perspective so foreign. But then I hit the last sentence of the first paragraph of the first chapter: "Meditation *is* awareness."

After the accident and the cosmic rays, after I got these powers, I had to learn to understand my body and what I was feeling. I had taken up long-distance running which can be meditative, very meditative if you let it. I didn't have a word for it before, but awareness was something I had been cultivating, something I needed to be Neutrinoman. Awareness of my flesh and blood body and awareness of my q-morph form. I was locked in a cell and the idea of becoming more aware was appealing—given, of course, that I had no fiction to read.

So I read. In fits and starts. Rereading, sometimes over and over. Learning about vipassana meditation and how the mind works. Wondering if this would help.

Eventually, I found the exact center of my cell—a little OCD, I will admit—took the thin, scratchy blanket off my bunk, folded it up, and sat there. I felt silly knowing I was being watched, knowing my every move was being evaluated.

I just sat there and paid attention to my breathing, feeling the stale air flow in and out of my nostrils, my eyes half closed, listening to my mind rebel.

This is stupid. How is sitting here going to help me? It's not. Sitting isn't going to get me out of here. I have to find a way to become Neutrinoman and blast my way out or I need to tell them everything and get this over with.

I made it maybe thirty seconds that first time. But really, all I had there was time. So I would go back to my bunk, read a little more, and then go back to the center of the cell and sit there cross-legged listening to my mind babble on.

Quinn is out there with Licia. He's pretending to be you. She may have decided she likes him better than you by now. You can't even remember what she looks like, you...

That wasn't even fifteen seconds. That voice was the one that hurt. It spoke in my mind like it wasn't me, like it was outside of me, like it knew things I didn't.

This time I didn't go back to the book, I started pacing. I needed out of this cell. I needed human contact. I needed Licia.

"How's it going?" Ronald asked from the bars of my cell. I hadn't heard him walk up.

"I hate that book," I snapped.

Ronald smiled. "Then it's doing its job."

I walked to the bars. Ronald smelled of Old Spice, which made me think of my father. "What do you mean?"

"Well, the novels help you escape out of yourself, provide some relief," he said.

I nodded.

"This one asks you to go into yourself, to confront the demons there, to understand how your mind really works. Not fun, but more useful in your particular circumstance."

He just stood there, a bemused smile on his old face. I didn't want to confront my inner demons. I just wanted the hell out of here. "I don't think I can do this much longer."

His eyebrows furrowed, and I swear his eyes misted up. "Keep practicing. If you do, I'll bring you another Reacher book tomorrow."

SUMMER 2005, LOCATION UNKNOWN

"WHAT ARE YOU READING NOW?" THE VOICE ASKED AS I slumped in that metal chair in the middle of that square room with white walls.

What I wouldn't give for a piece of art hanging on the wall. A landscape... hell, give me a finger painting by a five-year-old at this point and I would be happy. Something to look at. Something with life. Something with character.

"What puzzles me," I said, "is why you want me to read it."

"What do you mean?" he asked.

"You control everything here, including Ronald. Why did you send him down with that book? It doesn't make sense." I was having trouble reconciling Ronald and the positive effect he was having on me with the aims of the people that imprisoned me.

"Why do you think we did it?" the smooth voice asked.

"No," I said, standing up from the metal chair and going into the corner of the room without the camera. "None of the psychological mumbo-jumbo. Either answer the question or don't."

There was a lengthy pause. "What does Ronald look like?"

The room felt small to me, like the walls were closing in. Why the hell would they ask a question like that unless they were messing with me?

"What does Ronald look like?" the voice repeated with the exact same inflection and intonation.

"Bald. Old. Black... Why are you asking me this? You know what he looks like."

Another long pause. "Tell me about the book Ronald gave you."

I slid down to the floor, my back pressed against the wall, my breathing rapid, sweat pricking out on the back of my neck and my arm pits.

"What is the title of the book?" my interrogator asked.

Why were they asking me questions they knew the answer to? The room seemed smaller, the walls against my back hard and cool, the hum of the air blowing into the room loud.

"It's a simple question, you know," he said.

"What? What is?" I asked.

"What is the title of the book?"

I didn't answer, but slowly rose, my back pressed firmly into the corner. My heart was thudding in my chest, my face flushed. I reached up above me to the camera. It was small, mounted on a little metal bracket, just barely within my reach standing on my tiptoes.

I moved slowly, feeling for screws or another way to release it. I wasn't really thinking this through, I was just acting. I needed to escape the voice, the endless questions. The questions that he had to know the answers to.

As I was feeling around, I felt the two wires connected to the camera. One for power, one for the video feed. Electricity! My fingers were hungry. My cells had none, but this room did. I blinked and looked around the room carefully studying the walls. It was a foolish hope, but I was looking to see if there was a power outlet in the room.

Of course there wasn't.

"What is the title of the book?" he asked, his tone infuriatingly even.

Sweat was trickling down my back. How could I get the wires off quickly? Could I get enough electricity to change before they gassed me?

I should take my time, think about it, study the connections. But I didn't have enough will to wait. I jumped up with a grunt, got my hands fully around the little camera and pulled hard.

With a snap it came off the wall, the wires snaking out of their holes a bit. I yanked and the camera came loose from the wires and I let it drop to the floor.

The voice didn't speak, but I started to smell sour almonds again. I took a deep breath and held it, turning around and looking at the wires.

Both of them had copper exposed. Neither of them were large, not like a normal power plug. They didn't come very far out of the wall so I had to reach up to grab them. I pressed my fingers against the copper conductors.

I could feel it. Sweet electricity. Not much, it was low power and definitely DC, but it was electricity nonetheless. I almost shouted out in joy, but kept my mouth closed, holding my breath.

I willed the change, tried to flip the switch, as soon as the meager current started flowing through my veins. This was no power-up from Lightningirl—it was the drip-drip of a leaky faucet, where she was the roar of Niagara Falls.

It wasn't enough, but I tried anyway. I let the electricity flow through me while my lungs screamed for oxygen, while the voice— still maddeningly steady—asked me what I was doing, while the beefy boys in black busted into the room wearing gas masks and started shooting me with the alien energy weapons. Still I stood there, ignoring it all. The purple balls of energy didn't really do anything to me—I had no power to rob.

I twisted around, still holding the wires so I could see them.

Three men, one with the alien energy weapon—the silver tube and awkward backpack—and two with handguns.

"Step away from the wires," one of the men said, his voice muffled because of the gas mask. He raised his gun and pointed it at me. His voice was rough and he sounded scared and had a bit of a southern drawl. Not the voice of my interrogator. "Do it now or I will shoot."

I smiled. One of the guards had spoken to me. It was a tiny victory, but a victory nonetheless. They had left the door open and the smell of almonds was dissipating. I took a few breaths and felt lightheaded but it wasn't enough to knock me out. "No," I said, my voice as calm as my interrogator.

He took a step forward and cocked back the hammer on the gun. "I will shoot you."

"No you won't," I said. I didn't really believe what I was saying, but I wanted to. The way they had treated me was all about breaking my will but keeping me alive.

He pulled his gas mask off, the muscles of his jaw bunched and his green eyes connected with mine briefly, but then flicked away. I studied him. He had loose black pants on, a black long-sleeved shirt, with a black multi-pocket vest. On his belt was the holster for his gun, a walkie-talkie, and a Taser.

I almost cried out in joy. A Taser. Not much amperage, but 50,000 volts. That could do it. I had trouble making my eyes leave his belt and return to his face. I wanted that Taser like a drunk wants his first drink of the day.

Another thought occurred to me seeing that Taser. I'm not the only prisoner. If I was, they wouldn't have those. It's too dangerous to have them around me.

"Step away, right now." He lowered his gun, pointing it at my leg. He wasn't going to try to kill me, but he was willing to shoot me.

I took a deep breath and nodded slowly but didn't let go of the electricity yet. It wasn't much, just a few crumbs to a starving man. But it was something.

"What's your name?" I asked. "Tell me your name and I'll let go."

He blinked and looked up and to the right. He was going over his orders in his head. Knowing that he wasn't supposed to interact with me at all. But maybe preserving my life was a higher priority.

"Evan," he said as if revealing a secret. "Evan Saunders."

I still held onto the wire. "You married or got a girlfriend? Any kids?" Evan was about 5'10" and strong, with black hair, a square jaw, and pale green eyes. He was somewhere in his early thirties.

"Let go of the wires," he said. "Now!"

I bit my lip, hard. I had made a deal and it was hard to not do it. To not let go like I had said I was. "Just answer that question. I'll let go then. I promise."

"I had a girl but then I went to Iraq," he said, his voice even, but his eyes flicking around. "She didn't wait for me."

I almost smiled. Not because of his sad story, but because he was human. I was so relieved. He wasn't just a square-jawed beefy boy anymore. He was Evan Saunders with green eyes, the Iraq vet that missed his girl.

"Sorry about that, Evan," I said as I lowered my hands.

He gave me a sharp nod as he backed up. One of the other guards backed out of the room and came back with the long pole with the handcuffs on it. Evan held his gun on me while the other guard pointed the alien energy weapon at me. The third guard held the pole and got close enough so it was right in front of me.

"No," I said, looking from the handcuffs to Evan. "I think I know my way back to my cell by now."

"You have to," Evan said.

"I don't think I do," I said.

Evan held his finger to his ear and I noticed a black earbud in there. A thin wire snaked down to his walkie-talkie. He was receiving orders. "Very well," he said. "Let's go."

15 / YOU MUST SURVIVE

WILLIAMS STAYED TWO MORE NIGHTS. EACH NIGHT WE drank. Each night we signed. On our flagstone patio under the bright stars, our isolated high-desert home feeling less and less safe.

He made it clear to us that Project Vulcan was in place, that the powers that be were nervous about our current activity. He didn't know exactly what should be done, but he said that we needed to get to the bomb and do "something" about it.

That something was what was at question. Disarming it made sense, but I was no bomb expert. And could I really spend time on the internet learning about them? Wouldn't our guards figure that out? They listened to us, they watched us, surely they monitored our digital activity.

During those next two days we dug. Williams volunteered for the hard duty of helping us break ground. He grumbled and complained about the location, told us we should move it—again playing his part for our audience—but he swung a pick and wielded a shovel. He wasn't fast, but he was steady. Damn impressive for his age.

That last night, Licia brought up what I didn't want to talk about. We were back to Williams's Whiskey (as we had come to call it). Our mood was somber. We were physically tired, and for my part I wasn't ready to see him go. It had been nice to have company.

We were out on the patio, a fire blazing, and for once we weren't talking (verbally) very much.

What if we stop? No writing. No interviews, Licia signed.

I shot back some whiskey and grimaced. I didn't know if that was a life I could go back to.

Williams looked at me, a grim smile on his angular face. He rubbed at his brush-cut, a gesture so old and so familiar it made me smile despite myself. *Let's face facts*, he signed. *He's not going to do that, so I didn't bring it up.*

Licia looked at me, her brown eyes hard. She didn't need to sign. The question was obvious.

He's right, I signed.

"The smoke's a little much," Licia said, getting up. "I'm going to get some air." She walked quickly away towards the site of our excavation.

A noisy sigh escaped my lips.

"Glass is empty, I see," Williams said, refiling it.

It's too much, I signed.

That it is, he signed back.

What do I do?

You must survive, he signed. *The world may need you again.*

I groaned noisily and got up, those words curdling into something sour in my stomach. I was sick of people needing me to survive. I was sickened by being thought of as a savior, a hero. I know we would have failed without Colonel Williams and so many others, I just happened to be the one with some raw power. I couldn't stand the thought of anyone else sacrificing themselves for me, too many had already.

"I'm going to go check on Licia," I mumbled. I left Williams there and walked out into the night. The moon wasn't up yet and it was dark, the stars bright pinpricks of light above. I couldn't see very well, but I knew the way. I smelled her before I saw her. Alcohol mingled with sweat and the sour smell of fear. She hadn't been Lightningirl for a while so the ozone scent of her was missing.

My eyes were adjusting and I found Licia at our excavation site. It wasn't much yet, just a rectangle about eight feet on a side and two feet deep. We had a long way to go. My muscles ached from the digging, but it was a good ache.

I walked up next to her and just stood there. We needed to talk, to have the kind of long conversations we had had so many times in our relationship. The kind that starts on one topic and meanders for hours, that goes around and around a problem until you can finally see it, can finally talk about it. The kind of insight that can only come from a long talk with someone you love.

But we couldn't do that. We now knew we were being watched, recorded, and evaluated. 24/7. That we had no privacy. That this beautiful home we had built was just as much a prison as that twelve-by-twelve cell that they had thrown me in after the Hoover Dam incident.

Licia slipped her hand into mine and squeezed it hard.

"I love you," I said, hoping that those three words conveyed what I needed them to. That I was sorry that I had gotten us into this mess but didn't know what else to do. I've had my freedom taken away before and I couldn't keep living this way.

"I love you too," she said, her voice low and rough.

"I... I've been thinking about that Diane Madison interview," I said. It was a risk to say anything directly, but I had to say something. "Maybe we shouldn't. She's not the most trustworthy woman."

Licia snorted. "No argument there. But I disagree. We should do it. We need to get out of our shell here a little." She squeezed my hand hard again. She was telling me it was okay, that we would figure it out.

Without a word we walked hand and hand back to Colonel Williams. We made good use of his whiskey, our laughter ringing out into the night, and sent him off in style.

SUMMER AND FALL 2005, LOCATION UNKNOWN

"CAN YOU TELL ME ANYTHING ELSE ABOUT EVAN SAUNDERS?" I asked Ronald. He had asked me about the meditation work, but I was done with letting everyone else set the direction down here.

"Evan?" he asked, his wrinkled face putting on an impressive show through the bars as his forehead furrowed.

I nodded. "He's one of the guards. We met during yesterday's little incident."

Ronald looked briefly puzzled, like he didn't know what I was talking about. Then his face relaxed and he said, "With the camera?" he asked.

"How many exciting things happen down here every day?"

He chuckled. "Not many."

"So, what do you know about him?" I asked.

Ronald shrugged. "He's a soldier, follows orders, is from the south, loves soccer."

I nodded and smiled. It wasn't much, but a tiny bit more about Evan, making him a tiny bit more human.

"And the meditations?" Ronald asked.

"They suck," I said. And they did. The book talked about how you could get to this point where the mind shut up, but I hadn't. This morning's attempts were filled with remembering the incident in interrogation and wondering about Evan.

"Good," Ronald said and turned to go.

"You got a girl, Ronald?" It was the same question I had asked Evan, but Ronald's age made it sound a little awkward.

He turned, one eyebrow raised, his hand rubbing at his bald head.

"Or a guy, for that matter," I added. "Do you have somebody?"

He smiled, but it was bitter and wistful, his dark eyes darting away from mine. "She died."

"I'm sorry," I said.

I could see the emotions playing across his face. Pain, regret, grief. It was like looking at the foamy chop of a big lake on a windy day. I knew there was a lot more below the surface.

I felt for him, missing Licia as I was, but the added evidence of humanity down in this hole was uplifting.

"Maybe you need to meditate," I offered.

He chuckled and with a wave left me.

I went back to the wool blanket in the middle of my cell, crossed my legs, and tried to center myself.

IT HAPPENED SLOWLY. AT FIRST, I WASN'T AWARE IT WAS happening, that time had slipped by in the oddest way. I'd be sitting there on that scratchy wool blanket in the middle of my cell fighting to stay present with my breath, to note my thoughts and just let them go, and suddenly it would be later in the day.

No clock down there. No real sense of day or night except the light being on or off. It was my stomach that was my best guide to time. And my little meditations would last longer without seeming longer, my stomach clock told me the truth.

At first it was so subtle that I didn't notice. But then it became obvious. Dinner was coming much sooner than I thought it should (but not my stomach).

The meditations still sucked, my thoughts still ran around my head holding riots of guilt, grief, and condemnation. But time started to slip by more smoothly.

And when you are stuck in a cell with no one to talk to, that is a wonderful thing.

"You seem happy today," Ronald said after I had been trying my meditations for a month, maybe longer. I couldn't track the days very well either. I was pretty sure another season had passed outside while I sat in this cell learning about my mind. Summer to fall, and while part of me despaired that I would never leave, none of that mattered for those precious moments when I could really meditate.

I shrugged. I didn't feel happy. I had all the same problems. But I did feel a little lighter. As if the burden of the loneliness and isolation weren't so bad.

"Got a Grisham for you today," he said, putting a book in the pass-through. "*A Time to Kill*. It's his first novel."

"Thanks, Ronald. You're a good man."

Ronald did a half-snort that sounded like he doubted my declaration.

"You are," I insisted. I had noticed that he took back all the fiction I had been reading until I really started to meditate, then he would let me keep a few of my favorites. When he wanted me to meditate, he gave me nothing else to read. His ability to get me to do something good for myself made him the best kind of man.

Ronald gave me a weary smile on his aged face. "Don't know about that, but thanks."

"What do you mean?" I asked.

He stepped right up to the bars, his brown eyes locking with mine. I was standing in my cell a few feet back. He was my height so our eyes lined right up. "If I was such a good man, I wouldn't be stuck down here with you."

I stepped close and whispered, "Are there other prisoners down here." The Tasers the guards wore seemed to indicate there were.

His head bobbed up and down just the tiniest bit as he said, "Just you. All of this for you."

He turned and walked away.

"Why do they let you talk to me?" I called after him. It didn't make sense. It bugged me constantly. Our brief conversations and the books he brought me were lending me strength. They were helping me keep my secrets. Why would they do that?

Ronald didn't answer, he just held his hand up and waved without looking back.

17 / HUNGER

INTERROGATION TIME CHANGED AFTER THE INCIDENT WITH the camera. I would no longer wear the cuffs. This resulted in interrogation not happening for a few days. Evan Saunders and the other two guards had come for me as usual. Evan with a gun, another guard with the alien energy weapon, and the third with the handcuff pole.

"No," I said, looking at Evan. He had his dark sunglasses back on, his lips a tight thin line. "I'll go, but no cuffs."

They didn't speak, but when it was clear I wasn't going to cooperate, they left and didn't come back the next day.

When they did come back, Evan held up a sign at my refusal that said, "Cooperate or we will force you."

"Go ahead," I said.

They quickly departed. That night they didn't bring dinner and Ronald didn't show up. Punishment. I just meditated more.

The next day the same routine. I said no and they didn't feed me. And the next and the next.

The first two days, the constant gnawing in my stomach was

loud and unbearable. It just wouldn't shut up. Hungry. Hungry. Hungry. It's like my mind was a skipping record.

I took that into meditation and let it get as loud as it wanted. *We're going to die. We have to have food. Just put the cuffs on and they'll feed you.* On and on it went in endless variety. I just kept focusing on my breath, my eyes half slits gazing at the floor and the bars of my cell, noting the thoughts of hunger and letting them go.

I had meditated enough now to understand that most of my thoughts were boring and repetitive. I was still having the same thoughts I did before I started meditating, but I was taking them a lot less seriously. The good thoughts, the bad thoughts, and all the ones in between.

On the third day of this, I started to feel a lightness to my body and the hunger pangs stopped. I was surprised at first, I didn't expect it to feel good. The layer of belly fat that I still had was melting away—which was fine with me—but I knew that once the fat was gone this was going to start to get serious.

So I wasn't hungry physically, but I was worried.

I sat crossed-legged on that wool blanket and let those fears bounce around my head, just observing them as dispassionately as I could and coming back to my breath, my gaze soft, what I could see of my tiny cell, the bars, and the hallway blurry through my eyelashes.

I guess I could have stared at the wall, not had the bars of my cell in my field of view, but the cell door was the way out of here—it symbolized freedom.

No food. No Ronald. No voices but my own.

It drove me to meditate more and more. To seek solace in that still space between breaths.

The change, when it came, wasn't a lot, it wasn't like I suddenly felt a bolt of lightning come down from the sky and I suddenly knew everything. It was subtle, like every time I sat, every time I could endure my mind's jabbering, I would feel just a little lighter. Just a little bit better.

It didn't change my situation, it just made it bearable.

And fasting helped. A lot. My body wasn't digesting food anymore, and while I knew it would kill me long-term, short-term it just powered that sense of lightness.

I didn't care if Ronald came or if I got to talk to someone even if it was that bland voice of my interrogator. It didn't matter. I had my wool blanket. I had my breath. It was all I needed.

On the fifth day of my fast is when it happened. The guards had left, me having refused the cuffs yet again, and I sat down to meditate, knowing it would be another long day of isolation.

It was subtle at first. My eyes were a bit more open than usual, wanting to see more of the hallway and what it symbolized. I was staring at the wall at the end of the hallway where it turned to the right. There was a one-way mirror there and I knew there was a guard back there with an alien energy weapon.

When it happened, I could see something beyond the reflection of the mirror. I thought I could see that guard. Kind of.

He was in a sitting position, his body slumped forward, staring right at me.

I didn't think much about it. That meditative state is not about thinking. I just took another breath and watched. I was sure I was imagining it.

The figure I saw was just a ghostly outline in neon blue. He rocked back, rubbed at his face, and then leaned forward again. I hadn't thought much about my guards, about how boring it must be for them watching me all day long just in case I do something.

I let that thought go and went back to my breath. The guard resolved in more details. A neon-blue nimbus around him with thin veins of pulsing blue running through his body, a tight, bright nest of it in his head.

I took a deep breath and let out a long sigh. If I hadn't been so deep in my meditation, I would have questioned what I was seeing. I would have doubted myself. Well, I did doubt myself, and was fascinated by that too. But I just kept letting all those thoughts go.

They were just brief flickerings of the mind. I went back to the breath and kept meditating.

I don't know how long that meditation lasted. I was amused by what I had seen, but wasn't taking it seriously, wasn't seeing the possibilities. Yet.

ELECTROMAGNETIC ENERGY. IT'S WHAT LIGHTNINGIRL wields. It's what she can use to charge me when the neutron blast of an atomic reaction isn't available.

But it's all radiation. Electromagnetic radiation. Neutronic radiation. It's what I need to become Neutrinoman.

My fast lasted a total of ten days. During that time I lost about fifteen pounds and became as weak as a kitten. As I became weaker, I just meditated more. As I meditated more, I began to see more.

Ghostly blue lines snaking along the long hallway towards my cell. My guard behind the one-way mirror, a tracery of delicate blue lines with a blue nimbus around him, and a bright purple blotch of energy next to the guard representing the alien energy weapon, a thick pulsing blue line leading to it—they had figured a way to charge them up.

Pale blue auras around Evan Saunders and the other two guards, a bright blue splotch at their belts where their Tasers sat.

It was day ten of the fast and I sat on my wool blanket, my body weak but my sight strong. Evan had a grim look on his face. Evan, who likes soccer not football, who had a girl but she didn't wait for him while he was in Iraq. I thought these thoughts whenever I saw him. It gave me some small measure of comfort.

I let my soft, meditative gaze linger on him. I could see more than just the aura. I could see the tangle of blue in his head, and thin blue lines tracing their way throughout his body.

He unlocked the cell door, his gun trained on me the whole

time. One of the guards stepped forward holding the metal pole with the cuffs on the end. I just shook my head.

"Please," Evan whispered.

I looked at his eyes, but they were hidden behind the dark sunglasses. But no, I could see them now. Light blue orbs of energy, electromagnetic radiation, behind the plastic. I could see all of him. The bright blue of his pulsing heart, the solid blue trunk of his spinal column, nerve impulses racing back and forth, the dense, tangled blue of his mind.

I smiled. Electromagnetic radiation. He and the other guards were biological generators of this energy. I was a biological generator of it too. I looked down at my hand and saw the same delicate trace work of blue lines running through it and I laughed.

It all seemed so simple. I didn't need an external source of power to transform myself to Neutrinoman. I was that source of power. My body turned biological matter into electrical impulses to power my nervous system. It wasn't much power, but I figured it had to be more power than that damn camera I had tried to tap into.

"You've got to," Evan whispered.

I looked up, he was in the cell only a few feet away, the guard with the pole having backed off. His mouth was pulled down into a frown, his forehead creased, his gun lowered. He was worried about me. He was risking backlash by even talking to me. His voice had the slightest hint of a southern twang.

"Where are you from?" I asked, staring past the sunglasses into the blue tracery I could now see that were his eyes.

"They won't feed you until you collapse," he said. "Please, just let us cuff you and then they'll let us feed you."

Was I just being a stubborn fool? Was this line I had drawn an important one? In my starved and meditative state, such questions didn't mean much to me.

"Georgia, maybe," I said, trying to figure out where he was from. "Or South Carolina."

"North Carolina," he said.

I nodded knowingly, like he had just told me something epically important. "You like soccer," I said, "not football."

His brow furrowed. "How do you know that?"

"Ronald told me," I said.

"Who's Ronald?" he asked.

"He brings me books. Talks to me." I smiled broadly at Evan. At this point what we were having seemed like a good long conversation.

My mind slipped back to powering my transformation to Neutrinoman. I was weak, but still electricity flowed through my nervous system. Electromagnetic radiation emanated from Evan and the other guards, from the lights above. It seeped out of the power lines embedded in the walls. It was everywhere.

And then I found it.

"You better take a step back," I said to Evan.

"Why?" he asked.

"I don't want to hurt you," I said calmly.

He slowly rose, his gun trained on me as he stepped out of the cell.

I took it all in. The blue lines of electromagnetic radiation everywhere. Delicate lines running through the bodies of the guards. Bright balls of it where their Tasers were. A purple blob of it on the back of the guard with the alien energy weapon.

They look scared. I didn't blame them.

"Relax, boys," I said. "I'm not going to go anywhere, just going to prove a point."

I took a deep breath. I reached deep for that place within me. The trigger that turned me to Neutrinoman. I flipped the switch and...

And everything went black.

INTERLUDE 1: THE PAST

I have found that taking a long look at one's own past is not a comfortable thing. At least not for me. We tend to see our failures clearly and our successes, while seen, aren't dwelled on. Probably human nature, but this process is not comfortable.

I don't look back on my prison time fondly, but I managed to stumble into some things that proved to be very important. But it's the stumbling, fumbling nature of my performance here in the prison, and really throughout this story, that is becoming hard to watch. It's one thing to know I was faking it all those years, it's entirely another to record it in minute detail.

And sitting here typing away, having the perspective of time and not being in that difficult situation, I find myself having less compassion for the 2005 me than I probably should.

Couldn't I have just transformed into Neutrinoman my first day and flew out? Couldn't I have resisted my interrogator, not let that way-the-hell-too-steady voice get into my head? Couldn't I have been stronger?

Hindsight isn't really 20/20, is it? Twenty years later I am looking at my past as realistically as I can, but I am not that struggling young man that I was then.

Licia, who has a bad habit of reading over my shoulder when I write, just said, "No, dear, you're a struggling older man," with a merry laugh.

While I can see more clearly what was happening, what is less clear is who I was.

I think what I am trying to say is that while time has given me the distance of perspective, it has also dulled the empathy I used to have for that me.

Maybe the same is true for you as you reflect on your past. And I've been doing so much of it I have a bit of advice, if you will indulge me. Be gentle with yourself. You were doing the best you could no matter what it looks like now.

I was doing the best I could back then. I know that. I still wish I had done better.

But, frankly, here in 2025 things are anything but stable for Licia and I, so one kind of danger is past, but another kind is on us. I sit here typing away at my wife's insistence so I hopefully get my head on so we can take on this new challenge, find a new life. Again.

I need to take my own advice and be gentle with myself, I just don't know if we have that luxury.

I SAW HIM THROUGH THE WALLS FIRST, THAT BRIGHT BLUE trace work that is the electromagnetic radiation of a human body. The room I had awakened in wasn't my cell. It was a small room with two beds, white cabinets, a sink, and bright fluorescent lights. The infirmary.

I was strapped to one of the beds, an IV slowly dripping fluids into me. I couldn't move much, but I didn't care. I felt energy returning to my starved body. I could see the blue. A halo around the lights, a blue line leading through the ceiling to them.

I turned my head as much as I could to the closed door of the room. I could see the line of blue that brought electricity to the room, the lines of it snaking to the two cameras mounted at two corners of the room. Outside the room, on the other side of the door stood a guard. I could tell because of the ball of blue at his side, a Taser.

And I saw my visitor approaching before I heard his steps or saw the doorknob turn. He was tall and slim without a Taser at his side, so I didn't think he was a guard.

"And how are we feeling?" he said as he entered the room. His voice smooth and even and so very familiar to me. The voice of my interrogator.

He was tall, with sharp cheekbones, green eyes, and grey hair. He wore a white coat, like a doctor, over a white shirt and blue tie. He was neither the short bald man nor the smiling handsome man I had imagined him to be.

"Weak," I answered as I studied him. I still had the sight so it was a bit strange looking at him. The blue lines everywhere, the aura around him.

"Not to worry. You'll be feeling better soon." He was fitting a blood pressure cuff around my arm.

I felt my cheeks flush as I watched him. He wasn't a handsome man or an ugly one, just a regular person, if a bit older than I imagined. But I was mad. He was the one that had asked me all those questions. He was the one that seemed to be in charge. He was the one that had done this to me.

As my anger grew, the blue lines faded away and my vision returned to normal. My state was anything but meditative.

"Are you the one who decided to withhold the food?" I asked. "To do this to me?"

He pulled the blood pressure cuff off, his green eyes connecting with mine. I saw what looked like compassion on his face, but I didn't believe it. "I am," he said with a nod. "I am in charge down here, so it all falls to me." His shoulders slumped as if demonstrating the weight of his burden.

"Why?" I asked.

He sighed and pulled up a stool, slumping down onto it. "You were not cooperating. We needed you to cooperate." He said it as if it were as simple as a math equation. One plus one equals two. You don't cooperate, we withhold food.

"Needed?" I asked, noticing his use of the past tense.

He nodded. "We're releasing you as soon as you are well enough to travel."

I blinked and stared at him, imagining something much worse than this coming next. "Why?"

He smiled, but it was a bitter thing. "The military needs you back in action. From what I've heard there's been some 'chatter' that is disturbing them. For my own part, I believe we were very close to a breakthrough, but..."

"But what?" I asked.

He smiled again, but this time it looked wistful. "Well... This Ronald thing has gotten to be quite disturbing." His tone was still as even as ever, but his mouth puckered into a frown.

"What about Ronald?" I asked. "You sent him to me."

He looked away and shook his head. "I'm afraid that we didn't."

"What?" Ronald with his calming, elegant presence. Ronald who brought me novel after novel and that meditation book. Ronald who would make eye contact with me and talk to me. Ronald who made my stay bearable. It made no sense. "Who sent him?" I asked.

He leaned close, his tone low as if sharing a secret. "I'm sorry to tell you this, but there is no Ronald."

19 / THE BOMB

AFTER COLONEL WILLIAMS LEFT US, LIFE AT CASITA DE Soledad became somewhat stilted. Licia and I dug during the day, slept at night, attended to the plants and the many other things that you have to do when you live off of the grid. We didn't talk much, not about important things. We tried to keep up our normal banter but soon let that go as our fatigue from digging built up. We figured that would be enough cover for our watchers.

At first, under the stars at night, we would sign like we did with Colonel Williams, but soon we stopped doing that. There was nothing left to say. We were in an untenable situation and we didn't know how to get out of it.

So we dug our root cellar, the threat from Project Vulcan looming, and I did my best to reestablish my meditation practice.

Meditation is something that can be wonderful and amazing, but it has its price. You might not think so, I mean, you're just sitting there breathing, how hard can that be? Well, in this case, very hard. Meditation makes you confront yourself, your doubts and your fears.

And I had a lot of them out there in the high desert of central Arizona. I half expected them to trigger the bomb just because we were close. I began to have trouble sleeping, afraid that they would wait until they knew we were asleep and we were vulnerable and then just trigger it.

Boom! No more Neutrinoman and Lightningirl. No more powerful superheroes that are hard to control.

But I kept at it. I kept digging. I kept meditating. Until it was enough.

When the sight came, I was actually digging. Weeks had passed and the hole was six feet deep. I was working with a pick and shovel, filling a bucket, and Licia was raising it up out of the hole and disposing of it.

Physical labor can be meditative if you let it. Your breath becomes important, the stress to your body makes you let go of most of the babble of your thoughts—they're just not important—and you are just *there*.

I had slipped into it rather on accident. One of the basic tenets of meditation is that you don't chase thoughts away, you just know they are going to come up and you let them go. And that is what I had been doing for hours as I dug and Licia hauled. Just the effort and the rhythm of it, the heat and the work, time slipping away without me being very aware of it.

And then I saw it. A dim glimmer of purple far below me. It was small in my sight, but I could see its power. A purple ball of contained energy, waiting to be released.

I had thoughts about it. How far is it? Can I even dig that far? They'll know if I'm getting close. But I went back to my breath and let those thoughts go. I kept digging. I kept looking, as I moved around the pit, and I got a better idea of the bomb's location. We were off a bit. It looked to be about ten feet north of the pit and about fifty feet down.

Later I created a fire out on the patio and Licia and I signed under the moonlight, the cooling air a comfort after a long, hot day.

I told her I had found it and where it was.

What now? she signed.

I shook my head. *We can't dig that far by hand.*

You could get there quickly as Neutrinoman, she signed.

They would know. They would trigger it, I signed.

You could survive it.

I shrugged.

In the flickering yellow firelight, her face fell. I could relate, my stomach was rebelling against our dinner. I think maybe I had held out hope that Williams had been wrong. That Project Vulcan wasn't real, that our watchers wouldn't be willing to sacrifice us if we got far enough out of line.

All that time in prison sitting in that room being asked questions by my faceless interrogator came tumbling back on me. I wasn't isolated here like I was there, but it was similar.

I can't live this way, I signed.

She nodded, her lips a thin line, her face grim.

I stood up and pulled her close, hugging her fiercely.

"You need to leave," I whispered in her ear. "Zap out of here now."

She pushed away far enough to look in my eyes. I don't know what she saw, but her own eyes widened and her mouth opened. "Don't do anything stupid," she whispered.

"I can't live this way," I said.

"And I can't lose you," she replied.

That stopped me short. I was willing to risk my own life, but not hers.

"I'm not leaving," she added. "Whatever we do, we do together."

I nodded and took her hand, leading her through the moonlight towards the power lines. She squeezed my hand hard. We had done this before, gone into battle together, faced our enemies side by side, not knowing if we would survive.

We would live or we would die, but we would do it together.

When we got close to the power lines, we both transformed without a word. She extended her left hand, pulling a crackling bolt of lightning from the high-tension power lines, the energy flowing through her right hand into me, lighting up the night, throwing eerie shadows out across the desert.

"How much do you want?" she shouted.

"As much as you can give me!" I replied. "We're going to dig that thing up. One way or another this will be over tonight."

There is no Ronald. Strapped to that bed in the Q-morph prison infirmary, thoughts swirled through my head as fast as a tornado, whipping by at fierce speeds only to be quickly replaced by another thought. But there was a monotony to those thoughts, a uniformity that resolved into one thing: I am crazy.

My interrogator had explained in his calm voice that there was no one named Ronald down here. That they didn't employ an older black man. That they had been disturbed by all the conversations I had had with my "imaginary friend."

I didn't believe him. I got angrier until he grabbed a laptop and started showing me footage of me in my cell.

As the footage played, I'm slumped on my bunk and look up surprised and said, "Who are you?"

The camera changed to one from the back of the cell clearly showing me and the bars of my cell. I was alone. This was the moment I met Ronald.

On the screen I have a shocked look on my face. I said, "Um...

yeah..." got up, stuck my hand through the bars and shook the empty air. "I'm Nik."

My mind turned to mush as he showed me clip after clip. Me having conversations with the thin air. Me sitting in my bunk appearing to turn pages of a book that isn't there. Me sitting on my blanket in the middle of a cell on that scratchy wool blanket pantomiming the reading of a book before taking a heavy breath and flexing my shoulders.

I can't think. How could this be possible? I had never read any Jack Reacher novels, yet I could tell you the plots of the many that Ronald had brought me. I could describe to you exactly what Ronald's face looked like, the melodic timber of his voice, the slightly yellowish color of his teeth.

"But... I..." I said, my voice thick and pleading, so much so that I couldn't stand it.

My interrogator took a deep breath and let out a sigh. "It is concerning, isn't it?"

I looked at him. There was a sparkle in his eye. The bastard was enjoying this.

"Maybe we should go back to this Byte woman," he intoned, just like I was in the interrogation room. "Surely there is something else you can tell me about her."

I surged against my restraints, I wanted to hurt him. I wanted to punch him, to throw him across the room, to beat him until the tone of his voice showed some emotion. But I couldn't. I was strapped to the bed and could barely move at all. An inelegant grunt escaped me.

"Or we could talk about the conversation you had with Toxicwasteman after the breach of the Hoover Dam," he said calmly.

He hadn't told me that Ronald wasn't real or shown me that footage for my own benefit. He had done it to further unbalance me, to break me, to get me to spill the secrets he knew I was keeping.

He was cruel. And right then and there, I would have preferred

Tom Tyree over him. I would have rather been his prisoner. Tom's motives and methods were at least clear. This man was something I didn't understand and something I didn't want to understand.

My mind slipped back to when I was in the cell. When Evan Saunders actually talked to me. When I was convinced that I had found a way to turn into Neutrinoman without a nuclear reactor. When I had tried and blacked out and ended up here.

I turned away from my interrogator and took a deep breath, letting my eyes half close and staring up at the ceiling of the infirmary. He kept talking but his voice was just like the tornado of thoughts running through my head. I let them go and focused on my breath. I wanted to find that place again and hoped that now that I was a bit healthier, I could manage the transformation. That I could turn into Neutrinoman. That I could escape this prison and this man I had come to hate so much.

EMPATHY. IT'S AN IMPORTANT SKILL TO HAVE. ALSO, realizing that everyone is the hero of their own story. Tom Tyree, my interrogator when I was in prison, and whoever had their finger on the trigger of Project Vulcan. They had reasons to do what they were doing.

Maybe it was because I had just meditated, but after Licia charged me and we walked back to the excavation site, I tried to imagine the person that had conceived of and controlled Project Vulcan.

They must believe that we could easily become more of a threat than anything that we might be called to defend against. And I could see that. If Licia and I decided to go all Bonnie and Clyde, it would be bad.

They must believe that the alien threat is done, despite how things turned out.

They must be afraid of what we could do to usurp the status quo.

Having empathy doesn't mean you don't defend yourself. As

we walked, her electric hand in my neutrino hand, our yellow and blue-white glow lighting up the desert, I understood their motivation. I was hoping whoever was watching would understand mine.

"What should I do?" Licia asked. We were on the edge of the pit staring down. Now that it was time, we both were hesitating.

I looked at her scintillating face, at the worry there. "Stay alive," I said. She gave me a wan smile and nodded. I looked back to the home we had built with our own two hands. "We might lose everything, you know."

"The only thing I need is you," she said. It was sappy and romantic and filled my heart with joy. I kissed her, our bodies doing their energy exchange, taking our passion and our love and our worry and multiplying it. We took our time with that kiss, not knowing, yet again, if there would be another. When it was done, I jumped into the pit.

I took a deep breath and calmed myself. I don't have to breathe in the normal sense as Neutrinoman. I don't need the oxygen. But it helps even in my q-morph form to calm me. It took a few minutes but the sight came back, only more powerfully. I could see the purple ball of energy down and over. I could see a tiny line of blue leading to it—some kind of power or communication running to the east.

I went to the north edge of our pit, ramped up my reaction, and started melting the earth around me. I took my time. I knew they knew what I was doing. This was more about seeing if they had the will to pull the trigger. If preventing us from discovering it was more important than our lives.

Still, it was only fifty feet. It didn't take long. I melted a roughly cylindrical tunnel straight down and then I broke into a cavern. It was small, maybe ten feet in diameter, and there in the middle of it was an odd-looking shape, basically rectangular, but with a few non-right angles all covered in gleaming stainless steel. It was about the size of a VW Bug. Project Vulcan.

The cave didn't look natural. It had a uniform shape that made it look like it was mechanically excavated. There were metal supports lining the ceiling and unlit bare lightbulbs attached to the supports.

And beyond the cave, which was lit by the flickering yellow of my neutrino reaction was a tunnel, and I could faintly hear voices.

THE DRONE OF MY INTERROGATOR WENT ON, THE ASSAULT OF my own doubts and fears continued, time slowly slipped past as my half-slitted eyes gazed at the fluorescent light above, my body relaxed on the infirmary table, my ankles and wrists strapped securely.

Meditation is hard work. Really hard. It may not sound like it or look like it, but it is. In many ways I find it similar to running. Getting started on it is difficult, painful, and taxing, but once you get over the hump it remains hard, but it is rewarding. The meditator's high, if you will.

Meditating when some sick bastard is trying to break you, keeps reminding you that the man you've been interacting with for the last six months wasn't real, is all too happy to keep proving it to you, wants nothing more than to break your spirit, is beyond difficult.

But the level of difficulty was irrelevant, though. I had to do it. I had to calm myself and reach deep inside and find that trigger, turn myself into Neutrinoman.

While he continued to ask me about Byte and Tom Tyree and

the base they took me to, and the other members of LoVE I had met, I kept meditating, focusing on my breath, on that sensation as air passed in and out of my nose. While I worried that he would go nuts and kill me, that I would never see Licia again, or that if I did, she would either have not waited for me or not want me anymore. I kept letting those thoughts go and focused on my breath. While I worried about the alien threat to our planet and how powerless I was to do anything about it, I kept breathing deeply and evenly.

Our view of how our minds should work (neat, clean, and orderly) and how they really work (a chaotic swirl of everything from hope to despair several times a second) had become clear to me. That is the one thing I gained from Ronald (real or not) and my time in prison and my time reading *A Gradual Awakening* (real or not).

The human mind is a messy thing that by some miracle ends up working.

As I kept letting go and kept breathing, my body relaxed. I found myself not resisting my interrogator but becoming more open. So open that his words just passed right through, becoming insubstantial ghosts.

I felt the air flowing through my nose as it made its way into my lungs. I felt my belly expand with each inhale and grow relaxed with each exhale. I noticed the smooth texture of the sheet below me and the slight breeze from the room's ventilation.

Slowly I noticed a blue nimbus around the fluorescent lights, then I could see a pulsing in the ceiling of the wire that brought power to the light. I didn't dwell on it, I went deeper.

I heard the guard outside the infirmary door shifting his position, taking a deep breath, and sighing. My hearing became even better than normal.

I could feel the radiation emanating from the fixture. Visible light and electromagnetic radiation. Electromagnetic radiation coming from the man next to me.

I opened up to it. I breathed it in. I am Neutrinoman. I am the power of the split atom itself. Radiation is everywhere. It is enough to trigger my transformation.

And there it was. That switch. I could turn right then and there. I knew it. I finally had it.

"What did Tom Tyree tell you on the way to Yellowstone?" he asked. "We should go back there to the first time you were alone with him. Maybe that is where it all started."

His words didn't mean much to me and they were still smooth and steady, but in my state of heightened awareness I could hear the tension below the surface, I could smell his fearful sweat. He was about to fail. He was desperate.

It wasn't a thought, not really, it was more of a sense of empathy for my captor and a knowing that if I turned with him this close, I would hurt him, maybe kill him. A few minutes ago, that would have been fine with me, but now that I had heard and smelled his fear, I hesitated. His failure would have personal ramifications. Did he really deserve to die?

I was aware he had moved away from the bed, but it wasn't important. I was following my breath, letting go of my thoughts, trying to stay deep enough to flip that switch. So when I felt the prick at my arm, I was surprised.

"Shhh," he said, a wicked smile on his face. "Chemical inducements were forbidden—we mustn't risk real damage to our mighty superhero. But who could have imagined you'd fracture like this with your invisible friend and all? We don't have much time left, so what can it hurt? We'll let this be our little secret."

The syringe had a clear liquid in it and he quickly injected it. I felt a slithering cold invade my artery as my blood started mixing with the clear substance. What was it? His green eyes were alight. His mouth forming a childlike smile.

I knew I didn't have much time. I reached for that switch that would turn me into Neutrinoman. I flipped the switch. I triggered the transformation.

I AM A QUANTUM METAMORPH. I CHANGE AT A QUANTUM level, every cell in my body becomes this different thing. My basic structure is the same: two arms, two legs, two eyes, a lung cavity. But the function becomes different. I become a nuclear reaction, not a biochemical one.

When I am strong, fully powered, the transformation can be fast, like a fire through a parched forest. And when I am weak the transformation can be very slow, starting at a single point and spreading a millimeter at a time like a slow water leak on a bathroom floor.

In that underground prison with my interrogator desperate and injecting me with a clear substance, my point of focus was on that injection, that slithering sensation of cold. That is where the transformation started. The inside of my right elbow.

I was in a strange state. Half scared, half meditative. The threat seemed real and distant at the same time.

My nose was still biological, so I smelled the sharp scent of my neutrino-self combined with the smokey smell of the sheet below my arm starting to smolder.

My interrogator's eyes widened, and he stepped back. "No..." he muttered, some emotion finally entering his voice.

I kept breathing, kept willing myself to transform. First the inside of my elbow, then the yellow swirl of my neutrino form traveled down my arm to my wrist, the restraints there starting to smolder.

It was going so slowly. I needed to be out of here, I needed to be free.

Curiosity bloomed on his face, his green eyes going to my changed arm, his back against the infirmary's counter. "Did I do that?"

I almost laughed. He thought the injection had changed me, not my will. With the transformation starting there, I could see how he got that idea. I didn't correct him. I kept focusing on my breath, focusing on my transformation. My transformed right hand broke free of the restraint, smoke now visible in the air. I ripped off my other restraints and stood as my body continued its slow transformation, my grey prison jumpsuit starting to smolder.

"I'm leaving now," I said. I was still transforming, my right arm and leg now a pulsing yellow, the rest of me still flesh, my clothes burning off me. It was a strange feeling, this slow-motion transformation.

"I don't think so," he said with a grin.

A blaring alarm went off as I heard the slap of boots on the floor outside the room. At the same time the sprinklers above us opened up and water started raining down on us.

Two more breaths and the transformation was finally complete. I no longer felt the water that fell on me only to sizzle away as steam.

"Get out of my way. I don't want to hurt you," I said.

"We both know that's not true." He was standing in front of the door, daring me to go through him, daring me to hurt him.

While I was fully transformed, my reaction was low and tenuous. I didn't feel my normal Neutrinoman self.

I shrugged, turned to the nearest wall and plunged my hand into it and started cutting through.

I didn't have much of a plan besides escape.

My interrogator opened the door and let the guards in. It was the usual three. Evan Saunders with a rifle this time, the ubiquitous M4 carbine the military loves, and the two other guards with alien energy weapons.

"Stand down," Saunders yelled at me over the fire alarm, the water soaking through his black clothing.

I turned to them. "I don't want to hurt anyone. Just let me go."

"Can't do that," Evan said. He was back to being a soldier with orders. What he would do wasn't going to change by me giving a speech.

"Okay," I said, stepping away from the small hole I had made in the wall. I could see that there was a supply room on the other side. "But you'll have to do something for me."

"Stand down," Evan said. "Now!"

I ignored him and backed up to the bed I had been strapped down to. "All I want is to talk to Colonel Williams. If you can guarantee a face-to-face with him, I will cooperate."

Evan glanced at the other two soldiers. My interrogator was gone, he had slipped out of the room after the soldiers came in. They all looked scared. "Fire," Evan shouted and I ran for the hole I had created.

SUMMER 2025, CASITA DE SOLEDAD, CENTRAL ARIZONA

"WHAT SHOULD WE DO?" LIGHTNINGIRL ASKED, LOOKING AT the bomb that sat below our high desert home. There wasn't much to see, just a large, roughly rectangular shape covered in stainless-steel plates sitting in a rough-hewn cavern. No "Project Vulcan" on the side. No urgent red countdown lights. No switches or controls. I had flown up and brought her back down so we could investigate together.

"This thing has power running through it and leading to it," I said and then pointed to the thick black cable. "But it's not an active power." My sight, my EMV or Electromagnetic Vision, was still working. "There is an element to it that reminds me of the alien energy weapons, but I think there is more."

"Maybe you should open it up," she said.

I shook my head. "I heard voices before I came to get you. I say we leave this for now and find out what else is here."

She eyed the bomb again suspiciously and nodded. I took her hand, enjoying our energy exchange, and we slowly walked down the tunnel. I heard the faint voices again. They were low and urgent.

The tunnel was long, several hundred yards, and towards its end we could see light up ahead and I heard other sounds to go with the voices. The clacking of keyboards. Footfalls. The whisper of ventilation.

The tunnel stopped at an oversized metal door. I dampened down my reaction in my right hand and tried it. It was locked. The voices had stopped.

"What now?" I asked.

Licia shrugged and knocked on the door, the metallic clang echoing down the long tunnel behind us.

"I know you're there," I shouted. "I'd really rather not blast the door down."

There were furtive whispers, the sounds of boots, a scrape and a click as the door was unlocked, and then a groan as the big door was swung back.

When I saw who waited for us, my jaw dropped. It was Agent Peters, the Homeland Security agent that oversaw us. The bland, bald man that Licia charmed and I avoided as much as possible. The thorn in our side that insisted we fill out the proper paperwork and follow all the rules. I thought he was just a bureaucrat who got the crappy job of looking after us.

Licia didn't miss a beat, though. "I expect explanations, and I expect them now."

The room behind Peters looked like your average office building. Fluorescent lighting, linoleum on the floor, desks lining the walls with large monitors, it only lacked windows. The mundanity of it was very incongruent.

Peters looked back to the other three people in the room and then back at us. They were all dressed like him in black suits as the Homeland people always were. "Perhaps I should meet you back at your place," he said, his voice wavering.

"I don't know," I said to Licia. "I'd like a tour. Wouldn't you like a tour?"

"Yes, dear," she said with an electrical smile. "I'd like a tour too." She looked back to Peters. "Perhaps you can get us some robes or something so we don't do any damage while you show us around."

He didn't speak, his jaw silently moving. This was obviously not a contingency they planned for. "Alison," he said to a young, dark-haired woman I had seen a few times. "See what you can find our guests." She got up quickly and left through another door.

"Maybe we should all go wait by the bomb," I offered. "Or, maybe you should start telling us what is going on. Right now."

He went pale, which was quite satisfying, but didn't move.

"Come on, John," Licia said. "I think you owe us some sort of explanation."

His eyes were twitching back and forth between us. We were still in our q-morph forms, so maybe he was worried about radiation, maybe something else was going on.

A paranoid thought crept into my mind. What if he was stalling us until the bomb goes off. Maybe they were willing to sacrifice themselves too.

I thought back to the bomb. It had some of the latent energy of an alien energy weapon—that's how I saw it. Williams had characterized it more of an explosive device. It clicked in my mind. It was a huge alien energy weapon combined with a massive explosion. It would strip us of our powers so that the explosion would then kill us.

I squeezed Lightningirl's hand. "We're leaving now," I said to her and then turned to Peters. "Get your people out of here. I don't want anyone to get hurt."

"What? You can't..." Peters stammered.

"What is it?" Licia asked.

"Now!" I shouted at Peters. "We're coming in."

Peters's eyes kept ping-ponging between Licia and me. He

backed up a step but didn't go farther. The other two suits in the room were staring at us.

"Trust me, honey," I said. Her lips pursed, but she nodded. "Now get these people moving!"

She extended her right hand, tiny bolts of electricity stabbing out from her fingers to Peters and the other two agents. "You heard the man," she said. "We're leaving. Now! Lead the way."

With yelps of pain, the three of them scurried out of the room.

I closed the large metal door behind me and noticed that the entire back wall of this room was made of metal. It wouldn't be enough to shield from the blast, not completely. But it would be helpful if there was radiation involved. If the bomb had a nuclear component... well, a very small nuclear component.

Licia and the rest had left the room. I paused, looking at the flat screens. One had paused aerial footage of Licia and I digging the root cellar. Another showed the transcript of a recent conversation we had had. Yet another showed the exact route of a walk we had taken two days ago.

Anger welled up in me in this underground facility. It reminded me of the prison I had been "detained" in so many years ago. It brought back the sense of claustrophobia. I could almost hear the voice of my interrogator asking me about Tom Tyree and Byte.

With a cry, I shot each of the flat screens with a neutrino bolt, and then shot everything in sight. Sparks flew and a small fire started on one of the desks. I kept blasting, shouting words that I don't remember. When Lightningirl came for me, the room was dark except for the yellow glow of my reaction, the flickering of the fire, and the blue-white light her lightning form cast.

"Honey," she shouted. "We need to go!"

I could feel the tingle of her electrical touch, but I was far away. The remnants of fluorescent lights dangled from the ceiling. I blasted them into bits.

"Nik!" she shouted, pulling me towards the door and out of the room.

I would not be a prisoner, even in our lovely high desert home. I could not be a prisoner. Not anymore.

The thick bolt of lightning she struck me with got my attention. I looked back at her, her electrical hair haloed around her beautiful but worried face. She was tapping into the electrical supply of this facility, which must be considerable.

I took a deep breath. The hall behind her, again, looked like any other office building with linoleum and horrible fluorescent lighting that was flickering as Lightningirl drew power. It had a haze of smoke from the fires I had started, but was otherwise empty.

A small lightning bolt leapt out of the wall to her left hand. The power line must have been just below the surface. The wall was blackening and was now on fire too.

Another breath and I nodded.

"I want to bring this place down," I shouted so she could hear me above the crackle of the lightning. "Are they all out?"

She nodded, the worried look not leaving her face.

"Keep feeding me power." I turned my back to her and started blasting the ceiling as we walked backwards down the hallway. This was unacceptable. This I could not leave.

Rock fell as the hallway we had just left collapsed, dust engulfing us.

I had felt change was coming, but this was unlike anything I had imagined.

IN THE INFIRMARY OF THE Q-MORPH PRISON, THIS WAS NO longer me figuring out something crucial about my powers. This was now life and death. All three of them fired at once. Two alien energy weapons and one semiautomatic rifle.

As I hit the wall it slowed me down and two of the purple energy balls hit me. One in my right leg, one square in the back. I could feel my meager reaction dimming, my right leg going numb. Several bullets passed through me too, but this wasn't a problem. Yet.

Once the energy weapons turned me back to flesh, the bullets would matter.

Evan Saunders who likes soccer not football, whose girl didn't wait for him while he was in Iraq, was trying to kill me. This was war now. Could I take his life to preserve my own? A man who was just following orders?

And is that even an excuse? "Just following orders" has been used throughout the ages to justify a myriad of sins.

I was in a jumble in the supply room floor lying on top of metal shelves I had knocked over on my way through, rolls of toilet paper on top of me catching on fire. I shot several neutrino bolts through the hole in the wall up into the ceiling of the infirmary. At the same time purple energy balls came flying through the hole well above me.

The smoke was starting to get thick and the sprinklers went off in this room too. I rolled off the shelf, and staying low, made it to the door. My right leg was really slowing me down. While I blindly shot neutrino bolts through the hole, I looked at my leg. It was a duller yellow, the nuclear reaction there having slowed.

I had transformed without the tiniest bit of direct radiation, surely I could deal with this.

But there wasn't time. One of the soldiers peeked through the hole in the wall and fired, the coruscating purple energy ball flying right above my head. I fired neutrino bolts at him and he disappeared.

I needed a plan. I needed a way out. I needed a serious source of energy.

I yanked the door open, the metal melting under my brief touch, and hobbled out into the hallway.

They were ready for me. I didn't stand a chance.

FALL 2005, LOCATION UNKNOWN

DOWN IN THAT PRISON MADE FOR Q-MORPHS, FAR BELOW THE ground, two guards stood at each end of the hallway I had just hobbled out into, both of them pointing alien energy weapons at me. Big beefy boys dressed in black. Neither of them familiar to me.

They didn't wait. They didn't ask questions. They fired.

I went down, lying flat on the wet floor, steam rising up as my reaction touched the water from the sprinklers.

I felt the energy balls fly above me. It was a sensation very similar to the hairs on the back of your neck rising up. Except I had no hair, I was completely neutrino. I could feel their energy. I could feel my own energy wanting to go to it. Opposites attract. Those energy balls were the opposite of my neutronic energy somehow. That's why they affected me the way they did. I thought furiously about it. They were energy, surely there was a way for me to tap it, instead of its energy canceling out my own.

I didn't have long to think about it. Right after the energy balls passed above me, I heard high-pitched squeals coming from either end of the hallway and then there was an explosion.

The floor beneath me shook and I felt blast waves crash into me from either direction. I focused on maintaining my neutrino form, on remaining calm, remaining alive.

If I had been biological, I would have been dead. From the shockwave, from the heat.

Those energy balls that the alien weapons shoot don't always act the same. Well... they always tap my powers, but sometimes they explode on contact, like the first time I saw them in Yellowstone. I've also seen them do no harm whatsoever to physical objects. I also knew that they could fire orange energy balls that tapped Lightningirl's powers.

So when I heard the explosion, I was baffled at first. The coruscating purple color had been a bit pale, the variety that didn't do physical damage, so why would they explode?

From my prone position, I looked down the hallway. There wasn't much left of the guards and the floor. The walls and ceiling had been carved out in an eerily perfect, spherical shape, digging into the rock beyond the walls. I turned in the other direction and there was a spherical blast there too. I saw Evan and his two men coming out of the infirmary, shaking their heads, their eyes wide as they saw the guard's blast areas and what little was left of him. A hand, a foot with clean cuts, and no blood like they had been carefully cut off a department store dummy.

"What... What the hell?" Evan stammered.

"I didn't do it," I shouted. "They both shot those weapons at the same time... and... and..."

Evan wiped the falling water from his face and stared. This wasn't normal. He was trying to figure out what to do.

I was too. I decided to run.

THE BASE NEAR CASITA DE SOLEDAD WASN'T LARGE. THAT first room was the control room, and besides that it had a small kitchen, a dormitory, and some bathrooms and showers. And then a long hallway leading to a large garage.

I blasted all of it. Licia tried to stop me several times, but I couldn't do it. It was too much like that prison. I was too infuriated by what I had seen on those monitors.

We q-morphs had given all we could in our battle against the aliens, many of us our lives. We had saved the planet time and time again. It hadn't been perfect, and it hadn't been pretty, but this is how they rewarded us? Put us on our q-morph reservations and monitored our every move? Planted a bomb under us to take us out if we become a threat?

I had been so naïve to not expect that. I was mad at myself, not just them.

The garage was hidden in a cliff next to that poor excuse for a road that led to Casita de Soledad. We were less than a mile, as the raven flies, from our house, in a shallow canyon that Licia and I never roamed to, our wanderings keeping us closer to home and on more friendly terrain. I had always thought the agents had to drive a long way to get to us. But no. They had been in the neighborhood the whole time.

The agents were out of the garage and in their big black SUVs when we got there.

"Leave," I said to Peters who was standing in front of the first one. "I don't know what the radius of that bomb is, but I don't expect you want to be here when I deal with it."

"Stop now," Peters said, his voice calm, his spine erect. "The further you go, the worse this will be."

I walked up to him, banking my reaction way down. "I am going to give you some time to clear out. My wife is fond of you. But let me tell you this right now, this had best be the last time I see you."

His brow furrowed and his grey eyes pinched. "They are not going to like this," he said.

"Then have them come talk directly to me," I said. "Now go. I'll give you thirty minutes."

Peters's shoulders fell, and he got into the passenger's side seat of the SUV. The vehicles made their slow way down the road. I stood silently until they were out of sight.

When I turned back, I had the goddess of electricity staring at me, her stance wide, her hands on her hips. "You had best explain yourself," Lightningirl said.

FALL 2005, LOCATION UNKNOWN

As I ran down the hallway of my prison, my body the yellow motes of q-morph form, a purple energy ball clipped my left shoulder as I came to the pit that one of the explosions had created, I went tumbling in. It was a sphere about twelve feet in diameter, cutting deeply into the bedrock this facility was carved out of. I thought back to the guards' positions when I had come out into the hallway. They had been on either side of me in that long hallway.

Both guards had shot their energy weapons at me at pretty much the same time. I had ducked. The energy balls had gone over me and impacted the opposite guard.

That whining noise I had heard had been those huge power packs they wore on their backs. They had exploded and vaporized the guards and the hallway.

Shoot an alien energy weapon with an alien energy weapon and... boom.

There were bits of smoldering cloth and other things at the bottom of the pit that I didn't want to try to identify. I felt for the guards. I hated that they were dead, but this was not my doing.

As bullets and energy balls passed above me, I looked at the sides and top of the sphere. It was smooth like the blast had vaporized the rock, water dripping on me from above from the mostly sealed end of a water pipe. I was hoping for an escape route, but there was rock all around. I remembered the long elevator ride we had taken when they had brought me here. We were deep below the earth and I certainly didn't have enough power to tunnel my way out.

Casting about for a plan, I decided to fire neutrino bolts into the ceiling down the hallway, to create a barrier and buy some time.

I was about to proceed when I noticed that the firing had stopped. It was still noisy, water dripping on me and hissing up into steam.

"Nik, I have ordered my men to stop firing," my interrogator said, his voice smooth and confident. "I would like to talk before there is more loss of life."

"Tell me your name first," I shouted. "Your real name." It may seem like an odd request, but I needed some sliver of humanity from this man that had imprisoned me, isolated me, starved me, tried to drug me into talking.

There was a pause. I thought back to the interrogation room when I surmised that those pauses were him talking to his superiors, but when I had been in the infirmary, he had told me he was in charge. Maybe he just thought before he spoke.

The sprinklers suddenly shut off and the silence seemed vast, just the drip-drip of water.

"My name is Larry," he said.

"Tell me something about yourself, Larry." I said. The hallway was full of steam still and I couldn't see him.

"I don't see how that is—" he began.

"You said you wanted to talk," I said. "So let's have a conversation."

Another pause. "I like flowers," he said, a reluctance in his smooth voice as if talking about himself was painful. "I like to raise flowers."

I tried to imagine Larry with his green eyes and sharp cheekbones fussing over petunias or maybe orchids. The image was congruent, and I decided he was telling the truth.

"Thank you, Larry. So what is it you want to talk about?"

"I told you earlier you were going to be released." His voice was back to being as smooth as ever. "I wasn't lying. There is no need for this."

When he had injected me, it had been a desperation move. He wanted to get my secrets out of me before I left. Perhaps preserving his prison and his life had taken precedence over that need.

"What do you propose?" I asked.

"That you revert your form," he said. "That I walk you out of here right now."

"No," I said. "I don't trust you, Larry. You just tried to drug the truth out of me not ten minutes ago."

"And for that I am sorry," he said, the faintest trace of emotion in his voice. "I lost my way and won't try anything again."

I thought about it lying on the earth in the bottom of that sphere, my reaction low and tenuous. The water was gone, all having turned to steam.

"I want Saunders," I said. "I want to hear you give him orders to escort me out immediately, to not attempt me harm. And I don't want to see your face anywhere. Do you understand?"

Another pause. "Yes," Larry said. "I accept your terms."

That made me nervous. It was too easy.

I listened carefully as he issued orders to Evan and my other two regular guards. I didn't hear anything that bothered me, that might let them turn on me. And that really bothered me.

Our home seemed different after we walked back hand in hand, still in our quantum forms. It had a silence that made it feel like it had been abandoned for a long time. Our little adobe house, the two green houses, my tool shed, and the pit for the root cellar with its tunnel down to the bomb.

We stood there staring at that tunnel.

"Are you sure?" Lightningirl asked.

We had talked there in front of the base for a long time. I honestly expected them to trigger the bomb once their people were out of its radius. But they didn't. It had been an hour. It had been long enough for them to get clear.

I nodded. "We can't live this way, can we?" After I had explained how like the prison this was, she had agreed with my plan. I just wanted to hear her say again.

"No," she said, her jaw set. "We cannot."

"There will be consequences," I said.

"These are the consequences they brought on by doing this to us." The anger in her voice was palpable. I had told her what I saw on those screens, to what degree they had been monitoring us. Williams had told us as much, but seeing it made it that much worse, that much more real.

I nodded, walked over to our beautiful house that we built with our own two hands. I let go of my q-morph form before entering. I couldn't damage it, not directly, not intentionally. Licia followed, grabbing my hand after we entered. I felt eerily calm, and the sight, somehow, was still with me.

I quickly found the three cameras in our living room. I didn't have any idea if the feeds went beyond the destroyed base, but their presence was unacceptable. I pointed them out to Licia, she transformed just her right hand and she fried them, tiny lightning bolts jabbing from her finger to the cameras.

It didn't take long. We went through each room of the house and she destroyed any hidden electronics.

I felt the fool. I shouldn't have trusted them. I should have looked for them earlier.

And then finally, once we knew we were truly alone, I pulled the cookie tin from under our bed. It was a faded red with a picture of Santa Claus on it. I opened it up and pulled out the black metal case inside of it.

"One of Tom's many gifts," I said to Licia.

She smiled, a strained gesture, but didn't speak.

The black case was heavy and it clanged on our tile floor when I set it down. I opened it slowly, reverently. The walls of the case were thick, made of lead, and the inside compartment was small. Sitting there was a little black bag.

I pulled it out and poured the contents onto my hand. Little grey rocks, they didn't look like anything, but I could feel the energy in them, the power waiting to be unlocked.

They were from that LoVE base that I had visited and where Tom had tried to recruit me before I met the alien Sarah. These little rocks were uranium ore.

I stood and walked out of the house over to the pit.

"How much are you going to use," Licia asked.

We stood there naked under the summer sun. I knew they were watching now. They had cameras external to our house, but I didn't want to take the time to go find them and they certainly had drones, and what could I do about them?

Down through the dirt I could see the coiled purple ball of energy that was the bomb.

"All of it," I said as I turned into Neutrinoman. The uranium ore absorbing into my q-morph form.

This wasn't pure uranium, like what I had fallen in in the bottom of the pit in Yellowstone when we first encountered the aliens. But it was a significant charge. I hadn't felt this powerful in years. Not since I had had access to a nuclear reactor.

Licia changed to Lightningirl and I took her into my arms and flew straight up. Our property rapidly receded until we were about a thousand feet up. Everything looked small, like they were just toys, some kind of desert diorama made for a school project.

"Are you sure?" I asked her again. Sure that she was okay with me doing this. Sure that she wouldn't leave and get herself out of danger's way before I tried it. After Peters had left and I had explained myself, we had argued over this.

"I am still sure," she said. "We stand together, or we..." she trailed off, not finishing the thought.

"I love you," I said.

"I love you, too," she said.

I thrusted hard for several seconds then switched from thrusting to firing neutrino bolts. I rained hell down upon the pit we had dug, down the tunnel I had melted, all the way to that bomb.

It was time to be free.

THE SUN WAS BRIGHT, ITS RAYS HARSH ON MY EYES THAT HAD been underground and deprived of it for so long. But my skin, it reveled at the exposure of the UV radiation. I felt like a tourist coming out onto a Hawaiian beach after a long Midwest winter. The warm breeze felt like heaven compared to the stale recycled air down there.

Except I wasn't a tourist and this wasn't a vacation.

Evan Saunders and the other two guards had escorted me out of the prison. They had handguns and rifles, but no more energy weapons. After seeing what happened to the other guards, I couldn't imagine they wanted those energy packs on their backs.

I hadn't seen my interrogator, Larry, since we made our deal and the guards and I hadn't talked much on the long walk through the corridors or on the ride up the elevator. They had brought me another dull grey prison jumpsuit and I had put it on. I didn't have shoes, so I could feel every pebble under my feet.

The land was dry and flat in front of us with brown craggy hills poking out here and there. There was a large and very flat expanse of white not far in front of us, and past that an airfield and some squat buildings. We were just north of Groom Lake in Area 51.

I felt my face flush with anger. All that time Licia and I were training here, they had been building a prison for us.

"They're sending a jeep," Evan said, his chin poking out towards the military base. "It'll be a little bit. They weren't expecting us so soon."

Behind us was a small cinder block building with a single metal door and no windows. Innocuous. You wouldn't think it was anything. But I knew better.

I swayed and Evan grabbed my elbow, keeping me from toppling over. I was weak and dehydrated. Turning into Neutrinoman with no charge was, I now knew, possible, but it came with a price.

"Do you need to sit, sir?" he asked.

It seemed funny him calling me "sir."

I shook my head. I wanted to stay on my feet. "So who is your favorite soccer team?" I asked.

He smiled briefly before his eyes went back to the white expanse, searching for our ride. "I root for the US, of course," he said. "But I love the Brazilian national team. Such skill. Such passion."

"I've never watched much soccer," I began, so glad to just be chatting. "It seems a little tame compared to—"

"Incoming!" shouted one of the other guards. The one with brown hair that always had the cuffs on the pole when they came and got me for interrogation.

What was he talking about? Incoming? Did he mean a missile or something? My brain was sluggish and soon I was knocked over and felt a heavy body on top of me before I heard and felt an explosion behind me. Remnants of the brick building rained down on us. Evan grunted as he took the bulk of the impact.

Who would be attacking us here? We were on a military base, for God's sake. Was this part of my interrogator's plan?

I was still dazed as automatic gunfire rang out and I felt the spray of dirt on my face from bullets hitting the ground near me. Evan dragged me behind the rubble of the building. The attack was coming from the north, from the craggy rock that rose out of the desert on the far side of Groom Lake.

One of the guards was talking, calling for help. The other guard was firing his rifle, an M4 carbine, popping up from the rubble and shooting up into the hills, the shots barking out in short bursts.

Evan was talking to me, but I was still dazed and didn't understand him.

The guard with the gun popped up again but then he fell back in a jumbled heap, blood at this temple.

Evan was shaking me then, and his words finally reached me. "...change. You must change into Neutrinoman. You must do it now. You must survive."

The bright blue sky framed Evan's head and complemented his green eyes. He looked serious and scared. He looked desperate. He had been my guard, what did he care if I survived?

He slapped me, hard. "Goddamnit, snap out of it. The world needs you."

I nodded and took a deep breath. "I need a moment."

"I'll give you what I can," he said.

The remaining two guards started firing up at the hill. I didn't know how many assailants there were, but it seemed like a lot. I heard the faint roar of a helicopter in the distance, but it was going to be too late. I needed to change now.

But I couldn't find that switch. I was too weak. I was slumped in the sun and didn't know what to do.

Then I remembered Ronald, with his elegant demeanor and his long fingers. The meditation book. That is how I did it before.

I half closed my eyes and gazed up at the sun. Taking in every bit of radiation I could. I turned away from my tornado of fears and doubts and started focusing on my breath. Feeling the passage of air through my nose, feeling my belly rise and fall. I was aware of my other guard, the one that always had the energy weapon, going down. I let it go. I went back to my breath. I dove as deep and fast as I could.

"Now or never," Evan hissed. "I'm out of ammo."

The gunfire stopped and the silence hastened my descent into my mind. Time passed, I don't know how much, but I heard a helicopter getting closer, I heard the crunch of boots on the desert sand.

"Stand aside, son," a deep voice said. "I don't want you."

I was not looking at him, our attacker. I was vaguely surprised it was just one person, but I let that go and focused on my breath. I wasn't really looking at him, but I could tell that he was tall and strong, his presence looming over my emaciated form. Evan was there standing between the two of us.

Evan lunged at him and was thrown aside. I let it go, following my breath, looking for the trigger. I let the thought of looking for the trigger go and went back to my breath.

I knew I wasn't going to make it but let go of that thought too. The figure was pointing a gun at me, but still I wasn't looking at him. I was gazing up at the sun, my body still drinking in all the radiation that I could.

"Nothing personal," he said.

Things slowed down. I heard my heart beating in my ears. My mouth sour and dry. I felt the heat of the sun warming and energizing me. I heard the shuffle of feet and the cocking of a gun's hammer.

I was close. So close. But not there yet. I needed more time.

I let it all go and focused on my breath.

The hammer fell. The gun fired.

VULCAN IS THE ANCIENT ROMAN GOD OF FIRE. HE WAS associated with both the destructive and fertilizing aspects of fire. Fire, it can destroy, but it also can create.

Williams had called the bomb, "Project Vulcan." Maybe the Vulcan referred to me—I was the most fiery of the q-morphs. Maybe it referred to the fire the bomb would unleash. Maybe the name was chosen by someone who was into *Star Trek*. It didn't matter.

The first neutrino bolts didn't do much but extend the pit we had dug and collapse the tunnel I had melted. It didn't matter. I was well powered. I started a rhythm. Thrust up until we had good upward momentum and then shoot neutrino bolts out of my hands and feet.

Licia clung to the front of me fiercely. The girl hates to fly and this was the worst kind. We were flying then falling then flying again.

I maintained my altitude above one thousand feet. I had no

idea what the blast radius was. That was as high as I thought I could go and still hit the target.

I missed several times and took out our new greenhouse. Lightningirl didn't say a word, her strangling grip on my neck tightening only slightly.

I could still see the ball of restrained purple energy below the earth. I just kept at it. Flying, firing, flying, firing.

And then it happened.

The little purple energy ball began to expand rapidly, like a spring let loose from its containment. I stopped firing and flew up as fast as I could.

But it wasn't fast enough. Not nearly enough.

FALL 2005, GROOM LAKE, NEVADA

IT'S NOT LIKE DECIDING TO SCRATCH YOUR NOSE, TURNING into Neutrinoman, that is. It's an act of will, but a bit of a tricky one. It's more like sneezing. When the time is right, when the forces within you need it, sneezing is easy. When your nose is clear it's almost impossible to sneeze for real. I mean you can do an awkward ahh-choo, but that is no real sneeze.

Willing myself to turn into Neutrinoman is kind of like that. Easy and natural when I'm fully powered. Awkward and difficult when I am not.

And lying there in Area 51 not far from Groom Lake, my half-closed gaze on the sun, my body already spent from my time in prison and my recent unpowered change to Neutrinoman, it was more than awkward. It was nearly impossible.

When our attacker's gun fired, the sharp sound of it just about burst my eardrum and the sand of the desert splattered my face. He missed on purpose. The thought was a bright spark in my mind, but I let it go and breathed. Almost there.

"I expected more out of you," the attacker said. He sounded

sad, regretful. "Fight me, at least, will you? What the hell happened to you down there?"

He was talking like he knew me. That thought lingered briefly before I let it go too. There was one way out of this. I had to go deeper.

"Oh well," he said. It was time, but I wasn't quite there. Any attempt at change would still be like a fake sneeze, not a real one.

There was a grunt, the sharp retort of a gun firing echoing out over the land, and the sound of bodies falling to the ground.

Evan Saunders, who likes soccer, who had a girl once, had tackled our attacker, had saved my life.

I'm so close. I can feel the switch, just out of reach. I let the thought go and breathed.

They struggled and grunted on the desert floor. I saw bits of it in my peripheral vision, the sun still dominating my field of vision. One of them let out a feral scream. It was like an animal that wanted blood, that would kill to survive, that would do anything to win.

Another gunshot rang out, this one muffled. Then the attacker was standing over me again, blocking my view of the sun.

He was broad shouldered with round goggles on, like pilots of those old-fashioned crop dusters wear, with some kind of close-fitting helmet on his head. He was pointing the gun at me again. The prone form of Evan Saunders was in my peripheral vision. I smelled the iron tang of blood mixed with dust.

I knew he was dead, that he had died for me.

The knowing twisted in me like a knife.

I looked at him, for just a moment. He was on his back, his head pointed toward me, his legs splayed out awkwardly. I saw his empty, slitted eyes. Blood was still leaking from his chest and staining his dark clothing.

There was another scream, animalistic and primal. This time the scream didn't come from our attacker, it came from me.

I abandoned the peace of meditation and let my anger drive me to a different place in my mind. A more primal place. A desperate place.

The quality of my scream changed into something with a vague metallic edge as my grey prison jumpsuit began burning, as the man above me fired his gun, as the bullet passed through my neutrino form without hurting me, as I rose to my feet and leapt onto my attacker, the two of us going down in a jumble.

I was on top of him, not really knowing what had happened. My fist connected with his cheek and his skin sizzled away. He grunted, both of his gloved fists connecting with my chest. I went flying back and landed in the debris of the building.

"That's better," he said as he rose to his feet. I gawked as I watched the ragged ground-beef wound on his face heal itself. He was a q-morph. He was trying to kill me. Why?

He was dressed in rugged black clothing, with dull black armor over most of his body. His chest, his arms, his legs. His skull was covered with a sleek black helmet and his eyes covered by those aviator goggles. He had a thick belt at his waste that held several gun holsters, some small round devices, and some other pouches. His jaw was set, his mouth a thin, grim line. Honestly, he reminded me of Batman, but without the cape and with silly goggles.

He took one of the round black objects from his belt and threw it at me before running to my right.

I surged up into the air as the object landed on the rubble of the building and exploded. The explosion was small, hardly noticeable. And then a dark purple energy ball erupted from it, expanding rapidly. The energy ball quickly engulfed my legs as I flew upward. My legs went numb and I fell to a heap onto the brick rubble.

An energy grenade. I had never seen one of these before. It had to be something new created by the aliens. He was a q-morph and working for the aliens. It made no sense.

I sat up, my legs useless, and fired neutrino bolts at the running soldier. One of them clipped his leg and he went down.

"Why are you trying to kill me?" I shouted.

He slowly got up and smiled, his left hand going to his belt, his right hand grasping a gun.

"Why?" I repeated.

I hated that I couldn't see his eyes. Just like the guards down in the prison with the dark sunglasses. None of the guards had worn them as they escorted me out, as they fought and died to protect my life. They had finally been human to me. This soldier was not.

He threw another grenade at me and instinctively I extended both of my hands, and a yellow beam of neutronic energy stabbed out from my chest and formed a shield in front of me. The grenade sizzled when it hit the shield, the purple energy ball bursting from it. My shield sputtered out, consumed by the energy ball, but it didn't touch me this time.

I fired neutrino bolts at my attacker as he ran around the rubble that I sat on. He threw grenades at me two more times and I managed to block them with my neutrino shield. Each time the shield was smaller, and I was left feeling an exhaustion I had never known. My neutrino bolts became weak and anemic. I felt my reaction nearing failure.

He sensed this and stopped running and walked slowly towards me. A gun in his right hand, an energy grenade in his left.

"Why?" I asked again. I considered flying away, but my legs were still numb and I didn't think I had the energy for it.

"You're in the way," he said. His voice was even, all that running and he didn't seem the least bit tired.

"Of what?"

"Of the future," he said with a smile.

I laughed. I'm in the way of the future? What the hell kind of cryptic bullshit was that? His smile turned into a sour frown. He didn't like to be laughed at.

No more talking, he threw the grenade at me. This one, I noticed, was bigger than the last few had been. His aim was good, it was going to connect directly with me.

I didn't try to throw up a shield, I didn't think it was in me, but rolled awkwardly over the rubble away from where I had been sitting.

My legs were not strong, but I had just a touch of control of them and I was doing a strange log-roll down the pile of rubble when the grenade hit. This grenade was different. It sent out a ball of energy and then exploded for real, not a small explosion like the others.

He had waited until I was drained to throw this one. It was meant to strip me of power with the energy portion of it and kill me with the concussive portion of it.

The purple energy ball expanded rapidly, clipping my right arm as I rolled away, but I retained my form. The concussive component of it threw me and the rubble I was rolling on into the air.

Time slowed.

I was flying in the air, still doing my log-roll spin. My head was facing the soldier, my arms close to my body, my palms facing him. His left arm was still extended from his throw, his face grim and determined.

I knew there wasn't much left in me. I had been through too much today. I had turned twice without a charge. I knew I would be lucky to hold my neutrino form for even a few more seconds.

I tweaked the position of my palms and fired neutrino bolts from both of them.

In this slowed-down state, they erupted slowly and flew gracefully through the air towards my attacker, scintillating yellow balls of energy. Four in total, two from each palm.

All four were well aimed. All four plowed into his chest and burned their way through his armor and into his flesh.

And that was all the energy I had, my neutrino form fading as I fell.

33 / COERCED?

MY NAKED FLESH CONNECTED WITH THE HARD GROUND NEAR Groom Lake, rubble raining down on me, pain lancing through my body. All four neutrino bolts had hit the goggled soldier's chest. He should be dead. But I didn't think I was safe.

As the dust settled, I assessed my condition. I was dizzy and weak, a spiking pain in my head, I had lots of scrapes and blossoming bruises. My body hurt all over, but nothing seemed to be broken. I thought of staring up at the sun again, trying to trigger another change, but if the soldier survived, I didn't have time for that.

I raised my head and looked around. The soldier was lying still on the ground about ten yards away. The corpse of one of my guards was lying a few feet from me. The brown-haired one that always had the pole with the cuffs on it. I saw blood on his face and then noticed the gun on his belt. And the Taser.

I crawled over. I thought that if I stood, I would just fall down. As I did, I heard a groan from the q-morph soldier. He wasn't dead. He was going to attack again.

My mouth and throat were parched and dry. I was desperate for water. My stomach gnawed with hunger. I needed sleep. Crawling that six feet seemed more like climbing a mountain. When I got to him the first thing I took was his Taser. I pointed it at my chest and fired, the two metal connectors embedding themselves into my flesh, the voltage stored in the device pouring into my body.

Lightningirl wasn't here. I needed some kind of power.

My muscles contracted briefly as the energy flowed into me, but only briefly. My body recognized it for what it was and opened up to it.

I didn't feel good, but I felt a little better. I heard a scrape from behind me, grabbed my guard's gun, and still lying on the ground, turned.

The soldier made it to his feet, the hole in his chest closing itself up as he moved. "Much better," he grunted with a grin. "I'd have hated it for this to be easy."

I must have looked pitiful lying there naked with my stomach sucked in, my body ravaged from my long fast and my repeated transformations, my hands shaking as I pointed the gun at him.

"It'll be quick now," he said as he stood all the way up. "I promise."

I took a deep breath, pushing away the yammering of my mind. *You're going to die. Now. You will never see Licia again. He's one of them. This means the aliens are coming back. They will succeed. The planet will fall. You will fail.*

It wasn't a meditation, at least not like I had done it before. I remained fully aware of my surroundings, but I was following my breath, letting my thoughts go as they bubbled up.

"Leave now," I slowly said, "and I won't kill you." My voice seemed to come from far away in this semi-meditative state.

He laughed, his voice deep and rumbling. The sound of the approaching helicopter was getting louder, but if he didn't have senses like I did, I doubted that he could hear it yet. "Kind, you are," he said, "but I think I'll take this chance."

His hand went to his side and the gun holstered there. I fired, aiming for his chest. I knew how a gun worked, I knew how to fire one, but I wasn't very good at it. Guns had never interested me.

As I fired, I reached down and found my own trigger. To survive I had to. There was no time. I had the tiny boost from the Taser and with all my heart believed it was possible.

Most of my bullets missed, but one clipped him in the right shoulder and he hesitated for just a moment. By then I was Neutri-noman and standing in front of him.

He held up his hands away from his body, his mouth opening and closing in surprise or maybe fear. With his eyes behind those goggles it was hard to tell.

"The aliens... they've... they've got my son," he stammered, his deep voice sounding suddenly weak. "My wife. They're going to kill them if I don't kill you."

Part of me loved what he was telling me. That there was a reason a q-morph was trying to kill me, was working with the aliens. Another part of me didn't believe a word of it.

"What are their names? Where are they being held? Tell me everything you know and I'll do what I can."

"No," he said, his voice shaking now. "They're monitoring us. Right now. I..." His left hand was drifting slowly down.

I extended one arm, palm forward. "Get your hand back up or I will fire at you until there is nothing left." It was an empty threat. I didn't have that kind of energy.

He nodded as I heard the sound of sirens in the distance as well as the thump-thump of a helicopter. The cavalry was coming. All I needed to do was keep him here until they arrived.

"Tell me something about yourself," I said. It felt like the most awkward question in the world as I stood there, but I wanted to know he was real. Was human. I was looking for a reason not to kill him. I *needed* a reason not to kill him.

"What?" he asked, looking around as if my question was some sort if lame diversion.

"You know," I said with a nod, "if we met at a party, what would you tell me so I knew something about you. Who you are as a person?"

"Are you mad?" he asked. "I just tried to kill you. I just told you my wife's and child's lives hang in balance."

I shrugged. "We've got a few minutes. Tell me something about yourself."

His forehead furrowed deeply above the goggles. "Umm... I like to play checkers. My dad started teaching me when I was four years old. Still like to play."

I smiled. There it was—he was a real person now. Not just my enemy.

"Is your father gone?" I asked.

He nodded, a sly grin blooming on his face. "He is, as you will be too soon."

I was confused for a moment. Did he just threaten to kill me again? He shuffled his feet awkwardly, first his right heel tapping against his left and then he slammed his right heel into the ground.

A purple energy ball erupted from the heel of his left boot and engulfed both of us. My neutrino form fled, I collapsed onto the ground.

I knew it was time to die and my thoughts were all of Licia. I could see her face in my mind's eye again, her beautiful round face. Her coffee with cream skin. Her thick expressive eyebrows. Her deep brown eyes.

All the parts went together again. It wasn't much, but I clung to it.

A shot rang out and I tensed, but nothing happened. I heard the soldier grunt in pain and heard his retreating boots. The cavalry was here.

I was going to survive.

I unceremoniously passed out.

SUMMER 2025, CASITA DE SOLEDAD, CENTRAL ARIZONA

THE RADIUS OF THE ALIEN ENERGY EXPLOSION WAS MASSIVE AT our home of exile in the high desert of Arizona. It was the kind that didn't harm physical matter, but before I knew it was on me and Licia. It stripped me of my power and I was then naked and we were both falling.

It was one of the purple energy balls designed for me, not the orange ones that worked on her. This was why she wouldn't leave me, even though I asked her to. This was why she put up with the aerial acrobatics, even though she hated it so. She worried it would be like this.

As we fell, I felt her feeding me electricity. I saw the arc of lightning she drew from the nearby high-tension power lines.

We had about seven seconds before we hit the ground. She would survive as Lightningirl, I would not if I was still flesh and blood.

We were out of practice. We didn't train or do drills anymore. We made the occasional trip to orbit to piss off Homeland Security, but that was about it.

We tumbled and fell. Lightningirl fed me power. I changed several seconds before we hit the ground and thrust us upwards, but it wasn't enough.

We slammed into the ground hard in the bottom of the blackened pit that our excavation had turned into, the bomb, Project Vulcan, still buried beneath us.

I looked down, but the sight had fled, I couldn't see what was going on. I got up, grabbed Lightningirl and flew us low over the ground away from the bomb. We didn't get far before an orange energy ball engulfed us and suddenly Licia was flesh in my arms and screaming.

When she's Lightningirl, my energy can charge her up, just as hers can charge me up. When she's flesh and blood, my neutronic touch is destructive.

We were flying low over the ground and I dropped her. She hit hard and rolled awkwardly, the desert biting at her bare flesh. I landed in front of her, trying to look away from her damaged flesh, the red and blistered areas where I had been touching her, but I couldn't.

I didn't get us very far from the bomb, maybe one hundred yards. Licia cursed, reached out her left hand and drew a lightning bolt from the high-tension power lines and was back to being Lightningirl.

"I really want to hurt someone now," she said.

The bomb was made for us. They knew us and how we worked together.

"Thank God for the power lines," I said. I was looking towards them when the explosion occurred. It didn't come from the bomb, but from the tower closest to us. It was a small explosion, but enough to take out the tower. The giant metal structure began to screech as the metal bent and broke, as it fell, as power lines snapped, as Lightningirl was cut off from her power supply.

I opened my mouth to say something when the next purple

energy ball erupted, followed several seconds later by an orange energy ball.

Licia and I were left naked and without a power source. My uranium was gone, her electricity supply had been destroyed.

It was the end, I knew it. We had a good life, we had each other. But just because it's the end, doesn't mean you stop fighting. I grabbed her hand and we started running naked through the desert away from the bomb.

They had stripped us of our power, and we both knew it was time for the "vulcan" part of Project Vulcan.

LICIA WAS HOLDING ME THERE IN THE DESERT OF AREA 51, ON the rubble of the structure that had been the entryway to my prison. I was so glad that I think I wept. But I can't be sure, it's all fuzzy. My body had been through so much I was having trouble holding onto consciousness.

I heard sirens and the loud thrash of a landing helicopter, felt the hard ground underneath me, my mouth tasting of dust and blood. And then I felt her arms, the electric tingle of her touch, heard her voice. "I'm here, Nik. I'm here."

I opened my eyes, just a bit, and saw her face haloed by the sunlight. When she's Lightningirl, she looks like a goddess. That day she was an angel.

"God, you're beautiful," I said, my voice much weaker than I expected it to be.

She laughed nervously. "And you're a mess. What happened?"

I heard the baritone bark of Colonel Williams giving orders, boots scraping the ground, questions asked of me, but I only had eyes and ears for Licia.

"Attacked by a q-morph soldier. I need... to..."

"Save it, Nichols," Williams said, his lean, angular face entering my field of view next to Licia's, the light haloing him too. "This is no time for a debrief. You need medical attention first."

Williams's face was no longer in my field of vision and I heard him barking more orders. Something about securing the area.

Licia leaned close, her lips tickling my ear. "We have a plan. We won't be here long." She pulled away, but I signaled with my hand for her to come close. "What?" she asked, her breath smelling sweet.

"Pot roast," I said, uttering the agreed upon words when we had parted after the destruction of the Hoover Dam. Pot Roast, the meal my mother served the day I met Licia.

She pulled back, smiled, and nodded, and then the smile faded and tears were running down her face. She wiped them off and held a water bottle to my lips and I drank in huge gulps and ended up coughing most of it up.

Next thing I knew, I was in a jeep with a blanket wrapped around me, Licia still holding me. We were speeding across Groom Lake. Colonel Williams was driving.

"Is he well enough?" he asked, his head darting back to the two of us.

"Nik, can you hear me?" Licia shouted.

I nodded.

"I want to get you off this base. There's a vehicle waiting. Are you well enough to leave right away?"

I looked at her and smiled. The worry in her eyes was sobering. "All I need is you, my love," I said.

Licia snorted and turned to Williams. "He's fine. Get us the hell out of here."

—————

THE RV WAS LONG AND BLACK AND PERFECTLY POLISHED. IT

looked so out of place sitting on the narrow blacktop in the middle of the Nevada desert in front of the gate into Area 51.

It took both Williams and Licia to get me out of the jeep and headed towards the RV. I was not in good shape. I was weak, dehydrated, bruised, and battered.

After we got past the gate, two figures got out of the RV. A tall, middle-aged man in a black suit, the driver, and Jennifer Johnson, dressed in shorts and a blue T-shirt instead of her usual lab coat, with her nerd glasses on and her curly black hair pulled into a semblance of a ponytail.

Jennifer rushed over and took me away from Williams and Licia. We all stood there for a moment. I was trying to assimilate all of this.

"Will you be okay?" Licia asked Williams, her eyes straying back to the gate with its tall fencing, barbed wire, and guard's house.

He grunted and nodded his head. "You're both civilians. You asked to leave. I was following protocol."

A tear ran down Licia's cheek as she stood on her tiptoes and kissed him on his cheek. "Thank you," she whispered.

Williams blushed, his cheeks turning bright red. He quickly walked back to the jeep and drove back into the base.

"What is this?" I asked Licia, looking at the RV.

"It's a long story," she said. "One not suited to our current surroundings."

"Let's get you fixed up," Jennifer said, she and Licia and the driver helping me into the RV.

SUMMER 2025, CASITA DE SOLEDAD, CENTRAL ARIZONA

As Licia and I ran away from the next stage of Project Vulcan, fully human and naked, I kept thinking, *we've been through worse*. I thought it as my foot grazed a prickly pear cactus, as I fell and rocks bit into my bare flesh, as Licia went down and cried out.

But there was no time for thought. Only running. Only making sure Licia was with me, that I was touching her.

Our bodies didn't do their usual energy exchange. We were tapped. I noticed this too and pushed the thought away. I went back to my breath. I needed the oxygen to run.

Just my breath. Just the physical exertion. Just the touch of Licia. That was enough to keep me moving over the dry, rough land. That was all there was. That was my world.

The end comes to us all, even superheroes. I pushed that thought away too.

Just the breath. Just the run. Just Licia.

We didn't look back, only forward. We knew the threat was

there, no need to slow ourselves down imagining we'll see the explosion coming for us and somehow be able to outrun it.

Just the breath. Just the run. Just Licia.

My eyes slitted from fatigue. My lungs burning from the effort. Most of my mind in service of this moment, this need, this now. It wasn't a meditation, not how I had learned it, but running can be meditative.

And there it was, the trigger deep inside of me, the one I learned of in prison.

"Stop!" I yelled as I flipped that switch, as I drew from my internal reserves to once again become Neutrinoman.

Time slowed. I felt the earth rumbling beneath me. "Get down!"

I turned towards it. I extended both my hands in a defensive gesture. The beam of yellow extended from my chest and formed a shield in front of us.

The earth was disintegrating as the wave of energy hit the shield. I willed the shield into a sphere around Licia and me. The blast of energy parted at the shield and went around us, under us, disintegrating the earth below us.

I recognized this blast. I first saw it in prison when the two guards with energy weapons shot each other and were vaporized. Project Vulcan used two pieces of alien technology: the energy balls to strip our powers and the energy bomb to reduce us to atoms. They had somehow reproduced what happened in the prison, an alien energy ball hitting an alien energy source and vaporizing everything in its sphere.

We fell, the earth below us gone, the blast of energy past us, the earth all around us just gone. My spherical shield held. We were standing on normal earth inside the shield as it fell straight down like Wile E. Coyote falling off of a cliff in a Road Runner cartoon.

The epicenter of the bomb was far below the surface and it vaporized a spherical area about two hundred yards around it. We were near the edge of the blast radius far above the bomb, which left us with a long way to fall. Too far.

"You've got to change!" I yelled as we fell.

I stood in the middle of our little sphere with the neutrino shield still around us. Licia was off center and that imbalance in weight caused our sphere to tip. I was going to tumble into her.

But I was Neutrinoman, and unlike when we were flying, she had time. Not much, but some time. She thrust out her left hand, I felt her drawing power from me like she can from plants, people, or rampaging buffalo. The natural tendency of our bodies to feed each other was intensified by her will, yellow tendrils of energy flowing from me to her. I let the shield go, the dirt below our feet crumbling, and we fell into the empty space beneath us as she pulled energy from me.

It seemed like it took forever, although I know it was only a few seconds. I didn't thrust, I fell with her, and at the last moment she changed.

We hit the ground hard and tumbled to the bottom of the sphere.

THE RV WAS RIGGED FOR MEDICAL INTERVENTION. A HEART monitor, IV stand, even a defibrillator. I don't remember too much about those first few hours. Jennifer examined me, got me on to a bed, and hooked me to the IV. Licia fed me. I faded in and out of consciousness.

I felt terrible, but I was so grateful to be away from that prison, to be free of my interrogator, to be with people I cared about.

"I love you both," I mumbled once as consciousness began to fade again. I don't know if they heard me. I don't know if they replied. It didn't matter.

And then I was back in the prison in my grey jumpsuit, pacing my twelve-by-twelve cell, experiencing the colors and textures that I knew so well, my fingers touching the books on the shelf. I worried that I had dreamed that they had let me go, that I had had that battle with the q-morph soldier, that I was with Licia and Jennifer.

My little bookshelf was there with a few novels and my meditation book. I took the meditation book and went to my spot in the middle of the cell. My wool blanket was already there and folded up properly. I sat cross-legged and didn't open the book, just held it, looking at the cover with the tree and the mountaintop peeking out of the mist, letting my breath slide in and out of my lungs.

My thoughts were so clear. The real prison was inside. It didn't matter if Licia and Jennifer and the soldier were a dream or if this was a dream. I had the key. My breath was the way. It was all so simple.

"It's important you keep meditating," Ronald said, a smile on his kind face as he stood at the door to my cell.

"I hate it," I replied. "It's hard. Does it ever get easy?"

He shook his head. "Not really. It's not supposed to be easy."

I nodded and remembered what Larry, my interrogator, had said about him, those videos he showed of me reading a book that wasn't there.

"Are you real?" I asked.

He smiled. "One hundred percent," he said. "But I was never in this prison."

"What?" I asked. "How?"

He tapped his head with his index finger.

"You're a q-morph," I said.

He smiled. "That I am."

"So I'm not crazy," I said, a goofy grin on my face. "I just had a q-morph making me see things that weren't there."

Ronald's brow wrinkled. "Oh, everything you saw exists. I do, those books do. Reality isn't such a black and white thing."

I was dreaming, I knew it then. This was a dream of Ronald, my mind trying to make sense of what I had experienced. Giving me a story that would make it so I wouldn't think myself crazy.

Ronald took a deep breath and sighed. "You are dreaming, but you are not making this up. You didn't make me up."

I got up and opened the gate to my cell. It was a dream. I could do what I wanted. "Prove it."

Ronald shrugged his shoulders. "If I must."

We walked down the bland hallway past the door to the interrogation room, around a corner, to another door. I had never been in this door. He opened it and waved me to enter. In it was my interrogator, Evan Saunders, and another guard.

"His name isn't Larry," Ronald said, indicating my interrogator. He was seated at a desk with a large LCD monitor and a microphone. On the monitor I saw myself handcuffed to a chair in the middle of the interrogation room. "His name is Christopher Halifax. He used to work for the CIA and then did some black ops for a while. He lives in Laguna Beach, California, is on his third wife, has three kids and five grandkids." Ronald then proceeded to tell me his address, the name of all of his children, the address of the gym he uses when he's home, and a bunch of other things.

"Why are you telling me all this?" I asked.

"You wanted proof," he shrugged. "This is it. When you wake up, check it out. You'll find that every piece of it is correct."

I stood there staring at the scene. Ronald, my interrogator, Evan who died saving my life. I found myself believing him.

And then something clicked in my head. "You work for Tom Tyree." That first book Ronald had given me had a note from Tom in it. The book hadn't been there in my hands. Ronald had projected it into my mind.

Ronald smiled, his cheeks rising high. "Kind of. I'm not part of his gang, if that's what you think. I just owed him a favor."

I nodded. This time Tom's intervention didn't disturb me at all. I had needed Ronald.

"What's next?" I asked.

Ronald shrugged. "You get yourself better. You keep yourself away from the military. You save the world."

I groaned.

"Hell of a burden, isn't it, kid?" he asked, clapping me on the back.

I nodded.

"One more thing," he said as he turned and left the room,

looking at me over his shoulder. "You've got an offer coming your way. You're not going to like it, but keep an open mind."

I tried to ask Ronald another question, but he was gone.

"WHERE ARE WE?" I ASKED. I HAD SLEPT FOR WHAT FELT LIKE days, but we were still rumbling along in that fancy black RV. My mouth tasted like old socks and I was horribly weak but getting better. I had woken up in the bedroom in the back of the RV, managed to get myself to the little bathroom and walked up to the front. Out the window I saw desert and cactus that seemed to go on forever.

A tall man dressed in a black suit was driving, and Jennifer and Licia were seated at the little table towards the front. They both had laptops out.

"Mexico," Licia said with a smile. "Feeling better?"

I nodded and eased my body down next to her, a few tendrils of electricity jumping from her body to mine. No yellow neutronic energy jumped back—I still wasn't right. "Whose RV is this? Who's the driver?"

Jennifer smiled. "A gift from a fan." She reached across the table and put two fingers to my neck, checking my pulse.

"His name isn't Tom Tyree, is it?"

Licia shook her head. "No. Why do you ask?"

I shrugged, remembering my dream of Ronald. "That guy just keeps showing up. So, who's the fan?"

Licia took my hand and smiled. "Let's just wait on that. He'll be down to meet you when you're feeling a bit better."

"He's got an offer to make me, doesn't he?" I asked. The widening of the ladies' eyes told me I was on the right track. "And I'm not going to like it, am I?"

Licia shook her head, her silky hair sliding across her shoulders. God, that woman is beautiful. I laughed. It wasn't about humor, but relief. That was enough. I knew Ronald and the dream were real. I knew that I hadn't been imagining all of it.

I knew there was more to do, more to know, but I needed rest. A lot more rest.

I slowly got back up. "Help me back?" I said to Licia.

She smiled and nodded, letting me lean on her as we made our way back to the bedroom in the back of the RV.

"You okay?" she asked.

"I will be," I said, and I believed it.

WINTER 2005, SONORA, MEXICO

I HEALED SLOWLY, AND THAT WAS FINE BY ME. NO NUCLEAR reactor to help me out, only time, the sun, and gentle infusions of electricity from Lightningirl.

I've lived inland all my life, and after two weeks in Mexico by the beach I had come to love the water and the sun and the wonderful white noise of the ocean. The driver—his name was Valentine Oscar—had driven us across the border, past Rocky Point, and a few hours farther south to an empty stretch of beach with a little adobe casita.

He was more than a driver. He was bodyguard, cook, and companion to us. Another gift from my benefactor. My initial impression of him was terribly wrong. A middle-aged man in a black suit that drives vehicles for a living. It was a small description to capture the quiet, complicated man. Val was a gourmet cook, a martial arts expert, and also a very gentle man.

Well, I suspect he hasn't always been gentle, he carried a gun too. Maybe I should rephrase that. He was clearly a man capable of doing great damage and interacted with the world all that much more gently because of it.

I learned a lot by watching him.

In those two weeks we became something of a family. Jennifer was motherly, making me take vitamins, drink a lot of water, and constantly checking my vitals. Val was like a quiet father, watching over us all, attending to our physical safety. Licia and I, we were... We were in love, of course, but more than that, we had finally been through enough to get truly comfortable with each other.

I was happy. I was glad to be alive. I was with the love of my life and my best friend and making a new friend. I wasn't saving the world or fighting for my life. I wasn't dealing with the military or psycho-pathic super-villains. And, most importantly, I wasn't in prison.

It was idyllic except for the dreams. Every night I would be back in my cell alone, or back on the metal chair, the voice of my interrogator my only company.

On our thirteenth night there, it was particularly bad. I woke up, my body covered in sweat, crying out, ripping the covers from my body like it was trying to smother me.

"Honey, honey," Licia said, trying to hold me, but I shook her off. "It's okay. You're fine. You're with me."

My body shook with fear and I let her hold me until the shaking died down.

"I'm never going back," I finally said, my words thick, my throat raw.

"To the States?" she asked.

I nodded. "Can we stay here? What does this benefactor expect from us?" We still hadn't talked about it. I had been content to let time slide by pleasantly and avoid such realities.

The white noise of the Sea of Cortez floated in through the cracked window, the room simple and not much larger than the queen-sized bed. It had a dresser made of old wood and side-tables that were antique trunks.

"You can ask him when you meet him," Licia said.

"When is that?" I asked.

"I told him you would need at least two weeks," she said, her hand caressing my neck.

"I need more time than that," I said quietly.

"Okay. I'll call him tomorrow."

"Who is he?" I asked.

The curtains were open. I always had to have them open to not feel like I was trapped. The night was dark and the room was only vague shapes. In the darkness, I felt her shrug.

I was out of the bed before I knew it, looking around, my breath coming in ragged gasps. She didn't know who had given us these gifts. What would they want from me?

There was a soft knock on the door. "Is everything okay, Mr. Nichols?" Valentine asked.

I jumped. Who was Valentine, really? What would he do if I didn't cooperate with this benefactor?

I moved towards the window, it looked out over a dark expanse of beach, the Gulf of Mexico beyond.

Could we get away?

"Nik had another bad dream," Licia said. "We're fine, Val."

"Let me know if you need anything," he said.

"We will," Licia replied. "Thank you."

Licia joined me at the window, her arms resting on my shoulder, the tingle of our energy exchange starting to calm me.

"You don't know who he is?" I asked.

"Not really, no," she said, worry leaking into her voice.

"Then why?" I asked.

"He knew they were releasing you," she said. "Williams confirmed it. He knew you'd be a mess and would need to leave right away. He presented me with this plan. I had to do something. I..."

"It's okay," I said.

We were silent for a long time. She wrapped her arms around

me as I stared out the window onto the beach lit in the ghostly light of the moon. It doesn't get that cold down here in the winter, the nighttime temperatures in the high fifties. The window was cracked and the light breeze flowed through, the sound of the waves soothed my fearful mind.

I let myself slip into a semi-meditative state. The warmth of Licia's body against mine, the cool of the breeze, the gentle in and out of my breath. I hadn't tried to meditate since I had gotten out of prison—it had seemed like something that belonged in the past too. But there I slipped into it quickly and easily.

Minutes slid past and then my sight changed. I could see the blue lines of electricity in Licia's hands where they gripped me. A pulsing vibrant blue much brighter than I had seen from the guards in the prison. I turned and looked at her. It was like I could see Lightningirl beneath the flesh. It was there, hidden, ready. She said something, but I was somewhere else, somewhere where talking didn't matter.

I smiled and looked around the room.

I saw a trickling blue line of electricity snaking through the wall and cord to the alarm clock on our bed. Through one wall I could see the faint blue tracery outline of Jennifer asleep in her bed in the room next to us.

I looked carefully around the room looking for anything else that consumed electricity. A cell phone in Licia's purse. A charging laptop on the little wooden dresser. I went out into the living room and kitchen and looked there too. The clock on the stove. The flat-screen TV. Nothing strange, nothing unusual. Through another door I could see the electrical charge of Valentine asleep.

Licia was worried. I wasn't acting normal. I hadn't even gotten dressed, only pulling on a robe. She spoke to me again and I gave her a smile and signaled for her to follow me.

I couldn't speak. That would destroy the mental state I was in. When she hesitated, I took her hand and gently pulled her out of the house.

It was an adobe structure with a flat roof and rounded edges. Simple and lovely. Our refuge. It greatly influenced us when we built Casita de Soledad.

I walked slowly around the house looking for anything that might be a hidden camera or listening device and I couldn't find any.

By the time I was done, Valentine was out with us, keeping back several yards, but shadowing our every move.

I ignored him and led Licia down to the beach.

"What is it? Are you okay?" she asked. I had been silent long enough that she was very worried.

"I'm fine," I said quietly, letting myself come back to a more normal level of consciousness. I was sad to see the inner Light-ningirl fade away as my meditative state fled.

"Really?" she asked, her arms folded. "What the hell was that?"

I hadn't told her very much about my time in prison, about what I had learned, what I could do.

"It's a long story," I said. "Do you have a few hours?"

She smiled and nodded.

"But first things first. In the morning, call this benefactor. Tell him I'm ready to see him now."

SUMMER 2025, CASITA DE SOLEDAD, CENTRAL ARIZONA

CASITA DE SOLEDAD WAS GONE. THE LAND WAS GONE. IN ITS place was this huge, bizarre sphere of hollowed out earth that was melted and blackened at its edges. The alien bomb vaporized everything in its path.

"You okay?" I grunted after we stopped moving.

"Alive," she grunted back.

Our limbs were tangled together and all I could see was the blue sky above us framed by the eerily round sphere.

I started laughing. Not that there was anything funny about this. Our home destroyed. Our future unknown. It was more the stress.

"What's so damn funny?" Lightningirl asked as she stood up and looked around.

"Nothing," I said, trying to suppress my laughter.

"No, really," she said, her hands on her hips. "I'd like to hear what is amusing you right now. I could use a good laugh."

Her electrical face was serious. I knew I shouldn't be laughing, but I just couldn't help it. I got myself briefly under control and stood up, but then descended back into a gale of laughter.

Lightningirl wasn't talking anymore. She was staring at me, hands still on her cocked hips.

"I'm sorry," I said. "Really. This isn't funny. It's ridiculous. We've been living with this damn bomb under us the whole time. Look at what it did." I pointed to the smooth curved earth around us two hundred yards in diameter.

She pursed her lips. "And this is funny, why? What the hell are we going to do now? We have no home. No possessions. Nothing. Homeland Security will be here shortly to see if we survived. And when they find us, I don't think it will be all that pleasant."

The world doesn't want its heroes when it's done with them. Not when those heroes are powerful and dangerous. The world wants us to do our deed, to save them, and then just disappear.

"Well, at least you have me," I offered, trying to put a genuine smile on my face. She had told me that was all she wanted.

"For that I am grateful," she said with a small smile. "But, seriously, what are we going to do now?"

"We do what we always do," I said. "We survive."

She nodded and started pacing. As you might have noticed reading these memoirs, I'm happy to wing it. Not Licia, she wants to have a plan.

I let her pace. I figured we had a little time before Homeland showed up. They had clearly been caught off guard by all of this. She paced around me, our bodies close enough to do their energy dance, thin yellow and blue-white tendrils arching between us.

After several minutes she stopped. "Diane Madison," she said.

"What?" I asked.

"Our interview with her is in just over two weeks," she said. "So?"

She stared at me. "Live TV, Nik. We can make our case to the people. We just need a place to hide out until then, and we need evidence of what happened here, like some video footage."

I smiled. "Not only are you beautiful, you're smart too. I know who can help us get that footage, but I haven't a clue as to where we go."

"I have a place," she said shyly looking down, the comment not really registering with me.

"So there we go," I said. "A plan."

Licia nodded and came into my arms and I held her tight, feeling the increased energy of our q-morph forms close together.

"We'll get through this," I whispered. "Together."

"Promise?" she asked.

"I promise."

I then flew us out of the empty sphere that used to be our high desert home. The change I had feared and also wanted was now upon us. Our sheltered, small life was over, never to return. One way or another, things were going to be very different from now on.

I flew us low over the rolling desert landscape towards sanctuary, towards our unknown future.

WINTER 2005, SONORA, MEXICO

OUR LITTLE ADOBE CASITA IN MEXICO, WHERE I HEALED UP from my imprisonment, had a flagstone patio out behind it with a fine view of the ocean. On it was a black metal table and four chairs, the metal faded from wind, sun, and weather.

Valentine stood a few steps away watching us and our surroundings. I had asked him to sit, but he had refused. On my right was Licia and on my left was Jennifer.

We were all dressed for our location, looking like expats glad to be away from the stress of the States. Loose clothing, T-shirts or loose short-sleeved shirts, shorts or loose pants, all of it in one earth tone or another.

Across from me sat our benefactor.

He was short, maybe forty, with short brown hair that was making a quick retreat from his forehead. He was a bit overweight and his hands were always in motion. Rubbing the worn metal of the table, playing with the buttons of his white silk shirt, fiddling with his sunglasses.

There had been introductions, thank yous from us for his hospitality, and small talk. His name was Aaron Jordan.

"Shall we get started?" he asked as he reached into his briefcase that sat on the flagstone beside him.

"I have a question first," I said.

"Sure," he said, fiddling with his buttons again.

"Actually, a request and then a question," I said. He nodded. "Can you take off your sunglasses and tell me to exactly what extent Tom Tyree is involved in all of this."

His brow furrowed above his dark glasses. Under the table Licia squeezed my hand and Jennifer glanced at me and gave me a small nod. We had all talked about this approach.

"I'll know if you're lying," Licia told him, although it was a lie. "Both of us have new abilities emerging."

"And I'm sure Tom told you how much I value the truth," I added. "So you wouldn't even think of lying."

Aaron smiled and nodded as he took off his glasses, his light brown eyes meeting mine. "Tom did tell me that, and he has played a catalytic role here, but he's no longer involved."

"Why?" Jennifer asked.

Aaron smiled. I think he was enjoying the exchange. "This doesn't work with him involved. He's too much of a villain, and what we want to do is gather the heroes."

"It's a fine line between the two," I said, remembering how things had changed so abruptly for me after the Hoover Dam.

"That it is," he said. "For some, but not for you. You will always be a hero."

The word rubbed me the wrong way. I knew that I was considered a hero, a superhero, but the word seemed to hide the hard realities of having power and trying to do the right thing with it. But I let the comment go by. I didn't want to engage on morals or ethics. I wanted to get to the offer that Ronald told me I wouldn't like but should listen to.

"And what is it that you want from us?" I asked.

He pulled three glossy blue folders from his briefcase and handed one to each of us. On the cover was a round embossed logo that said, "Heroes Incorporated."

I almost groaned. The word "hero" was not something I liked or even understood anymore.

"It's pretty simple," Aaron began. "We have commitments of money, property, and services to start an organization for both of you and for the other heroes. A place where you can meet this alien threat without the burden of the military. An organization that will work with the military but not be controlled by them. Where you can set your own course, defend this planet, your own way."

He stood up and started pacing over the flagstone, his hands animated, his voice gaining strength. "I have commitments of five hundred million dollars to start this. If you sign on, I can triple that in a week. We can gather the q-morphs, train them, get them all the resources they need. We can meet this threat with our eyes open. This will be your organization to run as you see fit."

My mind was still stuck on "five hundred million dollars." That was a huge amount of money. What would I possibly need all that for? And how would we go about defending the planet from the aliens? How could that amount of money make a difference?

I was vaguely aware of the rustling of papers as Licia and Jennifer opened their folders.

"...as you'll see on this spreadsheet," he continued, "I've set up a preliminary budget. Most of it in creating a lab, hiring staff, creating a secure base of operations. I think if—"

"Wait," I said, holding up my hand.

Aaron stopped his hand in the air, his mouth open, a surprised look on his face. "Is there a problem?"

"Back up. Five hundred million dollars?"

He nodded. "Yes, not all cash. Some of it is services. We have offers of land too."

"What's wrong?" Licia asked.

"That's a crazy amount of money," I said. "Why would they

give us that much? What do they want from us?" The military spent tens of millions on me, I knew it. Taking over part of Palo Verde, training me, hiring people like Jennifer to deal with health and other concerns, flying me all over the place. And what had they wanted? For me to shut up and color in the lines. What would these people want that were planning on giving us hundreds of millions of dollars?

Aaron sat back in his chair and leaned towards me. "These companies are the biggest on the planet: Wal-Mart, GM, Apple, Google, Tesla, Amazon. There are only three small stipulations that come with the money. First, that the organization be called Heroes Incorporated; second, that you are the head of the organization; and third, that their involvement be public knowledge." He paused, taking a deep breath. "But what they really want, Mr. Nichols, is for you to save us. Not one dollar that they have matters if we don't survive."

My heart started thumping in my chest, an insistent and loud knock. The gentle crashing of the ocean suddenly seemed a roar. Aaron was talking, but I couldn't hear him anymore. Why was it always me that had to save the planet? All I wanted, all I had ever wanted, was love and work worth doing. I never wanted to be a hero. I never wanted to have to save anyone let alone the entire planet.

I didn't want this.

Aaron was talking, telling me it wasn't a rush, that they could start much of it without me, that I could stay here a while longer, but I couldn't really hear him. I surged up, knocking the chair down and stumbled past the patio and out onto the hot sand. I needed to be alone. I considered changing into Neutrinoman and flying off, but I wasn't properly charged, and I wasn't in the proper mental state.

"What is it?" Licia asked. She had her hand on my arm, but she seemed far away.

"I need to be alone," I said. "Please."

She nodded and walked back to the patio, pulling Valentine back as he was about to follow me. I turned my back and walked down the beach.

━━━

"A care package, sir," Valentine said, sitting a backpack in front me.

I was several miles down the beach from the adobe casita we had been staying in. It had been several hours since I had left the house.

"Jennifer asks that you remain hydrated," he said. "Licia said that you should eat something."

I smiled. My girls taking care of me. But the smile didn't last long.

"I'll be going now, sir," he said with a brief nod of his head.

I took a deep breath of the salty air and watched as the sun headed towards the horizon. "Is he gone?" I asked.

"Mr. Jordan? Yes. He left shortly after you did."

"And you work for him?" I asked, looking up at the tall man. He had short-cropped grey hair and he wore loose-fitting tan pants and a T-shirt over his fit torso.

"No, sir. I work for you," he said.

"But I don't pay you."

"No, sir."

"Does he?" I asked.

"No, sir."

"Then who pays you?" I asked.

"Not all actions are motivated by monetary remunerations," he said.

I sighed. "Tom sent you."

He nodded.

"Sit down," I said, patting the sand next to me.

He easily folded himself down, his legs crossed, his spine erect.

"And what did Tom give you?" I asked.

He shrugged. It was a minute gesture. "Nothing. He presented a compelling need."

"And that is?" I asked.

"That you needed a bodyguard," he said. "Someone that protects you from physical threats when you are vulnerable."

"Like now?" I asked.

"Yes, sir," he said, the breeze ruffling his short grey hair.

"And if I send you away?" I asked.

"I will monitor threats from a distance," he said, his tone flat.

"Why?" I asked, watching the waves gently caress the shore, breathing the moist air.

"For the same reason they want to give you all that money," he said.

I groaned. "So I can save the world?"

He nodded.

"It's too much, you know," I said, looking into his pale blue eyes. "What you all want from me is too much."

"Yes, sir," he said with a sharp nod. "I agree. But it is no more than you expect from yourself. And it is what is needed."

I remembered the meteor. Flying out to stop it, not believing I could make it back.

"And what if I fail?" I asked.

"You are not the only one in this fight," he said. "Protecting you is *my* best chance of affecting the outcome favorably. Those companies wanting to fund you, that is their best chance. Miss Lopez and Mrs. Johnson, this is their best chance. The other heroes that will gather around you will do so for the same reason. If failure occurs, it is not just you. It is all of us."

"It's too much," I said. "A little over two years ago I was a janitor. Now everyone wants me to save the world. How is that even sane or even possible?"

He smiled and the shadow behind his eyes made me think he had long experience with heavy burdens. "Then lead," he said.

"The leader carries the heaviest burden, but he does not do so alone. Let us stand with you. Let us fight together. And if we fail or succeed, if we live or die, at least we will have stood and fought. At least we will have lived a life we believe in."

He stood up and offered me his hand.

"Let me guess," I said. "That care package was misdirection. If you didn't bring me back, Licia was going to come down here and drag me back."

"Yes, sir," he said with a smile.

I took his hand and he pulled me up and we started walking down the beach.

"So, Heroes Incorporated," I said. "It's kind of a dorky name. I'm not at all fond of the word hero."

"Yes, sir," he said.

"Val, you have to call me Nik."

"Yes, sir," he said.

I laughed, feeling some of the tension ease. I wasn't alone. I had friends. I had Licia. I had a team to assemble, and a planet to save.

ELEMENTAL FACTORS

NEUTRINOMAN AND LIGHTNINGIRL: A LOVE STORY, EPISODE 6

1 / NERVES

I was an only child. I had great parents. I was curious and loved to tinker with things and take them apart, spending hours at this not even aware if someone was with me or not. You'd think that being alone wouldn't be that big of a deal for me, but the thought of going into the conference room was terrifying. I'd much rather face down aliens bent on our destruction or go up against Toxicwasteman.

I am Nik Nichols, aka Neutrinoman, I've saved the world a couple of times now but am afraid of a bunch of military brass and suits in a conference room.

I was standing there fidgeting while Licia was looking at me with those soulful brown eyes of hers, so full of compassion, and it's frankly hard for me to meet that gaze. We were standing in a nondescript hallway with short brown carpet and bright fluorescent lights. Down the hall I could see a window and a slice of the orderly streets of Phoenix, Arizona, with the craggy humps of Camelback Mountain beyond. The air-conditioning was humming, the circulating air playing with some of the fine black hairs framing Licia's round face and escaping her ponytail.

"You got this, honey," she said, touching my arm, a brief spark of our q-morph powers flowing between us. She stepped close and fiddled with my tie and smoothed the lapel of the suit jacket I was wearing, and I'm grateful that I don't have to meet those eyes.

Before September 10, 2003, when the cosmic rays hit and the power plant melted down and the rat bit me and I was transformed into Neutrinoman, I was a janitor working at the Palo Verde Nuclear Generating Station. Back then I was still finding myself, still fairly aimless and drifting along, working a low-paying job just so I could see the inside of a nuclear power plant. Back then you'd swear I was fine being alone, that I even enjoyed it.

I swallowed, trying to smile at Licia, my eyes flicking to the conference room door and then back down the hallway, wishing I was a janitor right now, not a superhero, and certainly not *this* superhero.

At Palo Verde, as a janitor, I was always moving, sweeping, polishing floors, taking the garbage out. It's not like you weren't alone walking down those large halls, hearing the slap of your feet on the polished cement echo through the large spaces, hauling garbage out into the Phoenix heat, looking around the flat, sandy landscape as the desert sucked the moisture out of you. Sure you saw people, but only for brief interludes.

"How're the kids, Frank?"

"Oh great, Nik. Little Fran's birthday is next week. Did you see the Steelers game on Sunday?"

"Sure did, the old man and I barbequed, tinkered with the Charger."

Simple interactions. Not that intimate, not when looked at one at a time. Just moments here and there. But you stack them up and you get to know someone, you can see their faces sagging when they've had a bad day, or their eyes bright when things are going good.

And I guess before Homeland Security arrested me, threw me into that hole for two hundred days, tried to break me by isolating me, I didn't think much about it. Being alone, that is.

As a janitor I had frequent interactions, I had the huge spaces of Palo Verde to wander through. I walked miles in a shift and wasn't locked in a cell walking around and around just for something to do.

As Neutrinoman I had spent a good amount of time off the planet, either in orbit, or farther out when I went after the earth-killing meteor that the aliens sent our way.

But I was never alone for long.

I saw other faces frequently.

I interacted with other humans all the time.

Try being locked in a cell with no human interaction, no smartphone, no internet, no books.

Well, there were a couple of books and Ronald, the kind man that brought them to me. Except he wasn't really there, a q-morph sent by Tom Tyree (Toxicwasteman) that could project his presence and the books he gave to me into my mind. He was there to keep me sane.

And he did.

But barely.

Back in that hallway, I took a deep breath and let it come rushing out, blowing more of those stray black hairs on Licia's head. The past, that imprisonment and all that happened around my release is haunting me. It keeps coming back to me.

She looked up and did her best to smile, but I knew her well enough to know it was not a real smile. Things have changed since we met and saved the earth from that meteor, since the aliens tried to kill me and Tom Tyree tried to recruit me, since Gaia destroyed the Hoover Dam, and since they locked me up.

It's not like I was going to be alone in that room. But... well... I wasn't going to have Licia by my side, and that now feels like being alone. She's been with me most every moment since I got out of that prison, since I fought the q-morph soldier, since we ran off to Mexico and agreed to start Heroes Incorporated.

I didn't used to be like this.

"It's going to be okay," she said, pulling me into a fierce hug. "You have to face them, you know this. And they have to listen to you."

I couldn't speak, I just nodded.

"You're my man, my Neutrinoman," she whispered.

"And you're my girl, my Lightningirl," I whispered back.

She loved me, I know she did, but I needed her too much. How long would she stick with the needy, afraid to be without her, version of me.

I took a deep breath, trying to still my mind, slip back into the meditation routine I started in prison, but it just wasn't working.

"I know it will be okay," I whispered back, telling her the lie we both needed to hear.

She let me go and I turned and walked into that conference room.

2 / A PLAN

LICIA HAD A PLAN.

Our world had fallen apart, our life in exile in the high desert of central Arizona vaporized, and my amazing wife had a plan.

And I had no idea. I was completely clueless.

After the war with the aliens, after all the madness, the Quantum Metamorph Accord of 2020 had separated us surviving q-morphs, hiding us away from the public, keeping us isolated. And our home had been Casita de Soledad. And the military had planted a bomb under us they called "Project Vulcan," and after I learned about it, I hadn't been able to live with it.

Project Vulcan, and my insistence on poking at it, had literally blown our home and our life up. There was nothing left of Casita de Soledad, just a perfectly spherical void in the ground, everything in the blast radius vaporized... nearly the both of us with it.

I kept seeing it, that spherical void in the ground where our home used to be. Bushes and trees on the edge sliced cleanly, inside the sphere, the ground smooth and a bit shiny like the explosion had polished it. A void where our home used to be, where our lives used to be.

I had hated our small pedestrian life, railed at the limitations, hated how Homeland Security kept us there, watched us, chided us when we used our powers. We had battled the Arcturian Alliance. We had saved the world over and over, and we had become their pet superheroes sent out to the high desert of central Arizona just in case we were needed again. Project Vulcan had been their insurance in case we got out of control.

And, I guess that is what I did... I lost control and brought this on us.

"They... I..." I mumbled as we trudged over the high Arizona desert naked and barefoot. We had both transformed to our quantum forms during the explosion—the only way we could survive—we had no clothes left to wear. Gone was my giddy laughter of relief right after survival. Reality had settled in on me. I had been in prison once after that mess with Gaia at the Hoover Dam, where they tried to break me through extreme isolation, and I suspected it would be worse if they caught us this time.

The sun was rushing down to the horizon, casting the cactus, sage brush, and brown wild grasses in a warm light that didn't cheer me like it usually did. The heat of the day would soon bleed off leaving us naked, hungry, and still running.

Anger was coming, brewing just below the surface, but not there yet. It was trapped like that super volcano under Yellowstone the aliens tried to get me to activate.

I was confused and lost trudging through the desert, walking around cactus and yucca on my battered feet, only barely aware that my beautiful wife was nude in front of me, but quite aware that she didn't seem nearly as heartbroken as I and wasn't loudly yelping at each bump and scrape to her feet.

She had a plan.

Her spine was erect, her shoulders squared, her long black hair sliding over her shoulders as she walked, her steady rhythm nearly metronomic.

"I can't believe they did that... I..." I continued to mumble, barely above a whisper. I was exhausted, I had depleted myself saving us from the explosion—or vaporization. Really, a better word for it.

The desert revealed itself slowly as the hills rose and fell under our feet, covered in dead grasses, prickly pear cactus, sage brush, and yucca plants with their sharp needlelike leaves here and there. It was beautiful land, land that I loved, but I wasn't feeling it.

We were in the high desert of central Arizona a few miles east of I-17, but Licia had us heading north. The direction didn't make any sense to me. To the west was I-17 and the possibility of help, and to the east was the high-tension powerlines that carried electricity to Flagstaff. Even though they had been severed where Casita de Soledad used to be, there might be power there to the south.

But she was walking north. With intent and purpose.

Homeland Security would be looking for us. We cleared their hidden base out before I triggered the bomb, so they know what happened. Although, since we barely survived, they must know there is a good chance that we were vaporized in the blast along with every single one of our possessions, along with the adobe house and greenhouses we had built ourselves, along with our lives that were small and boring, but comfortable and simple.

The summer evening was warm, a slight breeze licking the sweat off my bare skin, but I barely noticed as my mind went over what had happened, as that anger got closer to the surface. My foot landed on part of a decaying piece of prickly pear cactus. It was a dull brown and faded green, blending in with the sandy soil, and I hadn't seen it.

"Damn!" I cried, hopping on one foot while I raised the other and tried to yank it out. It was old and half decomposed, the once bright skin of the cactus now dull and flaking, bits of its harder skeletal structure a lattice visible through breaks in the skin. The needles were a tawny color, three long ones and many of the hair-like smaller ones embedded in my foot.

I hopped, I pulled at the cactus, and all I managed to do was come down on another piece of the decaying cactus with my other foot.

I fell hard to the ground, landing on some old grass. The grass broke my fall, but it also poked my bare behind in some very uncomfortable places. I just sat there, both feet lifted watching Licia walk away.

It was no use. I had flown us, low and fast, about a mile before my energy faded, before Licia and I had to surrender our quantum forms and become entirely flesh and blood. Homeland Security would be here any moment, but we were naked, we had nothing, and I couldn't even walk.

And yet she kept walking, her spine straight, her stride steady. She didn't even look back.

Licia had a plan and nothing was going to stop her, not even my little cactus mishap.

She didn't speak, she didn't encourage me, she just kept walking. And I knew that walk, that posture, she was furious. Definitely at Homeland because of the bomb, maybe at me for not letting things be, probably at the world for putting such a burden on us and then discarding us.

I smiled, just a tiny bitter little smile, as I watched her and thought those things. That's what *I* was mad about, that's what *I* was feeling. I've been married long enough to know it's not a good idea to project your own emotional state and foibles on your spouse. I'm sure Licia was feeling many things, and having known her for so long, I could guess that anger was primary, but it was best to let her tell me what she was feeling. But she wasn't talking, only walking.

But there it was, that spark of anger, some energy, something I could use.

I took a deep breath and let it out slowly focusing on my feet and the decaying cacti embedded there. I dug deep, like I had learned I could do all those years ago after I got out of prison and had to battle the q-morph soldier. The bottom of my feet glowed yellow, taking on the neutrino swirls. Not long, just for a moment, just enough to burn out the needles, and I let it go.

I stood up and took a deep breath and started walking after my wife.

I now had a plan, follow Licia, learn how she plans to get us to that interview with Diane Madison, do whatever it takes to make that happen.

But even below that, guiding that short-term plan was another plan. A simple plan. A one world plan.

Licia.

My love, my life, together we would figure this out, and if not, we would fight and we would fall, but together.

3 / A FREE AGENT

THE CONFERENCE ROOM DOOR CLICKED LOUDLY BEHIND ME
and I did my best not to jump, sweat slowly trickling down my neck
despite the excessive air-conditioning.

I felt Licia's absence. It felt like an ache that wouldn't go away,
like I wouldn't be all right until she was by my side again.

The conference room was on the twentieth floor of an office
building in downtown Phoenix. This floor was used by the US
Department of Housing and Urban Development. Not military,
not police, but government. Fairly neutral ground.

Out the floor-to-ceiling windows, I saw the flat grid of the city
laid out, the north-south, east-west flow only interrupted by the
small craggy protrusions of the desert that rose up in rounded
humps. Hunks of tan rock that reminded me of Gaia and her ability
to control the earth, like how she turned a sandstone canyon into a
giant rock monster and destroyed the Hoover Dam.

That destruction is what got me "detained" and what ended up
putting me here. It wasn't lost on me that Tom Tyree (Toxicwasteman) had lured me to Vegas to try to capture Chaosboy, had sent

me out to the dam to confront Gaia, had been instrumental in that "detainment." (Not to mention Ronald who got me through it fairly intact.)

The people sitting at the conference table were waiting for me, I could hear the squeak of chairs, the rustle of papers, and a few low sighs. The room stank of fear and not just my own.

"Thank you for coming, Nik."

It was Colonel Williams speaking. I would recognize that gravel in his voice anywhere.

I had my hands behind my back as I stood in front of the long conference room table, hopeful it seemed like a confident gesture and they didn't know I was clenching those hands. I could see them out of my peripheral vision, but I was still staring out at the window at the cars crawling below.

"Would you like to sit?" he asked.

I let my eyes focus on them. Colonel Williams was at the head of the table in a crisp blue dress uniform, his green eyes boring into me. Around the table were other men and women, some in military uniforms, a few in suits. I spotted a general, but not General Markus, which was one of the conditions of this meeting. I smiled, they looked more nervous than I did, the sharp scent of the nervous sweat clear to my rat-enhanced sense of smell.

"Thank you, Colonel Williams," I said, "but this won't take very long."

A thin woman in a dark blue skirt and jacket cleared her throat. She was in her fifties, her wrinkles and her tight ponytail giving her an elegant feel. "On behalf of the president," she began, "I would like to convey our nation's eternal gratitude for your actions in defense of this country and our most sincere apology for what happened at the Groom Lake facility. Mr. Halifax clearly exceeded his authority on numerous occasions. His actions are most regrettable."

She was a powerful woman. You could tell by how she held herself amongst all the uniforms that surrounded her. Her spine was erect, her gaze steady, her hands folded neatly on the table. Melinda Michaels, the Secretary of State, I hadn't expected anyone of her stature to be at this meeting.

"Did the president know of this facility and its intent?" I asked her, my insides quivering but my voice strong.

She nodded sharply. "Yes, he did."

I took a deep breath, my eyes leaving her and going back to that window, back to that view that confirmed I wasn't locked up, that I could jump out that window, turn into Neutrinoman, and fly away.

"I appreciate your honesty, Madam Secretary," I said, still not looking at her, "but perhaps you will understand that his apology feels political, not genuine." I turned back to her. "You, too, I assume, knew of the facility and its intent."

She nodded, pursing her lips.

"Honesty," I said. "This is a good start. Let me return some honesty." I put my hands on the back of the chair I had been meant to sit in, high backed and faux leather. I squeezed it as hard as I could without it looking obvious. I thought of throwing it through the window, letting in the hot dry air, making my escape route that much easier. "Let me tell you what Mr. Halifax so desperately wanted to know," I said. "Let me treat you all with the respect you have never shown me."

I licked my lips and almost didn't do it, didn't tell the truth, but I was tired of hiding. "I went to the Hoover Dam because Tom Tyree told me that Gaia was targeting it. I chose not to inform the military because I feared a heavy hand would be used. I had a discussion with Tom *after* the breaking of the Hoover Dam in which he encouraged me to feign chasing him so you all would go easier on me. I went to Las Vegas with Quinn Rask in the first place with the express purpose of capturing Chaosboy."

The room had gone silent, no more squeaking of chairs, no more sighs or coughs, all eyes were on me.

"And I was aided in your 'facility' by a q-morph sent by Tom who could project a convincing illusion of his presence into my mind. He's who I was talking to. It was through his power that I was reading books down there. He's the reason I held up so well."

Except it didn't feel to me like I held up well at all. I was sweating, surely they could see that. Surely they knew that I wanted to fly out of here, leave this planet with Licia and never return.

"Why are you telling us all of this?" Secretary Michaels asked.

I stopped, released my death grip on the chair and stood up tall. "Because I won't, under any circumstances, work directly for the United States government again. I'm sure you know about Heroes Incorporated. We are moving forward with it. Any future dealings you have with q-morphs that are part of our consortium will be through a negotiated legal contract. We will be treated fairly. We will not be kept in the dark. We will be partners not weapons you deploy at a whim."

Williams gave me a single nod, he had been expecting this, but there were mumbles and movement and more squeaking chairs.

I gave it a few moments to settle down before continuing. "And I wanted to give you a complete account of what happened in Las Vegas in case you do deem my actions criminal. If so, then do arrest me, but do so in the light of day. Do imprison me, but do so humanely."

Secretary Michaels was talking, something about how things had gotten out of control at the "facility." The general was shooting questions at me and several other people were speaking. Williams was looking at me calmly, his eyes locked with mine, his lips turned up in the smallest of smiles.

"Two more things," I said loudly and waited until the voices had died down. "Colonel Williams will be the government's liaison with Heroes Incorporated." A bunch of mouths opened up to speak, but I held my hand up. "And, any q-morph prisoners in that 'facility' will be released. Immediately. Any crimes you deem that any of us have committed must be dealt with publicly and transparently. These points are *not* negotiable."

They were all looking at me, different people from different lives with a different view of what I was, what I could do, what kind of threat I posed to the country and the world. What kind of help I could provide. They saw me as a hero and villain both.

"You're worried about the Arcturian Alliance," I said slowly. "I am too. You don't know if you can trust me. I understand that and relate. I'm *quite* sure I can't trust you. You fear a single person having this much power. I do too. I fear how much power many of you wield. You are worried about Tom Tyree and what kind of influence he has had on me. I get that."

The room was eerily silent and they all stared at me again like I was a mind reader or something, but all of this stuff was totally obvious.

I took a deep breath and sighed, my shoulders slumping. "But I care about this planet and its people. I want us, as flawed as we are, to survive. And I believe you all feel the same way. So we must find a way to work together."

Secretary Michaels nodded, Williams smiled, there were some other nods and a few yeses and then I could see all the questions on their faces and my knees went weak. They wanted answers. They were hoping that I could provide them.

They were faking this just as much as I had been.

"I'm sure you're aware of what Heroes Incorporated is doing in Ruby, Arizona. I would consider it an act of good faith if you aided us in getting our base setup. It's remote so we need transportation help."

"Of course," Secretary Michaels said. Her mouth opened to say something else, but I cut her off.

"Then we are done for today. We'll reach out to Colonel Williams soon to coordinate."

I stood up straight, turned my back to them, and walked out the door. When it snapped shut behind me, my knees turned to water and I almost went down, but Licia was there and put her arm around me.

"Valentine has the car pulled up in front," she said gently. "We'll be out of Phoenix in no time."

I nodded and held tightly to her, feeling her electric tingle, drawing strength from her presence. Valentine Oscar was my bodyguard, he had appointed himself the role and would not accept payment for his services. He had been there when I got out of prison and had been essential to my recovery.

"We have a lot of work to do," I said, my voice barely above a whisper.

"Yes, we do," she answered.

4 / THE SECRET CAVE

THE CAVE WAS DARK, BUT LICIA WITH HER RAVEN-ENHANCED eyesight walked ahead of me like she knew exactly where she was going until the darkness swallowed her and I was left at the edge of the light, cool stone under my bare feet.

The air was damp in my nose and without clothing I began to quickly chill down. Our march across the desert had taken over an hour and the sun was setting and I had heard the sound of approaching helicopters right before we reached the cave.

We needed shelter, for sure, but we also needed food and water and a way to escape Homeland Security. And I needed power, either some potent radiation, or a lightning powerup from Licia.

As we marched over the desert, Licia's straight-backed determination had never wavered. She was quiet, her eyes fixed on a low hill with a craggy face. This hill. This cave. She had a plan.

We hadn't talked yet, my self-recriminations were so loud in my own head I didn't need any conversation. They clanged around having long conversations with my self-doubt with a few timely interjections by my self-loathing.

This was all me, my freak out caused all of this. I couldn't calmly confront Homeland Security after finding the bomb, Project Vulcan, after seeing just how closely they monitored us, after feeling that I was in prison all over again.

I took another sniff of the air and smelled feces, some kind of animal had lived in here, probably a rodent. And below that I could smell food, stale crackers maybe, and just a whiff of rust, like there was something metal back there.

A raven was involved in Licia's transformation into a q-morph, giving her that great eyesight, and a rat mine, giving me a discerning nose, and an obsession for cheese.

I heard the snick of metal against metal, items shifting around, and then light blossomed bright at the back of the cave.

Licia was standing there, the harsh bluish light from a small LED lantern illuminating her naked curves, making her light-brown skin look a tad blue. She stood in front of a metal footlocker that was about three feet wide and stuffed to the brim with gear.

My wife, she had a plan.

A secret plan.

One she hadn't breathed a word of to me.

My mind turned over sluggishly as I celebrated her forethought and cleverness, but also ground into the fact that she hadn't told me a thing. Not one word.

She was staring at me, a question on her face and then she blinked and nodded. "I'm sorry I didn't tell you," she said. She knew what I was thinking, decades together will do that. Or, rather, a decent emotional intelligence, which she certainly has, will do that.

I took a few tentative steps towards her. "I'm just glad you did," I said.

She bit her lip and sighed, her head slowly wagging back and forth, her long hair sliding across her bare back.

"I mean," I continued, it wasn't time for half-truths, "I *am* glad you did, but why didn't you tell me?"

She swallowed and nodded, and I knew she was sorting through her own feelings, which couldn't be easy in our current circumstance. She was trying to get to the core of it so she could satisfy me and we could move on. Quickly.

And I felt bad that I needed satisfying here, but I did.

"I didn't tell you..." she began, setting the lantern down and walking the few steps that separated us until she was standing right next to me. I could feel her heat, but I couldn't see her face very well, the lantern lighting her from behind, its rays a halo around her, reminding me of the goddess she becomes when she transforms into Lightningirl. "I didn't tell you because I was worried enough to do something but didn't want to believe that anything like this would happen."

I nodded. "I get that, but..."

"You were writing, lost in the past," she continued, her cool hand taking mine. "It was going well, doing you a lot of good. I... I didn't want to disturb that."

And there it was, my wife was looking towards the future while I had my head in the past, trying to get it all sorted out, both of us missing the present.

And the writing had done me a lot of good, to relive it, feel it again and then move on. But right then, in the cool and dusty cave, dirt and rocks under my feet, it twisted on me. Maybe if I hadn't been so busy writing, I could have done a better job of this. It was the writing that led to agreeing to the interview with Diane Madison, that had made Homeland nervous, got them thinking about using Project Vulcan. Nervous enough so that Colonel Williams got wind of it and came out and warned us. Maybe if the crushing weight of the war and all that happened along with the Quantum Metamorph Accord hadn't made me satisfied to be alone in the desert with my wife, this could have been different.

And then Licia was in my arms and she was shaking. From the cold, from how close we came to dying, from the seemingly insurmountable task in front of us, from all of that.

Her skin was cold against mine and I held her tight. I took a deep breath, a meditative one, and brought myself back to the present, using what I had learned in that prison below Groom Lake at Area 51. I took another deep breath and told Licia that I loved her, that she was all that mattered to me. And both were true. I listened to her telling me the same in her own words and let it feed me.

Her shaking stopped and I felt a strange warmth on my face coming from the back of the cave. Not much, just the tiniest bit as if the clouds had just broken on a cold and rainy day and a single shaft of light lanced out from the grey and found me. The feeling was familiar and I smiled.

"Is there some uranium back there?" I asked.

She nodded her head still buried in my chest.

"You are brilliant!" I exclaimed lifting her up and twirling her around. She must have taken some of our secret uranium stash and moved it here.

She giggled in that girlish way that just made my knees weak and I put her down and kissed her hard. At the very least I could fly us out of here, although that could get very complicated very quickly.

"So, we need to get to Diane Madison," I said, once our brief celebration was over.

"Yes. You said you can get us footage of what happened."

I nodded. "I need the internet, though."

She went back to the footlocker and rummaged around, and I wished I could stop the moment. We had a sliver of hope, like that sunbeam breaking through the clouds. I was a bit more myself and actually noticed how beautiful my petite, well-proportioned wife was, her movements graceful, her smile dazzling as she pulled a smartphone out of the footlocker and plugged in an external battery.

Hope, when you are truly feeling it, seems like it's going to last forever. The same is true for despair. Right then it seemed like we could do this, it seemed like that feeling would last forever, but nothing does, does it?

I couldn't make the moment last, but I did savor it, did breathe it, steeling myself for the fight I knew would come next.

TIMOTHY TRAN HAD THIS WAY OF WALKING THAT WOULD make you think he either worked out all the time, drank way too much coffee, or both. He was short, maybe five-eight, with a compact, athletic body, and he liked to pace. All the time.

"The name is stupid," he shot off with such conviction it seemed like the statement was meant to end the conversation. He was wearing grey sweats and a Missouri Tigers T-shirt. He had jet-black hair with just a few grey invaders visible.

But it was his eyes that caught you. His irises were so dark you couldn't tell where they ended and his pupils started. When he looked at you, it felt like he was looking through you, into another world or something.

Licia and I sat at the small round table in his hotel room in Birmingham, Alabama, while he paced the short stretch between the door to the hotel room and the bathroom door, looking like he was going to wear a path in the uninspired grey carpet.

The room was messy, books and papers covering one of the two beds, the other bed had his suitcase on it with the clothing spilling out. There was room enough for him to sleep, but it was easy to believe that he never bothered with such things. The room stank of old takeout Chinese food and cigarettes.

"Sorry," Licia said with a smile, her arms crossed over her sweater like she was mad or cold or both. "The name Heroes Incorporated comes with the funding." It was damp, the patter of rain and the dripping of the gutter outside a constant white noise.

Licia hadn't wanted to come along on these recruiting missions, finding q-morphs to join Heroes Incorporated. I hadn't begged. We hadn't fought. I just told her that I needed her.

And I did.

I was having nightmares almost every night. Being alone—and at this point that meant being without Licia—left me prone to panic attacks.

"We need you," I said to Timothy when his restless course brought him close and his eerie dark eyes briefly connected with mine. He stopped, brushed his overlong black bangs back away from his face, gave me a sharp nod and continued to pace.

It seemed that was easy for him to imagine, that we needed him, but the question seemed to be, did he need us?

He stopped at an open laptop on his bed and poked at the keyboard briefly. It showed a map of the area with radar information overlaid in garish colors. He was a storm chaser and the q-morph known as Tornado. In 2003 when the cosmic rays hit, he was caught by a class-five tornado, his truck, with him in it, swept up in its embrace. He had gotten too close, the tornado had caught him.

Earlier, when he had told us about it, he had stopped his pacing, his eyes wide, his body still, his mouth open just a bit, his hand brushing at the tuft of black hair under his lip. "For a moment," he had said, his voice reverent, "it was perfect. I was weightless. I was in the storm. I *was* the storm. Time seemed to stop."

He had blinked and sighed.

"And then?" Licia had prompted.

"And then..." he shrugged. "My head slammed into the window and the next thing I knew I woke up naked, not a scratch on me, in the wake of the tornado's destruction with these weird eyes." He pointed at his black orbs, shrugged, and resumed his pacing.

After we had shared our transformation stories, after I told him just a bit about my "detainment" and the prison made for q-morphs, we had pitched him "Heroes Incorporated" and asked him to leave the military and join us. And all we had gotten was him telling us that the name was stupid.

And he had a point, but not a point that mattered.

"We're setting up a base in southern Arizona not far from the Mexico border," I said, trying to figure out what this guy wanted, what would entice him. That location, so close to another country, was important to me.

His lips took on a brief snarl. "Desert," he spit out, his pacing not slowing down.

Licia caught my eye, her eyebrows raising slightly. "It's just the base. The word is out about Heroes Incorporated. We are getting interest in your services from some exotic locations."

I nodded. "Retainer clients for hurricane season. Puerto Rico, Cuba, Hawaii. Florida."

"Hurricanes? They want me... I..." His pacing finally stopped and his normally barely-there accent thickened. Timothy was born in South Korea but moved to the United States with his family when he was seven.

Licia smiled. "Yes. Hurricanes. We don't expect you can absorb enough energy to stop them, but you should be able to blunt them, maybe tweak their course."

The military had him down here hoping to find a tornado even though it was fall not summer. In my mind they were doing it for two reasons, so he could power up if possible, and to keep him busy. He was horribly underused, we wanted to find out if he could do more.

If he could... well, this was important. He could save lives and give Heroes Incorporated a good stream of income.

"There's a class three hurricane approaching Puerto Rico," I said. "We can get you there with a team to support you. A ship, a plane, whatever you need."

"We can get you there, tonight," Licia added.

His eyes wide, Timothy Tran, the Tornado, smiled.

6 / TWEET TWEET

I TOOK THE CHEAP SMARTPHONE FROM MY WIFE AND MOVED to the entrance of the cave. We had a good line of sight, the Mogollon Rim unseen behind us, the rolling hills of our former home spread out to the south. Low hills covered in cactus and the dried grasses of summer, with the cut of I-17 visible here and there to the west. The sun, low on the horizon, was turning up the contrast with the western faces of the hills a warm yellow and the eastern faces slipping into darkness.

Three helicopters were hovering over our former home a few miles away and I could hear more coming.

Cell towers dogged the highway and we had signal.

I brought up Twitter and logged into an account that I never used, @aliensaintrealguy. There was a stream of stupid screed there, dumb stuff like "Moon landing = hoax. Arcturian Alliance = hoax. Superheroes = hoax. Grow up world, they're just trying to control us." Retweets of other conspiracy nuts and tweets about an unhealthy obsession with Nutella.

"What the…" Licia mumbled, looking over my shoulder.

292 / ROBERT J. McCARTER

I typed out a new message. "They're coming for me. Now. I have photographic evidence. Proof. They'll be coming for you soon. Run. We'll all burn. Help!"

"Byte," Licia said with a sigh.

I nodded. "One of her bots runs that account, any message that originates elsewhere will set off alarms. She'll figure it out."

I pulled the external battery and the phone died, my eyes going to the helicopters. One was hovering over what I knew to be that eerily smooth sphere of vaporized earth that used to be Casita de Soledad. Two others were slowly spiraling out.

I opened my mouth to apologize to Licia. I had never told her I had a back door to communicate with Byte, just like she had never told me about this cave. I hadn't wanted to worry her. I hadn't wanted to believe I would ever need to use it.

I looked and Licia was staring at me and before I could speak, she gave me a small nod. She had processed all of that already and was moving on.

"They're looking for us," she said.

I nodded.

"What are we going to do?"

I did the chopping hand gesture that means "stop" in American sign language and pointed at my ear. I needed to focus, I needed to hear.

Licia nodded, her eyes scanning the beautiful high desert land laid out before us. This wasn't one of our many sunset walks that we had taken here. This wasn't one of our long, lazy days that made up much of our forced retirement.

This was survival.

I deepened my breath and quieted it, holding it briefly at the end of the inhale and at the end of the exhale. I listened.

I heard the buzz of the highway to the west and of flies nearby. The chirp of bats sending out their ultrasonic radar as they roused themselves for the evening feeding. The scampering of a rabbit, the dried grass moving in the breeze, the distant yip of a coyote. The thump of the distant helicopters and the farther away thump of the approaching helicopters. I heard other vehicles, their engines quiet, their tires crunching over rock.

And I heard voices. Not close, just on the edge of my hearing, so distant that at first I thought I was making it up.

I closed my eyes and continued the slow, deep breaths. The crunch of feet on the ground, the muffled squawk of a walkie-talkie, voices speaking in whispers.

"They're almost here," I signed to Licia.

She nodded and pulled me back into the cool dark of the cave.

MY EARS POPPED AS THE PLANE SURGED INTO THE SKY, leaving New York City and the United Stated behind. I peeked out the window and saw the dark blue of the Atlantic below, whitecaps churning in the winds of the approaching nor'easter. I looked back and saw a thin strip of Long Island under a lead-grey sky.

I was in the plush blue seat of first class with mirror shades on and a blue New York Mets baseball cap pulled over my brown hair, dressed in jeans and sweatshirt. I slouched down in my seat and stared out, trying to ignore the fact that Licia wasn't in the seat next to me.

She was working a job for Heroes Incorporated, helping to repair a power plant in Oregon after the earthquake. She had been called out at the last moment, hopping a flight west while I headed east. If you're dealing with high-voltage power what could be better than Lightningirl, the goddess of electricity, who in her former life was a linewoman?

"You'll be okay," she had said when we parted in the Phoenix airport, a swirl of travelers flowing around us, the air dry, barely intelligible announcements coming in over the PA. Her round face was passive, no smile, no frown, no crinkled forehead. She was worried and the statement, while not a question, felt like an aspiration not a reality.

"I will," I had said with as much conviction as I could muster. My stomach felt hollow and I could smell the sharp scent of my own fear.

She held me tight for a long time, told me she loved me, and then I watched her walk down the long hallway that joined two of Sky Harbor's concourses.

The plane jolting pulled me back to reality and I sighed and looked around. First class wasn't full, the seat next to me, Licia's seat, empty. The other passengers were reading books, or tapping on laptops, or reclining and trying to sleep for the long flight to London.

I pushed the panic down and stared at the churning ocean below as the jet surged upward. Soon we were surrounded by grey as we moved into the clouds, more jolts of turbulence rumbling through the hollow tube with fuel-filled wings attached that we rode in.

Air flight is safe, a lot safer than car travel, I get that. I'm a q-morph that can fly, I get that too. But there is something about hurtling through the air at six hundred miles per hour in a heavy machine that can be unsettling.

Well, when you're halfway to a PTSD panic attack it can be. I've been in lots of military aircraft, jumped out of a few helicopters, flown myself into space, but right there, that day, I wanted nothing more than to get out of there and not be stuck for seven hours.

I felt hot and I was starting to sweat. I twisted away from the aisle, took my hat and sunglasses off, shucked my sweatshirt, leaving a plain black T-shirt. But I just felt hotter, my cheeks starting to burn, my breath going shallow. I fiddled with the controls above me, trying to get more air on me, but it wasn't enough.

Another jolt rumbled through the plane and my heart leapt. I looked around, expecting to see other people panicking, but it was just me.

This place was too small. That was it. It wasn't a twelve-by-twelve cell, it was a long hollow tube, but I couldn't get out. I couldn't leave. I couldn't even pace.

On the previous flights on this recruiting tour, I had had Licia with me, chatting, holding my hand, distracting me with news of her parents, talking about the dinner we had just had with my parents.

I hadn't even noticed how small these places were. How trapped I felt. I stared at the grey void of the clouds, hoping it would make me feel less claustrophobic, but it just made it worse. I needed to get out of here. Now. Even if I have to—

"I think you should put your hat and glasses back on, Nik," a voice said, a feminine voice. My heart leapt. Licia was here.

I turned, and a woman was in the seat next to me. She had bright red lips and long black hair, but her eyes were blue and her skin was too light. It wasn't Licia. Dressed in a black turtleneck she had an elegant air to her. I played back what she had said, and yes, there had been an English accent.

Byte.

She put sunglasses on and I spotted a few blond hairs peeking out from underneath what now was clearly a wig. She was in disguise, trying to look like Licia to the very casual viewer.

My heart fell, even though she was the one I was going to London to see. I tried to cover my disappointment by putting my hat and glasses back on.

"How did you..." I began, but trailed off. Asking Byte how she knew I was on this flight was silly. She was a q-morph who could hack the internet with her mind, control any computer with a thought. I'm sure she had a passable ID and a copy of Licia's ticket in her pocket.

She didn't answer me but slipped her soft hand into my sweaty hand and squeezed. "It's going to be all right," she said, her voice calm. Byte was part of Toxicwasteman's League of Villains Extraordinaire (LoVE), but this wasn't like when she tried to seduce me when we first met. This was motherly.

I nodded and took a deep breath letting it out slowly, her rose scent relaxing me just a touch.

"We were hoping this wouldn't happen," she added, her lips turning down into a frown. "But we have a plan."

That "we" meant her and Tom Tyree (aka Toxicwasteman).

I pulled my hand from hers, my cheeks flushed with anger. "It was you that had that last-minute job come up for Licia," I said, suddenly feeling alone again.

"It was necessary," she said. "They really do need her help, we just nudged them a bit."

I looked away back out into the grey, but Byte kept talking.

"I need you to close your eyes, Nik," she said, her voice taking on a quieter, lulling tone. "I need you to remember what you learned in that prison. I need you to deepen your breath, soften your mind. Breathe in and out."

I didn't want to, but I had learned something important there in that prison under Groom Lake. If you can free your mind, there is no prison.

I listened to her lulling voice, smelled her calming rose scent, and remembered what I had learned.

MY FEET WERE A MESS, BATTERED BY THE DESERT, PUNCTURED by cactus, and now the rocky floor of the cool cave poking into them. We don't think about our feet all that often, not when they are doing their job, not when things are going well. They're these complex biomechanical collections of bones, joints, ligaments, and muscles that let us run and walk, climb and swim. They are marvels really.

The soldiers were getting closer, the sounds of their boots pounding across the desert, the occasional whispered word clear to me. Licia would be able to hear them soon. She had pulled me to the back of the cave, to the warmth of the uranium hidden in that metal footlocker. She was talking, but I was just staring at our dirty feet.

Casita de Soledad was gone.

Homeland Security and the military were searching for us.

I flew us away from that strange sphere that Project Vulcan had created and yet they had tracked us quickly. They must have had some aerial surveillance in place.

They knew we had survived.

They were going to find us.

I had tweeted, attempted to contact Byte, but I had no idea if she would come through, if she would help me. She had set that account up almost two decades ago. We weren't exactly on friendly terms since things got crazy.

Licia is the practical one, I'm the romantic. She's all business in a crisis, I can often get distracted by the past, or by my worries or by—

"Take it!" Licia hissed, her hand holding a grey rock with gold flecks that was radiating a warmth that I could feel.

After surviving the meteor, what happened at Yellowstone, the damn prison, not to mention the war, here I was with my mind in neutral.

But I was cold, physically cold. We lost our clothes when we transformed earlier and hadn't put any of the clothing on from the footlocker. I grabbed the rock. I took a deep breath. I felt my mind coming back.

Colonel Williams had risked a lot to warn us about Project Vulcan. He wanted us to survive. We all knew the aliens might come back. And then I had gone crazy about the bomb planted below our desert home, about the degree of surveillance we had been under. I had blown it up. I had blown up Casita de Soledad and our lives with it. I had—

"They're almost here. Nik," Licia said, her cool hand on my shoulder. "Snap out of it."

We were out of power. Naked. Cold. All I had was a piece of uranium, its radiation slowly starting to fire me up. Slowly seeping through my hand into my body, reminding me who I was.

"I need a little more time," I said.

She nodded and said, "Don't take too long." She touched my arm with her cool hand. There was no exchange of our energies, no tendrils of yellow and blue-white, we were that tapped out. She grabbed a blanket from the footlocker, wrapped it around herself and walked to the front of the cave.

The blanket was one of those scratchy wool blankets, just like I had in prison. The uranium, while warming, wasn't enough. I had to dig deep like I did the day I got out of that prison.

I grabbed another blanket from the footlocker and put it on the cave floor and sat on it with my legs crossed, my eyes slits. I could see Licia with her blanket wrapped around her, framed by the orange tinged sky of sunset at the mouth of the cave.

I took a deep breath and held the uranium ore to my belly. I let go of everything, like I had learned. I let go of the past and the future, my world nothing more than Licia's silhouette through slitted eyes, my focus soft.

Licia was all that I could see. All my world.

I breathed and my guilt about Casita de Soledad bubbled up and I just noted, thinking "guilt" and letting it go. The traumas of the war, the indignities that I had been subject to, the many times I nearly died, all bubbled up. I noted them. Fear. Regret. Guilt. Worry.

I let it all go.

And I knew that I was just putting those things down, as I breathed in the dry air of the cave, felt the warmth of the uranium grow against my belly. They were not gone, I was still human, I needed to figure it all out. Just like overheavy bags I had been carrying for too long, I set them down. I relaxed.

I heard the soldiers coming close, their boots against the sandy dirt, their breaths quick from exertion. I heard a male voice speaking on a walkie-talkie, saying that we had been found and the high-pitched whine of one of the alien energy weapons charging.

But I didn't care. It felt so good to put all of that baggage down. To breathe. I felt the warmth at my belly, radiating out through my body and I wasn't cold anymore.

"Well, boys," I heard Licia say, her voice distant as if in a dream. "Are you going to just shoot me or are we going to talk first?"

I KNOW I'VE SAID IT BEFORE, BUT IT BEARS REPEATING. Meditation is hard work.

Byte's voice was lulling as the plane vibrated around me. All I could see through my slitted eyes was the back of the seat in front of me. With vipassana meditation, you don't close your eyes all the way, it is more about seeing the true nature of reality, not shutting yourself off from it.

As I breathed, I smelled the rose scent of Byte louder than all the other smells around me. Sweat. Coffee brewing. Alcohol. A random thought came up and I spoke it instead of letting go. "No patchouli today," I whispered to her, my gaze still forward.

She had smelled both of roses and patchouli the day we had met in the LoVE base near the Grand Canyon.

She chuckled softly. "Just breathe, Nik. Let that go, okay? Breathe in the air, feel it rushing in at the back of your nose, feel it filling your body, breathe out the thoughts and the worries."

Noticing it had pleased her, I could tell. And then I was amused at what I was noticing, and then I let that go.

Just the breath coming in, just the breath going out.

And then I could see. Blue tendrils of electricity all around me, running through the shell of the plane, up the back of the chair to the LCD screen.

I kept breathing, but slowly moved my head and saw her. Byte. Humans are a dense tangle of electromagnetic energy with a thick trunk down the spine and a tight blue ball in the skull, but Byte, she was different, or rather, more. The blue tendrils of energy left her head, winding out all over the place in graceful twists and curls. To the LCD monitor in the seatback in front of her, to the phone sitting on the tray table of the passenger across the aisle. A large tendril twisting out of her head and spiking down through the bottom of the plane.

"Good," she said with a smile. She looked so different with the blue lines I could see just below the skin. "You can see now. That's your EMV. Electromagnetic Vision. You must make this second nature."

I smiled, a silly smile, like I was an infant who saw everything as beautiful, like the trace work of blue running through the flight attendant's body as she walked down the aisle. The dense blue splotches of the other passenger's phone, the battery and electronics, with tiny pulses of blue radiating out, the Wi-Fi signal, the phone not in airplane mode.

Ahead, past the passengers whose energy I could see, through the seats, I saw the cockpit and its dense tangle of wires and electricity, its pilot and copilot.

It looked like they were having an intense conversation, their mouths moving rapidly, the copilot flipping switches, which sent out tiny pulses of blue down thin lines. He then looked out the window back towards the wing, and then was talking to the pilot some more.

"There's something wrong," I whispered, trying to hold onto this state, this Electromagnetic Vision.

"What?" she asked.

I slowly turned my head back so I could see the wing with my eyes and with my EMV. We were at elevation, the storm roiling grey below us, blue sky above. The clouds themselves had large blue veins and smaller tendrils flowing through them as electricity churned within the clouds. I could see the outside half of the wing with my eyes and I could see the tracing blue lines of electricity that went to the flaps, that wound around the engine.

There, in the middle engine, I saw the blue flicker, a sparking, and the blue winding around the engine winked out and all that was left was a blue blotch that scuttled along towards the back of the engine. The relentless white noise of the engines lessoned and I felt the plane slow, twisting slightly.

I stood, Byte was asking me what was going on, but I ignored her and moved into the aisle, with my EMV gaze looking at the opposite wing, which still had energy pulsing through it.

"This is not good," I whispered, glancing back at Byte. The blue tendrils coming from her head were stronger, pulsing brightly, more of them reaching out, connecting with every piece of electronics in the plane.

I felt the plane execute a slow turn, heading us back towards the west.

"Excuse me, sir," the flight attendant said when I got to the front of the plane, "you'll have to go sit down." She was all pulsing blue lines, my EMV making it hard to see what she really looked like. But I could still tell there was worry there written on her face.

I removed my hat and glasses and her eyes widened.

"We have a problem here," I said evenly. "I need to talk to the captain."

The blue bundle that was her brain sparked brighter at the front of her head.

"There's something out there," Byte whispered in my ear, so low that I doubted anyone else could hear it. "It disabled one engine and... it's moving towards the next."

Something out there? Was she talking about the scuttling blue blotch I saw? What the hell could it be?

I turned to her and saw that the blue lines and tendrils leaving her head were denser and brighter than everyone else's. She was a quantum biomorph, her form changed permanently on that day in 2003 when the cosmic rays hit. As I looked at her it became clear that controlling electronics with her mind was only the beginning of what happened to her. Her whole brain had changed. Her whole nervous system.

"Can you do something about it?" I asked

She shrugged and in my meditative, childlike state I found the firing of the nerves that sparked right as the muscles in her shoulders moved to be fascinating. "It's... I don't know what it is. It's not... normal. I don't know."

"Sir, you'll have to sit down," the flight attendant was saying, I think she might have said it multiple times, but she was keeping her distance from me, so I suspect she knew who I was.

I held up my index finger and in my calm state was able to spark the tip neutrino yellow for just a second, a very limited transformation, so there was no doubt.

"How far out are we?" I asked as the flight attendant gawked.

"Ninety minutes from JFK," Byte answered from behind, a strain in her voice. "This thing... whatever did this... It's at the second engine now. It's... I'm almost there."

The hum of the second engine died and I almost stumbled as the plane noticeably slowed. There were murmurs from the cabin behind us.

"Too late," Byte said.

We were ninety minutes out, a storm over the Atlantic below us, and no engines.

"How long can we glide?" I asked Byte.

She paused, her head tilted like she was trying to retrieve a distant memory. "Twenty minutes... tops."

The pulsing blue lines of electromagnetic energy faded as I

almost slipped out of my meditative state, almost lost my EMV. But I took a deep breath, noting the worry and letting it go.

"I think you better let me speak to the captain, now," I said to the flight attendant with the best smile I could offer.

"He's coming," Byte whispered, again so low that I doubt anyone else could hear it, but the fear in her voice clear. "But he won't be in time."

I knew she wasn't talking about the captain but about Toxicwasteman. Whatever was to be done, we had to do it.

THE DESERT HAS ALWAYS FELT LIKE MY HOME. I WAS BORN IN Phoenix and kicked around Arizona all my life until Licia and I ended up in the central Arizona desert for our exile at Casita de Soledad. The desert doesn't hide its dangers. It's full of spiny plants and fanged reptiles, dry air and relentless heat. You know exactly what you are getting from the desert. It's hard, but it's obvious.

But people... they are not like that, not at all. Not when it comes to groups when the dynamics of politics and bureaucracy creep in. They're nothing like the desert, their poison and danger largely hidden.

Like Homeland Security planting a bomb under our little piece of desert. Planting explosives to take out the high-tension power lines that could make Licia into Lightningirl. Having so much surveillance on us that even when our home and everything around it was vaporized they tracked us with ease.

Homeland is not like the rattlesnake whose tail warns you, whose fangs make it clear just what kind of danger you are in.

Homeland hides behind paperwork and "need to know" and layers of bureaucracy and security.

And they are not like Toxicwasteman whose hunger and danger were written all over his sickly green quantum form. With him, you knew it could go bad at any moment, get weird, you could rest assured he would do something unusual.

These thoughts were gnats as I meditated, as my EMV came to life, as I saw that there were four soldiers confronting Licia, as I heard the thump-thump of a helicopter closing in on our location.

They shot orange energy balls at Licia, they lit up the cave with garish light but I just closed my eyes.

They shot purple energy balls into the cave, seeking me, and in my flesh and blood form they did nothing to me, nothing to the uranium I held. I wasn't Neutrinoman, I was just Nik, thirsty, hungry, and naked in the middle of a small cave with beat up feet.

I took a deep breath, the scratchy wool blanket beneath me, the piece of uranium ore pressed to my belly, the warmth of it growing, making me feel safe when nothing should have made me feel safe right then.

The soldiers were in the cave now. Licia had talked to them, tried to stall them, but all their words had just slipped by me. The soldiers were talking to me, shouting words, fear clear in their voice, clear in their scent. Even with my slitted eyes I could see the blue tracery of their bodies, the tangled ball of their brains, the strong trunk of their spinal cords.

Three of them stood pointing their weapons at me. One of them fired purple energy balls into me repeatedly. The balls, I was curious to note, looked the same to my eyes as they did to my electromagnetic vision: coruscating, spiking balls of energy about the size of a fist.

I didn't think, but took another deep breath and pressed the uranium ore to my belly. It was hidden underneath my hands, they couldn't know it was there. I exhaled and I pressed harder. It didn't hurt, it felt good, it felt right.

And then their rough hands grabbed me, their scared voices tinged with fear. They pulled my hands behind my back to handcuff me, but the ore was gone. I wasn't quite sure how I did it, but it was in me. It was part of me and I felt warm... so warm.

IT ALL TOOK TOO LONG. SECONDS TICKING PAST FELT LIKE hours. This metal tube with fuel-filled wings attached was falling. Well, not falling, yet, not quite that. Without the engines it was slowing, the wings providing less lift, and we were gliding down to the storm clouds and the chaotic ocean below with over three hundred people on board.

The rumbling of the engines was long gone, the relative silence eerie. My EMV was still with me and I could see back to both engines, lifeless, no electricity running through them except for the odd blue blotch in one. I could see that the flaps were still operational.

The flight attendant had gotten on the phone and talked to the captain, but he wouldn't see me. She left and went back to deal with the scared passengers, their voices having become fearful.

Byte went after her, argued with her, and then gave up and came back and she was looking at me, still dressed in her black wig, her sunglasses still on. Even now with the future so uncertain, she wanted to retain her anonymity.

She had said, "He's coming, but he won't be in time." She had meant Tom Tyree, Toxicwasteman. He was flying towards us to... Not to rescue me, I didn't need rescuing, and surely not for the three hundred souls on board. He was coming for Byte. And that... it helped me somehow. He cared about her enough to risk himself. He "loved" her—whatever love meant to a sociopath like him.

"What can I do?" I asked, guilt lying on me heavily. I'm no Superman with powers that can be applied benignly. I'm a controlled nuclear reaction, my touch just as damaging as Toxicwasteman's. I could survive this. I didn't know about any of the others.

My EMV was fading and I could see her face clearer, her brow furrowed in concentration, several blue tendrils that headed into the cockpit getting more active, sparking blue lights zipping back and forth. She was doing... well, I didn't know what, but it seemed to relate to my questions.

And then her brow relaxed. "Be the engine," she said.

I smiled. Not because I was happy, but because I was relieved. I could do something besides go down with the plane.

I looked around, the hatch was there, but that would depressurize the cabin and slow the plane down. How to get out?

The flight crew would know, but that captain had refused to talk to me, the flight attendants were busy. There had to be a way.

My gaze wandered, my EMV fading in the worry, but not gone. I glanced down, there were blue lines of energy running down there. Of course. I was in a tube, the top half of a tube. If I could get into the lower half, the cargo hold, I could cut my way out without depressurizing the cabin. And then, somehow, I would have to be the engine.

Byte had beat me to it. She was on the floor of the mess opening a trapdoor, a strange look on her face. I would call it sheepish, but that's not quite right. It was a shy look as if she was asking a lot of me, but also as if she wasn't sure hope was even called for.

My stomach tightened and the EMV left.

"I can do this," I said as I crouched down beside her, wishing I could see the eyes behind her sunglasses.

She nodded, her cool hands pressing something into my ear. "If you can, keep from melting it," she began, "then I can talk to you." And then her lips didn't move, but I heard her in my ear, "To get this plane down safely, we'll have to communicate."

I nodded and pressed my finger to the metal she had inserted. It was cool and hard. The same kind of thing Toxicwasteman had in his ear when I saw him right after the Hoover Dam was destroyed.

"This is a fly by wire plane," she said in my ear, a smile on her red lips. "If they won't cooperate, I'll be taking it over."

I nodded, but hesitated for a moment. The pitch of the voices from the passenger section was getting strident and the sensation of the plane falling was getting more pronounced.

"Take care of yourself," I said.

She nodded. I climbed down the short ladder and she closed the hatch above me.

I THOUGHT WE WERE OVER THIS. BEING DRAGGED AROUND naked with scratchy wool blankets hastily thrown over us. Only the tiniest of gestures towards retaining our dignity that the military could manage.

The cloudless western horizon was tinged with orange, the kind of restrained sunset Licia and I had watched almost every night up here. The rolling desert was slipping into darkness, the yip of a coyote barely discernable over the shouts of soldiers and the thump-thump of the approaching helicopter.

Licia's black hair, rumpled and staticky, reminded me of what it looks like when she is Lightningirl. Her brown eyes caught mine and I gave her a small smile, hoping to reassure her. Her brow furrowed and she shook her head a tiny bit. We were just outside the cave surrounded by four soldiers, three with rifles pointed at us, one with an alien energy weapon strapped to his back, the silver tube pointing at me.

My EMV was still strong, the blue trace work of their nervous systems clear. Licia's, though, was different. It was much stronger, a deeper blue, with blue-white pulses zooming back and forth. And this is when she's completely tapped of energy.

We had learned, we had believed, that quantum metamorphs, like Licia and I, were normal flesh and blood before we transformed. And that quantum biomorphs, like Chaosboy and Byte, were transformed once, with Quin Rask being the exception and a little bit of both. Seeing Licia like this reminded me that it was just not that simple.

We had all changed permanently and some of us could transform into other forms.

"Gentlemen," I began. "I would appreciate it if you, at least, pointed your rifles down and let me have a moment with my wife."

I haven't described the soldiers yet, I haven't told you that two of them were white men, the third an older man of Latin heritage, and the fourth a woman. That they were dressed in fatigues, wore helmets, had gear strapped to their waists and tall boots on. That one had a deep gruff voice, another one a boyishly high voice, the woman hardly talking.

And they did have a lot of gear and they might have been as I just mentioned, but I don't remember. My EMV was strong, making ethnicity difficult to see. My mind was in a meditative state where I saw things more broadly and couldn't tell you if one of them had a mustache or if the woman's hair was braided.

But more than that, they were stand-ins for the forces that had kept us here for so long, kept us small. So even in my meditative state, I didn't want to know them.

This wasn't like it was back in the prison, where it was paramount to know something about one of my guards. That his name was Evan and he liked football not soccer, had lost a girl when he served in Iraq. Evan Saunders who had died saving my life. I needed to humanize the people around me then because I was starved of contact. Now, below the peaceful Zen state was that baggage that I had put down—the anger for what they had done and the shame for how I had handled it. The grief for what we had just lost.

I was desperate, surrounded by soldiers in the desert, our home just destroyed, my only hope a piece of uranium ore I had managed to somehow take into my body. My clearly never-quite-human body. The rock was whole and sitting just below the skin or in my stomach, or maybe my body absorbed the ore, so desperate it was for energy, pieces of it all through my body. I didn't know. I didn't think about it then. I just wanted escape.

They were talking to me now, these soldiers I didn't want to know, who were just following their orders. They were shouting, pointing their weapons at me, but still I walked to Licia. My hands were cuffed behind me, so I couldn't hold her, but I pressed myself against her. I smiled as I felt my body feeding hers, the old energy dance coming back.

She sucked in a breath, she hadn't expected it, and I whispered, "This will have to be fast."

I felt her head nod against my chest.

I didn't tell her it would be dangerous—she knew that.

I was about to do it, trigger the change, when I heard them. A low buzz rising above the gentle whisper of the breeze, barely perceptible against the thump-thump of the helicopter that was almost here.

I looked up and saw them. Drones. Quadcopter drones. Hundreds of them flying over the desert like a swarm of locust.

Byte. She got my message. Boy did she get my message.

INTERLUDE 1

"You gotta stop this," Licia said, her voice surprising me as I typed away on the laptop computer. Adrenaline dumped into my bloodstream, and I jumped and cursed.

"Stop what?" I asked, keeping my voice as calm as I could. I can't tell you where we were, but for the sake of the story let's say it was in a bland hotel room in shades of brown and off-white with an overloud air conditioner pumping dry cold air into the room to beat back the heat.

"This." She pointed at the screen where I was lamenting the loss of Casita de Soledad and all we had built. Feeling bad about my PTSD and lack of control.

Things were tense between us. We were in hiding (sort of, you'll get a glimpse of it soon) and we were still being hunted. I didn't speak, I just stared at her.

She sighed and bounced down onto the edge of the bed and held out her hand, a kind look on her round face. I took her hand and our bodies did their reassuring exchange of energy.

"Look, Nik," she began. "I know you feel bad about it. I know you need to write to get it out. It's just..." She trailed off, biting her lip.

"What?"

"Don't bore your reader. They get you feel bad. You don't need to bring it up over and over, even though that's what's going on in your head."

I blinked and wanted to jerk my hand out of hers, but I didn't. It was connection with my beloved and I needed that.

She smiled again, it was strained and tight, but filled with empathy. "I miss our home, too. I miss what we built and I miss the ease of those days, but..." She looked around the small room as if there was a magnificent landscape to see. "Look at what we are doing now," she said, her voice hushed. "It was hell getting here, but... This is better. You know it is."

I nodded slowly, my mind still in the past.

"You are certainly not bored anymore," she added.

I smiled in spite of myself. Boredom is not good for me, and this current adventure is certainly not boring.

"And thanks to Project Vulcan, your story got a hell of a lot better." She read my puzzled look and continued. "You started out writing about the past from a safe, secure position. The 'Interludes' of yours were minor, just a taste of our current lives. Well... now, both the past and the present are pretty amazing stories."

She stopped with a smile and the humming of the air conditioner seemed overloud.

"I still feel bad," I said quietly.

She nodded slowly. "I know. I do too. But for your reader, just get on with the story. They know you feel bad."

And Licia was right. What she was saying was in no way comfortable, but it was entirely true. So enough lamenting a single mistake. On with the story.

13 / DEPLANING

LIGHTS FLICKERED ON AS I DROPPED DOWN INTO THE 787's cargo hold, long strips of LEDs running along the low ceiling. I didn't know if they were motion controlled or Byte had turned them on for me, but I was glad I could see.

Not that there was much to see. I was stooped over and couldn't stand. This being the lower portion of the tube, the floor wasn't that wide. There was a diagonal section of wall that joined the horizontal floor to the vertical wall. This was because of the tube, trying to create a squarish space in a round object. Towards the back of the plane, I could see shipping containers that fit snugly into this space with only an inch or two between them. The floor was metal with regular divots that were used to anchor the cargo containers.

In front of me was a wall with a small door that led into an area under the cockpit. I assumed that had equipment in it.

For a moment, a thin second, I looked around with wonder at the scratched and well-used metal surfaces. At the door and the strange things that must lie beyond. At the shipping containers with luggage and who knows what else in it. I was the guy who took a janitorial job just so I could see the inside of a nuclear power plant. I wanted nothing more than to explore.

But there was no time.

Earlier, I mentioned fuel-filled wings, but I had no idea where else they might store fuel. Fitting something reasonably rectangular inside a tube meant there was space underneath the floor and past the walls. Would they store fuel there? This plane had to have enough to cross the Atlantic.

There was not time to debate or explore. I chose the diagonal section reasoning that since it was like that to accommodate the tube, there wouldn't be anything beyond it.

I crouched down, transformed my right arm, held my breath and punched through it.

There was no explosion, but the air in the small space whooshed out, sucking my breath away with it. Outside the hole was undifferentiated grey—we were flying in the storm clouds now.

"Hurry up," Byte said in my ear. "We've dropped into the storm."

"I'm working on it," I shouted against the roar of the wind.

"Go faster."

I transformed, slowly, keeping my reaction low, trying to not do too much damage in here, not wanting to melt the earpiece.

I widened the hole and marveled at just how thin this metal tube was that hurled through the air. There were ribs circling the tube and several layers of thin metal, but it wasn't much.

I shoved my head through the hole into the thick grey and saw the dead engine hanging lifeless on the port wing.

Now what?

To be the engine, as Byte had suggested, I had to get to the engine.

"I'm going out," I said, having no idea what I was going to do.

"Good luck," the reply quickly came back, her voice steady and emotionless as it had been before through the earbud. She wasn't actually talking, she was using her powers to transmit her voice to the earbud. It was kind of like a computerized version of her voice and right then it spooked me.

"What is your name?" I shouted, not sure how she could hear me with wind out here.

"Excuse me?" she asked, again no emotion.

I couldn't give her a long speech about how humanizing those who appeared to be my enemy had helped me survive prison. How I hated that LoVE had turned "Toxicwasteman" into "Toxic" and "Chaosboy" into "Chaos," seeming to discard their humanity with it. I couldn't tell her that before I thrust myself into the unknown, to attempt something that might not work, that she might not survive, that I wanted to know her name. That I needed to at least know someone's name on the plane.

"Please! Tell me your name." I shouted instead, shoving myself through the hole and falling into the grey.

14 / ESCAPE

THE DRONES WERE BUZZING ALL OVER THE DESERT, BUT THE bulk of them were coming towards us. A group swarmed the nearly-here helicopter, a UH1-D with the side door open and two soldiers with alien energy weapons pointed towards us.

At least a dozen descended on us, their cameras swiveling, catching the details of our capture, of our hastily covered nudity and our handcuffed hands.

"Hold still," I whispered, still pressed to Licia, feeling my body feeding her energy, seeing the tendrils of yellow pass from me to her and feeling the barest zaps of electrical energy coming back from her.

I thought of the drones as bats, not to be feared, knowing that they could fly with great agility, knowing Byte was behind them.

But the soldiers didn't react as well. They shouted. They started firing at them, but I just ignored it, breathing deeply, feeling the energy exchange, seeing my EMV deepen as I saw the darkening desert with new eyes. I could see the blue tracery of a rabbit sprinting away from us, spooked by the gunfire. The drones looking like some kind of blue fairies flying and bobbing in the air. Back towards Casita de Soledad I could see a few large blobs of blue, helicopters I presumed, being harassed by more sprightly pricks of blue, the drones.

Byte was getting the footage of what had happened. The military had clearly violated the Quantum Metamorph Accord of 2020 with Project Vulcan.

As the three soldiers fired, as the fourth one still kept the alien energy weapon trained on us, my smooth mind snagged on a thought, my EMV fled and I cursed.

"What?" Licia whispered.

"The drones. They got here so fast," I said.

"Oh..." She got it. Those drones getting here this quickly meant that the military had not been the only ones watching us closely. Byte had been too. She somehow got these drones in position with solar cells to keep them charged, hidden so that we didn't find them in our wanderings and neither did the military.

"Later," Licia whispered. She knew where my head was going, could feel the shiver pass through my body. I was no longer feeling so warm with that uranium ore inside me. "We should just go."

I nodded, but the Zen state was gone.

Around us the rifles fired, the drones buzzed, some falling to the bullets, and the helicopter fled like a hawk chased away by a group of sparrows.

"He can't get us both," Licia whispered. She was referring to the soldier with the alien energy weapon. It shot either purple or orange energy balls, designed to strip either me or Licia of our powers. It took a bit of time to switch.

And my best guess was they had it tuned to me, but that was a mistake. I couldn't stun them or do much without risking their lives, but Lightningirl could.

I took a deep breath, more drones falling around us, the helicopter getting farther away, my EMV returning.

I flipped the switch, transforming quickly, the handcuffs

sparking against the yellow of my neutrino form, the metal starting to glow. The wool blanket started burning, bits of it falling to the sandy soil below me.

I turned quickly and extended my hand in a defensive gesture, the yellow column shooting out of my chest, forming a shield in front of us.

He saw it all, of course, the soldier whose face I don't remember, the one with the alien energy weapon. He fired, purple energy balls as predicted, and I could feel them as they crashed into my shield, tapped my energy, but the shield held.

Behind me I could feel a sharp tingling as Licia found her q-morph form. At the same time, the other three soldiers ignored the drones and started firing on us.

It didn't matter, though. Neutrinoman and Lightningirl have always been better together than apart.

The drones buzzed, the bullets bounced off the shield, the orange energy balls slammed into it with a sizzle, the shield flickering, but holding.

I was well powered, that uranium ore giving me energy to spare. But when Lightningirl was fully transformed it was all over.

She stepped beside me, a blue-white coruscating electrical reaction in the form of a beautiful woman. She extended both hands, small tendrils of energy leaping from the four soldiers to her fingers. She wasn't zapping them with power, she was drawing energy from them. Just like she had first done in Yellowstone when we faced the stampede of Buffalo.

Soon the four soldiers were on the ground snoring.

"What now?" she asked.

And that was a good question. What now? It felt good to be Neutrinoman and Lightningirl again, but Casita de Soledad was still destroyed, Homeland Security would still be hunting us, and we still had an interview to get to.

A single drone hovered in front of us and I smiled and nodded at it, thanking Byte for her help.

"Anymore secret caches I don't know about?" I asked.

"Well…" she said with a sheepish grin on her electrical face.

I laughed. I loved my practical preparing wife more than ever. I took her into my arms and flew us away.

FALL 2006, OVER THE ATLANTIC OCEAN

I FELL, FIRST THE LONG TAPERING WING OF THE BOEING 787 passing within inches of me. I almost crashed into that fuel-filled wing with a dead engine attached. Then, the dark grey of the dense clouds took me, and I couldn't see the plane. Winds buffeting me and sections of the clouds lit brightly as lightning discharged.

"Shit!" I swore, jetting back to where I thought the plane should be, but it wasn't there. It was all grey, all clouds, nothing but the intermittent flashes to differentiate it.

What could I do? Fly below the clouds and wait for the plane to come out? By then it would have slowed more, making saving it much harder.

Not knowing what else to do, I tilted myself down.

"Your fifty... meters above," a bland voice crackled in my ear. "And... meters behind us."

Byte. She had access to the plane, access to their radar, could somehow see me. But the earbud, it wasn't working well. Was I melting it?

I flew faster, losing some elevation and tried to lessen the reaction around my left ear.

"Where are..." I began, just as the plane emerged out of the grey in front of me. "I see you... commencing with operation 'Be the Engine.'" I was trying to be flip, make light of it, but I was worried.

I had to push the plane to be the engine. I had to do that in a way that didn't directly threaten the passengers or the integrity of the plane, so that ruled out the fuselage. I couldn't use the wings, because, you know, fuel filled. That left the engine.

"I have done everything I can to shut off the fuel supply to both engines," Byte said in my ear, the static gone.

So the engine it was.

A jet engine is a big fan in front, a nozzle that expels hot gas in the back and a compressor, combustor, and turbine in between.

The combustor was my worry. If I melted my way to it, exposed the fuel line... well, that would be bad. This plane was fueled for a flight all the way across the Atlantic that we had barely started.

This also required some difficult modulation of my form. I had to tamp down the reaction where I met the engine but produce as much thrust as possible. So that means, you guessed it, time for the butt thruster.

I flew behind the engine and found that the exhaust cone, that round pointy bit at the back of the engine, was still rotating. Air was still flowing through the system, making it turn. I had been planning on melting the point off and pushing there, but how would that work if it was spinning? If I was off axis even a little bit, the thrust would be inconsistent.

The back edge of the engine cowling had a scalloped tooth pattern around and I saw there was space between the main part of the engine and the cowling where the front fan blew the air that didn't go through the main engine.

It was all I had.

I slammed myself into that gap, my reaction a little hot still, my arms by my side, burying myself in there.

There wasn't much to see, the dark inside of cowling on one side, and the exterior of the jet engine assembly on the other, with some struts joining the two. All of this illuminated by the flickering yellow of my reaction. I couldn't see anything up ahead. The sounds of the wind were strangely muffled and echoing in here.

"Here goes," I said, pulling my legs up and wedging myself in tighter and letting the butt thruster rip.

This was all Byte, and the flight crew if they had wised up, now. They had to use what thrust I could give them to get the plane closer to land.

"That's helping, Nik," Byte said in my ear. "But that's not enough. We need more... a lot more."

I nodded, although no one could see me, and steeled for the effort when in the dim light, I was confronted by a... I'm not sure what it was. A robot, I guess, but not like any I had seen before.

It was a silver-skinned, six-legged construct that moved with a fluidity I've never seen in a machine before. It glowed, filling the area with thin silver light that fought with my flicking yellow. Its body was about twelve inches across and it had something of a head jutting forth with a single rounded eye. It scuttled up to me, its head tilting this way and that, looking nothing less than curious. Its eye was reflective and I could see myself and the thrust shooting out my butt in it.

"Umm... I think I found what disabled the engine."

"What is it?" Byte asked in my ear.

"A... ahhh. A robot, I guess, but not like any robot I've ever seen."

This is what had done it, disabled the engine, I knew that, but it was... I don't know. Cute.

"What do you want?" I asked it.

It scuttled forward, another arm growing out of where its little neck was, on the end of this was a small pincher.

I saw my quizzical expression in its eye and then it danced

close, the pincher jabbing me and then it danced back, a sparking yellow bit of my neutrino form in the pincher.

What the hell?

It held it up to its eye examining it closely.

"It took a sample of me," I shouted. "It's examining me."

"This is not good," Byte's calm voice said in my ear. "It's sending out a strong signal. It's transmitting data."

THE SMELL OF COFFEE SLOWLY ENTICED ME BACK TO consciousness, but I resisted, pulling the blankets tighter around me, burying my head in the pillow, reveling in the soft comfort of the flannel sheets.

I listened for Licia, but she wasn't in bed with me, she must be up, that's who started the coffee. I wondered what we would do today, work on the new greenhouse, undoubtedly. We were still amending the soil and planting. I loved to watch Licia around the plants, how she would suck the life out the weeds, traces of electricity jumping to her outstretched fingers, and she would do the opposite to the plants she wanted to grow, feeding them trickles of energy that they would use to burst forth with fruit.

I turned over on my stomach, rubbing my face against the flannel sheets. They were musty, as if they had been in a closet for a long time. I could hear Licia's feet tapping on a wooden floor, it sounded like she was pacing.

Wait... flannel? It's too hot at Casita de Soledad for flannel. And we don't have wood floors.

And then it all descended on me. My mania on discovering Project Vulcan and the extent Homeland had been surveilling us. How badly I had handled it, setting the bomb off and vaporizing our home, destroying all that we had built together. The march through the desert to Licia's secret cache. The uranium ore. Contacting Byte via a fake Twitter account. The drones coming and our escape.

I groaned and sat up, my head thick, and looked around. Flannel sheets meant Flagstaff and there were pine trees out the little window, but the cabin was small and rustic and all I could see out the window were towering pine trees, all I could hear were birds.

It all came back to me.

After our escape, as the darkness descended on Arizona, I had flown us fast and low north up onto the Mogollon Rim, skirting Flagstaff and the San Francisco Peaks, over the lower expanses of desert that sat between Flagstaff and the Grand Canyon, and then into the Grand Canyon, zooming above the Colorado River, zipping through salmon-colored limestone canyons in the dying light, up long side canyons past the cream-colored Kaibab limestone into the ponderosa pine forest of the North Rim.

We flew fast, Licia shouting me directions the whole way, riding on my back and holding my neck so tight if I had been flesh, she would have choked me.

She hates flying and really hates riding on my back, but this was not a gentle jaunt into orbit. I was flying as low as I dared, well below radar, in the dim evening light, staying away from populated areas as much as possible. I had to go fast. I had to be maneuverable.

We flew until we found this isolated and rustic cabin where Licia gratefully hopped off my back, let go of her q-morph form, pulled a key from under a rock, and let us in.

"My cousin's," she said by way of explanation.

We talked, for a long time, our words carrying us around in

circles, and then she cried, and I cried, and we went to bed and held each other until sleep finally came.

This life had brought us much to grieve. I had hoped we were past losing this much, past this kind of grief, seeing all we had created destroyed, but we were not.

I moved slowly, my body feeling like it might break easily, like delicate stemware in rough hands. This wasn't because of yesterday's tangle with Project Vulcan, and my body was still fully charged from the uranium ore. This was my emotional state impinging on my physical state.

There was a ratty blue robe on the end of the bed and some slippers. I put them on and stumbled out of the bedroom.

Licia stopped her pacing and looked at me, but didn't look long, her eyes only flicking over me before she tightened the tie on her faded red robe and continuing her pacing.

The cabin was old, the wood paneled walls showing the patina of time, the tongue-and-groove floor scratched and scarred. There was a kitchenette on one wall, a couch, an old rocking chair, and that was it.

It was a bit cold, so I went over to the small iron woodstove that sat in the corner opposite the kitchenette, opened the squeaky door, and stacked some pieces of wood in.

"I'm so sorry," I said, my eyes locked on the wood. Her pacing stopped for just a moment and then resumed.

The words seemed hollow. I wanted to elaborate in a way that defended me, something like, "I'm sorry I have PTSD from all we've been through and can't stand the thought of being watched 24/7." But that wasn't an apology and I gulped it down like a pill nearly too large to swallow.

I wanted her to rage, to be mad, to throw things at me. She was the practical one, she kept her head all during yesterday's madness when I nearly lost mine. But today, I knew she would be feeling it. The adrenaline was gone... and so was our lives as we knew it.

I stuck my index finger out, held it near the wood, and shot out some neutrino thrust, just like I shot from my hands and feet (and sometimes by butt) when I fly. Yesterday's madness had helped me remember some of my long unused abilities. The wood quickly caught fire and the crackling noise was some small bit of comfort. It was summer and would be warm outside today, but any comfort seemed in order.

"The interview is when?" I asked, watching the yellow fire dance hungrily over the dry wood. I knew when it was, I just needed to hear her talk.

"Want some coffee?" she asked, as her socked feet continued their back and forth trajectory.

I nodded and walked over to the kitchenette, timing it so I didn't interfere with her pacing. The counters had dust on them, the cabin not seeing much use. We were at the end of a rutted dirt road way off the grid. The solar panels didn't work anymore, but Licia had charged the batteries last night, which apparently worked well enough to power a coffeemaker.

I poured coffee into the mug sitting there by the coffeemaker and promptly burned my mouth, but I didn't care.

The interview was still a week away. Could we stay here the whole time? How long would it take the military and Homeland Security to find us?

"They know we headed north," I mumbled, half to myself.

"And it's not like there won't be reports of Neutrinoman sightings," Licia added. There were numerous websites setup that tracked us, and this sighting will be an unusual one.

We had used the Grand Canyon like someone evading a tracker would have used a river. We immersed ourselves into it, trying to throw off our pursuers. We had made sure we were seen heading both upstream into Utah and downstream farther into Arizona.

"I'm sorry," I said again. I was standing in front of the crackling fire hoping its primal pleasure would help.

Licia stopped pacing and her eyes finally met mine and what I saw there made my stomach tumble. She wasn't sad and she was far past mad. She was furious.

"For what?" she asked, cocking her head.

She knew for what, but wanted to hear me say it. Why did she want to hear me say it?

I swallowed hard. "For destroying our home. For..." I wanted to say more, but couldn't. The shame and the guilt felt like they were smothering me, this great weight on my chest that made it hard to breath.

Her hands balled into fists and tears formed in her eyes. Furious yes, but there were other powerful emotions at play.

"Don't apologize," she said, her right foot creeping forward as if the need to pace was irresistible.

"If... I... Maybe..." I sucked in a breath. I didn't want the tears of last night to come back. I didn't have the strength.

Licia chewed on her lip, staring at me, her hands still fists at her side. "Don't apologize," she said, but quieter this time. "I can't..." She looked away, shaking her head. "Just don't apologize."

I nodded, feeling sick to my stomach, my mind screaming at me that I had destroyed not only our home, but also our marriage. That my weakness, my inability to let it be, had just cost me what I valued most in this world. Licia.

I put the coffee down on the windowsill. "I'm... I'm going to go for a walk," I said.

"That's a good idea," she replied.

I couldn't look at her, I stumbled outside in a worn robe and slippers into the forest.

"WE NEED MORE THRUST," BYTE SAID IN MY EAR, THE computerized version of her voice much too calm and kind of freaking me out. "We need it now."

I was wedged between the main jet assembly and the exterior surface of the 787's jet engine, a support strut against my shoulder, trying to replace the thrust of two dead engines. I also had an unwanted companion.

The glowing silver alien robot danced forward, its pincher jabbing my head, taking another sample of me. A larger one, the size of a pea, yellow motes of a piece of my neutrino form dancing in its pincher, somehow not melting them, its single bulbous eye staring at the sample and then at me, the strain on my face reflected in its eye.

"Can't you do something about this thing!" I shouted.

I needed to focus, but couldn't with this alien construct taking samples of me, transmitting data out, undoubtedly about what it was learning.

The alien Sarah had said the hostilities would end while she "spoke," while the council debated the fate of the Earth. Then why had this little beast disabled the plane and started taking samples of me?

"I can feel it," Byte said in my ear. "I can see its transmission, but I can't quite break through. It's different. It's still transmitting... a lot of data."

And then it dawned on me. The two were linked. It disabled the plane *so* it could take samples of me.

Maybe the council had finished. Maybe our fate had been decided and this was preparation for their final assault.

I shook my head. I didn't have time for this. I ignored the robot for a moment and focused on heating up my internal nuclear reaction to produce more thrust, but then the sample the robot held winked out into nothingness and it danced forward towards me, the small pads on the end of its feet somehow holding fast to the metal against torrent of wind passing through.

"No!" I shouted, and much to my surprise a yellow shield sprang forth from my forehead and shoved the robot back. That shield had always come out of my chest, it had always happened when my hands were thrust forth in a defensive gesture, not when I was thrusting as hard as I could with my hands pinned to my side, and not from my head.

The robot landed on its back, its six legs flailing in the air, but it didn't last long. Without its padded silver feet keeping it anchored to the metal, the wind picked it up and threw it at me, some silver, alien, robot, spider thing.

I reacted again, my mind wanting to lash out and my neutrino form following. The shield dropped, and a sharp beam of yellow jabbed forth, stabbing the robot in its center, running clean through it, the hole glowing orange around the edge. The construct went limp and bounced off my neutrino form on the way out.

"I got it!"

I smiled, but only for a moment.

That thing that I had just done, that neutrino laser was brand new, and it was just like a laser. It passed right through the robot and jabbed into a tube running to the interior assembly of the engine and fuel started spewing forth, mixing with the air and combusting when it hit me.

"That's a little better..." Byte's calm voice began. "Oh. We're losing fuel out of the port wing."

Yeah. No kidding. I couldn't see anything through the flames, and while this was apparently adding a little to the thrust, I worried about the additional heat this was producing. How long could the engine hold up?

"I can't shut it off," she said, "the leak is past any valving I control. I can pump some of the fuel out, but that will unbalance the plane. Do you know what's going on?"

Again, her voice was too damn calm. My face was full of flames. I needed to think.

"No. Wait." I shouted, my mouth opening and filling with flames. Not that it mattered. I wasn't human. I had an air cavity in my neutrino form, but I didn't need to breathe. I used it to pull air in so I could speak, so I could feel normal.

Something tickled in my brain. Shields popping out of my head. Yellow lasers shooting forth. These were new things that I could do. There must be more new things. Byte's words "Be the engine" mixed in and...

"Neutrino, it's me, Toxic." Tom Tyree's voice was a surprise, and chased off my coalescing thoughts, like a kid running at a flock of seagulls on the beach. "I asked Byte to patch me through."

It was too much. Dampening the reaction of my upper body so I don't just melt through the engine, thrusting harder than I ever had before, dealing with an alien robot, and now Toxicwasteman wanted to have a little chat?

"Listen, brother," he continued. "I need you to find a way. I need you to save Gayle. You asked her what her name is. It's Gayle and..." His voice nearly broke. Unlike Byte, this was really his voice, he must have one of the earbuds like I do and has been talking to Byte—no, Gayle—as he flies toward us.

"Look, I'll do anything you want, anything you ask, just find a way to save her and I'll..." He trailed off.

"I'm trying!" I shouted, pushing harder, engulfed in flames, knowing there was no way I could do this for over an hour and get us back.

The flames. There was something about the fuel and the flames, how the jet fuel mixed with the torrent of air before hitting me and burning. If I could just get my mind to work.

"I know you are," he said, "but I need you to reach deeper. I need you to find more. Not for me, but for Gayle."

But it was for him, I could hear it in his voice. He needed Gayle. The sociopathic villain Tom Tyree needed someone. I didn't understand it, but I dug deeper. I thrust harder.

"That's a little better," Byte's computerized voice said, "but we will still come down a hundred miles from shore."

I knew the nor'easter was raging below us, the waves churning and choppy. They might not even be able to send out rescue. Survival would be very questionable.

"Anything, Neutrino," Toxicwasteman said in my ear. "I'll do anything."

I ignored him, trying to get my brain back on track, trying to tickle out that idea that was just below the surface.

"I'll turn myself in," he said, his words coming fast. "I've never lied to you, Neutrino, you know that. If you get this plane to land, I will turn myself in."

Time almost stopped. The yellow flames engulfing me no longer an annoyance. Neutrino shields and lasers. Fuel mixing with air and combusting. The fact that I hadn't melted the metal earbud Byte had given me. *Be the engine.*

"I have an idea," I shouted, "but I won't be able to talk anymore. Byte, I'm going to need you to slowly shuttle all the fuel over to this wing. Tom, get out here and now, I don't know if this will be enough."

"What are you going to do?" Tom asked, his voice sounding like a scared child's.

"I'm going to be the goddamn engine."

A RAVEN WAS CAWING IN THE DISTANCE AND PINE NEEDLES kept sticking into my feet as I stumbled around the forest feeling sorry for myself.

Don't get me wrong, I had plenty of reason to feel sorry for myself, but that still doesn't make it useful.

The slip-on slippers left enough of my feet exposed so that as I walked on the thick carpet of dried pine needles a sharp end would poke me every once in a while.

I had started down the rutted and rock-filled dirt road, but looking up at the clear blue sky, I worried about satellites and the powers that be looking at every image they could take of the area and noticing a bedraggled man with brown hair in a ratty blue robe and knowing it was me. So I wandered out among the pine trees not paying any attention to where I was going, plodding around downed trees, avoiding the occasional gambel oaks, getting my feet poked by pine needles.

The pine needles weren't the straw that broke the proverbial camel's back, but something like that.

I had no home. I had no life. My wife appeared to be furious with me. And our whisper of a plan was to do an interview with Diane Madison, the reporter that had caused me so many problems over the years.

It was ridiculous.

I was, it seemed, the most powerful man in the world and I had nothing, could do nothing, and was just hoping we weren't found before we left to, somehow, get to this interview.

A raven, high up in a dead pine tree that had shed its needles but was still standing, squawked at me, seeming to be insulted by my mere presence.

"Me too," I mumbled to him. I was insulted by my presence.

I think it's a trick of the human psyche, perhaps a flaw, that when we are up we think we will always be up, and when we are down we think we will always be down. Those extreme states feel like they will last forever, but they don't. They can't.

And I was down, thinking it could only get worse.

I sighed and sat on a boulder, light green moss clinging to one side, and raised my head to the sun. The life-giving sun. I took a deep breath and let out a long sigh. I didn't try to chase away the fears or the, let's face it, depression. I just breathed.

Above me I could hear squirrels scampering in a tree and that raven continued to squawk at me from the dead tree.

I narrowed my eyes and deepened my breath, slipping into that meditative state with much more ease than I had before. Maybe the old skills were coming back.

Images of Licia's balled fists and hard expression came to my mind and I let them, but I kept breathing. I saw Casita de Soledad with our adobe house and greenhouses nestled in the high desert. Images of the prison and Evan Saunders and the battle with the q-morph soldier flicked by. Gaia at the Hoover Dam. Toxicwasteman, Lightningirl, and I at Yellowstone flying above a buffalo stampede. Sarah the alien in her crashed alien craft, and more. Pictures of the war. Images of when Licia and I got married. My parents. Ashely

Long. Diane Madison. Chaosboy. Dr. Cheese. Quinn. On and on the images rattled through my brain and I breathed.

And then a new image came into my mind, of a future that I feared. Soldiers surrounding the old cabin armed with rifles and alien energy weapons. Knocking the door down. Killing Licia.

I kept breathing, but that image stuck, it wouldn't leave me. And it wasn't a ridiculous thought... well, the killing likely was. They would drag her off and throw her in the prison I was in so many years ago below Groom Lake at Area 51.

We shouldn't be apart right now, no matter how bruised we were from what happened yesterday. Licia and I, we are better together. That is the way it is for couples that work. For us, more so because of how our powers complement each other.

Without thinking about it, I got up, pine needles poking my feet, but I didn't care anymore. I walked back the way I came, except... I didn't know what way I had come.

The raven perched in the dead tree, squawking at me, seeming to tell me what a fool I was.

I was lost.

The thought of Licia's capture played in my head repeatedly like a skipping record. My heart pounding and my meditative deep breathing turning into desperate gasps as I started to sweat.

I couldn't think. I needed to get back to her. I thought of taking to the air, I could find the cabin easily that way, but that would risk exposing our position.

It seems silly in retrospect, but I was losing it. Nothing had happened, aside from getting lost, except in my mind. I was in a forest that was almost all pine trees, one portion of it looking very much like another. It was easy to lose your way if you didn't pay attention, and I most definitely had not.

19 / HERE IS WHERE IT GETS WEIRD

Me becoming Neutrinoman, changing on a quantum level from flesh and blood to a contained nuclear reaction, honestly, sounds like a bunch of mumbo-jumbo. I get that. I do. But you all have seen it. I can do it.

I can fly, shooting yellow jets out my feet and hands (a la Ironman in the comics) and out my butt (most definitely not Iron-man). When I fly, I work in a similar way to a jet engine, I release pressurized gasses, the result of my internal nuclear reactions, in a controlled fashion (and I'm sure you see why the butt makes so much sense here). Those yellow jets are hot expanding gasses just like a rocket. Well... mostly. I mentioned when I first started writing about all of this that when I transform, I am governed more by quantum physics, than Newtonian physics, but you get the idea.

I can also go "elemental," losing my human form completely and exploding with nuclear force.

Until now, crammed in the engine of the 787, I hadn't found any states, besides flying and shields, between the human Neutrinoman and the elemental, exploding Neutrinoman.

And that is what came together in my mind. The neutrino shield meant I could create hard surfaces, which is why the earbud hadn't burned up, why my shoulder, pressed against that beam that joined the inner and outer portions of the jet engine hadn't melted. They hadn't because I hadn't wanted them to, and my form obeyed me. It created something akin to my shield so they could survive my touch.

Toxicwasteman was still talking in my ear, begging me to save his precious Gayle (aka Byte), promising to turn himself in if I did save her. No talk of aliens or how this world was his not theirs, just deep worry that he was about to lose something precious to him.

The flames from the leaking fuel combusting against my nuclear reaction were all around me, but I ignored them too. I focused on making my entire upper body firmer, less hot, covered in a "shield."

And it worked, the flames from the aerated fuel started occurring towards the back half of my body. That alien robot had disabled the jet engine's combustion chamber, where air and fuel mixed, burned, and released compressed gasses into the turbine which turned the front fan of the engine.

I had to become the combustion chamber. There was no turbine behind me, but if I could control the ignition of the fuel and the release of the gasses... well, that just might do it.

So I imagined myself as that combustion chamber. A shield all around my exterior, another shield, shaped like a funnel extending forth to capture the aerialized fuel and channel it deep into my body. There inside me, the fuel would combust and add to my nuclear reaction and expanding gases would pass out a small nozzle at the back of me.

I couldn't see myself as this transformation happened, and I am so glad. I think it would have so freaked me out and it wouldn't have worked. But I felt it. I felt myself filling up the space in a different way, getting larger, expanding. I saw a yellow, cone-shaped shield extending out in front of me. I felt the air enter and the fuel adding to my own internal reaction and then the gasses flying out behind me.

I had no legs, no hands, and even my sense of vision became vague, not that there was much to see in here.

I focused on taking in as much air as I could and releasing it out a narrow nozzle to produce as much thrust as possible.

"It's working," Byte's calm voice said in my ear. "Oh, my God, it's working. You're doing it."

Tom's voice was edged with manic relief. "I knew you could do it, Neutrino. I knew you could."

I couldn't talk, because I didn't have a mouth per se, but by some miracle of intention the earbud still worked, and I could hear them. And a thought burrowed into my head, a sick little worm of a thought. What if all of this, the robot, the disabled engine, the emergency, was arranged by Tom Tyree and Byte. What if Gayle wasn't her real name and this was just another one of the ways they were "training" me. Using Byte's simulations to plan this "attack" and manipulate me, to build me into what they wanted me to be.

"Wait. What happened?" Byte asked. "Our speed is going back down."

I felt the plane shudder as it hit some turbulence. I turned away from the thought. Now wasn't the time. And I focused on being the engine, combusting the fuel, keeping the plane in the air.

We were still a long way from land and I had no idea how long this would work.

20 / JUST A LITTLE FREAKOUT

MY EXHAUSTED BRAIN KEPT IMAGINING MORE EXTREME scenarios as I ran through the forest in slippers and a robe trying to find the cabin, sweat trickling down my back, my breath coming fast.

As I imagined it, there would no longer be trained troops with alien weapons coming to capture us, but by the time I got back to the cabin it would be all ash, Licia having been obliterated by some missile.

The slip-on slippers were really slowing me down, so I took them off and subjected myself to constant pokes by pine needles, rocks, and sticks, but I could move faster.

It hurt, a lot. My recent transformation had been extreme, and I had come back with baby-soft feet, all my callouses gone, my body consuming any unneeded materials in the transformation, including those callouses.

It didn't matter. Licia was all that mattered. All that ever mattered. I ran, still not really thinking, hoping my feet would find their way back.

And then, in my mind, it wasn't even the military coming for her, it was one of the oblong, silver, alien spacecrafts, like Sarah had been flying when I met her. They had kidnapped Licia and were doing horrible experiments on her. A rogue alien leftover from the war exacting their revenge on me.

My exhausted brain kept spitting out scenarios as my feet got further banged up. I ran until... I was there at that dead pine tree again, the raven squawking at me.

I had run in a circle.

I sank to the ground. The truth was, I wasn't ready for this. While our exile had been difficult in many ways, it was also exactly what I needed. I had seen enough war and adventure, and while it was hard being so small after those crazy years, it was also safe.

It was a simple life building things and growing food, each day spent with the woman that makes this world make sense.

And I had ruined it.

I started gasping for breath. Even though I was sitting, my heart was racing. If I couldn't handle one simple thing, like being lost in the woods, how was I to handle getting Licia and I back to a life we could live? How was I to deal with the forces arrayed against us?

I had been fooling myself sitting in our adobe casita typing away about the past, feeling assured of our present, acting like I knew what the hell I was doing and what the hell had actually happened.

The raven continued to caw at me from its high-up perch on a dead limb as I struggled for air. I felt too hot in the old robe, but I had nothing else on so I kept it.

My sweat had soaked into that robe and the sweet smell of the forest, which I usually loved, seemed wrong.

This wasn't a prison, not like the one below Groom Lake, but I felt trapped. I couldn't escape.

The trees were closing in.

I couldn't breathe.

I had to get out of here.

I had to find Licia.

But in the state I was in, that was beyond me. I knew it. A dim part of me was still sane, aware that I was having a panic attack, that I needed to calm myself. That transforming into Neutrinoman and flying away would be foolish. That my paranoid imaginings of Licia's capture or murder were just that, imaginings. She was probably still pacing, stopping only long enough to take a sip of coffee.

I pulled a stick out from under my butt and crossed my legs. I closed my eyes most of the way and started observing my gasping breath. Not judging it, just observing it. The raven kept cawing, which I tried not to fight. I let my breaths slip into the same rhythm as the caws. Still too fast, but slower.

I breathed, not trying to chase my demons away, but not playing with them anymore either.

I breathed. It was the only thing I could do.

INTERLUDE 2

I'm having trouble here. Yes, I'm lost in the forest, desperate to find Licia, worried that I've made another colossal blunder. But that's not what I'm talking about. I'm having trouble writing about this.

I do worry about what people will think of me. Neutrinoman lost in the forest, depressed, in an old bathrobe and slippers about to lose his mind. But that's not it either.

(Well, I could be fooling myself about this, but I don't *think* that's it. I can't really tell this story without looking fairly silly at times.)

What I really worry about is that I'm now boring you. That you don't want to hear about the personal struggles. You want to hear about superpowers and daring do and alien threats and maybe even a few grand romantic gestures to sweep my beautiful superpowered wife off of her feet.

You might have noticed, but I usually write these "interludes" as a conversation between Licia and I. Because these usually are conversations and this one, in fact, was a conversation we had. But I'm not going to write it like that.

For one, I can't tell you where we are. Our future is still uncertain, and it would be foolish to even hint at our location and I don't want to fake it like I did for the last interlude.

Also, Licia is not in the mood. She's still reading these chapters as I write them and it's clear now that it's not going to work if another one of them feels like when we were safe, if not content, at Casita de Soledad. Now is not that time for an adorable interaction between us—the loss of our home is too fresh.

But I digress. And perhaps the digression was boring too but hear me out. Please.

I'm writing about these small, human moments because they happened... Well, not *just* because they happened, but because they are important. My struggles with PTSD probably aren't what you are after here, but it's real. I won't detail every last piece of it, every time I struggle with shame and guilt, but my humanity, as demonstrated by my simple freak out in the forest, is very important to me.

Just because I can rocket into orbit at will doesn't mean I don't have the most down-to-earth problems.

And here I am breaking all the storytelling rules. "Show don't tell" they say. Okay, then, I'll get back to showing, but bear with me a while I'm just so very human.

I WASN'T ME ANYMORE, THE FUEL AND AIR MIXTURE funneling into me through my "head" combusting inside of my "body" and hot gasses spewing forth out a narrow nozzle at my back end. I had no head. No legs. No arms.

I had a vague sense of sight and I could hear just fine, Byte giving me updates on our progress, but my mind wasn't the same.

When I transform into Neutrinoman, I am "me." I mean, except for the flying and neutrino bolts and stuff, I still feel like me. I can't smell, and my sense of touch is numb and imprecise, but I have my memories and my thoughts. I feel like me.

When I go elemental and explode, I am most definitely gone. The elemental me guided by whatever intent I had before, but I am most definitely not conscious. My mind, which is present in my normal Neutrinoman q-morph form is absent as an elemental.

There, crammed into the 787's jet engine, I wasn't me, but I wasn't gone either. I was something more primal, hungry, fierce, single-minded.

I was the fire, seeking fuel, reveling in the flames. Eating. I felt strong and powerful. I felt indestructible. I felt so very sure of myself.

That last part... I have to tell you, it felt so good. After my time in the q-morph prison and being so clingy with Licia, feeling like I was alone when she wasn't with me, this was something I really needed.

I've never been the kind of person that felt sure of themselves. Ever. I doubt myself. All the time. Quite the opposite of Tom Tyree, who never has any doubt. But then again, he's a sociopath and I am not, so there is that.

"You're doing great, Nik," Byte's computerized voice said in my ear. I was back to thinking of her as Byte. Part of it was the primal state I was in, the other part was my doubt that Gayle with a "y" was her real name, that this whole thing wasn't some crazy Tom Tyree training program.

"I think I've got the rate down," she continued. "I'm moving fuel over from the starboard fuel tank. We're hitting a lot of turbulence and still losing altitude, but at this rate, we'll make it back to JFK."

It was the nor'easter that was the cause of the turbulence, but I was the engine, I was fire, I cared not for such things. I couldn't answer, and it was fairly miraculous that I could still hear her, that I had preserved my sense of hearing in this transformation and kept the earbud in place.

She was going to continue to supply me with fuel and that made me happy. As much as fire can be happy.

"I should get there a few minutes before you get back over land," Toxicwasteman said in my ear. The manic relief from earlier was gone from his voice. But I didn't like him. His voice, although it was real and not synthesized like Byte's, grated on me. I didn't trust it. I didn't need his help. I was the fire. I was the engine. I could do this.

"Wait," Byte said. "Oh hell. There's another one of those robots. It just activated. Nik, can you do something? It is crawling out the hole you made in the fuselage and is heading towards the port wing."

They didn't understand. I wasn't Nik. I was the fire. I was the engine. If I stopped being the fire the plane would fall—I had a strong sense of purpose. And, if I stopped being the fire, I would lose my sense of purpose and confidence—I knew that feeling was special and worth keeping.

But there was enough of my mind left to know that the alien robot was on my wing and could interfere with my purpose.

I let go of being the engine, so I could do battle with this foul robot, but I wasn't quite back to being myself.

SUMMER 2025, NORTHERN ARIZONA

THE RAVEN WAS THE KEY. ONCE I CALMED DOWN, SITTING ON the pine needles, feeling the panic and trying not to judge it, focusing on my breath, the regular caw-caw of the raven slowly becoming reassuring.

I heard a bird in a tree in the middle of a forest on a beautiful summer's day, me sitting and breathing, letting my imagination run wild, but not focusing on it. Just the breath. Just the in and out, feeling the air pass through my nostrils.

And then I remembered. I heard that same raven cawing when I left the cabin. It was distant and to the left of the road. I slowly rose, keeping my breath steady, my eyes not quite open all the way, and walked back, keeping that sound of the raven to my right and behind me.

It didn't take long, not in that state, time didn't really matter. Soon I was back to the cabin, the sun shining, the gentle breeze bringing the vanilla scent of the pines to me. The cabin was intact, there were no soldiers, no alien spaceships, no obvious threats.

But then I blinked open my eyes all the way, my heart starting to thump again. Licia was there. She was furious. We were still in this untenable position.

I took a deep breath and shook it off. If Licia was all that really mattered, then I best act like it.

I walked in and found Licia slumped in the rocking chair rubbing at the tears on her cheeks and sniffing. My wife is strong, so strong, that it's hard for me to see her like this. Not that she doesn't get to feel her feelings, not at all, it just scares me when the strongest person I know doesn't appear to be strong.

My stomach fell, and I felt like I was standing on the edge of a cliff looking over. I swayed as if I were really on that cliff, feeling dizzy and realizing that I was starving, my blood sugar well on the way to an epic crash.

But I didn't move. I stared, her brown eyes not meeting mine.

"I'm sorry," I whispered. And I was, but the words felt hollow and wholly inadequate.

"I'm angry," she said, her tone quiet but fierce.

I nodded. I wanted to go to her, to touch her, to hold her, to beg her for her forgiveness. But I didn't. I knew that wasn't the best thing right now. If I did that it would be about me and not about her.

"I'm sorry," I repeated. It felt even more hollow this time.

She rose, biting her lip, her arms hugging her chest, her eyes finally meeting mine. "I am so angry, Nik, I want to burn this forest down. I want to break everything I can find. I want to lay waste to the world. I want to…"

Her voice faltered, and she took a deep breath and sighed.

I looked down. I could not meet the fierceness in her eyes. I had only shame, and shame is no defense against anger.

"But I'm not mad at *you*, Nik." She was suddenly next to me, less than an arm's length away, but she didn't reach out.

"What?" I looked up, and even though she wasn't Lightningirl, I saw the eyes of a goddess. The fire, the fierceness was there, but so was compassion. Tears were slowly rolling down her cheeks.

"After the war was over," she began, quietly, but her words gaining strength, "they trapped us in their legal net, they coerced us into signing the Accords, and then they forced us into our desert exile, but first they planted a bomb underneath us and then they watched our every move, listened to our every word.

"I'm angry, Nik. I'm furious... but not at you." She paused, looking down, and then took my hand and squeezed it. "I grieve our loss, our beautiful home, our simple life, but I'm grateful the charade is over. I'm not going down without a fight. *We're* not going down quietly. We obeyed the rules, they did not."

I nodded, feeling her anger sparking my own, starting to wear away at my shame.

She shook her head, her long hair waving behind her. "I don't know if we'll survive, I don't know how we find a life after this, but..." And then she was in my arms and I held her tight.

"But we will do this together," I said, finishing her sentence.

I felt her nod and held her tight, hoping we would be enough for this challenge, hoping we would find a way.

23 / BEAST MODE

Beast mode. That's what I've come to think of the state I was in after I stopped being the engine and flew to meet the robot threat.

Beast mode. I was more myself than when I was sucking on fuel and taking the place of the airplane's engine, but I wasn't my normal self yet. I was bigger, eight feet tall, with a flatter face and huge hands. My mind was in a state to match my body, just like when Quinn turned into the Hammer and attacked Gaia at the Hoover Dam. I was aggressive and angry. This was my plane, and the silver alien robot was clinging to it, attacking it. I didn't want to be here, I wanted the simple life of being the engine, and I was angry about it.

I spotted the foot-long robot scuttling on the port wing as I flew. The clouds were thick and grey, laced with flashes of lightning, the wind blowing hard against me, but I didn't care. I had an enemy and a mission. A simple one. Preserve the plane and destroy the robot.

There was some benefit to thinking less, or rather, not over-thinking like I often do. My neutrino form changed quickly, did what I needed it to do without any fuss. No deep breaths, no concentration. I was elemental enough that I didn't need to "think" about controlling myself.

Look at it this way. When you learn to ride a bike, you have to really think about it. It's awkward and difficult and you fall a lot. After you learn, when you really are riding a bike, you aren't thinking about it, you are just doing it.

In beast mode I was just being Neutrinoman, not thinking about it.

In my ear, I could hear Byte's computerized voice, but I wasn't listening. She was saying something about the loss of speed, the time until the plane crashed into the ocean, things like that. My brain, such as it was, took it in, but it really just added to the urgency I was already feeling.

The robot had placed itself on the middle of the wing about sixteen feet from the fuselage and sprouted some kind of proboscis and poked it through the wing, its head starting a rapid sawing motion.

I wrapped my form in a protective shield, except for the jets coming out of my legs and hands. I did not want to harm the plane, *my* plane. I flew fast directly towards the robot.

As I got closer, I saw that the proboscis was serrated, it literally was a saw and as I approached, it reached its target and fuel started flying up from the wing, that fuel hitting me, rolling off the shielded parts of me and igniting at my hands and feet, a long tail of flame trailing behind me.

If the beast-me was mad before, now it was furious. The robot had damaged *my* plane. I flew up out of the way of the fuel and zoomed in front of the wing, timing my approach carefully, which was not easy. The plane was slowing, but it was still going several hundred miles per hour. It's not like I could just land on the wing (neutrino jets, you know). So, I zoomed just ahead of the wing, cut all jets, tightened my shields, twisted around, and landed on the wing and slid right towards the robot.

This is the kind of "just riding the bike" maneuver I couldn't have made if I had been thinking about it. It was instinct.

But the robot wasn't there when I slid to the mid wing, it had danced aside, its wide silver feet somehow sticking to the metal skin of the wing and I slid past and off the wing, the robot resuming its position and its sawing.

I tried again, flying ahead, cutting the jets, tightening my shield and landing on the wing, but the little guy was too fast. It just moved out of the way.

My anger mounted and my form grew bigger as I became more of a beast.

You must have seen the videos some of the passengers shot as I got bigger, more primal and more elemental. The yellow neutrino swirls are there, but blurred by the translucent shield that covered my body. Normally, looking at me as Neutrinoman, you wouldn't call me muscular. If you were being kind, you'd say I have well-defined muscles. The same is not true for beast mode. My form ripples with muscles, even though that doesn't make a lot of sense. I am a controlled nuclear reaction, I don't literally have muscles, but my form follows my mind and my mind was a lot less Nik Nichols and a lot more the Incredible Hulk.

I roared in rage as I slid off the wing. This wasn't working. I had to think, apply logic, be rational, but... beast mode, you know.

A third time I flew ahead, dropped onto the wing and slid down to where the robot had just been, but this time I lunged out with my arm and clipped the sucker as my fist tried to close on it. I tore off two arms and slid off the wing.

I glanced at the robot's arms as I briefly fell. They appeared to be metal, shiny silver, but as I watched them, they changed, they melted, turning into this dark purple liquid that began sizzling against my shield, like acid eating through metal.

The first robot I had encountered had taken samples of me.

Even with my blunted intellect, I saw this as related. The purple liquid metal, or whatever it was, was designed to hurt me.

And it was painful, a fierce burning sensation even when I had little sense of touch as Neutrinoman.

As I fell, I yelled at the purple stain and my hands they... Well, my hands exploded. Just a little bit, just in the area of the liquid. The shield I had been producing absorbed back into my neutrino form and then the pain got bad. But it was only a moment and the yellow of my palms got blindingly bright—although I didn't have physical eyes, so it didn't blind me—and small explosions erupted expelling the foreign substance.

Another new ability courtesy of beast mode and not over-thinking everything. This didn't take long, only a few seconds, and I flew back to the plane, my anger even greater. When I got to the plane, the damn robot had grown its arms back and was sawing again, the amount of fuel leaking out becoming substantial.

I had to try something else. I had to think. My plane was going to fall into the ocean and that was not acceptable. Not at all.

I flew forward in front of the wing, but this time I twisted my neck and watched the robot. As I cut my jets, I noticed it pulling its saw out of the plane and moving to scuttle farther out on the wing. As I fell, I used my right hand to change my trajectory, keeping the neutrino jet small and pointed away from the wing.

This time I ran right into the robot and knocked it off the plane.

I smiled as I watched it disappear into the grey of the clouds, just a brief moment of victory, and then I was flying behind my plane seeing the huge fuel leak and finally having enough of a mind to hear Byte's words.

"...got to stop the leak now or we're going to crash. Nik, we don't have much time, can you hear me?"

The clouds below us thinned and then were gone and I could see the roiling Atlantic Ocean below. Byte was right, we didn't have much time. I had to find a way to stop the leak and be the engine at the same time.

I VIVIDLY REMEMBER *THE INCREDIBLE HULK* TV SHOW starring Bill Bixby. That sad and plaintive piano playing at the end, time after time seeing Bruce Banner with an old coat and a backpack along some lonely road with his thumb out, trying to get a ride to the next place, the next chapter, the next chance at redemption.

I was born in 1974, so I was seven and eight watching the show towards the end of its run with my father. It wasn't my mother's kind of thing, so the two of us would watch it together on the old brown couch while he drank a beer and I sipped on a root beer. Every week as I watched, I was a little bit conflicted. I was, of course, hoping that Bruce could find the peace that he craved, but I was dubious that he would like his life without the Hulk being a part of him. He did good with the monster within, he had power with the monster within, he would have been dead so many times over without that monster transforming him at the most dire of times.

My mind was thinking of Bruce Banner as I stuck my thumb

out on a twisting section of blacktop that ran through the pine tree forest of the Kaibab Plateau north of the Grand Canyon. Licia was next to me, her brown eyes staring up at the blue sky, lost in thought.

We had left that day I had gotten lost. After breakfast we put on backpacks and started walking north through the forest. The cabin was remote, but it being summer there was plenty going on in the forest. ATVs ripping along the dirt roads, campers set up here and there. But we avoided everyone and had camped under the stars the previous night, eating cold beans and getting up in the morning and making it here to 89A.

Licia had a wig on now, short blond hair, and I had on sunglasses and an old cowboy hat we had found in the cabin. We looked dirty and bedraggled, which we let be so it could add to the disguise.

We had a plan... well, something of a plan. The interview with Diane Madison was thirteen days off. Our plan was to lie low, get out of the area, keep moving, and show up to the interview and tell the world what was going on. We needed to get a burner cell phone so we could have Byte arrange a few things for us. It wasn't much, but it was a plan.

As I stood there, my thumb out, the cooling breeze welcome, my nose full of the sweet scent of the pine trees, I thought about Bruce Banner and his quest to rid himself of the Hulk. Would I be better without Neutrinoman, living a simple life during these difficult times? If this was a TV show about our story, would the music playing be lonely and plaintive? Would the camera zoom out showing the remoteness of our location making the task in front of us seem that much larger? Illustrate how far we have fallen.

I smiled as the thoughts bounced around my head, because the answer was easy. No, the music wouldn't be lonely because while there was a huge challenge in front of us, there was an "us." Licia was here. She's not going anywhere. I have a partner, someone that makes me better and stronger.

And then the smile faded. I'm not alone, but I couldn't see a way out of this, a way for us to have a life, be in this world, be happy. I just couldn't.

So maybe sad music, maybe plaintive, but not lonely.

FALL 2006, OVER THE ATLANTIC OCEAN

THE WAVES WERE DARK, TIPPED WITH WHITE FOAM, THE winds of the nor'easter churning them into a froth. The plane bucked in the winds as I flew towards the port wing with its gushing fuel leak, Byte chattering in my ear.

"Tom is still a ways off," her calm, computerized voice said. "You've got to stop the leak. You've got to get our speed back up. There will be no rescue in these conditions."

Byte's voice was calm and computerized because she was not actually speaking but sending her synthesized voice to my earbud with her mind. But her sentences had gotten short and to the point. Even in beast mode, I could feel her anxiety and didn't need her encouragement. This was my plane, my fuel that was leaking. I wanted nothing more than to be the simple purposeful engine again.

And it was the engine that I summoned... no, that's not the right word. I didn't summon the more elemental me, it was still there, right below the surface, eager to return.

I can't watch the videos of this. It makes me profoundly uncomfortable to think of what I became. But I will do my best to describe it.

The leak was a third of the way out the port wing. As the huge beast-mode Neutrinoman flew closer, his head became large, his body swelling behind him, his mouth opening and extending like a toothless crocodile.

Okay... okay... I am describing myself in the third person. I did say "profoundly uncomfortable" up above, didn't I? Okay, let me try again.

My mouth extended and elongated as I approached the wing, my body fully shielded except for my hands and feet where the fuel ignited and a long flame blasted out into the wind.

It didn't last long. My now huge mouth clamped down on the wing and contained the leak, the fuel pooling inside my form. My legs had fused together, and I was a yellow tube with a tapering back end. The top of my "head" grew, like some sort of weird tumor and then it opened up so it looked something like an air intake on a muscle car. And that's what it was. Flames started shooting out my back end, as I combined the fuel with air and combusted it inside of me.

The flames were yellow and long, but as I got the mixture right, the flames virtually disappeared in the air behind me shimmered with heat.

I was a yellow cylinder clamped onto the wing. There was nothing recognizably human about me. If you saw a picture of it without knowing the story, the yellow motes and swirls beneath the translucent shield would remind you of me, but you wouldn't say, "Hey, is that Neutrinoman?" There was no "man" involved anymore.

But I was happy. No, that's not the right word. I wasn't really capable of happiness, but I was whole and complete with a purpose I knew I was fulfilling. I was the engine. I was the fire. I could feel the plane speed up as it continued to buck against the wind. There was hope.

I had a sense of sight, but I could see all around me. Below the plane to the churning ocean, above the plane to the dark clouds, and I could see the passengers staring out the window at me. At first, as I transformed, their looks were looks of horror and fright. When they saw it was working, those faces changed to hope. And this pleased me deeply.

"...we've lost a lot of fuel," Byte was saying. By some instinct I was still preserving that earbud, still hearing her, even though I didn't have a head much less an ear. The metal earbud was still embedded in the front portion of my engine form, still working. "But we don't have enough fuel now. I hope you can hear me. I hope you can find a way."

26 / ROAD TRIP

IT TOOK HOURS FOR SOMEONE TO STOP FOR US. 89A HERE RUNS from Jacob Lake to Fredonia, not exactly a major thoroughfare. It was a lovely summer day with the temperatures among the pines up in the seventies, the sky filled with high, thin clouds blunting that startling blue color you often get at eight thousand feet in elevation.

Licia and I talked, but not about much of anything. We remembered some trips together to this area in happier times, but we didn't go too far with that. These were not happy times and we were still processing what had happened.

Or, at least, I was. I could still hear the piano playing the theme from *The Incredible Hulk* as I stuck my thumb out for the intermittent vehicles roaring by. Since Licia and I couldn't get lost in conversation or nostalgia, it was my way of band-aiding the psychological wound until it could be attended to... whatever the hell that means. As I write this, I have more distance on what happened, a lot more perspective, but it's still a difficult thing to bear.

So my mind is occupied with Bruce Banner on his lonely quest to free himself from the inner monster, instead of Nik Nichols who just got his home vaporized and has no idea how he and his wife will ever find peace.

The couple that stopped for us looked to be in their seventies, with snow-white hair, wrinkled faces, and a fair amount of extra weight. They were driving an old RV, the kind built on a van frame, not one of those huge behemoths.

"Where y'all headed?" the man asked from the rolled down driver's side window as we walked up.

"West," I said, because I had to say something, and it was the way the road was headed.

"Just to Fredonia," Licia added. When the man's wrinkled forehead furrowed further, she added, "It's only thirty miles down the road."

"Well hop on in then," he said with a smile, his head nodding towards the other side of the RV.

"Fredonia?" I whispered to Licia as we walked around the back.

She nodded. "We have to pick up something there."

I wanted to ask her what she's talking about but there wasn't any time. And then I was worried. We spent all this time hiking and standing by the side of the road and we didn't talk about the next step except me asking Licia which way we should go and her telling me west. She had a plan after what happened at Casita de Soledad, she still had a plan now, and I still had no idea what it was.

We were both still in shock by what had happened, but I needed to do better. We needed to start acting like a team again.

"Welcome aboard the Polar Express," the white-haired woman said from the passenger's seat. She had bright blue eyes and a nice smile. "I'm Jean, this my partner in crime, Alan." She extended her hand which was soft and warm. I shook hands with Alan, but didn't say anything, my mind slipping.

I needed to introduce myself, but I couldn't use my name. We should have talked about this too.

"Thank you for stopping," Licia said, a big smile on her face. She still had on her sunglasses and her shoulder-length blond wig. "You are so kind. My name is Lee, this is Neil."

"What are you two doing out on this lonely stretch of road?" Alan asked.

Licia laughed, it was quiet and shy. "Well, Neil here bet me that we couldn't make it from our home in Yuma all the way to my uncle's house in Fredonia just by hitchhiking."

I nodded, warming to the charade. I didn't want to be myself right now, so why not be this "Neil"? "Yes, sir," I said. "I was convinced that we wouldn't find enough kind people like yourselves after... well, you know." I ended in a shrug.

Jean nodded her head and sighed. "That alien war was an awful thing and all that terrible finger pointing afterward. It didn't always bring out the best in us."

"And I was sure we would," Licia said, her smile bright, but I knew she was faking it. "And I'm about to win that bet." She turned and punched me in the shoulder. It looked playful, but it hurt.

"Well, buckle up, you two," Alan said, starting the van up. "We've got to win Lee a bet. The Polar Express will get you there!"

Jean smiled. "We call it that because... well, we're headed towards Alaska and we're not very creative... or geographically accurate."

Licia laughed and this time it hurt in my gut. It wasn't a real laugh, she was playing a part. What did we have to laugh about?

TIME SLIPPED PAST IN THE ODDEST WAY AS I SUCKED THE FUEL out of the wing, mixed it with air, ignited it in my body, and spewed the hot gasses forth keeping the damaged 787 aloft.

I was aware of the passage of time, the chop of the sea below, the spasms of turbulence that shook my plane, the looks of the passengers as they would stare out the window, the worry written clearly on their faces. But I wasn't aware of how much time had passed, if that makes any sense. I was not concerned with the future or the past. Just the now. The mixing of fuel and air, the ignition, the flames, the thrust.

Byte would talk in my "ear" from time to time, encouraging me. Toxicwasteman chimed in a couple of times reiterating his promise to turn himself in if I got the plane back to land. Their words, their pleas, felt familiar, felt like they should mean something, but I didn't care. I couldn't reply and continued executing my purpose.

Until...

The fuel ran out.

And my purpose was no longer achievable.

And land was not yet in sight.

And the plane started to head towards those stormy seas.

That's the thing about being the engine. What are you if you can't do your job? Just an empty container longing for fuel and air. Just a lifeless cylinder that has no purpose.

I wasn't fully elemental—thankfully—but I was far enough on that side of the spectrum that at first the lack of fuel was puzzling and then it was infuriating, but I was stuck. I had been the engine for so long, loved the single-minded focus and purpose, that I was lost. I didn't know how to change back into Neutrinoman, much less Nik Nichols.

"Nik, please hear me," the ever-calm voice of Byte said in my ear. "Come back to us. Please. Can you hear me, Nik?"

She didn't call me Neutrinoman or even Neutrino like Toxicwasteman would have. She called me by my real name. My human name. My mundane earthling name.

"Tom is still ten minutes out," she continued, the plane bucking violently against the force of the storm. "The airports are closed. The coast guard is at dock. We need to get this airplane to land. Nik? Can you hear me, Nik?"

The dark, churning ocean was coming near. My plane was falling, it would die. And that is the word that I felt, "die." My plane. My failure. My death.

But I was just an engine without fuel, what could I do?

"Honey, it's me." It was Licia's voice in my ear now. "I'm sorry I left. I should have been there with you." Unlike Byte, her voice was normal, filled with an emotion I couldn't quite identify in my current state. "Can you hear me, Nik? Byte has told me what you've done, what an incredible thing you managed to do getting everyone this far. But you are so close. I know you, Nik. I know you can do this."

Her voice was smooth, too smooth, something she would do when she was trying to hide her worry. But that voice was so familiar that with each time she said my name, I felt myself return a little bit more. A little less engine, a bit more Nik.

"I love you, Nik, you know that, right?" Licia asked, her voice getting thick. She was worried, but why? I couldn't understand that, but I wanted to. "We've been so busy lately, maybe I haven't said it enough. No matter what happens here, I love you. Do you hear me, Nik? Nik!" Her voice was edging higher. Was she worried that I would never recover, that in being the engine I would go down with the plane. That I would die, too.

Those were barely thoughts in my state, but it was what she was worried about. I was doing things the military had never conceived of. Byte didn't have enough data to run an accurate simulation, but the ones she had run had worried her enough to contact Licia.

"Remember the first time we kissed," Licia said with a sniff. "At the winery with Oak Creek below us, the grape vines planted on the hill above us. Do you remember, Nik? Can we take a break from all this recruiting and go back there? There's a place near there that has cabins. We could go incognito and just forget the world for a few days. Just you and me. Just us."

Licia was waxing romantic and the waves were getting close, too close. Licia wasn't the romantic and planes fly in the air, they don't go into the ocean. My plane... no, "the" plane was going to go down. I had to do something.

"Nik?" Licia said, and I could hear the tears in her voice. "Come on, Nik? Say something. Please."

I can't tell you how I did it. How I stopped being the engine and started being Neutrinoman again. How I left that simplicity of a single-minded purpose and returned to my decidedly difficult and chaotic life. It was Licia, for sure, giving me something I wanted more than being the engine, but I can't tell you "how." When I go from flesh and blood to my q-morph form it is like a switch, an act of will. Here, one moment I was the engine and the next I was

Neutrinoman falling towards the ocean feeling weak and disoriented.

"Lower the landing gear," I said as I flew back towards the plane. There was shouting in my ear, both Byte and Licia speaking their relief, but I didn't have time to listen. The plane was only hundreds of feet above the churning water and land was nowhere in sight.

FALL 2006, OVER THE ATLANTIC OCEAN

I WAS DOING MY BEST ATLAS IMPRESSION, NOT HOLDING UP the entire earth, just the plane, my shielded shoulders crammed against the axel between the front two tires of the port landing gear while I thrusted with my hands, my feet, my butt... with everything I had.

I wasn't trying to be the engine, I was just trying to slow the fall, make the plane lighter, hoping Byte and the pilot could use that to get us farther.

I wasn't in beast mode but back to regular old Neutrinoman and I was running out of power. I had been transformed for ninety minutes or so, expending energy the whole time, I could feel my nuclear reaction waning.

And still the dark oceans churned, slowly getting closer, the wind blew and the plane bucked and I thrusted.

"Will you come work for me?" I asked Byte. Licia wasn't on the line anymore, she was back to helping out at the power plant having gotten me back to myself. She was physically taking the place of some burned out transformers, powering hundreds of thousands of homes to keep them warm during a blizzard in the Pacific Northwest. She had more important things to do than to talk to me.

"What?" Byte asked. I was so sick of her calm, computerized voice.

"Surely you knew," I said.

"I don't know that I do now."

"That's why I wanted to meet you. To ask you to come work for me at Heroes Incorporated."

And I guess this might seem strange. I'm in the middle of a crisis and I'm trying to recruit a q-morph onto the team. And it was strange. But I hadn't asked her when we had been on board, having the big fat panic attack I was having, and right then I really needed a distraction. I didn't want to think about how hard this was, or how I was probably going to fail, or about how Licia had to stop helping so many to help me.

"That is interesting," she said.

"I would be hiring Gayle—sorry, I don't know your last name—not Byte. Your identity would remain secret. You would head up the IT department, ensure that the military is keeping their end of the bargain, get us some simulations up and running to help guide our decision making."

There was silence and, frankly, that wasn't good for me. "You could help liaison with strategic partners," I added. I didn't come out and say it, that I wanted her to coordinate with Toxicwasteman and his gang at LoVE. For a few reasons. I had been through enough to worry that we might be overheard, even though this was Byte I was communicating with. But mostly because I didn't want to say it out loud.

I mean, I believed that we would need everyone to defeat the aliens if they came back. What I didn't want to admit out loud is how deeply Tom Tyree had influenced me.

"You can't have her!" Toxicwasteman said in my ear, his voice no longer calm, no longer pleading, but full of energy and anger.

So that was the delay—she was talking to him.

"I'm not asking you," I shot back, a groan in my voice as the weight of what I was doing became difficult to bear. Planes are heavy, you know. "Let the lady speak for herself."

"Forget it, Neutrino, it's not going to happen." There was an implied "she's mine" in what he said in the way he said it, and that made me angry.

I wanted to shout back, tell him how Byte was not his property, how she was a powerful woman and could make up her own mind, that he should butt out and let me assemble my team, this whole Heroes Incorporated being something he catalyzed.

But I didn't. I heard how that would play out in my head, two men talking about a woman and what they thought was best for her. If I was ever in such a conversation and Licia ever found out... well, let's just say that it wouldn't go well for me. But that wasn't the reason I held my tongue. My mother is the reason. While she was often the definition of a helicopter mom, had a way too intense love of tchotchkes, and changed her hair color way too often, she was a strong woman. She ran my father's accounting business, doing everything but the accounting. She helped my grandparents, in their eighties then, remain in their home by doing everything they couldn't do anymore. She volunteered at the soup kitchen and had helped my uncle—my father's brother who she didn't like at all —through his cancer treatments. She didn't go to college. She didn't have any flashy skills or talents, and yet she, single-handedly, held the family together and made it work.

As the silence went on, and these thoughts flitted through my head, I really missed my mom and would like nothing better than to have her doing or saying something that, like mothers were so good at doing, deeply embarrassed me. Since my time in prison, since we started Heroes Incorporated, I had been staying away. I didn't want to see the worried look on her face as she asked me how I was doing, insisted I wasn't eating enough, told me that I should slow down some.

And I should slow down. Get away with Licia, go spend some time with my mom, help my dad tinker with his Charger.

But the potential alien attack, the needs of forming a team to meet them, it seemed like I was always carrying this huge weight, and right then, I literally was carrying a huge weight, a 787 airplane.

"Gayle," I said quietly, hearing the emotion of all that had just run through my head clearly in my voice. "I need you."

That was it. Three words. Just the truth.

I AM A ROMANTIC, THAT IS CERTAINLY CLEAR BY NOW, BUT I also live in the real world.

My world was walking behind my wife as she marched east down Pratt Street in Fredonia, Arizona. Her steps metronomically steady, her head straight ahead, her voice silent. The backpack made it hard to tell, but I'm pretty sure her back was straight and I could see that her fists were balled up.

Gone was the pleasant chitchat with Jean and Alan who had let us off in front of the Grand Canyon Hotel, the faded red fifties-style sign out front topped awkwardly with a wagon wheel.

I'm romantic enough to believe with all my heart that I am a better person with Licia, that she makes my life worth living, that I would literally be dead a dozen times over without her. But—and here's the "real world" part—I didn't feel that connection then. Not since Project Vulcan vaporized our home. We were not on the same wavelength, or however you'd like to put it. We were a couple, we were together, but we were not one.

And when you're used to feeling that togetherness, it's very disorienting when you no longer feel it.

What I wanted to do was pepper her with questions, find out exactly how much escape planning she did without breathing a word to me.

Don't get me wrong, I'm glad she did it. But it's hard to feel your partner is your partner when this level of deception comes to light. Maybe deception is the wrong word. She didn't actively deceive me—I don't think—but she sure did hide a lot from me.

After ten minutes, the small, scattered houses fell away and the road continued through flat desert, short weeds trying to survive in the reddish, sandy soil.

Another minute or two and we were standing in front of the Fredonia Cemetery, a generous plot of land out here separated from the rest of Fredonia, as if the growth of the town was stunted and it never grew out this far like in most towns.

The cemetery had a low chain-link fence that met a short flagstone wall on either side of the entrance. A wrought-iron gateway framed the entrance with the letters spelling "FREDONIA CEMETERY" backdropped by the darkening sky as the sun headed towards the horizon behind us. Below the entryway was, and I'm not kidding here, a cattle guard. Most of the plot was empty with several rows on the far side green-brown with struggling grass and some granite and flowers sticking up. Nice of them to protect the grass and the flowers from cows, but I guess it says something about Fredonia that they needed to.

We were not there long. I helped Licia pull a large limestone rock up, just on the other side of the wall. She dug, pulled out a small metal box, and stowed it in her pack. We put the rock back and soon we were marching back west on Pratt Street.

"I appreciate you not asking all the questions I know are driving you mad right now," she said from in front of me.

I smiled. There was distance between us and that feels profoundly uncomfortable, but my wife still knew me and I knew her. "No problem," I said, although it was anything but. "I do hope there is room for food in our itinerary soon, though."

She chuckled and shook her head, her metronomic pace not wavering one little bit.

It wasn't much, just a second of almost laughter, but on a day like today it was a lot.

Toxicwasteman came roaring in, a sickly green streak with a trail of coal-black smoke behind him.

He was mad.

He was just in time.

The churning ocean was a hundred feet below us and my Atlas impression was just about to end. It had been radio silent since I had tried to recruit Byte, told her that I needed her. I was pretty sure they were having their own discussion and I doubted that Toxicwasteman was using his inside voice.

His swirling green face was hard as he took position on the starboard landing gear between the two inner wheels just like me and started doing his own Atlas impression. As he flew in to take his position, I did notice that his upper body, where it pressed against the axle of the landing gear, had a translucent green layer. His version of a shield. He was a contained chemical reaction while I was a contained nuclear reaction... we were more alike than I liked to admit.

. . .

"DON'T TALK," BYTE'S ENGLISH-ACCENTED, COMPUTERIZED voice said in my ear. "Just listen, please. He's mad, but he'll get over it. Thank you for your kind offer, but I must politely decline."

"No," I said it quietly and then I turned and shouted it at Toxicwasteman. "No!"

He turned, the strain on his face obvious, from our effort to keep this 787 aloft, yes, but maybe from what I was asking. His pleas earlier made it clear that he needed her. The psychopathic villain needed someone and at first that had heartened me. But now, it seemed that he needed her to be exclusively his. Byte's assertion that "he's not the jealous type" in the LoVE base near the Grand Canyon had either not been correct or something had changed.

"Care to elaborate, Neutrino?" His eyes were hooded and his trademark wolfish grin was not decorating his lean face.

I hesitated. I didn't want to have a fight about Byte with her listening, with two men talking about her like she wasn't present. But what could I do?

"No," I repeated. "You don't get to decide for another human. No."

"I didn't decide, she did." His upper lip curled back as he groaned from the effort, green flames and black smoke pouring out his hands, his feet, and yes, his butt.

"I don't believe you."

"Please let it go," Byte said in my ear.

"No!" I shouted.

When I had met Byte in the LoVE base, when they were trying to recruit me, when she tried to seduce me, she had told me how she had gone mad after her transformation, how she got locked up and Tom Tyree had found her and helped her. I remember the look she had given Tom had been one of love and admiration. But what I was seeing now disturbed me.

"All this time. All this effort," I shouted at Toxicwasteman.

"You've been trying to mold me into a weapon that can defeat the aliens. I'm sure Byte's simulations are nearly certain they're coming back, it's not like the human race is going to suddenly get its act together. And yet here I am trying to form my team, trying to get *your* Heroes Incorporated off the ground, and you're blocking me. Why?"

He looked at me, his eyes wider, his face slack, almost innocent, and then he looked away.

"Why?" I shouted it this time.

The plane shuddered, the vibration reaching me through the axel my shoulders were pressed against. The ocean was still coming closer despite our combined efforts. Snow had begun to fall, the white flakes melting on contact when they reached the churning sea. None of this mattered. We weren't going to make it.

"Please stop this. Both of you," Byte said in my ear, and his too, I presume. "I am begging you. Save your energy for—" her voice cutoff suddenly like the connection had been dropped. "Land. I see land on the radar. We are almost there."

"You can't have her," Toxicwasteman growled. I glanced over, and his eyes were now feral and wild. "She's mine."

I opened my mouth to speak when a sharp pain lanced through my head and I heard a sizzling sound over the wind. I looked up and in the well of the landing gear was another silver alien robot, but it was different. It was the same size, its body a foot across, but it only had four legs, its body wide in the back and tapering into a log proboscis. As I stared, it shot a purple ball out its proboscis and hit me square in the forehead, feeling like I had been struck by a rock, the sizzling sound starting again.

The first robot had sampled me when I was in the engine, the second's legs had turned into this purple goo when I fought it on the wing, now this one was shooting the balls at me.

I couldn't keep holding the plane up and fight this robot. Why did they want to take the plane down?

And then it hit me. They didn't care at all about the plane, whether it landed or not. This was all about finding out more about me, learning better ways to stop and hurt me.

Could there be any doubt the aliens were coming back?

31 / A BEAUTIFUL MACHINE

THE MINI STORAGE PLACE IN FREDONIA, ARIZONA, WAS NOT much to talk about. Grey cement blocks, cheap metal overhead door. In the metal box she dug up was a wad of cash and a key. She pocketed the cash and used the key to unlock the storage unit. She paused and looked at me in the dimming light. I could see the emotions at play. She was worried, but I didn't think it was the larger how-do-we-survive worry, it was something more personal.

"Listen..." she began, licking her lips, her arms wrapped around her chest despite the warm evening.

This was it. If I wanted it, she would tell me everything. All the plans. All the things she hadn't told me. That look was part worry and part guilt. And I wanted it. I wanted to know everything, and it made me feel good that she wanted to tell me, but... well, it just wasn't the time.

"Let's get safe first," I said, doing my best to give her a relaxed smile, hoping it wasn't one of those crazed, fake, I'm-totally-freaked-out smiles. It wasn't time for that either. "Then we will both have a lot to talk about."

She paused, her eyes searching my face and then she nodded, so I guess my smile wasn't that bad, or the poor dusk lighting explained it—the storage place's lights hadn't gone on yet.

The door rumbled up, puffing out dust to reveal a most atypical storage unit. In other words, there wasn't much in there. In the dim light I could see some cheap metal shelves along one side, some jerry cans, and in the middle of the unit something covered in a sheet that looked just like a—-

"No..." I said, a smile blossoming on my face.

"Yup!" The worry and guilt were gone and on her round face was a look of pure joy. Like a kid in the candy store, or like a girl with her motorcycle.

Well, not to say like *any* girl with her motorcycle, but like *this* girl with her motorcycle. Like *my* girl with a motorcycle.

She stepped into the dark space, went to the metal shelves and turned on a battery powered lantern there, which threw out bluish illumination.

Licia pulled the tarp back, dust filling the air, to reveal a Harley-Davidson Sportster 1200. It was a twin cam beauty, long and sleek with two chrome exhaust pipes curling back on the right side, and the tank and the fenders painted an electric blue. It had leather saddle bags and a two-up seat.

It was up on a stand, keeping weight off the tires. It had been properly stored for the long term.

I have flying, I love it and she is terrified by it. She has motorcycles, she loves it and I'm... well, not quite terrified of it, but I don't love it.

Not that there's been much time for motorcycles since we met and all this madness started.

I rode bicycles like a maniac when I was kid, which was my downfall with motorcycles. When I was nineteen, I tried out Robby Holmes's Kawasaki dirt bike and I absolutely loved it. Except the rear brake control was at the foot, not on the handlebar. I was having a great ride through the desert when I had to brake fast for a rabbit, locked the front wheel and went flying.

I broke my right arm and my collar bone. After I recovered, I did ride a little more, just to "get back on the horse," but that early injury spoiled it for me.

From another perspective, though, I do love motorcycles, and that's really about the motor. It's displayed there, all chromed and beautiful. I spent a lot of time working on cars with my father and helped Robby with his motorcycles even after the crash. The Sportster is a particularly beautiful machine.

"The gas has a stabilizer and is about a year old," she said, shaking one of the jerry cans. "You think she'll start up?"

"New oil put in and the gas drained?" I asked.

She nodded.

I checked the exhaust pipes and pulled the rags out—they were put there because rats are notorious for nesting in pipes. I squatted down, looked at the engine, and then looked up at her and the shyness was back on her face. The prep was at least a year old, so there were other people involved in this escape plan. Licia and I had spent the last five years at Casita de Soledad with rare outings and none to this part of Arizona. She had a team that had helped her, and knowing her it was family members. It seemed everywhere we went she had a second cousin or an old friend of her father's.

"Normally," I said with a smile, "the battery would be an issue, but I think we have that covered."

The smile on her face was bright and I realized something. This is what Licia would have wanted back in 2020 if we had gotten the chance to choose. A simple life on the road, just being tourists, just seeing what was around the next bend, the wind ruffling our hair and the scenery whipping by.

The theme from *The Incredible Hulk* played in my head and I imagined Bruce Banner with a gorgeous Harley hitting the road in search of redemption. It didn't quite work, the tune was a bit too sad and a bit too plaintive, but it was a fun idea.

"So..." I began. "The plan is we're riding to the Diane Madison interview. Is it in Los Angeles?"

I knew the answer, but just wanted to see her face.

She shook her head, even in the weird bluish lantern light she suddenly looked younger. "The interview is in New York. We've got to get all the way across the country." She stalked up to me, like she was a big cat after prey, her hand landing on my shoulder, the electric tingle of our energy exchange making me smile. "Won't that be a chore?"

I nodded, not turning around. "A terrible chore. I'll be stuck on that bike behind you, holding on to you for hours a day on that tiny seat."

She ran her finger across my shoulder, her hand resting on my neck, playing with my hair. "Come on, Nik. It'll be fun. We'll make it fun."

And yes, the entire military apparatus of the United States was after us and my wife was flirting with me in a dusty storage unit in Fredonia, Arizona.

I nodded, her tingling hand still on my neck. "I think we should head north first, get out of the area, not take a direct route."

"Cheap hotels along the way," she said, leaning down and whispering in my ear, her breath sweet and warm. "Cash only. Arriving under the cover of darkness. Wine and takeout Chinese food. Backrubs and doing whatever else we can to relieve the tension of a long ride."

I wanted to turn around and grab her, close the door to the unit, and see what kind of tension could be relieved right here and right now. But after our decades together, I knew what this was. A promise. If I could get the motorcycle working, if I could handle the long days riding on it despite my past trauma and the narrow seat, she would make it well worth my while.

"I like this plan," I said and got to work getting the motorcycle running.

I WAS SO SICK OF SILVER ALIEN MORPHING ROBOTS. I WAS SICK of this 787 and the nor'easter and the struggle to get it back to land. I was tired of the months spent in meetings getting Heroes Incorporated off the ground, negotiating for land for the base, negotiating with the military for autonomy, hiring people, reading contracts. I was even tired of these recruiting trips, trying to convince people that our mission was worthwhile, that banding together was our only chance, that the military wasn't the only way.

And I was so sick of Toxicwasteman and his constant manipulations, his molding of me into what he thought could defeat the aliens and save "his" planet. He wasn't doing this for humanity. He was doing this because aliens invading earth felt personal to his sociopathic brain.

This whole thing felt like a setup. Licia being called away at the last moment so I was alone on the plane. The robots, while clearly alien, showing up time and time again to make this harder, forcing me to find new capabilities. Even this fight for Byte. Was this all a ruse to get me to want Byte more, give her more responsibility, more access? How could I have surprised them with this?

But mostly I was just tired. I had been Neutrinoman—normal, beast mode, or engine—for far too long. I was running on reserves and knew at this point I would be a mess when I became flesh and blood again.

The silver alien robot, clinging to the upper portion of the landing gear, spit another piece of purple goo at me out of its long proboscis. This stuff was purple like the energy weapon that so effectively sapped my power, but it was solid, goopy like jelly. It hit my shoulder and started sizzling, pain spiking through my body.

I pulsed my upper body, just like I had when I tore off the robot's legs on the wing. The pulse worked—it repelled the goo but it also further melted the rubber wheels of the front axle. The robot and I had done this repeatedly, the front two tires were practically gone, and the metal was beginning to pucker and fatigue.

Each of the aft landing gear have two axles with two tires with a large shaft between them. My shoulder was pressed to that central shaft as was Toxicwasteman on the other side. We were a pair. Yellow and green.

"Don't you have a shot?" I yelled at Toxicwasteman.

"No," he shouted back, his voice a growl. "It's up in the well. I can't see it. Don't you have a shot?" We hadn't talked about Byte since this attack started, but the animosity of it lingered.

"Yeah, I have a shot, but you know, holding the plane up, fuel supplies that could ignite. Little problems like that."

I missed being the engine, life was so simple then. I missed beast mode, too, just feeling my way through it.

The robot spit on me again, a spike of pain, the sizzle, and I pulsed it off, feeling my energy wane even further.

I looked at the forward landing gear, but that was the wrong place to apply lift—I'd probably just end up shoving the nose up and destabilizing the plane. I looked over at the starboard engine, the cowling melted back when my reaction had gotten too hot. The alien might be able to follow me there, but at least it would be more exposed.

"Going to the engine," I said as I stopped all the jets, fell away from the landing gear and flew over to the engine. I flew hard up into the forward part of the engine. The exterior metal is just an aerodynamic wrapping around the more complicated interior, but I slammed into it with my upper body fully shielded, making a big dent and resumed my Atlas impression.

The landing gear was behind me, so I couldn't see what the robot might be doing. I was also too far away from Toxicwasteman to shout at him or hear him over the wind and that gave me some small amount of joy.

Below, the ocean was getting choppier, the plane bucking in the wind, the snow getting heavier only to be consumed by the hungry seas. The plane was less than fifty feet above the water and through the grey I couldn't see land yet.

"How far?" I asked quietly. I was talking to Byte.

"Too far," Byte replied.

THE THROATY RUMBLE OF A MOTORCYCLE IS A THRILLING thing. I would rather experience that kind of rumble behind the steering wheel of a car, like my father's vintage Dodge Charger, but an engine and a long strip of blacktop is... well, that evening roaring out of Fredonia, Arizona, it sounded like hope.

The vibration of the engine, humming right below us, felt like it was shaking the last few years in Casita de Soledad right off us, dislodging the cramped feeling of being restricted and watched by Homeland Security. The high, scattered clouds hid most of the stars and the dim light turned the rising mesas into dark ghosts on the horizon.

Licia was driving the Sportster and I was perched on the thin seat behind her enjoying her closeness. We had helmets on and well-worn leather jackets with the orange Harley Davidson logo emblazoned on our backs.

"Driving" sounds kind of awkward there, doesn't it? It's usually "riding" when it comes to motorcycles, but that takes away from the skill and precision needed to hurl us down a two-lane road through the desert at night at ninety miles per hour. I was "riding." Licia was "driving."

Licia still had her blond wig on, poking out underneath the helmet, and this made our disguise complete. We weren't two superhero fugitives on the run, we were a couple hitting the road for a long summer adventure.

A couple where the petite woman was the master of the motorcycle and the man was holding on for dear life. We might get some second looks for that, but no one would suspect that the man was Neutrinoman.

I could feel Licia's tension ease as the miles flew past. We headed north out of Fredonia and were into Utah and through Kanab in no time. This is a scenic route that weaves in between Zion National Park to the west and then Bryce Canyon National Park to the east. The perfect route for summer vacationers in Southern Utah.

There is a simplicity to being on the road. Your life just gets smaller, but in a good way, in the best way. It's about getting to your destination without the load of all the usual possessions and things to do. It's about enjoying the journey and seeing new things. And for us, it was about a lot more than that. It was about our future and our survival. And that was there, but back in the background. The rumble of the motor and the hum of the tires on the pavement eased all of that away.

Soon the desert gave way as we climbed, sagebrush and pinon trees flickering by in the headlight of the Harley. We zipped past Mount Carmel Junction and through several other tiny little blips of civilization as the road continued to rise and we started to see pine trees instead of pinons.

The night was warm, in the lower sixties, and the wind felt good. We soon climbed all the way into the pine trees, the landscape looking very similar to Flagstaff. We were cutting through a corner of Dixie National Forest, dirt forest service roads diving off here and there. Our plan was to drive all night, get well clear of the area, before finding some takeout Chinese food, some wine, and a cheap hotel.

We zipped past an RV just off one of the Forest Service roads. The RV's headlights were on and I caught a glimpse of some sharp movement from behind it. It was one of the smaller type RVs, built on a van frame. It was only a glimpse, the bright lights hitting my eyes as we flashed by.

It took a few breaths as my mind tried to piece the shadows together, tried to make sense of the blur of motion.

"Turn around!" I shouted, my heart thumping hard.

"What? Why?" Licia asked.

"That was the Polar Express," I said, and I could feel her shoulders rise and fall in a "that's nice, but we're trying to escape here."

"I think they're in trouble," I added, my heart pounding harder. In that glimpse, I had seen four people and the way they moved wasn't right. Someone's hand was reaching out and someone else was throwing themselves towards them.

It could be nothing, just my imagination, fueled by recent experience. But Jean and Alan had been such a nice couple. If we kept on going, I would always wonder.

I didn't need to say anything else. Licia turned so fast I had to hold tight to her waist and soon we were roaring back towards them, the growl of the Harley taking on a more urgent tone.

THE TERM "LAND" AS A NOUN REFERS TO TERRA FIRMA, BUT AS a verb it's about something coming down from the air onto the ground. But what do you call it when something is coming down from the ground onto the water? That can't be landing, and "water landing" just sounds stupid if you think about it. Maybe water should be used as a verb. As in the 787 airplane Toxicwasteman and I were trying to keep in the air was about to water onto the ocean.

No, that sounds stupid too, if descriptive.

Chop from the stormy ocean was close enough now that it was splashing the underside of the fuselage, sloshing into my neutrino jets and turning to steam. The view from this elevation was so very different. From up high, the seas had been a churning, but undifferentiated, mass. As we descended, the waves resolved into individual features, and now I could see the swells were ten feet tall, some larger, the space between the top of the waves and me less than twelve feet.

"Five thousand meters," Byte said in my ear. She had been

counting off the distance for a while. And not the distance to JFK, but the distance to Jones Beach State Park on the outer edge of Long Island. The plan—if you can call it that—was to beach the plane there.

Hey, "beach" works fine as a verb, but water sure doesn't. Bad for the plane, bad for the English language.

Except we couldn't keep the plane aloft that long. It just wasn't going to happen. And a few thousand meters from shore in this weather would be as bad as a few hundred miles.

"Come on, Boy Scout," Toxicwasteman said in my ear. "I know that's not all you got. Come on! Remember my promise. I'll turn myself in. I swear to god that I will turn myself in. I've never lied to you."

And he hadn't lied, that I know of, but that didn't mean that I believed him. It was the "swear to god" part that ruined it for me. You could almost hear the lowercase "g" when he said "god." I was pretty sure he didn't believe in a power higher than himself. But the time to fight over Byte or anything else was past. For me, talking was pretty much past. Every ounce of energy I could come up with was in service of staying in my Neutrino form and keeping the airplane in the air.

I wanted to shoot something pithy back like, "Great. You turn yourself in and Byte will be free to come work for me." But I didn't have the energy for it and I didn't want to destabilize him enough so he stopped doing his part over on the landing gear.

The metal of the engine groaned as I thrust harder, the wing creaking, and I was worried that it might snap off. A wing is designed to hold the plane up, but with the lift of the flowing air applied across the entire surface of the wing, not me and my Atlas impression at the engine.

I don't know if you've ever noticed it, but wings have quite a bit of flex. I've seen it plenty of times on the runway, planes taxiing and the wings flexing in ways that are a bit disconcerting.

Wings are not designed for this kind of concentrated force.

"Four thousand meters," Byte's computerized voice said in my head.

I glanced ahead, but I could not see any land, only the grey sky and the grey ocean through the steam.

My mind drifted to Licia as I worried that I wouldn't be able to hold onto my neutrino form long enough, that I would be lost in the ocean below before the plane, that I wouldn't get to see her again.

And how was I to defend the human race from an alien attack when a couple of stupid robots had made saving this plane nearly impossible? Even with all the new tricks I discovered. There was at least one robot still onboard, it hadn't followed me from the landing gear, which was good. I didn't think I could withstand another attack.

"Three thousand meters."

Was that a slash of brown on the horizon? Was land finally in sight?

Endurance running was part of the training the military had me do. Learning how to push when it seemed there was nothing left and then pushing some more. I missed those early days when I had less freedom, yes, but a lot less responsibility. I didn't have to recruit or make hiring decisions or worry that each choice I made would be the mistake that would lead to humanity's disaster.

But humanity was a disaster already. The microcosm of Toxicwasteman and I fighting over Byte without her saying more than a few words about it. The cliché of powerful men fighting over the limited resources that is this particular woman. Misogyny. Attachment. Ego.

And that was just this one little battle. Humanity was battling all the time. Genocide. War. Murder. Violence. Not to mention the ugly blood sport of politics.

Maybe the aliens are right about us. Maybe we should be eliminated for the good of all.

The waves were now cresting just below my feet, the low elevation and the rising steam destroying my visibility of anything but the angry ocean.

"Two thousand meters."

Byte wasn't even offering encouragement anymore. Just stating the facts. As if she was exhausted with this fight. The fight for survival, the fight for her.

And while humanity was a mess, there was Licia, my own representative of what was right in this world. Love. Intimacy. Caring for someone else more than you care for yourself.

And did Toxicwasteman, the villain and sociopath, care for Byte more than he cared for himself? Or was she just a possession he was attached to, something he "owned"?

My mind raged as I struggled to keep the plane from the water, struggled to keep my form and then—

The waves receded and weren't peaking just below my feet, the steam dissipating and I could see land ahead and I could also see... Well I couldn't believe what I was seeing.

The nor'easter choppy sea was calming and quickly. The wind hadn't stopped, the snow was still falling, but a strip of ocean right below the plane and running to the beach became significantly calmer. The wind was still whipping at it, but the waves receded and that strip of calm water looked eerily like a runway welcoming us back to land.

This wasn't natural. This wasn't possible.

What the hell?

LICIA WASN'T HOLDING BACK AS SHE DROVE US BACK TOWARD the Polar Express. She was hunched down and going fast. I leaned down too and held on tight.

The whine of the engine told me she was pushing it hard and I had this terrible thought. What if I hadn't seen anything at all in the flash of light as we passed the RV? What if it wasn't even Jean and Alan and the Polar Express? What if my paranoid mind had made all of this up for reasons that would take years of therapy to understand?

My stomach was tight from those thoughts and the adrenaline of the ride.

"Two men with them," Licia shouted as the RV first came into sight and I couldn't distinguish any individuals, but she could with that raven enhanced sight of hers. "I can't tell if they are harmed. Jean and Alan look terrified."

More adrenaline dumped into my bloodstream. What I wanted to do was change into Neutrinoman and fly to the rescue. But that wouldn't be a good idea. First of all, we were on the run from the entire US government, and secondly, I didn't have a spare set of clothing.

That last one, admittedly, sounds a bit shallow, and it is. But time after time I've been in the strangest of circumstances without any clothing. That kind of thing can really worm into your psyche.

"Valentine," Licia shouted. Thoughts of not using powers must have been running through her head too.

Valentine Oscar, the man who served as my... God, what do I call him? He was part bodyguard, part confidant, part moral compass. I know I haven't written much about him yet—we're not to that part of the story—but trust me when I say that the utterance of his name made me feel even more than what I had already been feeling.

Many didn't survive the war and I've been careful not to share too much, but Valentine is one of those and that is all I can say right now.

Right then, Licia was saying "Valentine" because it was the easiest way to convey that we would have to do this battle as mortals. Valentine's mission was to keep us safe and part of that was training us in hand-to-hand combat.

Licia drove at top speed, like we were going to pass the RV by. It was parked right off the pavement just down the dirt forest service road. But she braked hard, the rubber squealing against the pavement, and then the hard-packed dirt as she took us off the road and brought us to a stop on the other side of the RV in a cloud of dust.

We didn't talk. She put the kickstand down and went towards the front of the RV as I went towards the back, keeping my steps soft, my center of gravity low. I took my helmet off, but kept ahold of it thinking it might be useful as a weapon.

The truth here was that I wasn't needed. Licia could handle this, being able to use her powers in a limited and non-lethal way without transformation. Like in Fredonia when she had charged the battery just by touching it.

By saying "Valentine" she had been telling me that she was going to try to not use her powers. We were undercover, after all.

I sneaked around the back of the RV and paused. I could smell sweat, unwashed bodies, cigarettes, and overcooked meat. I could hear the rustling of clothing and boots shifting on the dirt, and a man whispering, "One word, Pops, and she dies."

More adrenaline, a righteous fury fueling me, waking me up, making me feel alive. This was worse for Jean and Alan than I had thought, making it a fight worth having. A plan clicked together in my mind, one that I couldn't tell Licia about, but hoped she would follow my lead.

"Not tonight," I said loudly as I stepped out from the back of the RV.

There was a small folding table set up in front of the RV, on it was a lantern and a propane stove with two overcooked hamburgers.

Jean and Alan were there, tracks of dried tears on Jean's wrinkled face, Alan's shoulders stooped and his back bent. They looked much older than when we had met earlier that day. Fear was written on their faces, but also confusion. The look one gets when the world suddenly turns and it isn't quite what you thought it was. I've had that look on my face many times.

There were two men with them. The one had Jean's hair in his fist and held a 9mm to the base of her head as he pressed her against the door of the RV.

The other man had his gun pointed at my head and slowly pulled back the hammer. "You don't want to do this," he said. He was tall and thin with stringy brown hair down to his shoulders, the lantern light making his face seem downright cadaverous. Alan was sitting in a chair next to him, the man's hand on Alan's shoulder.

The one with Jean was shorter and plumper but had a

hollowed-out look on his face that made me think they were in withdrawal.

Twenty years ago, drug use went up considerably when the alien threat came to life. People acted differently, some turned to God, some turned to the bottle or drugs, some pretended it wasn't happening, and some fought. That trend lingers today as the world tries to put the trauma of the war behind us.

These two looked like tweekers, desperate for the next hit of crack or meth or speed. The forest is not a usual hangout for them, just bad luck for Jean and Alan.

"Oh, I think I do," I said with a smile. "Jean, Alan, you guys all right?" If these tweekers had any brain cells left, I wanted them to know that I knew these people and wouldn't be leaving.

"We most definitely are not," Alan said, his voice shaking and barely above a whisper.

My plan, as most of my plans are, was quite simple. Keep the men distracted while Licia takes them out. If I kept all eyes on me, she would feel free to use her powers and to draw electricity from these boys until they passed out like those buffalo at Yellowstone.

"I think we can work this out," I said slowly. "We've got a bike. A nice one. A Harley. How about I give you a hundred bucks and the bike and you let these folks go?"

Tweeker two's eyes flicked from me to the RV, towards the bike on the other side. He licked his lips. "Let me see the money."

I nodded and slowly reached into my front pocket. Licia had given me some of our cash reserves. I could hear her moving, her footsteps faint on the dirt, too quiet for them to hear. I pulled out a sizable wad of cash and both of their eyes lit up. I had their full attention.

I slowly pulled one and then two hundred-dollar bills out. "Let's make it two hundred. I'm feeling generous." I gestured with the money and their eyes were following it like I was holding a fresh soup bone in front of a hungry dog.

"Now," I began, hoping that would signal Licia as I stepped closer waving the money around even more, "I'm sure we can—"

Licia stepped into view, lightning arced from their bodies to Licia's outstretched hands and they both went down with a thud.

So much for hand-to-hand combat. So much for our cover.

FALL 2006, OVER THE ATLANTIC OCEAN

The stormy ocean was calming, but just below the low-flying 787 and extending like a runway to the beach. The waves shrank, until it was only the wind frothing up the water at the surface. Beyond the runway of water, the ocean was a chaotic mess with twelve-foot swells.

I was imagining it. That had to be the explanation. The only place you hear about water doing something like this was in the Bible where Moses parted the Red Sea.

"What the hell?" I mumbled.

"I'm not doing that," I heard Toxicwasteman say in my ear. "Neutrino, are you doing that?"

So I wasn't imagining it. I craned my neck around looking for the reflective silver of an alien robot, thinking maybe I wasn't imagining this and it was the next challenge the alien robots were setting for me.

But no robots.

"I'm not doing that," I replied.

"Well, then who the hell is?"

And then the water runway began to rise, closing the six feet that remained between the plane and the ocean as if it was reaching out for the plane.

I looked around for robots again, scanned what I could see of the skies for alien ships. What kind of power would it take to move this much water? It wasn't human, that was for sure.

"Don't worry. It's okay," Byte's perfectly calm computerized voice said in my ear.

"Don't worry?" Toxicwasteman shouted. "Are you out of you mind? What do you mean don't worry? There's a goddamn runway made out of water below us."

"Yes," Byte continued. "I know. I need the two of you to cease your lifting activities and move to the front of the plane in ten seconds. You will need to slow it for the landing."

I was as confused as Toxicwasteman, who continued to ask Byte questions which were not answered, but I didn't have any questions of my own. I stared at the dark water and felt... well, it was clearly a runway after all, it was reaching for the plane, the beach was getting closer.

As the plane continued to fall and the ocean grew closer, Toxicwasteman's queries became louder.

"Five. Four," Byte said, ignoring him, her computerized voice completely calm. He didn't seem to be enjoying this. I didn't know if this was all part of their act, but he sure didn't seem to know what was going on.

"Really, Byte?" he said. "You're going to ignore me. You're going to act like this is all normal to you. Well, I'll tell you one thing. This is *not* normal!"

It wasn't lost on me, even in the chaos of the situation, that he was calling her Byte not Gayle. Was this from habit or was it because Gayle wasn't her name?

"Three."

The water runway had risen and the plane had fallen, the calm water rising above Toxicwasteman's feet. He was lower than me, still on the landing gear, his green thrust producing so much steam I couldn't see him.

"Two."

I caught a flash of something moving rapidly in the water. Was it a dolphin or a pod of dolphins?

"One."

I gladly stopped my Atlas impression and flew right above the water to the front of the plane. Through the cockpit window, I could see the captain, a look of terror on her face as she stared down at the water. However Byte was coordinating this, it was clear she hadn't involved them. I guess she had taken the plane over.

Toxicwasteman and I arrived at the front of the plane at the same time, his green face forming the most sour expression.

"Welcome to my world," I shouted cheerfully. I wanted to make sure he heard me over the wind in case Byte wasn't patching our voices through our earbuds anymore. I think Toxicwasteman had spent most of this time thinking he was in charge and he had just discovered that his partner and mate had a lot going on that he didn't know about.

"Shut it!" he growled.

The landing gear retracted into the fuselage and the flaps on the wings went down a bit as the plane gently touched the water with a splash and then bounced back into the air like a rock skipping on calm water.

My fatigue forgotten, I flew ahead a bit for a better view and watched as the water reached up even farther and embraced the plane, this water runway rising well above the swells of the nor'easter beyond it.

Intelligence was guiding this, an intelligence that Byte was not afraid of and knew something about. I was all smiles as I flew and watched, Toxicwasteman barking out obscenities.

The wave or water runway or whatever it was effectively caught the plane and slowly lowered it as the beach approached.

When we were a few football fields out, Byte said in my ear, "Position yourself at the nose of the plane and slow it. Now."

I twisted around in the air and slammed into the nose of the plane, metal crunching beneath me, my shoulders shielded. Toxicwasteman did the same far enough away so we didn't touch—our quantum forms don't mix will.

We both thrusted, my yellow neutrino jets mixing with his green jets and black smoke.

Jones Beach State Park sits off of Long Island right on the Atlantic and is one of the most popular beaches in the New York area. It's got a wide sandy beach, broad parking lots and roads, and the Theodore Roosevelt Nature Center. But it's not a very wide piece of land and the plane needed to be stopped.

Byte spoke continuously. Counting off our distance from the land, telling us to increase or decrease our efforts. Too much and the plane wouldn't make it, too little and we'd plow through the sand and scrape along the parking lots or crash through buildings.

At the end, as the water became shallow and the beach approached, it was... well, I couldn't see it clearly from my vantage, and no one was out in this weather with a camera, but picture a 787 airplane, all two hundred feet of it, surfing on an incoming wave with the wind whipping and the snow pelting down.

The "water runway" effect went away for those last few yards, the raised water crashing like any other wave. The noise of the 787 smashing into the beach was deafening. The sand flying up, the sound of crunching metal loud against the background din of the storm, the plane bucking and groaning, the screams of the passengers barely audible against it all.

Toxicwasteman was bucked off the nose, but I held my position.

"More," Byte said. "We need more."

I thrust with all my might, adding my yell to the din of noise as the plane scraped over the sand.

We were positioned perfectly. The West End parking lot had a huge tongue of sand extending from it to the beach and the plane slid off the water-soaked sand near the ocean to the dry sand behind and onto the wide tongue of sand leading to the parking lot.

Byte had aimed well. This trajectory was about as safe as it could be for a 787 landing on the beach.

I screamed and thrust and gave it all I could, the crunching noise of the metal of the plane bending further against my force, effectively burying my face and shoulders in the metal.

It wasn't enough to get the plane to dry land, it had to be stopped before it took too much damage. Toxicwasteman had been thrown off, it was just me. I had to do it. I had to stop it. Fatigue didn't matter. Aliens and their robots didn't matter. Heroes Incorporated didn't matter.

The front part of me buried in the plane, I switched into a more elemental state. I wasn't quite the engine, but the need drove me to something primal, something more elemental.

My screams of exertion melted into the roar of my effort. My plane. I must stop it. I must succeed.

Time slipped away from me and I gladly fell into the single-minded purpose of stopping the plane.

"... is enough, Nik. You did it. You stopped us. Nik. Please. Stop."

Byte's words came to me as if from a dream and I returned to myself and stopped thrusting, pushing myself back out of the cratered front of the plane.

I felt my deep fatigue again, barely holding onto my neutrino form. I fell to the sand, turning to flesh and blood halfway down and landing hard, the wind icy cold, snow falling on my bare skin.

But there it was, the 787 after its beach landing sitting right in front of the snow-covered parking lot.

I laughed, a manic, high-pitched sound, and then the cold truly reached me and I began to shiver.

I could hear sirens in the distance—help was on the way.

Which was good. I would freeze in no time out here.

I WAS STUMBLING AROUND NAKED OVER THE COLD, SNOW-covered sand, snow sticking to my hair, my teeth chattering, the wind howling as I gawked at the 787.

The nose was pushed in, a crater about four feet deep... I hoped the crew got out of the cockpit in time. The path the plane had carved in the sand extended beyond the nose. In my mania to stop it, I had pushed the plane backwards and I was paying the price.

Besides the chattering teeth, my head spiked with pain and my gut was sucked in. I think I had lost five or ten pounds of muscle. This is how it works. During my reaction, the nonessential me will be consumed—including much of the bacterial colonies in my gut, leading to all kinds of fun in the bathroom later on. And, I was learning that if I kept pushing, if my will held, the reaction would start to consume more essential parts of me, like fat and then muscle.

Before the transformation, I was well-hydrated and healthy. After this long one, I was dehydrated and looked like I had been very ill for a long time.

I heard voices inside the plane and the sirens were getting closer.

"You can't have her," Tom Tyree said as he strode across the sand naked. He was much taller than me, his shoulders back as he marched across the snowy sand. He was gaunter than usual. He had been transformed for a long time too, and it must have taken its toll on him.

"Sh... Shut up, Tom," I said, my teeth chattering, my arms hugging my bare chest.

"You ca... can't have her," he repeated, walking boldly towards me like it was a sunny day on a nude beach even though his teeth were chattering too.

Tom never cared about his nudity. If there is one thing I could take from him, that would be it. Not his endless confidence, there's something wrong with you if you think you are always right. Not his complete lack of morals in pursuing his goals. I would just like to not be worried about being naked.

"I ddd... don't want to possess her," I said. "I want her to work for mmm... me."

"No!" he yelled as he reached me, his chest puffed out, his green eyes fierce.

And then it dawned on me. The emergency was over and he hadn't fled. Was he really going to turn himself in?

"Why nnn... not?" I yelled back.

"She's mine!"

"You keep saying that, but what the hell do you mmm... mean by it?" Part of me knew I should be paying attention to the plane, worried about my own survival, but there in front of the beached 787, I just kind of lost it. I was dehydrated and starving and freezing, my head pounding. I had been through way too much and I was just over him.

"Can you tell mmm... me that?" I yelled. "Are you saying that you own her? That you control her every action? That you make her every decision? Are you saying that she is your property, Tom, because I really hope that is not what you are saying."

"She's mmm... mine," he said quieter, his eyes flicking from me down to the sand, his thin shoulders slumping.

"You've nnn... never needed anyone before, have you?" I asked, my voice back to a normal tone, loud enough for him to hear me over the wind. Behind me I could hear sounds coming from the plane but I didn't pay attention. This seemed important.

He hugged his chest and shook his head, still not looking at me.

"And you nnn... need her."

He nodded.

Tom Tyree was like a child when it came to this. He didn't know how to act. But that doesn't mean I was going to teach him.

"And none of that matters when the aliens come bbb... back and we aren't strong enough to sss... stop them," I said.

He looked up, his wolfish grin appearing briefly but then melting away. "You said *when* nnn... not *if*."

I did. The damn robots had pushed me over the edge and I couldn't really hope that the Arcturian Alliance would somehow find humanity worthy of preservation. There were plenty of days when I doubted it myself.

"And that is why I need her to be part of Heroes Incorporated, which was *your* ddd... damn idea anyway."

He bit his lip and shook his head. "Nnn... no. *Her* idea." He nodded back at the plane and I turned around and saw that they had opened the hatch. A woman with long dark hair was the first to slide down the orange emergency slice.

It was Byte still in her wig, her hands full of blankets and she ran towards us over the snow and the sand.

I had forgotten about the earbuds. She had heard everything we had said. I remembered when she had told me that Tom Tyree had found her after her transformation, when she didn't understand what had happened to her. She told me how he had saved her.

Maybe she was the one saving him now.

"Here," she said, handing us both three of those thin airline blankets. It wasn't much, but at least it helped.

"Www... will you work for Heroes Incorporated?" I asked. I wasn't going to let it go.

She nodded away from the plane and walked swiftly towards the ocean. Tom and I shared a puzzled look and I began to wonder who had been in charge of LoVE all this time. Was it the psychopathic Tom Tyree or the clever Byte whose real name may or may not be Gayle?

We followed her down to the beach, the ocean roaring as huge waves crashed onto the sand, all signs of the water runway gone.

"Of course," she said with a wan smile before turning to Tom. "And I will keep working for LoVE."

I nodded, a stupid smile on my face feeling in that moment that I had won some kind of victory, but had I?

She turned to me. "My identity must remain secret. Do you understand?"

I nodded. Behind us I could see that a growing group of passengers had slid down the orange slide and the emergency crews had just reached the parking lot.

She took a step towards Tom, rose onto her toes, and kissed him on the cheek. "Now, neither of you follow me. Okay?"

We both nodded and then she walked into the ocean. When the wild waves had reached her calves she turned back. "Seriously. Don't follow me."

I just stared. What the hell was going on?

A huge wave, like some giant hand, rose up from the ocean, twice as tall as any previous waves. It crashed over her and then she was gone.

SUMMER 2025, SOUTHERN UTAH

ALAN HADN'T SEEN A THING, BOTH THE TWEEKERS HAVING been behind him, but a look of recognition was blossoming in Jean's face as she stared at Licia.

I was using some duct tape and binding both the tweekers at their hands and feet.

Licia had grabbed one of the guns quickly, waved it around briefly, and told Alan it was a tranquilizer gun. He was in shock and was so glad to be alive he would have bought anything, could dismiss the sizzling sound of the lightning as something he imagined, could ignore the sharp scent of ozone that still lingered in the air.

Jean, on the other hand, had seen that lightning, at least out of the corner of her eye.

"What now?" Alan asked. He was wandering around the fold-up table, his path erratic as he kept mumbling "Oh, my." I felt for the guy, this was not normal, not the kind of thing you can—or should—plan for.

And "what now" was the question of the hour.

"Take a moment," Licia said, calmly going over to Alan and putting her hand on his shoulder and guiding him towards his wife. Jean's eyebrow arched and she watched them like a hawk. "Just take a moment. Get your feet underneath you and then you guys can get back on the road."

They had parked right off the road, not in the kind of place you would camp in. You'd go farther down the dirt road, find a secluded spot. It looks like they had just stopped for a meal.

"What about them?" Jean asked, her tone a half an octave higher than normal.

"We'll take care of them," I said.

Her eyes widened as she looked more closely at me, her mouth forming an "O," another look of recognition on her face.

Except for my books, the world hadn't thought much about us or seen us for years. With the Quantum Accords of 2020 we were shipped out to the desert, the lawsuits against us settled, as the world tried desperately to forget what had happened and get back to normal.

There had been a lot of shouting and a lot of blaming after the war. Us surviving q-morphs didn't end up on the right side of all of that. Jean's recognition was quickly turning into distrust.

"How did you find us?" she asked quietly, her arms around her husband protectively.

I shrugged. "Just luck. I noticed the Polar Express as we rode by and something just didn't look right."

"And what a piece of luck that," Alan said. "You guys... you saved us. Jean, Lee and Neil just saved us."

I was glad he mentioned the names Licia had made up for us when they picked us up near Jacob Lake. I had forgotten them.

"After you guys are on your way, we'll call the cops and take care of them," Licia said with a smile. "No need to ruin your vacation."

Alan nodded enthusiastically, but Jean shook her head. She probably thought we would do something horrible to them.

"I think they'll want our statement," Jean said slowly.

Licia shrugged. "Okay, then." She turned to me. "You done? Are they secure?"

I had them leaning up against the back tire of the RV. Their wrists were taped together behind their backs and their ankles were taped together. I had checked their pulses, and they were fine. They would have a hell of a headache on top of their withdrawal symptoms when they woke up, but they would live. "Yup. Secure."

I had also searched their pockets and found a sock stuffed with jewelry and Alan's wallet which I had returned. It was a simple robbery. I'm guessing if we hadn't come by, they would have stolen the RV.

"Good," Licia said with a nod. "We'll be going then. We've got a long way to go yet tonight. Good luck, you guys." She said it sweetly, but it was clear she had seen Jean's looks. We couldn't stay until the cops came.

Alan protested, wanted to thank us, made Licia write their cell phone down and insisted that we call them if they could ever help us. Jean was restrained, but thanked us too.

Soon we were back on the road, Licia driving the Harley even faster. We had no idea when Jean was going to tell the authorities about us, but it was pretty clear she would.

I felt a little bit like Bruce Banner hitting the road once again. We had done the *right* thing, of that I had no doubt, but it clearly wasn't the best thing for us.

THE OCEAN DOESN'T ACT THIS WAY. IT DOESN'T CALM AND form a runway in the middle of a nor'easter. Rogue, handlike waves don't rise up and snatch people off the beach right after they tell you not to follow them.

I rushed towards the ocean, my bare feet on the wet sand where Byte had just been.

"Don't bother," Tom growled from behind me.

I turned. "Ddd... didn't you see what hhh... happened?"

He rolled his eyes and sighed. "She knows what she's doing. Believe me, Neutrino, she knows what she's doing."

My teeth chattering, I babbled on about the ocean and the weird waves and he just sighed and rolled his eyes again. "Byte is fff... fine," he finally said, turning and looking back at the plane. The beach was flooded with people, with flashing lights in the parking lot beyond. Police, paramedics, and firefighters were there, escorting people away.

"Excuse me," he said slowly, looking at the scene, "but I've got to go keep my promise."

"What?" I asked. "You're really going to turn yourself in?"

He turned back to me, his wolfish grin back and a sparkle in his eyes. "I told you, Neutrino, I've never lied to you and I will always keep my word. You got the plane back. Byte is safe. I'm turning myself in now, and I'll give you all the credit."

I just stared as Tom wandered back towards the plane. "I am Tom Tyree," he shouted, his voice rising above the storm, "the q-morph known as Toxic, and even though I just helped save the lives of every person on this plane, I am turning myself in."

He raised his hands, the blankets falling from his tall, gaunt body, and there were gasps. Several police officers were on him in seconds and had him on the ground and were cuffing him. He turned and looked back at me after they got him standing again. His green eyes drilled into mine and he nodded once before they hauled him away.

It was a brief, dramatic scene, just what you would expect from him. And it felt like a scene, part of a play, something designed with a specific outcome in mind. Tom's stated objective was clear: defeating the aliens, saving the world, and using me to do that. How the hell did Byte getting swallowed by the ocean and Tom getting led off in cuffs accomplish that?

A young police officer jogged down to me. "How did you do it, Mr. Nichols?" she asked breathlessly, handing me a winter parka which I gratefully pulled on over the blankets. "How did you get him to come in peacefully?"

I shook my head. "No idea."

She looked puzzled. "We should go, sir, the storm is only going to get worse."

I nodded, my gaze being drawn back to the ocean. "Can you give me a minute?"

She smiled, it was one of those star-struck smiles, and I hated it. I didn't want to be looked up to like that. I had powers, yes, but I was as insecure as the next human and was faking it just like the rest of us. She jogged back to the plane and I took a step farther into the water, the waves reaching my calves as they hungrily licked the beach.

The ocean was a churning mess. What had happened? What was going on?

I saw the wave form, out about fifty yards, the chaotic chop coming together and forming a bigger wave right in front of me, the same kind of wave that had taken Byte.

I sighed. I was so tired, swaying as the wind buffeted me. The roar of the ocean was soothing and I didn't move, not one bit. Not when the water receded as the wave approached, not when it rose up like a giant hand, and not when it crashed down and pulled me into the cold, churning ocean.

THE HARLEY SPORTSTER HURLED DOWN THE TWO-LANE blacktop of Utah Route 12, the headlight stabbing out and revealing juniper and pine trees growing from salmon-colored soil. We were near Bryce Canyon National Park, having headed east as soon as we could instead of going north on 89.

If I thought Licia had driven fast before, I was wrong. The motorcycle's engine howled and the miles whipped past. We had to assume that Jean had told the police about us, that the net was closing in.

And if she did and if it was, going faster probably didn't matter much. There just weren't that many roads in this part of Utah. It wouldn't be hard to watch for a couple on a Harley on all of them.

Her back was tense as we whipped around a corner, dove into the left lane and passed a pickup driving at a sane speed, and then zagged back into the right lane.

It's gorgeous country we were driving through, forests and deserts in shades ranging from taupe to ochre, mesas and canyons everywhere. Some of the most beautiful land in the country. I wished we really were tourists taking our time during the day, stopping to see the sights, staying at the kind of funky old motels you can find in the little towns that are sprinkled around out here.

"I love you," I shouted loud enough so she could hear me.

It's what I say when I have to say something and I have no idea what it should be. I say it because it's true. I say it because it is something that should be said, but still it feels empty sometimes.

"I love you, too," she shouted back. And I knew she did, but there were no assurances added that we would figure this out, that we would make it, that everything would be okay.

Everything wasn't okay, and we had no idea if we would make it.

I appreciate that about her and about our relationship. I don't want assurances that aren't based in reality. I would have loved it right then, believe me, a kind lie to soothe my worry, but we didn't do it that way, so we declared our love and kept going.

What else could we do?

The guilt tried to creep back in as the wind whipped by. Guilt over what just happened at Casita de Soledad, but other guilt, older guilt—a war can leave you with a lifetime of things to second-guess.

Maybe if the war hadn't gotten so messy, maybe we could have had a normal life in 2020 instead of our isolated desert home. No drowning in lawsuits. No Quantum Metamorph Accord. No Project Vulcan. No constant surveillance. No running for our lives through this beautiful land instead of being tourists.

And that's the thing about guilt, you let a little in and it brings all the other guilts with it.

Without thinking about it, I sat up a little, pulling away from Licia a bit.

"Don't!" she shouted as we pulled out of a tight turn.

She was referring to my shift in position. We were going so fast that changing the bike's center of gravity was dangerous. But she might have been talking about where my head had gone. She knows exactly what my lame "I love you" meant.

I leaned forward into her and gave her a tiny squeeze, just enough for her to feel it. Another way to say "I love you."

I pushed back the guilt and tried to think. We had to get to the interview with Diane Madison in New York. We had to plead our case in public, reveal how we had been treated, hope that it would go our way.

But if Jean said anything, we would end up in an untenable encounter with the police or, worse yet, the military. And this was something we couldn't plan for—not really much more than we turn into our q-morph forms and I fly us out of here.

As I worried and pondered, we roared through the Grand Staircase-Escalante National Monument, turned on Route 24 and went past Capitol Reef National Park and down into the Utah desert.

It was still dark when we made it to I-70, the gas tank low and our exhaustion high. We were about 250 miles away from where we left Jean and Alan. Licia pulled us to the side of the road right before the on-ramp, the lights of the cars cutting through the night.

This is dry desert with lumpy hills and mesas in tan to reddish tones, all of them like hulking ghosts in the dark.

"Maybe she didn't say anything," I offered, referring to Jean. It had been hours and no signs of military helicopters or one police car.

Licia shrugged.

"We should rest," I added.

She shrugged again.

"And eat." My stomach was a tight knot and my head was light. You really want to be in good shape physically before transforming. I was still vibrating from all the miles and my butt really hurt from being perched on the narrow seat.

When the silence stretched out, I said the other stand-in phrase, the one that was not nearly as positive as the "I love you" one. "I'm sorry," I whispered.

"Me too," she said, not turning, still looking at the highway.

And that's really the worst response. "I love you" echoed back can build you up. "I'm sorry" coming back does the opposite.

And as much as my ego wanted to take it all on, make it all about me, my rational mind fought back. I wasn't responsible for the cosmic waves or the accident at Palo Verde Nuclear Generating Station that changed me. I didn't make the aliens try to eradicate us. I didn't make the military do all the stupid things they did. I didn't plant Project Vulcan underneath us. I wasn't the only one that fought the war.

But this, today, sure felt like it was all my fault. First with blowing up the bomb under us at Casita de Soledad and then having us turn around and help Jean and Alan.

And that's the thing about ego and guilt. I think the ego feeds off of it, because even though it sucks, it is all about you. That previous statement assumes that Licia didn't have any say in either blowing up Project Vulcan or helping Jean and Alan, which of course she did.

"Let's risk a stop," I said gently. "We need food and rest."

She nodded, not turning around. "Next town, then."

We got on I-70, the traffic almost nonexistent this early in the morning, and headed east into the unknown.

THE OCEAN TOOK ME, AND I DIDN'T FIGHT. PARTIALLY because I was beyond exhausted, partially because I didn't want to face crowds or reporters or police, and partially because I knew something was going on and I wanted to understand it.

How much energy does it take to create a runway of smooth water in the middle of a nor'easter? What kind of intelligence would have to be behind that?

Well... there would have to be a high level of intelligence and a massive amount of energy. It's the latter that was driving me to distraction. What could possibly have enough power to control the ocean like that?

It didn't hurt when the wave crashed into me. In fact, I didn't feel wet... well, any wetter than I already was from the snow that had been falling.

My eyes were shut and I felt intense pressure and my empty stomach lurched like I was on a high-g amusement park ride. I held my breath and heard the sound of water all around me. It wasn't like the white noise of crashing waves or the slosh of water in a bathtub, it was more than that and subtler at the same time. It was a lot like those sounds compressed and happening very fast all at once.

I was moving. The water was moving.

I kept my limbs close and didn't move my body and it almost felt like something huge and amorphous was carrying me.

As the seconds ticked by, my lungs began to burn and I heard a voice that came out of all those water sounds. It was distant, but close, strangely musical. "Breathe..." it whispered.

I exhaled and carefully sipped air in through my mouth and... no water. There was air around me and I began breathing again, the sense of motion accelerating.

I slowly opened my eyes and saw... amorphous grey, almost black. I couldn't make out anything, but the grey wasn't still, it was moving like when you squeeze your eyes shut tight and see unnamable patterns in the dark. This was like that but soot gray, not pitch black.

Seeing the movement increased my sense of vertigo and I squeezed my eyes back shut. Whatever this thing was, this power and intelligence, it had me and it didn't feel like it was going to let me go anytime soon.

THE NEXT TOWN, AS IT TURNS OUT, WAS ONLY A FEW MILES down I-70. Green River, Utah. It's just a blip in the road with a population of less than a thousand, one of those forgettable southwest desert towns except for one thing. It sits on the Green River as it flows lazily towards the Colorado River.

It felt perfect to me. Just the kind of stop we needed.

We pulled into a truck stop right off the highway, gassed up and walked into the restaurant, a greasy-spoon style diner that had my stomach jumping for joy. Not that exciting for Licia, her being a vegetarian and much more health conscious than me.

It felt strange not to have the rumbling Harley beneath me, and the world seemed to be moving even when I was still. This restaurant served truckers, so it was actually open at the predawn hour.

We slipped into a booth and ordered coffee and omelets from the tired, middle-aged waitress and I got a side of bacon. We didn't talk much, both of us keeping an eye out, but it was just the one waitress and a few truckers, the hiss of cooking food in the kitchen wafting in with the smells, mixing with the sounds of trucks and the faint whiff of diesel fuel.

No one here was living the dream, we were all just getting through another day, getting ready to put in more miles or working to pay the bills.

"Any emergency and we turn and fly away," I said to Licia when the food was most of the way gone and my hunger was no longer screaming in my ear. "We don't give them any time. We go fast and straight up."

She nodded, her tired brown eyes finding mine. "And the interview?"

I shrugged. "I think we have to take on one problem at a time."

Her mouth twisted into a frown, which she tried to cover up by taking a drink of her coffee. I could hear, loud and clear, what she hadn't said. Dealing with one problem at a time, Project Vulcan in particular, is what got us into this mess.

"Okay," I said with a nod. "That hasn't been going so well. What do you think our next step should be if that happens?"

"Anything else for you two?" the waitress asked. Her name tag said "Harriet." She had a simple wedding band on her left hand and her grey hair lay flat against her head. She was tired. I doubted that she would remember us, just two more bikers taking a break from the road.

"Apple pie, if you have any," Licia said with a smile. "A la mode for him. And the name of a decent place to crash."

"You got it, hon," she said, plodding back towards the kitchen.

"Switzerland," Licia said once the waitress was out of earshot. "Or Thailand. Hell, I don't care. If we go up, we come down fast in a country that will welcome us."

Suddenly the clanking of dishes in the back was loud and the squeal of a semi's brakes put me on edge.

Licia had a pained look on her face and I understood it. Completely. "Leave the country..." I mumbled.

She nodded sharply, sipping more coffee.

For her to even suggest this was... it was nothing short of desperation. I was an only child, but she had a big family, cousins, seemingly, everywhere.

Our parents, while all still alive, were getting old, all of them approaching their eighties. We had talked to them a lot at Casita de Soledad and once or twice a year Homeland would let them come visit. We had assurance that we would be able to leave—escorted of course—in case of medical emergencies.

Leaving the country meant leaving our parents to live the ends of their lives without us. I mean, that had obviously changed with setting off the bomb, but this made it real, way too real.

And another layer of guilt descended on me. I hadn't given them one thought when I was so desperate, feeling so trapped.

"Here you two go," Harriet said, setting the pie down in front of us. "Best place in town is the Green River Inn. It's on the main drag, right on the river, you can't miss it. Tell 'em Harriet sent you."

And then she was gone and I was staring at the apple pie, watching the vanilla ice cream slowly melt, the food I had already eaten feeling like a lead weight in my stomach.

Licia reached out and grabbed my hand and squeezed it. She didn't say "I'm sorry" or "I love you," but I could feel both.

It dawned on me that she had been so silent since our escape partially because she had figured this out way before I did.

"We... we can't leave them," I said looking up from the pie to Licia's compassionate brown eyes. "Everything else, but you, I can let go of, but we can't just leave our parents."

She nodded and sniffed, her eyes moist. "So let's get back on the road and get closer to that interview."

Licia pulled out enough cash for the meal and we walked out into the lightening sky as dawn approached. "What about that motel?"

Licia shrugged as she put her helmet on. "Just in case, to throw them off the scent."

I got on the Harley behind her and it roared to life. No more thoughts of sleep. We needed to get somewhere where it would be easier to hide. No turning. No flying away. We had to get to that interview.

43 / NEPTUNA

I OPENED MY EYES AND SAW SWIRLING GREY AROUND ME. There was very little light and the dark grey shapes gave me a greater sense of motion which just made the vertigo worse. On top of my starved, dehydrated state, that was just too much and I closed my eyes again, breathing shallowly.

I was under the water, but there was air around me. It didn't make sense, but then again, very little had in the last few years.

It was hard to track time. I was so exhausted that I fell asleep as I was swept along in my bubble of air, that watery sound becoming lulling as I got used to it.

As consciousness returned, I heard the watery sound again, but it was much more normal. Water flowing and sloshing. I wasn't moving anymore, and I could sense light through my closed eyes.

I slowly opened my eyes, blinking against the brightness. I was... well, there is no easy way to explain this, and many of you may doubt this, but like everything I've told you it is true.

I opened my eyes and found I was still in a bubble of air, still under the water, but dappled shafts of light flowed down through the deep blue water. A movement to my right caught my attention as a pod of dolphins swam by and I swear they were looking at me.

I was floating... somehow... in the middle of the air bubble that was, maybe, thirty feet below the surface. I could see the waves playing with the light above me. A thin tube of air extended from the bubble up to the surface, providing me with fresh, cool air.

I was no longer in a nor'easter. I was no longer freezing cold. The sleep had refreshed me, but I was still very dehydrated—my head spiking with pain—and starving.

A dolphin came close, straight towards me with something dangling from its mouth. She poked her nose through the air bubble and dropped a small rubbery bag into my hands before chirping and backing out of the bubble and just staring at me as if she was asking me whether I was going to open it or not. The dolphin was a she, I was sure of it.

Thoughts of Aquaman and Doctor Dolittle came to mind. I didn't know it yet, but I was not, bizarrely, that far off.

The bag was made of rubberized nylon with a top that rolled down and clipped together. It was some kind of dry bag. A school of small silvery fish swam by as I opened the bag. Inside were two water bottles and a ham and cheese sandwich. A dolphin had just delivered me lunch.

I shrugged and smiled, still in the parka the policewoman had given me, figuring if I was in a dream, I might as well enjoy it. I sipped the water and slowly ate the sandwich, not wanting to overdo it with my much-abused body. And I watched the show.

Dolphins swam around me, schools of fish swam by in the distance, below me were craggy boulders on the sandy floor of the ocean with fish darting in and out.

I wasn't in the tropics or anything, but after all that I had just been through with the airplane, it was pretty wonderful.

When I had drunk all the water and eaten the food, my body starting to revive a bit, she appeared.

Well, really, she made an entrance. Dolphins had been circling me the whole time I had been there, a pod of ten or twelve. The first thing that happened was they shot off quickly as if something had spooked them, or maybe someone had called them.

Soon they came back, an obvious gap in the middle of their formation and in that gap was... a swirl of dark, denser water. A shape. A presence. The form wasn't still enough to describe a shape, its size wasn't consistent either, but it was clearly there as if the ocean itself had taken on a watery form.

I bet this isn't making any sense. This is really hard to describe, but let me try again. If you've ever seen the water from above, warmer portions will appear lighter, you can see how it's not all the same depth or temperature, not all moving the same way. That was happening here, but much more intensely. The water the dolphins were escorting was much denser, probably warmer, light more reflecting off of it than going through it. It was water, but it wasn't the same as the rest of the water.

The dolphins came straight towards my bubble, splitting around it and the watery presence didn't turn but entered the bubble, becoming more solid as she approached. As the watery form came close, began to change, her feminine nature was very clear.

As her form became denser and more human, the dolphins swam swiftly around the bubble and then more joined them and all I could see outside of the bubble were the sleek grey forms of the dolphins.

But my eyes were on her. As her form became more human, I saw that she was tall with graceful, athletic limbs and long seaweed-green hair that flowed in sheets covering her breasts. Her eyes, though, were blue like the waters of the Caribbean.

"Hello, Nik Nichols, the one they call Neutrinoman. He that is the fire to my water," she said, extending her hand. "It is high time we met. I am Neptuna."

SUMMER 2025, DENVER, COLORADO

WE STAYED ON I-70 UNTIL WE GOT TO GRAND JUNCTION, Colorado. As the sun rose, the road got busier and the miles stacked up. We didn't talk much, there wasn't much to say. Licia focused on driving and I kept a lookout, every time I saw the highway patrol or the police, my heart thumped in my chest.

They were looking for us. They had to be looking for us, even if Jean and Alan hadn't said anything. It began to bother me that we weren't meeting any opposition or having any close calls.

It was just Licia and me on the Harley, my butt slowly going numb.

At Grand Junction we headed southeast, opting to get off the highway in favor of smaller roads. It would slow us down, but we hoped there would be fewer watching.

The forests and the little towns and the miles all blended together with our fatigue. We stopped for gas, caffeine, and quick food. Me, I would have survived on chips and hot dogs, but Licia insisted we eat fruit smoothies and simple things like bagels.

Seven hours later, early in the afternoon, we hit Denver, both of us too weary to put together a coherent sentence. The I-25 corridor south from Colorado Springs, through Denver and north to Fort Collins, is a dense stretch of humanity, the cities much like any other except for the looming Rocky Mountains to the west. We headed north and got off the highway and headed towards Henderson and picked an old motel at random. Licia checked us in and then we stowed the Harley at a park a few blocks away and stumbled back and passed out on the old brown-and-orange toned bedspread of the queen bed.

Sleep. We had to sleep. There was no choice.

This wasn't the romantic Chinese food and fun that Licia had promised in the storage unit in Fredonia several states and a thousand miles ago. This was our fatigue growing large enough to take over our desperation.

The plan, or more honestly put, the hope, was that we would be very hard to find in the middle of this metropolis. Anonymity was our shield, whether Jean had told the cops about us or not. Whether the military was looking here or not.

I woke up with a start, drool pooling on the bedspread below my face, the hum of the city alarming me after waking up for so many years in the middle of nowhere.

I looked around and Licia walked out of the bathroom, her long black hair wet and a white towel around her torso offsetting her olive skin. She looked better, but still tired.

"We have to leave the Harley," she said.

My brain wasn't working yet. For a moment I was just waking up to see my beautiful wife just out of the shower, a most happy way to wake up, and then it all came back in a rush and I groaned.

"I know," she said, thinking my groan was about leaving the Harley, but I hadn't processed that yet. I was groaning because of the mess we were in.

I pushed myself up, still fully clothed, my hand going to my cheek and the imprint of the bedspread's fabric that was there from not having moved for so long. My stomach was growling, my bladder full, and my mouth was dry. I looked at the clock and it said 8:02—I must have been out for sixteen hours.

She sat down next to me with a sigh and I took her hand.

"I'm sorry," I said. My butt would love to leave the Harley behind, but I understood. It would be like me leaving my dad's Dodge Charger behind. That Charger, by the way, he was still tinkering with it and hadn't fully restored yet all these years later.

She gave me a wan smile. "We'll leave it where it is and hide the key around here. I've got a second cousin close and I'll send him a postcard, so maybe..."

She didn't finish. She didn't say that maybe someday we'll be in a position where she could get it back, because that just didn't seem possible today.

"We buying a car then?" I asked.

She shook her head. "Buying a car with cash could draw some attention."

"Then what?"

"Amtrak," she said with a whisper of a smile. "We get a sleeper compartment and don't come out until we get to Chicago."

I nodded. There was risk. In every direction there was risk. We could be recognized. I grabbed the remote from the bed, pressed the microphone icon and said, "Play WNN."

The TV came to life and on the screen was a female anchor—I didn't watch much news and wasn't familiar with her. She was blond and perfectly quaffed in that oh-so-plastic way. To her left were photos of Licia and I, not very flattering ones. Licia's was an overexposed picture of her some paparazzi got off at night with a flash in which she looked ghostly white. Not flattering. My picture had me with my mouth tight as if I was about to yell at someone, probably the guy who had shoved a camera in my face. The choice of those photos told you a lot about what they thought about us.

"...source exclusive to WNN say there is direct evidence that the attack on the Nichols/Lopez compound was alien in nature."

"Compound?" That had a sinister ring to it. Maybe my books hadn't made the kind of progress I had hoped... or maybe it was just making the divide in opinions greater.

The image switched to an overhead view of our former home with the eerily round scoop taken out of the desert, like some giant ice cream scooper had come down and carved it out.

"Where are Nichols and Lopez?" the anchor continued. "Are they still alive? Agent Peters with Homeland Security had this to say yesterday evening."

The view switched to Peters, his bald head shiny in the sun, sweat running down his cheek, the desert laid out behind him. "We have found no evidence of Nichols or Lopez," he said, swallowing hard. "We don't know what caused the blast and we don't know if they lived or died. There's nothing..." he looked off into the distance, his eyes haunted, before clearing his throat again and continuing. "There's nothing left. Not one trace of any of the buildings, any of their possessions, or them."

"Bastard," Licia growled at his lie. She had been kind to him for many years.

The image switched back to the blond anchor. "Does this mean the end of Neutrinoman and Lightningirl? Stay tuned to WNN for around the clock coverage of this breaking story at the top of every hour."

Licia grabbed the remote, turned the TV off and stood up, her arms hugging her chest. "Shit!"

We had been so focused on escape we had—if we had even been thinking about it—assumed Homeland would cover this up, that it wouldn't be a huge news story. We didn't expect them to get ahead of the story, lay down their own narrative. We didn't think everyone in the world would like being reminded again of exactly what we looked like.

Shit!

"There goes our interview with Diane Madison," I said.

And then it occurred to me that Byte and her drones were the reason for this ground they were laying. They knew someone knew about what had happened, so they were establishing the story before we could.

Once again, this all felt like my fault.

45 / UNDER THE SEA

SHE WAS BEAUTIFUL, WITH HER FLOWING GREEN HAIR, LITHE limbs, full lips, youthful features, and piercing Caribbean-blue eyes. But then again, goddesses should be beautiful. Lightningirl, goddess of electricity, or perhaps ether if you're thinking in traditional terms. Gaia, goddess of the earth, and now Neptuna, goddess of the sea.

But the name... "Neptuna" was... it just seemed off to me. Too much like the fish "tuna" or maybe thinking that a goddess's name shouldn't just be a small tweak to the Roman god's name.

I shook her hand, her grip strong, but not in a showy way. "Hi..." I began. I mean, what do you say to a naked woman who, somehow, has transported you through the ocean, has created you an air bubble so you can breathe, and had a dolphin deliver you lunch. "I'm sorry. I feel like you know a lot about me, but I've never heard of you."

The sound in the bubble was echoey and strange, a constant gurgle of water in the background.

"Yes," she said with a pleasant smile, "and let's keep it that way, shall we. My friend, Byte, who commands all things technological, is the only one, besides you now, that knows of me."

Well that helped put some things into place, like the magical water runway and the wave that helped take the 787 to shore. Byte had a way to communicate with her. Also, Toxicwasteman's puzzlement over all of it and Byte's dramatic "don't try to follow me" exit into the ocean. He didn't know about Neptuna.

She didn't have an accent, not really, but she put together words in an odd way. "The fire to my water," "who commands all things technological." It was almost as if she was a queen and used to addressing her subjects.

"Then why did you bring me here?" I asked.

"You gather the heroes, do you not?"

I nodded. "Heroes Incorporated. We are preparing to meet the alien threat."

"Thus our meeting," she said, gesturing to me and the water around us. The dolphins still swam all around the air bubble as if they were guarding her.

"You want to join?" I asked.

"Well, Mr. Nichols, I believe I already have, helping you and the chemical man land that plane."

Something wasn't right. Byte was on that plane, and while Neptuna did help, I was sure it was about Byte.

And then it hit me. The name.

"Can I ask you a question? It will help me in understanding if you are the type of q-morph we are looking for," I asked. Yes, she clearly was a q-morph, an elemental like Licia and Tom and myself.

Her smooth brow furrowed but she said, "Ask me anything!"

"Your name, 'Neptuna.' Can you tell me how you came to be called that?" Her eyes narrowed and her brow furrowed even deeper. "I know it's a weird question, but I've found it helpful in illuminating the person behind the name."

She folded her arms, her head cocked and she stared at me. I was taking a risk, I knew that. I might have recovered enough to turn briefly, but if I was far out to sea, I wouldn't be able to make it to land. I might be the fire to her water, but I had only a spark left and we were surrounded by water. It would really be best not to make her angry.

"This ain't working, is it?" she asked, her lips pursing, her skin darkening slightly, her face transforming into something that looked Asian and about ten years older. I'm embarrassed to say I couldn't really tell you if she was Chinese or Japanese or Korean. I blame it on growing up in the Desert Southwest of America. Her voice changed to, gone was the regal tone, and while it was mildly accented, I couldn't tell you what Asian country it was from. "Byte, she said this might help, throw you off my identity, but she also said that you weren't dumb."

I just blinked, not knowing what to say.

Neptuna got a sheepish look on her face. "The name... well, my daughter's five. She came up with it." She ended with a shrug. "She also came up with Waterwoman, Seagirl, and Fishlady. So you might see why I went with Neptuna."

I smiled.

"So, am I in?" she asked, a cheerful look on her face. "My identity really does need to remain a secret, you'll have to communicate with me through Byte, but... well, I can do some stuff."

I nodded, still processing. That landing had certainly been "some stuff."

"You know I helped Tornado with that hurricane a couple of months ago." She leaned close and got a conspiratorial look on her face. "Don't tell him, the delicate male ego and all, but isn't he dreamy?"

Now it was my turn to furrow my brow. "Delicate male ego." Was that a cut at me? After all, she had brought me, and effectively trapped me, here. And that comment was sexist to boot.

"See, right there," she said gently. "That's your delicate male ego at work. I can see it on your face."

"Umm..." I only spoke because it seemed like I should be saying something, but I had absolutely nothing to say. I mean, I am well aware of being male and having an ego and egos in general being very delicate things.

"Not that women don't have egos," she continued. "We do, believe me. It's just that... well, look around, Nik Nichols, this world is run by men, and women are still constantly objectified and earn much less than men. And that's in the developed world. Forget about how women are treated in the rest of the world. So yes, while we have egos, they have become strong because of all that we have had to go through. I stand by my statement. Don't tell Timothy Tran, the Tornado, that I helped him. Delicate male egos and all."

She paused and the gurgle of water seemed louder than it had before. I got what she was saying, but I have to say that my delicate male ego did not like it at all.

"So am I in?" she asked with a bright smile.

FALL 2006, THE ATLANTIC OCEAN

NEPTUNA HAD RULES. PARAMETERS. SPECIFICALLY, HOW AND
when she would participate in Heroes Incorporated. Always
anonymously. Always through Byte. Always in ways that did not
involve her appearing physically like she was to me right now in
that gurgling bubble of air under the ocean with the dolphins
circling us.

I began to doubt that I was even looking at the real woman with
her Asian features and hint of an accent. The royal Neptuna was a
ruse, this likely was too.

But I didn't really care. She had immense power and it could be
useful to Heroes Incorporated and doing our paid jobs. She could
cool ocean temperature enough to blunt hurricanes and change
their paths. Tornado would be the above ground, the visible source
of the work, but she would be below the waves doing even more.

And we would protect Tornado's "delicate male ego," true, but
it was mostly about her anonymity. Here was a q-morph that even
Tom Tyree didn't know about. Although with what we saw getting

that 787 to the beach, he has to suspect, but that was Byte's problem, not mine.

Actually, it's not either of our problems, because he turned himself in and he had much, much bigger fish to fry.

"I have several conditions," I said with a smile which I hoped was charming, but I still was clothed only in a winter parka and a few thin airline blankets. I was still undernourished and dehydrated.

"Conditions?" she asked, her head tilting and her eyes narrowing. That royal air of hers was certainly not gone, there was some truth to it. And I guess if you can control the oceans and talk to dolphins you might feel kind of special.

"Yes," I said. "I think they will be simple for you to provide."

She made a casual rolling gesture with her hand as if I were a servant and she was impatient for me to get to the point.

"One, since Byte is how I communicate with you, I am assuming you can guarantee her wholehearted participation in Heroes Incorporated."

Puzzlement passed across her face, but only briefly, as if she had believed that Byte was already wholeheartedly a part of Heroes Incorporated. Which made me wonder, again, whether this whole plane thing wasn't some kind of setup, but I wasn't believing Tom Tyree was behind it all anymore.

"Of course," she said with a confident smile. "Anything else?"

"I need you to find Gaia and bring her on board," I said.

"Gaia?"

I smiled, not buying her feigned innocence. She said she had a daughter, and I believed her, which meant she had a life above the waves. Everyone saw the footage of the seven-hundred-foot-tall rock giant that destroyed the Hoover Dam. Everyone knew about Gaia at this point. She wasn't a very good liar, and I liked that about her.

"The earth to your water," I offered.

"Oh yes... of course," she said. "We have not met. I am not sure how I can help you there."

I sighed and nodded. "Very well. It was really good of you to help with getting that plane to the ground. You saved a lot of lives." I looked around as if I was in a conference room looking for the door. "I really should get back to the plane. I'm sure the authorities have some questions for me."

She sighed and nodded. "I can't guarantee her participation, but I can arrange a meeting with her for you."

"Thank you," I said. "And can you at least get her to stop her activities until we talk? No more earthquakes, no more sink holes."

She shrugged. "I will try."

"Thank you." I extended my hand. "Welcome to Heroes Incorporated."

"THEY'RE PLANNING ON KILLING US," LICIA SAID AS SHE PACED the worn brown carpet of our Denver motel room.

I nodded. The conclusion was pretty inescapable. Agent Peters —whose life we saved along with the rest of the Homeland agents who had been spying on us by making them evacuate—was laying the groundwork, convincing the world that we were already gone.

The only sliver of a doubt was that he was just covering his own ass and not acting on orders. But that was just a sliver, there were a number of other agents in that base that all knew what really happened.

If they found us, they could kill us and no one would be the wiser. It would be an alien attack on Casita de Soledad that did it, not the bullet from a Marine. A nice clean end to the difficult task of keeping us around.

And I could—almost—see their point. If we resurfaced, if we convinced the world it was the military's Project Vulcan, a use of alien technology, that they had created in violation of the Accords, it wouldn't go well for them. Byte had evidence of our survival, of those soldiers trying to capture us after the incident.

It wasn't enough evidence, not really, but enough to show that they were lying about what had happened at Casita de Soledad.

As Licia paced, I stumbled into the bathroom, took care of my urgent needs, drank a bunch of water, and got into the shower. I let the hot water pound on my head, hoping it would wake me up, but my thoughts were disorganized. It was just too much. Too many things arrayed against us with nothing on our side.

Byte had helped us escape, she might be able to help us survive, but she wasn't exactly my greatest fan anymore. She, like everyone else, only wanted to keep me around just in case the aliens came back.

But would that be enough? And, besides, I was frankly sick of being kept around like that. A weapon you lock away and bring out only in dire circumstances.

"I've got it!" Licia cried as she ripped the shower curtain back.

I squinted at her, soap in my eyes. "We need Byte," I said, tentatively, my thoughts not yet clear.

"Yes!" she said, her voice loud. "And we need to bring back Heroes Incorporated."

My jaw dropped. I was just thinking about using one of the online drops I set up with Byte to have her figure out how to get us out of the country, but this...

I cleared the soap from my eyes and smiled. "This is going to be *so* dangerous," I said, seeing a glimpse of what she was talking about.

She nodded, a gleam in her eye and a wicked smile on her face.

"We need Jean and Alan to talk about what we did," I offered, finally catching on.

"Oh, yeah," she said, a smile lighting up her face. "And we're keeping the goddamn Harley!"

"We'll need a semi, I think, and some support staff," I said, my brain finally engaged. This was a little bit the Incredible Hulk and a lot the former Heroes Incorporated.

Licia smiled widely. "We'll probably go down in flames."

I shrugged. "At least we'll be fighting for a good cause."

And then the tears were running down her face and I knew it wasn't because she was scared, but because she was relieved. This new Heroes Incorporated would be a fly-by-night, low-key, vigilante-type operation, but we could help people and the world would know that Neutrinoman and Lightningirl were not dead and gone. God only knows how Homeland will spin that, but one step at a time.

She was crying because now we could actually do something, actually have a life, actually use our abilities to help people again. It wasn't the freedom we needed to be with our families, but it was a lot more freedom than we've had, and maybe, just maybe, a step towards a normal life.

I grabbed her and pulled her into the shower and ripped that towel off of her. She giggled and I kissed her hard.

Time to embrace our powers and not run from them anymore. Time to be heroes again.

48 / TORPEDO TIME

I never wanted to be a torpedo, slicing through the water at a blinding pace. After Neptuna was done talking to me—and that is exactly what it was, this royal dismissal—she said, "Best get rid of that parka before the water hits." And then I was suddenly horizontal and moving fast, the dolphins making room for me as me and my bubble of air headed out into deeper water.

I watched, but not for too long. The bubble became smaller, occasionally joining with other air bubbles that I ran into, refreshing my air as older air was released and floated to the surface. I saw fish and sharks and then nothing as the bubble headed into deeper, darker water. The speed, it was dizzying, and I was still a complete mess despite the water and sandwich the dolphin delivered. I squeezed my eyes shut and just wished for solid land.

This time the ride lasted less than an hour and suddenly the bubble was gone and I was deep under water, the pressure hurting my ears, the parka sucking the water in and weighing me down.

The water was icy, sapping my strength as I struggled with the parka, got it off, and started swimming up.

Neptuna had taken me from the shore, why couldn't she deliver me there? Was this another whiff of her royal manner, did she want to prove her power over me?

When I bobbed above the surface, I sucked in cold air, a sandy shore and sand dunes beyond. This wasn't Long Island. Where the hell was I?

The cold was numbing as I started to swim, unsure I had the energy to get to shore, fairly sure I didn't have the energy to turn into Neutrinoman and fly to shore. So I swam, the water gently swelling underneath me, turning into waves and then breaking ahead.

The salt stung my eyes, but the effort helped with the cold water. It wasn't warm here, by any stretch, but there was some blue in the sky amidst the high clouds and I clearly wasn't in the middle of a nor'easter.

I did fairly good until the waves started crashing on me, pushing my head under, shoving the saltwater up my nose, and just as I started to panic, strong arms grabbed me.

"I got you, brother," my rescuer said. His voice was deep and he had an odd, vaguely European accent.

"Quinn?" I sputtered.

"At your service!" he said, way too enthusiastically. He put me on my back, his arm over my chest and started swimming strongly for the shore. I was exhausted and let him.

"I'm here, Nik. I'll always be here," he said, and in my desperation and exhaustion it didn't sound the least bit creepy.

I was soon coughing on the shore, the dregs of the waves washing over me, and I got a good look at Quinn Rask. He was 6'4" and muscular with jet black hair and blue eyes. He was also as naked as I was.

"How?" I spat out, panting.

He shrugged, an elegant gesture, his breath easy as he sat on the sand.

"A woman with an English accent called me, said you would need some help. Told me to get here. Aren't you glad to see me, Nik?"

I did my best to smile and nodded. "So glad, Quinn." I crawled a little farther towards the dry sand. "Where is here?"

"North Carolina."

Quinn got up, jogged to the dry sand and brought back a towel and helped me get up. He was still very naked, and given his abilities, I'm sure not the least bit cold. I was having a hard time keeping my shivering down.

"Www... When did the woman call? What time?"

He shrugged. "I don't know, about four hours ago. She told me exactly where to go."

The sun was getting low on the horizon and I did the math and realized that he had been called before the mysterious runway had appeared. My encounter with Neptuna and my deposit here several states away was all planned.

Byte and Neptuna had planned it.

Up the beach, Quinn had a blanket laid out with a bunch of power bars, bottles of water, and clothing for me to wear. "She said you would be hungry," Quinn said when he saw my eyes light up. "You look like feces, by the way. What happened?"

I grabbed a water bottle and nodded at him. "Put some clothes on and I'll tell you."

The click-squish sound of Quinn using his powers to change his appearance gave me the usual queasy feeling and soon he looked like he was wearing a black tuxedo.

"Nice, but that's not clothing," I said.

"You hurt me, Nik," he said. "I save your life and again you reject what I am with your stupid American prudishness."

I shook my head. He appeared to be clothed, but it was all him, his flexible form looking like clothing now. In my mind he was still as naked as he'd been when he rescued me, but I didn't have the energy for this old argument.

I put the clothes on and told him the story while I devoured the food and water, while he sat there relaxed in a freaking tuxedo.

"What happened to that robot?" he asked at the end. "The one that attacked you from the landing gear?"

My mouth dropped open. I had completely forgotten about it. I had no idea. I shook my head and washed down my third power bar with some water.

"Okay," he said nodding his head. "Alien robots attack plane. Byte helps you become the engine and discover beast mode so you can keep it in air. Toxicwasteman joins at end, but day really saved by mysterious underwater force. Toxicwasteman turns himself into authorities. Alien tech robot gets away. You are mysteriously transported here. And, it now appears that Byte may be in charge of LoVE not Toxicwasteman. Did I get it all right?"

I nodded slowly. I hadn't told him about my meeting with Neptuna and told him I wasn't sure how I ended up down here. He wasn't completely buying that, but him laying out what had happened in the last few hours left me breathless.

He patted me on the back. "This has been a good day for our little enterprise. I was listening to the news on the way in. They are talking about how you saved the plane and convinced Toxicwasteman to turn himself in peacefully. What's next, boss?"

Good day? Sure, hundreds of lives were saved which does make it a good day, but what about Neptuna and Byte? It's clear that Byte arranged much of what happened, but did she know about the robots in the first place? And if so, how did she get them, and was she actually working for the aliens?

I shook my head. I couldn't believe that. I saw Toxicwasteman destroy an alien ship in Yellowstone, his animus towards the aliens was not an act. Byte couldn't be in league with them, she must have just used the attack opportunistically to push me further—and to survive.

"Well?" Quinn asked, staring at me. "Tiger got your tongue?"

I smiled at his mangled idiom and took a deep breath and looked around. The cold beach was deserted. "How did you get here? Do you have a car?"

He nodded and pointed towards some steps that led between a couple of sand dunes.

"I need a phone," I said. "We need to see if there is any sign of that robot. I'll need to brief Colonel Williams. I want to check on Licia." I pushed myself up, and the beach started to spin and I would have fallen, but Quinn caught me.

"I got you, Nik. What I think you need is Jennifer Johnson. She'll know how to make you not so skinny."

I nodded and let him help me up the beach.

There was a lot to do yet. More heroes to recruit. A base to build. So many preparations to make.

But right then, what I needed was a nap.

FALL 2006, AFRICA

THE GOOD NEWS WAS THAT THE AIRLINE THAT FLEW THAT 787 that we saved was so grateful that they became a sponsor of Heroes Incorporated and provided us with gratis flights around the world.

The bad news was... all those flights around the world.

When Byte transmitted Neptuna's message that Gaia wanted to meet in Africa, it's not like I could claim that the flight was too expensive and couldn't we just meet in Arizona somewhere... or really anywhere within the continental United States that I could fly to easily under my own power.

Add onto my prison-induced phobia of small spaces, the fear that any flight would soon be sabotaged by some morphing silver alien robots and I would be forced to push myself way past the extremes to save it.

I don't think you can call that paranoia. I mean, those little robots *were* out to get me. The military *had* imprisoned me. The aliens *were* out there deciding the fate of our planet.

I can report, though, that beside my low-grade panic attack, the flight was very long, quite boring, and without incident. Licia held my hand. Valentine Oscar, my self-appointed bodyguard, sat calmly and stoically, having made it quite clear that after the incident with the 787 he planned to never leave my side.

Nevertheless, I was more than glad when the jeep driver dropped us off in front of a large expanse of African savanna. He looked at us, his eyes wide, and he said, "No farther. This land, it is hers. No farther."

So comforting.

Yet there was sky above us, the ground below us, grasslands sweeping away to the horizon dotted with those umbrella-shaped acacia trees, and a small herd of zebra in the distance.

"What now?" Licia asked, adjusting her backpack.

I nodded towards the zebra. "We walk south, we're looking for a cone-shaped upthrust of rocks."

"She's messing with us, you know," Licia said.

I nodded and smiled, still glad to just have my feet on the ground. "I don't blame her," I replied. "Our encounter at the Hoover Dam didn't exactly go well."

"Damn Hammer," Licia growled.

"Quinn is working on a less aggressive version of the Hammer," I said.

Licia just shook her head. There were stories there, stories of the time when Quinn posed as Neutrinoman while I was in prison. Stories Licia still hadn't shared with me. What with the recovering from the trauma, breaking from the military, and the Heroes Incorporated madness, we hadn't had time.

I glanced at Val, he had binoculars out scanning the landscape. "No rocks in sight," he said. Val was taller than me, an athletic middle-aged man with short grey hair and sharp pale blue eyes.

"So let's walk," I said, happily striding out into the savanna in search of Gaia, goddess of the earth, the last q-morph elemental we needed for Heroes Incorporated.

GAIA WAS MESSING WITH US. VAL WOULD SPOT AN ODD stacking of rocks on the horizon with his binoculars, we would hike towards it for an hour, maybe two, and then it would be gone.

The day was hot, but not oppressively so and it wasn't an unpleasant way to spend the day. We spotted elephants and giraffes, I heard some roars that I suspected were lions, but no wildlife approached us.

I'm sure we were an odd sight for the animals. Humans out here were generally in jeeps, and in larger groups ready to defend themselves against the wildlife.

With Licia here, I wasn't worried. She could suck electricity from any attackers. We avoided the termite mounds and watched for snakes, and let Gaia lead us on a circuitous route deep into the savanna.

Towards the end of day, as low mountains were becoming visible on the horizon, we finally reached an odd upthrust of rock. My feet were sore, my clothing sweaty, but I was actually happy. No board meetings. No decisions made. No dire emergencies faced. I'd spent the whole day with Licia and we had enough time for our conversation to wander away from the immediate madness on to simpler things. The kind of common intimacy that couples often fall into but we just hadn't had the time for.

Val fell back and gave us space when this happened. We held hands and talked quietly. We laughed. She told me that she really wanted a dog... or moreover, a life that could properly support a dog. A house and a place to walk the dog. A schedule that was normal. A simpler life.

I told her that sounded like heaven and hugged her on the African grassland for a long time, no longer caring about today's particular mission.

It was then that Val spotted the rock upthrust, this time closer than before. Gaia had been watching us, obviously, maybe even listening. I wonder if that interchange Licia and I had was why she finally let us find her.

When we got to the rocks, I was a bit disappointed that it was over, or at least I thought it was. The rocks were just that, rocks. Tan boulders naked of vegetation rising up about thirty feet, roughly cone shaped and forty feet in diameter at the base and about ten feet in diameter at the top.

This didn't look natural, but there was no sign of Gaia and the rocks didn't move.

"Look," Val called from the other side.

Licia and I walked over and saw what he was pointing at. There was a slice of this thing made of smaller rocks and formed what was clearly a staircase winding up to the top. The staircase wasn't cut into the rocks but was made up of smaller rocks.

"She's messing with us," Licia said again, but this time with a smile on her face.

I nodded. "I can't say I mind."

"You can't go up there," Val said mildly. "It could be a trap."

I shrugged. "Val, my friend, it's all a trap. But I don't think she means us any harm."

I got on the first stone step and extended my hand to Licia.

———

GAIA WAS THERE, OF COURSE. HER NAKED SKIN A DEEP BROWN in the waning sunlight, her feet buried in the soil of the flat top of the rocky upthrust. Her eyes met Val's when he got to the top and she slowly shook her head, her lips forming a thin line.

"We'll be okay, Val," Licia said, putting a hand on his arm. "Wait for us on the ground."

His eyes narrowed as he assessed the naked woman and the rocks she had so easily assembled with her thoughts. He had seen the video of the rock giant she was when she wrecked the Hoover Dam. She was clearly a threat to us, and to him, but still you could see the calculation in his eyes as he weighed the risk.

Val was a different kind of man. I was not his boss, he had no boss, really. He was here on his own because he felt this was the best way to contribute to the war against the aliens. I had come to trust him and appreciate his calm presence.

He smiled at Licia. It was thin and brief, and I swear his body looked more poised for action than usual. That smile wasn't of resignation, it wasn't an admission that he could do nothing to us powerful q-morphs. That smile was a calculation that Gaia didn't mean us any harm.

After he made it to the ground, Gaia spread her hands, palms up and said, "My friend Neptuna said you wished to talk. I hope that we are not rudely interrupted this time."

I smiled because this was a different kind of greeting from her. More Jena Grange than Gaia.

The elements are thought of differently by different traditions, but for us q-morphs it is: Gaia is the earth, Neptuna is the water, Lightningirl is electricity, Tornado is air, and I am fire.

Five elementals. Six if we add in Toxicwasteman and the element of chemicals, provided he is out of jail by the time this all happens.

If we could work together, if we could combine our powers, it seemed to me like that would have to be enough to defend this planet. To give humanity, as flawed as it is, time to sort its problems out.

THE ARIZONA HIGH DESERT SUN HUNG IN THE WASHED-OUT blue sky, a light breeze licking at the sweat on my forehead, my breath coming fast and my mind calm at the end of a long run.

As I gazed past the busyness of Ruby, Arizona, and the under-construction home of Heroes Incorporated at the craggy upthrust of Montana Mountain, I couldn't help but think of Gaia. We spent three days talking with her. At night she would descend into the ground and Val would come up and be with us as we made a simple camp safely on the top of Gaia's rocks.

For a long time, the three of us elemental q-morphs talked as friends might talk. About our pasts and our doubts and our fears, and even our dreams. We were just Jena, Licia, and Nik. And then on the last day we talked about Heroes Incorporated and the existential threat that the aliens posed to all of us.

Gaia wanted to also talk about the existential threats of climate change, deforestation, species going extinct, human rights violations, and all the other challenges facing our world.

These were not easy conversations. I wanted her on our team and she wanted us on her team.

We were preparing to fight the aliens and she was trying to save the planet... all of it, not just taking on this single threat.

We made plans, we set things in motion, including taking ten percent of the Heroes Incorporated seed money and starting a nonprofit. But it wasn't clear how any of it would play out yet. Would Gaia be with us when the fight began? Could our little nonprofit really do much good against the huge problems that faced us?

It was a lot. All of it. Too much, really.

The ever-present sound of construction equipment beeping brought me back to the Arizona desert. The sound was starting to get on my nerves, especially the beep-beep-beep of heavy equipment backing up.

I was finding, and this was no surprise to anyone, especially not Licia, that I was something of a hands-on leader.

Heroes Incorporated had purchased Ruby, Arizona, a ghost town southwest of Tucson and four miles from the Mexican border. This put me close enough to Palo Verde Nuclear Generating Station if I needed to charge. It also put us close enough to another country in case things got weird with the US government again.

Ruby sits in rolling high desert hills near Montana Mountain at four thousand feet elevation with two small lakes and a flat area of old mining tailings that remind me of Groom Lake in Area 51. This made Ruby spotable from orbit, another plus. Two UH-1 helicopters, on loan from the military, sat on the far end of tailings next to a fuel tank.

Ruby was a mining town, once the home of the Montana Mine that pulled gold, silver, lead, and more out of the ground. There's old mine shafts, schoolhouses, a mercantile, and more buildings on the property in various states of decrepitude.

Some of these have been torn down, making way for the large

concrete building with a large circle-H symbol on the side and a flat roof.

It looked nothing like a superhero base in the movies would look like. Heroes Incorporated has money, but this is about speed and economy. The building was a hulking rectangle made out of bland, grey, concrete slabs. It will contain offices and workspaces. It sits next to a smaller version of itself which was setup a few months ago and right now Jennifer Johnson was transforming it into our medical facility.

At the near end of the tailings flat, just below Town Lake (which, this being Arizona is more the size of a pond) mobile homes were being put in place for housing and near it a new well was being drilled and large septic tanks were being put in.

The rattling hum of a generator mixed with the noise of the construction. APS was in the process of getting more power to us, but that would take time. We had several wind turbines planted on the hilltops and solar panels on every available roof, but Licia needed all the power she could get.

It was a strange sight. I was on the north end of Ruby, on the recently widened dirt road taking it all in, pulling in deep breaths, dressed in shorts, recovering from a long run on the dirt roads around here.

I always stopped to look at the rapidly changing tableau when I got back. One of my rare moments of stillness. Somehow all the new buildings seemed to fit right in with the buildings from the past, a new boom town that will fade back into obscurity before too long.

It's not that I was pessimistic or anything, it was just reality. We would either win the war and Heroes Incorporated would not be needed anymore, or we would lose and... well, none of us would be left.

Our newly minted, Gaia-inspired nonprofit was based in Phoenix. We were housing the hero operation out here because we needed the room and the privacy, and we feared direct alien attack and didn't want to be near any population centers.

Valentine Oscar was standing next to me, his knees bent, his eyes scanning the landscape. He was dressed in his usual black, running shorts and a T-shirt this time, his short grey hair bright in the sunlight. I've had a hard time convincing him to leave me since the incident with the 787, not that he could have done much in that crisis. He took his self-appointed job of bodyguard very seriously and never let me out of his sight. He was quite a bit older than me, but a better endurance runner and had been helping me clean up my sloppy form.

I tried putting Val on the payroll, now that my father had the accounting department up and running in Phoenix, but he wouldn't hear of it. He said, "I don't need the money and I will not sully this effort with something so base."

There was more to it, though, I was sure of it. Since he was on no payroll, he had no one to answer to but himself, and that is what he wanted. I admired his position, and it put into stark contrast the hundreds of millions of dollars being given to fund Heroes Incorporated.

Down on the flats, I could see a glint of red hair as a woman did a lot of pointing, instructing some of the workers. My mother had taken it on herself to run the HR department and anything around here that has to do with quality of life. She's a redhead now, something I haven't gotten used to yet, but it was good to have her here.

Quinn was with her in his Hammer-light form carrying things, tweaking the position of trailers, doing whatever my mother told him. This was a smarter, not quite as strong version of the Hammer that caused such a mess at the Hoover Dam. I smiled as I watched. He stepped first one way and then the other. I could just imagine my mother telling him to do three things at once.

Near the crane as it lowered in another concrete section of the new building stood a short, broad-shouldered man in a yellow hard-hat. John Lopez, Licia's father. He was directing the construction effort and his wife, Elena, was organizing the kitchen, currently a cluster of food trucks down on the tailing flats near the trailers.

And yes, we took a lot of heat about nepotism when the media found out, but frankly, I didn't care. I still don't. We needed those that we trusted close to us, as many as we could get.

But I worried about the danger, not just for our parents, but for the q-morphs assembled and everyone else. The different types of danger. Not just the Arcturian Alliance, but the growing backlash from q-morphs doing damage when they were helping people or the intensifying media scrutiny and the paparazzi that assailed us whenever we were in the real world.

Like the lawsuit filed against me concerning the damage to Las Vegas when the remnants of the meteor hit. Or the rumblings from the United States Bureau of Reclamation about the cost to rebuild the Hoover Dam. Heroes Incorporated had money and that changed everything, and often not in a good way.

We had a team of lawyers on the payroll and those kinds of costs just rubbed me the wrong way. That meteor had been a planet killer, the pieces that had gotten through were nothing compared to what it would have done. If we hadn't been at the Hoover Dam, Gaia would have completely destroyed it and who knows what else.

We had to convince the world that things were much better with us here, thus the PR department working out of Los Angeles.

My rumination continued. This new life was a lot more stressful than before the break with the military, trying to balance getting the enterprise up and running with all its myriad of details *and* thinking about how we deal with the aliens if they come back.

I wasn't a janitor anymore with a simple job that I could leave behind after the end of the workday. It was all meetings and reports and conference calls. Plus training, public appearances, and the occasional operation.

This hadn't left much time for Licia and me since our trip to the savanna a few months ago and that had been bothering me more and more, but of the many problems I had, I hadn't been able to figure that one out.

She was on the Heroes Incorporated board of directors, so she had to sit in on plenty of meetings and read some of those boring reports, but she was spending a fair amount of time out in the field doing the kinds of money-generating jobs we needed done for the income, and for the good will it produced.

When the military was in charge, I hated being kept in the dark, now... I longed to know a lot less.

Val's phone beeped and he looked at it. "Diane Madison and her escort have left the Tucson airport. They'll be here in approximately ninety minutes."

"Very good," I said, nodding.

"Excuse me, but do you think this is a good idea?" Val asked. "She is the one that revealed your identities and has been relentless on breaking news about you."

I sighed. "Of course I'm not sure. But what is that old saying? Keep your friends close and your enemies closer. We need to let the media further in. We'll see how she does."

Optics. Public perception. Appearances. All of these things drove me crazy. What we needed to do was focus on the job of keeping the human race alive, not focusing on the latest news cycle and what the world thinks of the latest half-truths the media is serving up about us.

But I was naive then. In retrospect I think this all would have gone better if I had spent more time focused on the optics.

I chuckled as I watched my mother have the Hammer move a new trailer back to the exact same position it used to be in.

Val's phone chimed again. It wasn't really the role he wanted, but since he was with me most all the time, he served as something of an assistant. "Ms. Lopez has requested a few minutes of your time down on the flats. She wishes to meet you there in five minutes."

I smiled, and we started down the dusty road towards the mine shaft and buildings. This issue that Licia and I faced felt big. We were trying to save the world *and* be in love at the same time. But I knew, for the most part, it was the challenge that all couples face. How do you take care of life's voracious needs for your time and have the space and focus for intimacy and connection and love? And, no, I'm not talking about sex... at least not just about sex. Physical intimacy, in general, is a lot more straightforward than emotional intimacy, a lot easier than finding the time to beat back the urgent and just talk with your partner.

We walked past the construction site and I waved at Mr. Lopez who gave me a curt nod in return. Frankly, I didn't think he was happy about this enterprise, and the danger to his daughter. I had pondered reminding him that she was in it before we met, but I didn't think that would help.

Beyond the building was the renovated mine shaft with steel girders and a working elevator instead of a rickety wooden contraption. Gayle Smythe, our head of IT, and I am quite sure not Byte's real name, insisted on this. We have some underground storage and some emergency shelters built in the old mine and our servers are being installed down there.

She wasn't here much, she conferenced in for meetings, and spent more time in our Phoenix offices where a lot more servers were located.

Licia knew who she really was, but no one else did.

Tom Tyree was currently being held at Luke Air Force Base. I'd visited him a few times. This was a whole thing between the military and me. They wanted to put him in the facility at Area 51 and I had to threaten breaking ties to stop them. I demanded that the remaining q-morphs there be released, but they told me there were no other q-morphs, despite the evidence I saw of it during my stay.

The world didn't know about that facility, and they really couldn't yet, but I'd be damned if I'd see someone else thrown into that hole. That prison was firmly in the "Deal with later" column of my extensive to-do list.

The road ran next to Town Lake (really it was just a pond) under the thin shade of some mesquite trees and onto the flats. We had the tailings tested, thoroughly, and it was a boon to have this large, flat area for our temporary buildings.

Licia was standing there smiling like she was a kid with a secret she just couldn't keep anymore. It made me smile. Her long black hair was pulled into a ponytail and she had on khaki shorts and a white tank top.

She was so beautiful. More beautiful than when I met her. And you all might be getting tired of me saying how beautiful she is, but it's just a fact. I will admit, though, that the more I know her, the more I see her strength and her heart, the more beautiful she becomes.

As I write this, Licia looks, maybe, five years older than she did then. I imagine when enough time has passed to counteract the anti-aging effects for our q-morph transformations, when she is wrinkled and truly looks old, I will still find her just as beautiful. Different, yes, but still beautiful.

Isn't that the way it should be? The years change your love's appearance, but if you are lucky, they are still your love and you've found a way to stay together and stay intimate through all those changes.

"Come on," Licia said, taking my hand, a glint in her eyes. She gave a pointed look to Val who got the hint and hung back.

Mom waved at me from a few trailers away and the Hammer gave me an exasperated nod, but I was focused on Licia. She was excited, walking fast, a spring in her step.

She took us through the twenty or so trailers there to one on the edge of the flat with a hearty juniper that was growing at the edge of the tailings. She smiled and nodded at the trailer, beaming.

I smiled back, but I didn't quite get it. It was one of the many single-wide trailers set up here, painted grey with some metal steps leading up to the door. It wasn't anything special. I mostly slept in my office, which was a horrible habit, but Licia had been gone a lot lately and there was so much to do.

"Really?" she asked, letting go of my hand and crossing her arms.

I was tired. Clearly she had done something nice and really wanted me to notice it. I took a step back and really looked at the trailer, letting my breath deepen and slow. I hadn't been making enough time to meditate and I really needed to do that.

The living room window had some blue curtains and I could see that electricity, water, and sewer connections were complete, the pipes and the wires snaking down in the tailings.

There was a simple wooden sign on the door with names engraved there. Each trailer had one, so you could tell them apart.

This one said "Lopez / Nichols."

My heart started beating hard and there was no chance of meditation anymore. Was she saying that...?

"Are... are we living together now?" I asked.

She looked away, suddenly shy. "If you want to."

I swallowed hard. I was in prison for six months, and then the long recovery, and the recruiting, and the 787 and recovering from that, and building Heroes Incorporated. When we were together, we stayed together, but we never had a place, "our" place.

When I blinked back tears and sniffed she looked back at me, tears pooling in her eyes as she nodded.

This, right here, this is what I wanted. I wanted her to be front and center and the world and all its problems to be second. I wanted to do simple things like plant a garden together, get that dog she so wanted, read the paper over leisurely breakfasts.

I didn't talk. I grabbed her and pulled her off her feet in a fierce hug. I didn't have the words.

"Come on," she said after I put her down. "Let's go look at our house."

Tears flowed down my face as she showed me *our* house. I felt

464 / ROBERT J. MCCARTER

no shame for more tears, only love for Licia and hope. This here, this is what could keep me together while the madness raged. The world and all its demands wouldn't go away, but this tiny sanctuary with her would give me strength to do what needed to be done, to endure the meetings and the media and all the demands of Heroes Incorporated. To help find a way to defeat the aliens. This would be enough.

It had to be enough.

EPISODE 7
HEROES INCORPORATED

THERE IS MORE ADVENTURE, MORE FUN, MORE *NEUTRINOMAN and Lightningirl* coming soon in episode 7, *Heroes Incorporated*. Sign up for my newsletter at RobertJMcCarter.com/newsletter and don't miss a thing.

And for the same kind of romantic adventurous fun as *Neutrinoman and Lightningirl* set in post-apocalypse Arizona, check out *Woody and June versus the Apocalypse*. Join the fan club at Woody-AndJune.com and get the first two episodes for free!

WOODY AND JUNE VERSUS THE APOCALYPSE

Love and the Apocalypse

When Woody Beckman meets June Medina, neither expects the adventures that will follow. Dedicated go-it-alone survivors, they've learned not to trust anyone in post-zombie-apocalypse Arizona.

But when regular-guy Woody must save tough-as-nails June, they realize that to survive they must learn to trust each other.

As the pair deals with everything from zombies to psychotic, petty, wannabe warlords to the harsh Arizona deserts, they start to realize that they might just prefer facing this crazy world together.

A story of adventure and love and taking things (even the apocalypse) in stride.

Get the first two episodes for free by joining the fan club or go grab Volume 1 with all 7 episodes!

ACKNOWLEDGMENTS

Writing a series is its own adventure, especially over a span of years. I am changing personally and as a writer as my characters are changing. And the world is changing, which is always true, but feels way more true here in 2020.

The writing of *Meteor Attack!*, the first episode, goes back to 2011. I set the "future" timeline as 2025 and that seemed like a long ways off. But now it's 2020 and we are rushing right up onto it. We'll likely be past it before I finish the series. Which is weird. I'll go from looking towards the future to looking at the past as I keep writing.

All of that is to say it's been a wild adventure so far with more to come. As always, I get a lot of help along the way.

First and foremost, my wife, Aleia, for being my rock, my inspiration, and my first listener. These stories would not exist without you.

Next to my super team of beta readers: Roni Hornstein and Peter Klein. Thanks for making each of these better.

Thanks to Diana Cox for your excellent proofing and using your grammatical superpowers to save me from myself.

And special thanks to Elizabeth Fitzekam for putting together the Neutrinoman and Lightningirl series bible. There's a lot of moving parts here and I couldn't keep track of them without it.

And last, but not least, thank you for reading.

If you are not part of my newsletter, you can join at RobertJMcCarter.com/newsletter and be the first to find out when Neutrinoman flies again. Feel free to reach out with your thoughts or comments, you can find me online here:

Facebook: facebook.com/robertjmccarterauthor

Twitter: twitter.com/robertjmccarter

My website: RobertJMcCarter.com/contact

ABOUT THE AUTHOR

Robert J. McCarter is the author of seven novels, three novellas, and dozens of short stories. He is a finalist for the *Writers of the Future* contest and his stories have appeared or are forthcoming in *The Saturday Evening Post, Pulphouse Fiction Magazine, Fiction River, Andromeda Spaceways Inflight Magazine,* and numerous anthologies.

His latest effort is a serialized novel called *Woody and June Versus the Apocalypse,* a story of adventure and love and taking things (even the apocalypse) in stride. Of his novel, *Seeing Forever,* Kirkus Reviews says, "Sci-fi as it should be: engaging, moving, and grand in scope."

He lives in the mountains of Arizona with his amazing wife and his ridiculously adorable dogs.

Find out more at:
robertjmccarter.com

BOOKS BY ROBERT J. MCCARTER

NEUTRINOMAN & LIGHTNINGIRL: A LOVE STORY

- Meteor Attack!
- Toxic Asset
- Protocol X
- Season 1 (Omnibus edition of Episodes 1 - 3)
- Off Book
- Hard Times
- Elemental Factors
- Season 2 (Omnibus edition of Episodes 4-6)

Find out the latest at Neutrinoman.com

WOODY AND JUNE VERSUS THE APOCALYPSE

1. Woody and June versus the Wannabe Warlord
2. Woody and June versus the Fungus-Head Zombies
3. Woody and June versus the Grand Canyon
4. Woody and June versus the Ex
5. Woody and June versus the Third Wheel
6. Woody and June versus Phantom Company
7. Woody and June versus the Daring Rescue
8. Volume 1: Episodes 1-7 (all seven episodes for a great price)

Join the Woody and June Fan Club at WoodyAndJune.com

NOVELS IN THE "GHOST'S MEMOIR" WORLD:

- Shuffled Off: A Ghost's Memoir, Book 1
- Drawing the Dead
- To Be a Fool: A Ghost's Memoir, Book 2
- Of Things Not Seen: A Ghost's Memoir, Book 3
- A Boy, a Girl, and a Ghost

OTHER NOVELS:

- Seeing Forever

For a complete list, go to RobertJMcCarter.com

www.ingramcontent.com/pod-product-compliance
Lightning Source LLC
Chambersburg PA
CBHW020628020726
47494CB00001B/102